# ADVENTURES

*Full of Stories a Lifetime Shouldn't Miss*

# ADVENTURES

## PEOPLE AND STORIES THAT SHOULD NOT BE FORGOTTEN

Winter 2024




**ISBN: (PAPERBACK) 978-1-950464-74-6**
**ISBN: (EBOOK) 978-1-950464-77-7**


**WWW.ADVENTURESBOOKZINE.COM**

# ADVENTURES

### *FULL OF STORIES A LIFETIME SHOULDN'T MISS*

**WINTER 2024**  **ISSUE #14**

## WHAT



## WHERE

# Editor's Note

WELCOME TO THE WINTER ISSUE OF ADVENTURES, WHICH, APPROPRIATELY FOR the season, is full of stories to warm your heart as well as stories to chill you to the bone.

For starters, we have two Christmas-themed stories that will put you back in the holiday mood: "Twas the Day Before Christmas" by Kyle Owens and "The Christmas Masquerade" by Mary E. Wilkins Freeman.

Owens is the author of the Vegas Chantly Mysteries series, and he wrote this original story for Adventures, and we think it will become a new Christmas favorite of yours. Freeman's story is a bit older - it was published in the 1890s - but it's another fun heart-warming tale that you're sure to fall in love with.

If you're in a mood for something a little less "cozy," we invite you to check out "New Bodies for Old" by Maurice Renard. This author, although not widely known today, was essentially the French H.G. Wells (who was an Englishman, for the record). He wrote stories about mad scientists, invisibility, body switching and more. Body switching is, perhaps obviously, the theme of "New Bodies for Old," and if you've never read anything by Renard, you're in for a treat.

Speaking of Wells, we have a story of his as well in this edition: "A Story of the Days to Come." This novella takes place in a dystopian future in London and depicts an over-populated, over-urbanized society where class warfare is the norm. Like other works by Wells, it's a piece that seems hauntingly modern.

This story goes hand in hand with "When the Sleeper Awakes," a short work that Wells wrote in the same year as "A Story of the Days to Come." The novellas can stand on their own, however, and we decided to run one in this edition and one in the spring edition so you can get the complete experience. Generally we don't want to run cliffhangers between editions, but we think the stories are complete enough to stand on their own.

There's more in this edition of *Adventures*, including old photos, a poem and another story. So we invite you to grab a mug of your favorite hot beverage, settle into a cushy chair and read whichever one of these stories strikes your fancy!

On a more personal note, we know 2024 was a challenging year for many, whether it was personal health issues, economic hardships or something else. We certainly had our share of challenges, and one way we deal with difficult times is immersing ourselves in a good story. It is our sincere hope that our Adventures issues help distract you from your troubles and give you unadulterated enjoyment for at least a couple of hours.

Here's to a great 2025.

Cheers!

Michael Brian

*Michael Brian*

# NEW BODIES FOR OLD

## BY MAURICE RENARD

To H. G. Wells:
I beg you, Sir, to accept this book.

Of all the pleasures that its writing gave me, that of dedicating it to you is assuredly not the least.

I conceived it under the inspiration of ideas that you cherish, and I could have wished that it had come nearer to your own works than it does, not in merit—that would be an absurd pretension—but, at any rate, in that pleasant quality shown in all your books, which allows the chastest minds, as well as those that exact the greatest realism, to have communion with your genius—a communion which the ablest people of our time can acknowledge without feeling its charm lessened by such considerations.

But when Fortune for good or ill allowed me to discover the subject of this allegorical novel, I felt bound not to set it aside because of a few audacities which a faithful rendering involved and which an arrest of development alone—that is, a crime against the literary conscience—could avoid.

You now know—you could have guessed as much—what I should like people to think of my work, if by chance any one did it the unexpected honor of thinking about it at all. Far from desiring to arouse the creature of instinct in my reader and amuse him with scandalous descriptions, my work is addressed to the philosopher anxious for Truth amid the marvels of Fiction and for Orderliness amid the tumult of imaginary Adventures.

That, Sir, is why I beg you to accept it.
M. R.

# INTRODUCTION

It all happened on a certain winter evening more than a year ago, after the last men's dinner-party I gave to my friends in the little house which I had taken furnished in the Avenue Victor Hugo.

As my projected move was nothing more than the gratification of my vagrant fancy, we had celebrated my house unwarming as joyfully as we had celebrated the warming of yore, and the time for liqueurs having come (and also the time for jokes) each of us did his best to shine—more especially of course, that naughty fellow Gilbert, Marlotte, our paradoxical friend, the "Triboulet" of our band, and Cardaillac, our licensed wizard.

I cannot remember now exactly how it came about, but after an hour spent in the smoking-room, somebody switched off the electric light, and urged us to have some table-turning; so we grouped ourselves in the darkness round a little table. This "somebody" (please observe) was not Cardaillac; but perhaps he was in league with Cardaillac—if indeed Cardaillac was the guilty party.

We were exactly eight men in all, eight skeptics _versus_ a little insignificant table which had only one stem divided off at the end into three legs, and whose round top bent under our sixteen hands placed on it in accordance with occult rites!

It was Mariotte who instructed us in these rites. He had at one time been an anxious inquirer about witchcraft, and familiar with table-turning, though merely as an outsider, and as he was our customary buffoon, when we saw him assume the direction of the séance, every one just let himself go in anticipation of some excellent clowning.

Cardaillac found himself my right-hand neighbor. I heard him stifle a laugh in his throat and cough. Then the table began to turn.

Gilbert questioned it, and to his obvious stupefaction it replied by dry cracklings like those made by creaking woodwork, and corresponding to the esoteric alphabet.

Mariotte translated in a quavering voice.

Then everybody wanted to question the table; and in its replies it gave proof of great sagacity. The audience became serious; one did not know what to think. Queries leapt to our lips, and the replies were rapped out from the foot of the table, near me—as I fancied—and towards my right.

"Who will live in this house in a year's time?" asked in his turn he who had proposed the spiritualistic amusement.

"Oh, if you question it about the future," said Mariotte, "you will only get back thumping lies, or else it will hold its tongue."

"Oh, shut up," interposed Cardaillac. The question was repeated— "Who will live in this house in a year's time?"

"Nobody," said the interpreter.

"And in two years' time?"

"Nicolas Vermont."

All of us heard this name for the first time.

"What will he be doing at this very hour on the anniversary of to-day? Tell us what he is doing—speak."

"He is beginning ... to write here ... his adventures."

"Can you read what he writes?"

"Yes ... and also what he will write."

"Tell us the beginning, just the beginning."

"Am tired—alphabet too tedious—Give typewriter ... will inspire typist."

A murmur went round in the darkness. I rose and went to fetch my typewriter, and it was placed upon the table.

"It's a 'Watson,'" said the table. "I won't have it. Am a French table. Want a French machine ... want a 'Durand.'"

"'A Durand?'" said my neighbor on the left, in a disillusioned tone. "Does that brand exist? I don't know it."

"Nor I."

"Nor I."

"Nor I."

We were much vexed at this untoward circumstance, when the voice of Cardaillac said slowly:

"I use nothing but a 'Durand,' would you like me to fetch it?"

"Can you type without seeing?"

"I shall be back in a quarter of an hour," said he—and he went out without answering.

"Oh, if Cardaillac is going to take it up," said one of the guests, "we shall have a merry time."

However, when the lights were turned up, the faces seemed sterner than one would have expected. Mariotte was quite pale.

Cardaillac came back in a very short time—an astonishingly short time, one might have said. He sat down in front of the table facing his "Durand" machine, and darkness was once more established. Suddenly the table declared: "No need of others.... Put your feet on mine ... type."

One heard the tapping of the fingers on the keys.

"It's extraordinary!" exclaimed the typist-medium, "It's extraordinary! My hands are writing of their own accord."

"What bosh!" whispered Mariotte.

"I swear they are, I swear it," said Cardaillac.

WE REMAINED A LONG TIME LISTENING TO THE TAPPING OF THE KEYS WHICH was every now and then broken by the ringing of the bell at the end of the line and the rasping of the carriage. Every five minutes a sheet was handed to us. We decided to retire to the drawing-room and to read them aloud as Gilbert, getting them from Cardaillac, handed them to us.

Page 79 was deciphered in the morning light and the machine stopped.

But what it had typed seemed to us exciting enough to make us beg Cardaillac to be good enough to give us the sequel.

He did so. And when he had passed many nights seated at the little table with his typing keyboard, we had the complete story of M. Vermont's adventures.

The reader shall now be told them.

They are strange and scandalous; their future scribe is _bound_ not to think of printing them. He will burn them as soon as they are finished; so that, had it not been for the complaisance of the little table, no one would ever have turned the leaves. That is why I, convinced of their authenticity, consider it piquant to publish them beforehand.

For I hold them to be "veridical,"—as the elect call it—although they have some of the characteristics of wild caricature, and rather resemble an art-student's funny sketch penciled by way of commentary on the margin of an engraving representing Science herself.

Are they possibly apocryphal? Well, fables are reputed to be more seductive than History, and Cardaillac's will not seem inferior to many another one.

My hope, however, is that "Dr. Lerne" is the truthful account of

real happenings, for in that case, since the little table uttered a prophecy, the tribulations of the hero have not yet begun, and they will be running their course at the very time that this book is divulging them—a very interesting circumstance indeed.

At any rate I shall certainly know in two years' time if M. Nicolas Vermont lives in the little house in the Avenue Victor Hugo. Something assures me of it in advance—for how can one accept the idea of Cardaillac—a serious-minded and intelligent fellow—squandering so many hours in composing such a fable? That is my principal argument in favor of its truthfulness.

However, if any conscientious reader desires to find reasons for the faith that is in him, let him betake himself to Grey-l'Abbaye. There he will be informed about the existence of Professor Lerne and his habits. For my part I have not got the leisure for that, but I entreat any one who may undertake the search to let me know the truth, being myself very desirous of getting to the bottom of the question whether the following tale is a mystification of Cardaillac's, or was really typed out by a clairvoyant table.

# CHAPTER I

## NOCTURNE

The first Sunday in June was drawing to a close. The shadow of the motor-car was fleeting on ahead of me and getting longer every moment.

Ever since the morning, people had been looking at me with anxious faces as I passed, just as one looks at a scene in a melodrama. With my leather helmet which gave me the look of a bald skull, my glasses like portholes, or the eye-sockets of a skeleton, and my body clothed in tanned skin, I must have seemed to them some queer seal from the nether regions, or one of St. Anthony's demons, fleeing from the sunlight towards the night, in order to enter therein.

And to tell the truth, I had almost a soul like that of one of the Lost; for such is the soul of a solitary traveler who has been for seven hours at a stretch on a racing-car. His spirit has something like a nightmare in it; in place of thought, an obsession is settled there. Mine was a little peremptory phrase—"Come alone, and give notice"—which, like a tenacious goblin, worried my lonely mind, overstrained as it was with joltings and speed.

And yet this strange injunction "come alone and give notice," doubly underlined by my Uncle Lerne in his letter, had not at first struck me excessively. But now that I was obeying it—being alone and having given notice—and rolling along towards the Castle of Fonval, the inexplicable command insisted, so to speak, on displaying all its strangeness. My eyes began to see the fateful expression everywhere, and my ears made it sound in every noise in spite of my efforts to drive away the fixed idea. If I wanted to know the name of a village, the sign-post announced "Come alone"; "Give notice" followed in the wake of a bird's flight, and the engine, unresting and exasperating, repeated thousands and thousands of times: "Come alone, come alone, come alone, give notice, give notice, give notice." Then I began to ask myself the wherefore of this wish of my uncle, and not being able to find the reason, I ardently longed for the arrival which should solve the mystery, less curious in reality about the doubtless commonplace answer, than exasperated by so despotic a question.

Fortunately I was drawing near, and the country growing more and more familiar spoke so clearly of the old days, that the haunting question relaxed its insistence. The town of Nanthel, populous and busy, detained me, but on coming out of the suburbs I at last perceived, like a vague and very distant cloud, the heights of the Ardennes Mountains.

Evening draws on. Desiring to reach the goal before night I open out to the full. The car hums, and under it the road is engulfed in a whirl; it seems to enter the car to be rolled up in it, as the yards of ribbon roll themselves up on a reel. Speed makes its hurricane wind whistle in my ears; a swarm of mosquitoes riddle my face like small shot, and all sorts of little creatures patter on my goggles.

Now the sun is on my right; it is on the horizon; the acclivities and declivities of the road, raising me up and sinking me down very quickly, make the sun rise and set for me several times in succession. It disappears. I dash through the dusk as hard as my brave engine can go—and I fancy that the 234 XY has never been excelled. This makes the Ardennes about half an hour away. The cloudy offing is already putting on a green tinge, a forest color, and my heart has leapt within me. Fifteen years! I have not seen those dear great woods for fifteen years—they were my old holiday friends.

For it is there, it is in their shadow that the château hides in the depths of an enormous hollow.... I remember that hollow very distinctly and I can already distinguish its whereabouts—a dark stain indicates it. Indeed it is the most extraordinary ravine. My late aunt, Lidivine Lerne, who was fond of legends, would have it that Satan, furious at some disappointment, had scooped it out with a single blow of his gigantic hoof. This origin is disputed. In any case the metaphor gives a vivid picture of the place, an amphitheater with precipitous walls of rock, with no other outlet than a large defile opening on the fields. The plain in other words penetrates into the mountain like a gulf of the sea; it there forms a blind-alley, the perpendicular walls of which rise as it spreads, and whose end is rounded off in a wide sweep. The result is that one gets to Fonval without the least climb, although it is right in the bosom of the mountain. The park is the inner part of the circle, and the cliff serves as a natural wall, except in the direction of the defile. This latter is separated from the domain by a wall into which a gateway has been let. A long avenue leads up to it, straight, and lined with lime trees. In a few minutes I shall be in it ... and soon after I shall know why nobody must follow me to Fonval—"come alone and give notice"—why these orders?

Patience. The mass of the Ardennes cleaves itself into clumps. At the rate I am going, each clump seems in motion; gliding rapidly; the crests pass one behind the other, draw near or draw off, seem lower and then rise again with the majesty of waves, and the spectacle is incessantly varying like that of a titanic sea.

A turn in the road unmasks a hamlet, I know it well. In the old days, every year, in the month of August, it was before that station that my uncle's carriage, with Biribi in the shafts, awaited my mother and me. We used to go there for the holidays. All hail Grey-l'Abbaye! Fonval is only three kilometers distant now. I could go there blindfold. Here is the road leading straight to the place, the road which will soon plunge into the woods and take the name of Avenue.

It is almost night. A peasant shouts something at me—insults probably. I'm accustomed to that. My hooter replies with its threatening and mournful cry.

The forest! Ah, what a potent perfume it has for me—the perfume of the old-time holidays! Can their memory bring any other odor than that of the forest? It is an exquisite odor.... I should like to prolong this festival of scent.

Slowing down, the car goes on gently. Its sound becomes a murmur. Right and left the cliff walls of the wide gully begin to rise. Were there more light, I should be coming into sight of Fonval at the end of the straight line of the avenue. Hullo! What's up?...

I had almost upset; the road had unexpectedly made a bend.

I slackened off still more. A little further on another bend—then another....

I stopped.

The stars one by one were beginning to shed their luminous dew. In the light of the Spring evening I could see above me the high mountain-crests, and the direction of their slopes astonished me. I tried to back, and discovered a bifurcation which I had not noted in passing. When I had taken the road to the right, it offered me after several windings a new branching-off—like a riddle; and then I guided myself in the Fonval direction according to the lie of the cliffs that ran towards the château, but new cross-roads embarrassed me. What had become of the straight avenue?... The thing utterly puzzled me.

I switched on the head-lights. For a long time by the aid of their light I wandered among the criss-crossing of the alleys without being able to find my way, so many various offshoots joined the open places, and so balking were the blind-alleys. It seemed to me I had already passed a certain birch-tree. Moreover the cliff walls always remained at the same height; so that I was really turning in a maze and making no advance. Had the peasant of Grey tried to warn me? It seemed probable.

None the less, trusting to chance, and piqued by the contretemps, I went on with my exploration. Three times the same crossing showed in the field of light of my lamps, and three times I came on that same birch-tree by different roads.

I wanted to call for help. Unfortunately the hooter went wrong, and I had no horn. As for my voice, the distance which separated me from Grey on the one side and Fonval on the other would have prevented its being heard.

Then a fear assailed me ... if my petrol gave out!... I halted in the middle of a cross-road and tested the level. My tank was almost empty. What would be the good in exhausting it in vain evolutions! After all, it seemed to me an easy thing to reach the château on foot through the woods.... I tried it. But wire-fences hidden in the bushes blocked the way.

Assuredly this labyrinth was not a practical joke played at the entrance of a garden, but a defensive contrivance to protect the approaches of some retreat.

Much out of countenance, I began to reflect.

"Uncle Lerne, I don't understand you at all," thought I. "You received the notice of my arrival this morning, and here am I detained in the most abominable of landscape-gardens.... What fantastic idea made you contrive it? Have you changed more than I thought? You would hardly have dreamt of such fortifications fifteen years ago."

... "Fifteen years ago, the night, no doubt, resembled this one. The heavens were alive with the same glitter, and already the toads were enlivening the silence with their clear short cries, so pure and sweet. A nightingale was warbling its trills as that one now is doing. Uncle, that evening of long ago was delicious too. And yet my aunt and my mother had just died, within eight days of one another, and the sisters having disappeared, we remained face to face, one a widower, and the other an orphan—you, uncle, and I."

And the man of those far-off days stood before my mind's eye as the town of Nanthel knew him then, the surgeon already celebrated at thirty-five for the skill of his hand and the success of his bold methods, and who in spite of his fame, remained faithful to his native town—Dr. Frédéric Lerne, Professor of Clinical Medicine at the "Ecole de Médecine," corresponding member of numerous learned societies, decorated with many divers orders, and—to omit nothing—guardian of his nephew, Nicolas Vermont.

This new father whom the Law assigned me I had not met often, for he took no holidays and only passed his summer Sundays at Fonval. And even these he spent in work—ceaseless and secret work. On those days his passion for horticulture, suppressed all the week, kept him shut up in the little hothouse with his tulips and his orchids.

And yet, in spite of the rarity of our meetings, I knew him well and loved him dearly.

He was a sturdy man, calm and sober, rather cold perhaps, but so kind. In my irreverent way I called his shaven face an "old wife's face," and my jesting was quite misplaced, for sometimes he would turn it into an antique visage, lofty and grave, and sometimes into one of delicate mockery ("Regency" style). Among our modern shavelings my uncle was of the few whose head and face by their nobility prove their legitimate descent from an ancestor draped in a toga, and a grandfather clothed in satin, and would allow their scion to wear the costumes of his ancestors without putting them to shame.

For the moment Lerne appeared to me decked out in a black overcoat rather badly cut, in which I had seen him for the last time—when I was setting out for Spain. Being a rich man, and wishing me to be one too, my uncle had sent me into the cork business as an employee of the firm Gomez & Co. of Badajoz.

And my exile had lasted fifteen years, during which the position of the Professor had certainly become better, to judge by the sensational operations he had performed, the fame of which had reached me in the depths of Estremadura.

As for me, my affairs had come to grief. At the end of fifteen years, despairing of ever selling safety-belts and cork on my own account, I had just returned to France to seek another trade, when Fate procured me that of an independent man. It was I who won the lucky number for a million francs, the donor of which wished to remain incognito.

In Paris I took comfortable rooms, but without luxury. My flat was convenient and unpretentious. I had the bare necessaries plus a motor-car and minus a family.

But before founding a new family, it seemed to me the right thing to renew relations with the old—that is to say with Lerne, and I wrote to him.

Not but what after our separation a regular correspondence had been established between us. At the beginning he had given me wise advice and had shown himself pleasantly paternal. His first letter indeed contained the announcement of a Will in my favor hidden in the secret drawer of a desk at Fonval.

After the rendering of his accounts as guardian our relations remained as before. Then, suddenly, his messages became different in character, and grew fewer and fewer, their tone becoming that of boredom, then of annoyance. The matter was commonplace, then vulgar, and the phrasing awkward; the very writing seemed to alter. Each time he wrote, these things became more marked, and I had to limit myself every 1st of January to sending my best wishes. My uncle replied with a few scribbled words.... Wounded in the only affection I possessed, I was much afflicted.

What had happened?

A year before this sudden change—five years before my return to Fonval and my wanderings in the labyrinth—I had read in the "Epoca":

"We have received the news from Paris that Professor Lerne is saying good-by to his patients in order to devote himself to scientific research begun in the hospital of Nanthel. With this aim that excellent physician is retiring to the neighborhood of the town in the Ardennes, to his château of Fonval which has been arranged for that purpose. He is taking with him among others, Dr. Klotz of Mannheim and the three assistants of the _Anatomisches Institut_ founded by this latter at 22, Friedrichstrasse, which has now closed its doors—when shall we have results?"

Lerne had confirmed this event to me in an enthusiastic letter, which, however, added nothing to the bald facts in the paragraph. And it was a year later on, I say again, that the change in his nature had taken place. Had twelve months of work ended in failure? Had some bitter disappointment so gravely affected the Professor that he should treat me like a stranger and almost as if I were a bore?...

In defiance of his hostility I wrote respectfully and with the utmost possible affection from Paris the letter in which I told him of my good fortune, and I asked his leave to pay him a visit.

Never was invitation less engaging than his. He asked me to give him warning of my arrival so that he might order a carriage to go and fetch me from the station. "You will doubtless not remain long at Fonval," he added, "for Fonval is not a gay place. We are hard at work. Come alone and give notice."

But, Heavens! I had given notice and I was alone!—I who had considered my visit as a duty! Well, well, that was merely a piece of stupidity on my part.

And I gazed in bad humor at the star of light on the roads where the exhausted head-lamps were casting no brighter an illumination than a night-light.

Without doubt I was going to pass the night in that sylvan jail; nothing would get me out of it before day. The toads of the pool in the Fonval direction called me in vain; vainly the steeple clock of Grey rang out the hours to tell me of the other resting-place—for belfries are really sonorous lighthouses—I was a prisoner.

A prisoner! It made me smile. Long ago how frightened I should have been! A prisoner in the Ardennes! At the mercy of Brocéliande, the monstrous forest which with its cavernous shade held a world in darkness between its boundaries, one being at Blois and the other in Constantinople! Brocéliande! that scene of epic tales and puerile legends, country of the four sons of Aymon and of Hop-o'-my-Thumb, the forest of druids and goblins, the wood in which Sleeping Beauty fell into slumber while Charlemagne kept watch! What fantastic stories had not its thickets for a stage—were not the trees themselves living persons? "Oh, Aunt Lidivine," I murmured, "how well you could give life to all those nonsensical tales every evening after dinner! The dear lady! Did she ever suspect the influence of her stories? Aunt, did you know that all your astounding puppets invaded my life by passing through my dreams? Do you know that a flourish of enchanted trumpets still sounds in my ears sometimes; you who made my nights at Fonval resound with the oliphant of Roland and the horn of Oberon?"

At that moment I could not check a movement of vexation; the head-lamps had just gone out after an agonized throb. For a second the darkness was total, and at the same time there was such a profound silence that I could well believe I had suddenly become blind and deaf.

Then my eyes gradually became unsealed, and soon the crescent moon appeared, shedding its snowy light on the cold night. The forest became lit up with a frozen whiteness. I shivered. In my aunt's lifetime it would have been with terror; I should have beheld in the darkness, where the vapors were creeping, dragons wallowing and serpents gliding. An owl flew off. I should have considered that bird the winged helm of a paladin— an enchanted paladin. The birch tree, standing straight up, shone with a lance-like gleam. An oak tree—a son perhaps of the magic tree which was the husband of the Princess Leélina—quivered. It was huge and druidical—a bunch of mistletoe hung on its main branch, and the moon cut through it with a shining sacred sickle.

Assuredly the nocturnal landscape was like an hallucination. For want of something better to do, I meditated on it. Without understanding why as well as I do to-day, I used to experience all its suggestiveness, and at nightfall I only ventured out unwillingly. Fonval itself was, I think, in spite of its countless flowers and its beautiful winding alleys, a most forbidding place. Its pointed windows, its hundred years old park inhabited by statues, the stagnant water of its pond, the precipice which closed it in, the Hell-like entrance, all these things made that ancient abbey (transformed into a château) peculiar even in daylight, and one would not have been surprised to learn that everybody there talked in fables. That would have been his real language.

That at any rate was how I talked, and still more how I acted, during my holidays. These were for me a long fairy tale in which I played with imaginary or artificial personages, living in the water, in the trees, and under the earth oftener than upon it. If I passed the lawn galloping with my bare legs, my air clearly showed the squadrons of knights were, in my fancy, charging behind me. And the old boat I masted for the occasion with three broomsticks, on which bellied nondescript sails, served me as a galleon, and the pond became the Mediterranean bearing the fleet of the Crusaders. Lost in thought and looking at the water-lily islands and the grass peninsulas, I proclaimed: "Here are Corsica and Sardinia!... Italy is in sight.... We are sailing round Malta...." At the end of a minute I cried "Land!" We were landing in Palestine—"Montjoye and St. Denis!"—I suffered on that boat sea-sickness and home-sickness; the Holy War intoxicated me;—I learnt in it two things—enthusiasm and geography....

But often the other characters were represented. That made it more real. I remembered then—for every child has a Don Quixote in him—I remembered a giant Briareus who was the summerhouse, and especially a barrel which became the dragon of Andromeda. Oh, that barrel! I had made a head for it with the help of a squinting pumpkin, and vampire wings with two umbrellas. Having ambushed my contraption at the bend of an alley, leaning it up against a terra-cotta nymph, I set out in search of it more valiant than the real Perseus, and, armed with a pole, I went caracoling on an invisible hippogriff. But when I discovered it, the pumpkin leered at me so strangely that Perseus almost took flight, and the umbrellas owed it to his emotion that they were broken to pieces in the yellow blood of the facetious vegetable.

My puppets did indeed make an impression on me by reason of the rôle I assigned them. As I always reserved for myself that of protagonist, hero, conqueror, I easily surmounted that terror during the day, but at night, though the hero became little Nicolas Vermont, an urchin, the barrel remained a dragon. Cowering under the sheets, my mind excited by the story which my aunt had just finished, I knew the garden was peopled with my terrifying fancies, and that Briareus was mounting guard there all the time, and that the dreadful barrel, resuscitated, hiding its claws with its wings, watched my window from afar.

At that age I despaired of ever being, later on in life, like other people, and able to face the dark. And yet my fears did vanish, leaving me impressionable no doubt, but not a coward; and it was indeed I who found myself without dismay lost in the lonely wood—all too empty, alas, of fairies and enchanters.

I had just reached this point in my reverie, when a sort of vague noise arose in the Fonval direction; an ox's lowing, and something like a dog's long mournful howl. That was all—and then the sleeping calm returned.

Some minutes elapsed, and next I heard an owl hoot somewhere between myself and the château; another raised its voice not so far away as the first; and then others took flight from places nearer and nearer me, as if the passage of some creature were scaring them.

And indeed a light sound of steps like the trot of some four-footed animal, made itself heard and drew nearer on the roadway. I listened for some time to the beast moving to and fro in the labyrinth, losing itself like me perhaps, and then suddenly it appeared before me.

One could not mistake its spreading antlers, the height of its neck and the delicacy of its ears; it was a stag of ten. But hardly had I perceived it than it made off in a sudden volte-face. Then—had it gathered itself in to spring?—its body seemed to me strangely low and paltry, and was it a mere reflection?—seemed to me to be of a white color. The animal disappeared in a twinkling, and its little galloping steps died quickly away.

Had I at the first glance taken a goat for a stag? Or had I at the second glance taken a stag for a goat? To tell the truth, I was much interested and puzzled; so much so that I asked myself whether I were not going to resume the soul of the child I had been at Fonval.

But a little reflection made me realize that hunger, fatigue and sleepiness, helped out by moonshine, may easily cause one's eyes to be deceived, and that a ray falling on an object and transforming it is no unwonted phenomenon.

I rather regretted it; for, having lost my terror of the mysterious, I had still kept my love for it. I am one of those who are sorry that "Philosophy has clipped an angel's wings," and yet I cannot let a mystery remain a mystery for me.

Now this beast was really a very extraordinary beast.

Wandering as it was through the incomprehensible labyrinth of the wood, it seemed to me an elusive riddle in a problem, and my curiosity was aroused.

But utterly wearied as I was, I soon fell asleep pondering detective ruses and subtle logical methods of investigation.

I AWOKE AT DAWN, AND IMMEDIATELY I HAD A GLIMPSE OF A POSSIBLE END TO my imprisonment.

Not far from where I was, some men, hidden by the underwood, were walking and talking. Their steps came and went like those of the stag(?) treading, doubtless the same winding ways. At one moment they passed, still hidden, a few paces away from my car, but I could not understand their conversation—it seemed to be in German.

At last they stood before me at the very place where the animal had appeared. There were three of them, and they were bending down as if they were following a trail. At the spot where the beast had turned, one of them uttered an exclamation and made a gesture as if they should go back. But they perceived me and I advanced towards them.

"Gentlemen," said I smiling my best, "could you kindly show me the way to Fonval? I have lost myself."

The three men looked at me without replying, in an inquisitive and shy way.

They were a very remarkable trio.

The first possessed on the top of a massive and squat body a round and calamitously flat face, the thin pointed nose on which, as if it had been shoved into it, made the disc into a sundial.

The second had a military air and was twisting his mustache, which was on the German imperial model, and his chin stuck out like the toe of a boot.

A tall old man with gold spectacles, gray curly hair and an unkempt beard, made up the trio. He was eating cherries in a noisy way, as a bumpkin eats tripe.

They were obvious Germans, doubtless the assistants from the Anatomisches Institut.

The tall old man spat out in my direction a salvo of cherry-stones, and in the direction of his comrades, one of those Teuton phrases, in which a hail of shrapnel-like words mingles with other nameless noises.

They exchanged in their own way some remarks which resembled so many broadsides, without paying the least attention to me, and then after cleverly imitating with their mouths the sound of a battle going on beside a waterfall—having held a council, in fact—they turned on their heels and left me astounded at their rudeness.

But I had to get out of that fix somehow or other. My adventure became hourly more ridiculous. What was the meaning of all this? What comedy was I playing? Was I being made a fool of? I was furious. The would-be secrets I had fancied I scented now seemed to me mere childishness caused by weariness and the dark. The thing was to get away—to get away at once.

Raging and without reflection I made the contact which set the car going, and the 80 horse-power engine started to work in the bonnet with the humming of a hive of bees. I seized the starting lever—and then a great guffaw of laughter made me turn round.

With his cap over his ears, in blouse of blue, and with his letter-bag on his shoulder, hilarious and triumphant, a postman came on the scene.

"Ha, ha! I told you last night that you would lose your way," said he in a drawling voice.

I recognized my villager of Grey-l'Abbaye, and bad temper prevented me answering him.

"It's to Fonval you want to go, is it?" he went on.

I cursed Fonval in some very profane language in which I consigned it and its inhabitants to the Devil.

"Because," went on the postman, "if you are going there, I'll show you the way. I am taking the letters there. But make haste, I have double load to-day; for this is Monday and I don't come on Sunday."

While saying this, he had drawn his letters from his bag, and was arranging them in his hand.

"Show me that," I cried sharply, "Yes, that yellow envelope."

He looked me up and down distrustfully and then let me look at it from a distance.

It was my letter—the announcement of my arrival, which followed it by a night, instead of preceding it by a day!

This untoward circumstance absolved my uncle and drove away my rancour.

"Get in," I said. "You shall show me the way and then... we shall have a talk!"

The car set off in the freshness of the morning.

A mist was just melting away, as if the sun after whitening the dark had still to dissolve it, and as if this faint fog, now almost nothing, were a portion of the darkness remaining in the form of vapor, an evanescent remainder of the night within the day, the vanishing specter of a vanished phantom.

# CHAPTER II
## AMONG THE SPHINXES

The car slowly wound its way among the twists and turns of the labyrinth. Sometimes in presence of a cluster of roads the postman himself hesitated for a moment.

"Since when have these zigzags taken the place of the straight avenue?" I asked.

"Four years ago, Sir—about a year after the settling in of Mr. Learne in the château."

"Do you know the meaning of them? You may speak freely. I am the professor's nephew."

"Oh, well, he's... he's, well an eccentric man."

"What sort of unusual things does he do?"

"Oh, well, nothing. One hardly ever sees him. That's just the funny part of it. Before he took this higgledy-piggledy into his head, one met him often. He used to walk about in the country, but ever since then ... well, he does take the train to Grey once a month."

So all my uncle's eccentricities came to a head at the same epoch; the maze and the different style of his letters coincided as to date. Something at that time had profoundly influenced his mind.

"And what about his companions?" I went on, "the Germans?"

"Oh, as for them, Sir, they are invisible. Moreover, although I go to Fonval six times a week I do not remember when I last clapped eyes on the park. It's Mr. Lerne himself who comes to the gate for his letters. Oh, what a change! Did you know old John? Well, he's gone, and his wife too. It's as true as I'm talking to you, Sir. No more coachman, no more housekeeper … no more horses."

"That's been so for four years, you say?"

"Yes, Sir."

"Tell me, postman, there's game about here, is there not?"

"Faith, no. A few rabbits, two or three hares—but there are too many foxes."

"What, no roe-deer? no stags?"

"Never."

AND NOW I FELT A STRANGE THRILL OF JOY.

"Here we are, Sir!"

After a final bend, the road did open out on the old avenue of which Lerne had kept this little bit. It was fringed by two rows of limes, and from the end of the two rows they formed, the door of Fonval seemed to be coming towards us.

In front of it, a carriage-sweep in the shape of a half moon widened the avenue, and beyond that one saw the outline of the blue roof of the château against the green of the trees, and the trees themselves standing out on the somber flanks of the gully.

In the midst of the wall which joined the cliffs on either hand stood the door with its tiled porch. It had aged, and the stone of the lintel was worn away; the wood of its panels was worm-eaten and crumbling into powder here and there; but the bell had not changed. Its sound came from my distant boyhood, so bright and clear that I could have wept at it.

We waited for a few moments.

At last some wooden shoes clattered.

"Is that you, Guilloteau?" said a voice with a trans-Rhenish accent.

"Yes, Mr. Lerne."

Mr. Lerne! I looked at my guide with eyes wide with wonder—What! Was that my uncle speaking like that?

"You are early," went on the voice. There was the metallic sound of moving bolts; then the door was opened ajar, and a hand was passed through it.

"Give me them."

"Here they are, Mr. Lerne. But there is some one with me," said the postman in an insinuating and timid way.

"Who is it?" cried the other—and in the fissure formed by the hardly opened door, he appeared.

It was my uncle Lerne. But life had laid hand on him, had made him much older, and turned him into this wild unkempt individual whose straggling gray hair covered his shabby clothes with dirty grease. He seemed smitten with premature old age, and there was an unfriendly gleam in the evil eyes which he fixed on me, from under their knitted eyebrows.

"What do you want?" he asked me rudely.

He pronounced the words like a German.

I had a moment of hesitation. The fact was that his face could no longer be compared to that of a kind old woman; it was a Sioux visage, hairless and cruel, and at the sight of it I experienced the contradictory sensations of recognizing it and not recognizing it.

"But, Uncle," I stuttered finally, "it's I.... I have come to see you—according to leave given by you. I wrote to you; but my letter ... here it is! my letter and I arrive together. Excuse my carelessness."

"Ah, you should have told me. It is I that ask pardon of you, my dear nephew."

A sudden change this! Lerne showed eagerness to welcome me! he blushed and seemed confused and almost servile. This embarrassment, misplaced with regard to me, shocked me.

"Ha ha! you've come with a mechanical carriage," he added. "Hum, there's a place to put it in, isn't there?"

He opened both folding-doors.

"Here one has often to be one's own servant," he said, while the old hinges creaked.

Thereupon he burst into an awkward sort of laugh. I could have wagered, looking at his perplexed expression, that he had no desire to do so, and that his thoughts were far away from joking.

The postman had taken his leave.

"Is the coach-house still there?" I said, pointing to the right at a brick building.

"Yes, yes. I did not recognize you because of your mustache—hum! Yes, your mustache. You hadn't one long ago ... had you? Well, and how old are you?"

"Thirty-one, uncle."

At the sight of the coach-house my heart stopped.

The dog-cart was moldering there, half buried under logs, and there, as in the neighboring stable which was full of odds and ends, the spider webs were hanging whole or in shreds.

"Thirty-one, already," went on Lerne in a vague and obviously distracted manner.

"But, Uncle, say tu and toi to me, as long ago."

"Ah, yes, dear ... Nicolas, eh?"

I was very ill at ease, but he did not seem more at his ease than I was. My presence clearly annoyed him.

It is always an interesting thing for an intruder to learn why he is so,—I seized my valise. Lerne observed my gesture and seemed to form a sudden resolve.

"Let it be—let it be, Nicholas," he said in a tone of command. "I'll send to fetch your luggage shortly. But first we must have a talk. Come for a walk."

He took my arm and drew me towards the park. He was still reflecting, however.

We passed near the _château_. With few exceptions the shutters were closed. The roof in many places was sinking in, sometimes even broken, and the moldy walls from which the whitewash had disappeared in large flakes here and there showed their masonry. The plants in boxes still surrounded the house, but, to tell the truth, for several winters no one had thought of putting the verbenas and orange-trees and laurels under cover. Standing in their battered and rotten tubs they were all dead. The sandy carriage-drive, of yore so carefully raked, might have imagined itself a second-rate meadow, there was so much grass growing there mingled with nettles and hemlock. It was like the castle of "Sleeping Beauty" on the Prince's arrival. Lerne, clinging to my arm, walked without further talk.

We got to the other side of the dreary pile, and the park lay before our eyes. A jumble. No more baskets of flowers, no more wide, sandy paths like winding ribbons. Except just in front of the château, the lawn—which had been metamorphosed into a paddock fenced with wire and given up to some cattle to feed in—had been encroached on by the valley which had relapsed into its wild state. The garden was no more than a great wood with open spaces and green paths in it. The Ardennes had reassumed their usurped domain.

Lerne thoughtfully filled an immense pipe with feverish fingers, lit it, and then we went under the trees into one of the alleys that were like long caves.

Once more I saw the statues and with a disillusioned eye, the statues which a former master of Fonval had erected in profusion. Those magnificent dumb personages of my dramas were as a matter of fact wretched modern figures, suggested to some commercially-minded magnate of industry of the Second Empire by Rome or Greece. The tunics of concrete swelled out into crinolines, the drapery of the cloaks was like that of a shawl, and the divinities of the woods—Echo, Syrinx, Arethusa—wore low chignons which filled their bag-like nets—in the Benoiton manner. Those hideous representations of exquisite fantasies, of forest charms transmuted into Dryads, were to-day more passable in their mantles of virgin-vine and clematis, although certain heroes were no more than ivy-clad figures of fun, and although a mere moss-clad attitude represented Diana.

After walking for some time, my uncle made me sit down on a bench of stone covered with a coat of lichen, under the shade of flourishing hazels.

A little crackling sound made itself heard in the bower right over our heads.

Lerne jumped convulsively and raised his head.

It was merely a squirrel watching us from the top of a branch.

My uncle darted a ferocious glance at it, fixing it as if he were taking aim at it; then he began to laugh in a reassured sort of way.

"Ha, ha, ha! it's only a little ... thing," said he, unable to find the word.

"Really," thought I within myself, "how queer one may become as one gets old. Environment, I know, is the cause of many evolutions; one adopts the ways and manner of speech of one's familiars in spite of oneself; the surroundings of Lerne might suffice to explain why my uncle is dirty, expresses himself ill, speaks with a German accent and smokes that huge pipe.... But he has ceased caring for flowers, he no longer looks after his property, and at this moment looks extraordinarily nervous and preoccupied. If one adds to that the happenings of last night, it all seems something less than natural."

Meanwhile the Professor looked at me in a disconcerting way, and eyed me up and down as if here were sizing me up and had never seen me before. I began to lose countenance. A fierce debate was going on within him which was reflected on his face. Every moment our looks crossed, but at last they met, and joined, and my uncle, not being able to hold his peace any longer appeared for the second time to make up his mind.

"Nicolas," he said, patting me on the thigh, "I am a ruined man, you know."

I understood his plan, and was revolted.

"Uncle, be frank with me; you want me to go!"

"I want you to go! What an idea!"

"I am quite sure of it. Your invitation was rather discouraging, and your welcome hardly hospitable. But, uncle, you must have a very short memory if you think me avaricious enough to have come here merely for your money. I see you are no longer the same—your letters indeed made me fear that—and yet it utterly bewilders me that you should have thought of this clumsy subterfuge intended to drive me away. For during these fifteen years I have not changed. I have never ceased venerating you with my whole heart, and have deserved better at your hands than those icy epistles and, above all, better than this insult."

"There, there! Gently!" said Lerne, much annoyed.

"Moreover, if you want me to go, just say the word and I'm off. You are no uncle of mine now."

"Don't talk such blasphemous nonsense, Nicolas." He said that in a tone of such alarm that I tried intimidation.

"And I shall inform against you, uncle, you and your acolytes and your mysteries."

"You are mad, you are mad. Hold your tongue. There's an idea for you!"

Lerne began to laugh loudly, but I don't know why, his eyes frightened me, and I regretted my phrase.

He went on.

"Look here, Nicolas, don't get excited! You are a good fellow. Give me your hand. You shall always find in me your old uncle who loves you. Listen, it's not true; no, I am not ruined, and my heir will certainly get something—if he acts as I desire. But, as a matter of fact, I think he would do better not to stay here.... There's nothing here to amuse a man of your age, Nicolas; personally I am busy all day long."

The Professor might talk as he liked now. Hypocrisy showed itself in every word; he was nothing but a contemptible Tartuffe; he was fair game. I determined not to leave till I had completely satisfied my curiosity. So, interrupting him, I said in a tone of deep dejection:

"There you are making use of the inheritance business again to make me decide to leave Fonval. You have clearly no trust in me."

With a gesture he deprecated the idea. I went on:

"No, allow me to remain in order that we may renew our acquaintance. We both need to do so."

Lerne knitted his eyebrows, then he said in a mocking tone:

"You insist on renouncing me?"

"No; keep me beside you, otherwise you will hurt my feelings deeply; frankly," this in a bantering tone, "I should not know what to think."

"Stop," rejoined my uncle with energy, "there is nothing wrong to suspect here—far from it."

"No doubt. All the same, you have secrets—as you have every right to have. If I speak to you of them, it is because I must resign myself to assure you that I shall respect them."

"There is only one! A single secret. And its aim is noble and salutary," said my uncle sententiously and with animation: "One only, I tell you— that concerning our work; a blessing to humanity—glory too and gold! But we must have silence assured us. Secrets! Everybody knows we are here, that we are working. The newspapers have said so—there is no secret in that."

"Keep calm, uncle, and tell me how I am to behave in your house. I am entirely at your disposal."

Lerne resumed his inward debate:

"Well," said he, raising his brow, "it is agreed. Such an uncle as I have always shown myself towards you cannot possibly drive you away. That would be belying all my past. Remain then, but on the following conditions:

"We are pursuing researches here that are about to come to their fulfillment. When our discovery is a fait accompli the public will hear of it in its entirety. Till then, I do not wish it to be informed of uncertain attempts whose revelation might raise up rivals capable of anticipating us. I do not doubt your discretion, but I prefer not to put it to the test, and I entreat you in your own interests not to try to surprise any secrets, rather than to be obliged to hide them. I say, 'in your own interests'; not merely because it is easier not to pry than to hold one's tongue, but also for the following reasons: Our business is a commercial one at bottom. A man of business like you will be very useful to me. We shall become rich, nephew—millionaires! But you must let me forget the instrument of your fortune in peace, you must show yourself a man of tact and respectful of my orders—in a word, the man I want as an associate. You must know, I am not alone in this enterprise. They might make you repent of your acts, if you transgressed the rule I am laying down for you—cruelly repent— more cruelly than you imagine. So practice indifference, my dear nephew. See nothing, hear nothing, understand nothing, in order that you may become very, very rich—and remain alive!"

"Oh, indifference is not so easy a virtue at Fonval. There have been things going about here since last night which should not be here and only find themselves here through some bit of carelessness."

At those words an unexpected rage seized Lerne. He flung out his fists and growled: "Wilhelm! Fool! Ass!" What I now felt sure of was that the secrets were considerable and would give me fine surprises were they discovered. As for the doctor's promises, and his threats, I did not believe in either, and his speech had neither aroused covetousness nor fear in me—the two passions that my uncle wished to make my counselors to obedience. I rejoined coldly:

"Is that all you ask of me?"

"No. But the next prohibition is of another kind, Nicolas. You will be presented to somebody in the château; it is a young girl I rescued...."

I made a movement of surprise, and Lerne guessed my imputation.

"Oh!" he exclaimed, "she is like a daughter—nothing more. But her friendship is precious to me, and it would be painful to me to see it lessened by a sentiment which I can no longer inspire. In short, Nicolas," he said quickly and with a certain shamefacedness, "I ask you to swear not to pay court to my protégée."

Astounded at such a degraded view, and still more so at such a want of delicate feeling, I told myself, however, that there is no jealousy without love any more than there is smoke without fire.

"What do you take me for, uncle? It is sufficient that I am your guest."

"All right—I know my physiology and how to use it. May I trust you? You swear it? Very well."

"As for her," he added with a crafty smile, "I am easy for the time being. She has lately seen my way of treating suitors. I advise you not to make trial of it."

Having got up, with his hands in his pockets, and his pipe between his teeth, Lerne looked me up and down in a jocular and provocative manner. This physiologist inspired me with an unconquerable aversion.

We continued our walk round the park.

"Ah, by the way, do you know German?" said the Professor.

"No, uncle; I only understand French and Spanish."

"No English either? That's not much for a future merchant prince. You have not been taught much, I fear."

"Tell that to the Marines, uncle," said I to myself. "I had begun to keep wide open those eyes you commanded me to keep shut, and I saw just then that your satisfied expression gave your words the lie."

We reached the end of the park by way of the foot of the cliffs and came in front of the château which seemed stretching its two wings towards us and dominating the underwood with its ruinous façade.

And it was at this exact moment that my eye was caught by an abnormal bird, a pigeon, which was wheeling in the air, and flew upwards with ever-narrowing and giddy circles.

"Just look at those roses on that long branch of briar; they are pretty and interesting," said my uncle. "Left to grow wild, they have become dog-roses again."

"What a curious pigeon!" I said.

"Just look at those flowers," insisted Lerne.

"One would think there was a drop of lead in its head. That happens sometimes when one is out shooting. It will tower and tower, and then fall from as high as possible."

"If you don't watch your feet, you will fall head over heels into the thorn-bushes. It's a breakneck place, this, nephew."

This useful bit of counsel was growled out in a menacing tone that sounded strangely out of place.

Then the bird attained the center of its spiral and began not to mount, but to come down with wild tumblings, and whirling over and over. It hit a rock not far from us and fell, an inert thing, into the thick herbage.

Why did the Professor suddenly become more restless? Why did he hasten his steps? That is what I was asking myself, when the big pipe fell from his mouth. Having dashed forward to pick it up I could not restrain a look of stupefaction; he had snapped it off sharp with a furious bite.

The scene ended with a German word—doubtless an oath.

As we returned in the direction of the château we saw running towards us a fat woman who seemed bursting out of her blue apron.

She was evidently unused to such athletic exercise and it went against the grain, for it shook her dangerously, and as she trotted along, she kept herself together by means of her arms and hands as if she were pressing some precious, huge and unwieldy burden against her person. At the sight of us, she stopped all of a piece—a thing that seemed almost an impossibility—then she seemed to want to retrace her steps. However, she came on with a guilty look on her kindly face, a look as of a school-girl caught in a fault. She awaited her fate.

Lerne scolded her:

"Barbe! What are you doing here? You have forgotten. I forbade you to go beyond the paddock. I'll end by sending you packing, Barbe, after punishing you—you know."

The fat woman was very much afraid. She tried to bridle, made a mouth as if she were going to lay an egg with it and excused herself—she had, from her kitchen, seen the pigeon fall and thought she might brighten up the bill of fare with it. "You always have the same dishes to eat."

"And then," she added stupidly, "I did not think you were in the garden, I thought you were in the lab...."

A brutal slap in the face interrupted her on that syllable—the first syllable of "labyrinth," as I imagined.

"Oh, uncle!" I cried indignantly.

"Look here, you! Hold your tongue, or off with you! That's clear enough, isn't it?"

Barbe was terrified and no longer wept. Her suppressed sobs made her hiccup. She was very pale, and on her cheek the bony hand of Lerne remained printed in red.

"Go and take this gentleman's luggage from the coach-house and put it in the lion-room."

(This room was on the first story of the western wing.)

"Won't you give me my old room, uncle?"

"Which was that?"

"Which? Why, the one on the ground floor, the yellow room, in the East wing, you know."

"No. I use that one," he said sharply. "Off with you, Barbe."

The cook decamped as fast as she could.

On our right the pond was lying there stagnant. Our silent passage flung its shadow into it, and it looked there like a dream in a lethargy.

My astonishment was growing every moment. However, I kept myself from seeming too much surprised at the sight of a new and spacious building of gray stone built against the cliff. It consisted of two blocks separated by a courtyard. A high wall pierced with a carriage-gate, at the moment shut, hid it from one's eyes, but the clucking of fowls escaped from it, and a dog, having scented us, raised his voice.

I flung out a plummet at a venture:

"You'll take me over your farm, won't you?"

Lerne shrugged his shoulders:

"Perhaps," he said. Then turning towards the house, he shouted:

"Wilhelm, Wilhelm!"

The German with the face like a sundial opened a little window and the Professor apostrophized him in his mother-tongue, so violently that the poor fellow trembled all over.

"By Jove!" I said to myself. "It's owing to him and his inadvertence that there are going about outside since last night, things that should not be there_—that's certain."

When the execution was over, we went round the paddock. It contained a black bull and four cows of various kinds, the whole lot of whom, for no particular reason, followed after us. My dreadful relative began to joke:

"Nicolas, let me introduce you to Jupiter; and here is the white Europa, the dun-colored Io, the fair-skinned Athor, and Pasiphaë clad in her robe of milk stained with ink, or ink stained with milk—whichever way you prefer."

This reference to libertine mythology made me smile. To tell the truth, I should have seized the first pretext to have a laugh; I had physical need of it. I also felt a hunger so intense that to satisfy it seemed the only question of any interest. The château was the one and only attraction. It was there I should eat! And the attraction it exercised on me almost made me fail to examine the hothouse, its neighbor.

That would have been a pity. They had added two halls of glass to it which flanked the original rotunda with their domed naves. Under its lowered outer blinds the building seemed to me to form a whole that was "perfect of its kind." It suggested something between a Crystal Palace and a glass melon-bell; it had quite a grand and out-of-the-way appearance, if I may so say.

A hothouse of this kind in this thicket! I should have been less astonished to find a love-philter in a monastery!

IN THE DAYS OF MY LATE LAMENTED AUNT, THE LION-ROOM WAS RESERVED FOR guests. It had—it still has—three windows, with deep recesses as deep as alcoves. One of them looks out in the direction of the conservatory and has a balcony attached; the second opens on the park; I saw the paddock from it and further away the pond, and between the two that summerhouse which once was Briareus. The third window faces the eastern wing; from there I saw the window of my old room—shut—and the whole façade of the château blocking the view on the left.

I felt as if I were in an hotel. Nothing there recalled anything to me. A Jouy wall-paper stained with damp from the wall and hanging loose in one corner, covered the walls with a host of red lions each with a cannon ball fixed under its paw. The bed curtains and window curtains showed, in distortion, the same subject. Two pictures balanced one another: The

Education of Achilles and The Rape of Deianeira, in which the damp spotted the faces of the four subjects with red and dappled the cruppers of the Centaurs, Chiron and Nessus; there was also rather a fine Norman clock which looked like a coffin set on end, the emblem and at the same time the measures of Time—and the whole furnishing of the room was commonplace and out-of-date.

I splashed my face with cold water and put on clean linen with pleasure. Barbe brought me, without knocking at the door, a plate of coarse broth, and made no reply to my condolences on her inflamed cheek; then she waddled out of the room like a gigantic sylph.

There was no one in the drawing-room—unless shades are people. O little black velvet armchair with your two yellow tassels, hideous piece of squat puffiness, so well termed a crapaud, could I behold you again as of yore without imagining seated on your toad-like form the shade of my anecdotal aunt? And you, my mother's chair—an austerer one, and one I cannot jest about—will she not always be in my memory leaning over your back as long as you shall be an armchair, if indeed you ever really were one?

Not a detail was altered. From the unspeakable white paper on the walls down which hung garlands of flowers trussed like sausages, to the hangings of sulphur-colored damask draping their fringed basques in a row, the work of the former owner—a contemporary of the crinoline— had admirably stood the effect of time. A swollen stuffing puffed out the sofas single and double, and nothing had succeeded in deflating the inflamed chairs or the blistered settees.

From the wainscot smiled down on one all my dead and gone ancestors: my great-great-grandfathers in chalk, my grandfathers in miniatures, my father a schoolboy in daguerrotype; and on the mantelpiece (duly petticoated with puffed-out fringed flounces) a few photographs were sticking to the mirror. A large-sized group claimed my attention. I took it up to look at it more carefully. It represented my uncle surrounded by five gentlemen and a big St. Bernard dog. The group had been taken at Fonval; the wall of the château made the background, and a rose-laurel in a tub figured in the picture. An amateur's work and unsigned. Lerne beamed with kindness and mental energy, resembling, in a word, the savant I had expected to find. Of the five men, three were known to me, the Germans; I had never seen the two others.

Then suddenly the door opened without my having the time to replace the photograph. Lerne was ushering in a young woman.

"My nephew, Nicolas Vermont—Mademoiselle Emma Bourdichet."

Mlle. Emma had apparently been undergoing one of those sharp lectures that Lerne distributed so prodigally. Her frightened expression showed that. She had not even the courage to make the conventional grimace usual in cases of constrained amiability, and merely made an awkward sort of bow.

As for me, after bowing, I dared not raise my eyes for fear my uncle should read my soul in them.

My soul? If by soul one means (as is generally meant) that ensemble of faculties which result in man's being a little above the other animals, I think I had better not compromise my soul in this matter.

Oh, I'm not unaware that, if all loves, even the purest, are originally animal desires, esteem and friendship sometimes add themselves thereto to ennoble the relations of man and woman.

Alas! If some Fragonard wished to commemorate our first interview and, in the 18th century manner, depict Love as presiding over it, I should advise him to study a certain little Eros with goat's feet and thighs, a faun-like Cupid unsmiling and wingless; his arrows should be wooden and in a quiver made of bark, and should be dripping with blood; he might indeed pass under the name of Pan. He is Love universal, Pleasure that is unintentionally fecund, the Master of Life who takes equal heed of lairs and eyries, beasts' dens and bridal beds.

Are there degrees of femininity? In that case, I never saw a woman who was more a woman than Emma. I shall not describe her, having scarcely noted more in her than an abstraction and not an object. Was she beautiful? No doubt; most assuredly desirable.

Yet, I do remember her hair. It had the color of fire, a dull red—possibly dyed—and the image of her body passes even now through my dead passion. It would have put all flat-figured ladies to shame.

Well, this adorable creature was at the height of her charm.

The blood beat against my brain pan, and suddenly a fierce jealousy possessed me. In truth I should willingly have given up this girl, provided no one else should touch her ever. From unpleasing, Lerne now became odious to me. I should remain now—at any price.

Meanwhile we did not know what to say. Thrown off my balance by the suddenness of the incident, and wishing to hide my confusion, I stuttered out anyhow:

"You see, uncle, I was just looking at that photograph."

"Ah, yes! Me and my assistants, Wilhelm, Karl, and Johann. And this is Macbeth, my pupil. It's very like him. What do you think of it, Emma?"

He had put the photograph under his ward's eyes and pointed out to her a man close-shaven in the American way, slim, short and young, with a distinguished bearing, who had his hand on the back of the St. Bernard dog.

"A handsome, intelligent fellow, eh?" said the Professor in a mocking voice. "The ace of Scots!"

Emma never changed her look of terror. She articulated with difficulty:

"His Nelly was very amusing with her performing-dog tricks."

"And Macbeth," said my uncle in a jesting voice. "Was _he_ amusing?"

There were symptoms of tears coming, and I saw Emma's chin quiver. She murmured:

"Poor Macbeth!"

"Yes," said Lerne to me by way of answer to my puzzled looks, "Mr. Donovan Macbeth had to give up his duties as a result of some unfortunate occurrences. May Fate spare you such unhappiness, Nicolas!"

"And the other?" I asked, in order to turn the conversation. "The other one, he with the brown mustache and whiskers, who is he?"

"He's gone, too."

"Dr. Klotz," said Emma, who had drawn near us and was regaining her calm. "Otto Klotz; oh, as for him...."

Lerne silenced her with a terrible look. I do not know what punishment she foresaw, but a spasm rendered the poor girl rigid.

Hereupon Barbe introduced slantwise half of her opulent form and murmured that lunch was on the table.

She had only set three places in the dining room; the Germans, I fancied, must live in the gray buildings.

The lunch was gloomy. Mlle. Bourdichet never ventured a word, ate nothing, and so I could not make out what was the matter, terror making all creatures alike.

Besides, sleepiness was overwhelming me. Immediately after dessert I asked leave to go to bed, begging to be allowed to sleep till the next morning.

Once in my room, I immediately began to undress. To tell the truth my journey, the night and the morning had worn me out. All those riddles, too, worried me, first because they were riddles and then because they presented themselves so confusedly. I felt as if I were enveloped in smoke wherein riddling sphinxes kept turning their vague faces towards me.

My braces were just going to be flung off—and were not flung off.

In the garden Lerne was making his way towards the gray buildings accompanied by his three assistants.

"They are going to work in there," said I to myself. "That's clear. I am not being watched; they have not had time to take many precautions; uncle is persuaded I am asleep. Nicolas, this is the time for action, now or never. But what to start with? Emma, or the secret? Hum ... the little girl is utterly gorgonized to-day.... As for the secret...."

Having put on my coat again, I went mechanically from window to window.

There between the wrought-iron stanchions of the balcony the Conservatory showed its mysterious additions. It was shut, forbidden, attractive.

I went out stealthily and noiselessly, like a wolf.

# CHAPTER III
## THE CONSERVATORY

Once outside, and without cover, it seemed to me that everything was spying on me; so I flung myself headlong into a little wood near the conservatory; then through the thorn and creepers I made my way towards my objective.

It was very warm. I advanced with great difficulty and taking thousands of precautions to avoid scratches and tell-tale rents.

At last the conservatory with its central dome and one of its bulging flanks loomed large before me. It was a side view that first presented itself. I thought it would be wise to reconnoiter it before leaving the shelter of the wood.

What struck me immediately was its appearance of cleanliness, its perfect upkeep; not a paving-stone of the encircling footway displaced, not a brick of the foundation broken; the blinds which were well fastened had all their laths, and in the narrow open spaces of their shutters the window-panes flashed in the sun.

I listened. No sound came to me from the castle or from the gray buildings. In the conservatory there was complete silence. One heard nothing but the vast hum of a burning afternoon.

Then I summoned up my courage, and approaching stealthily, I raised one of the wooden sun-blinds and tried to look through the panes; but I could see nothing; they had been smeared on the inside with a whitish substance. It seemed more and more probable that Lerne had diverted the conservatory from its original use, and now abandoned himself there to any other culture than that of flowers. The idea of microbe broths simmering under the warm light seemed to me quite a happy inspiration.

I moved round the glass house. Everywhere the same stuff smeared on the window-panes intercepted the view—rather thick stuff it appeared.

The ventilation windows stood open but beyond my reach. The wings had no doors, and one could not get into the central part from the back.

As I kept moving round scrutinizing the brick and the no less thick glass, I soon found myself on the château side opposite my balcony. This position being unsheltered was dangerous. I thought I should have to return to my bedroom, and give up the supposed palace of microbes without examining the front. I limited my investigation therefore to a most disappointed glance—a glance, however, which suddenly let me know that the mystery lay open to me.

The door was only pressed against the door-post, and the bolt which was quite free showed that some careless person had thought he had barred the door securely. Oh, Wilhelm, you priceless donkey!

The moment I entered, my bacteriological hypothesis was at once destroyed. A whiff of floral perfumes welcomed me—a moist and warm whiff with a touch of nicotine in it.

I paused in wonderment on the threshold.

No hothouse—not even a royal one—has ever given me that impression of riotous luxury which I at first experienced. In that rotunda in the midst of all those sumptuous plants, the first sensation was that of bedazzlement. The whole gamut of greens was played in a chromatic scale on the keyboard of leaves, amid the multi-colored tones of flowers and fruit, and on tiers which climbed up to the cupola those splendors surged magnificently upward.

But one's eyes became accustomed to the sight, and my admiration grew somewhat less. Assuredly, however, for this Winter-Garden to arouse my admiration so immediately, it must have been composed of plants very remarkable in themselves, for in reality no attempt at harmony had brought about their arrangement.

They were grouped in disciplinary order and not in accordance with a spirit of elegance—like some Eldorado confided to the care of a gendarme. Their ranks separated themselves brutally from one another, like so many categories; the pots stood in military array, and each of them bore a label, which had to do with botany rather than with gardening, and gave evidence rather of science than of art. This circumstance gave one food for meditation. After all, could I admit for a moment that Lerne could possibly do gardening for pleasure?

Prosecuting my researches, I let my charmed eyes wander over all those marvels, incapable in my ignorance of naming any of them. I tried to do so, however, mechanically, and then that luxuriance, which on a cursory general look had shown a sort of exotic character, began to appear to me as it really was....

Incredulous, and a prey to a fever of curiosity, I looked at a cactus.

In spite of my want of expert knowledge, I could not be mistaken, but its red flower utterly puzzled me.... I looked at it minutely, and my perplexity only grew.

There was no possible doubt: this demoniac flower with its insolent look, this rocket which soared up green to break in fiery stars, was a geranium!

I went on to the next flower: three bamboo stalks rose out of the soil, and capitals which crowned their slim columns were—dahlias.

Almost afraid, breathing in the unnatural perfumes in short breaths, I looked questioningly at the place around me, and its miracle-like incoherence clearly showed itself.

Spring, Summer, and Autumn reigned there in company, and Lerne had doubtless suppressed Winter, which extinguishes flowers like flames. They were all there, and all fruits too, but neither flower nor fruit had grown on its own tree!

A colony of cornflowers garnished a stalk ceded by moss-roses, and which now waved about, a thyrsus thenceforward blue. An araucaria unfolded at the tip of its bristling branches the indigo-colored bells of the gentian, and along an espalier among nasturtium leaves and on the loops of its serpentine stalk, camelias and parti-colored tulips blossomed fraternally together.

Opposite the entrance-door, a clump of bushes rose up against the glass wall. The shrub which stood highest drew my attention. Pears were hanging from it, and it was an orange tree! Behind it two vine-stocks with branches worthy of the land of Canaan flung their garlands round a trellis; their gigantic clusters differed as their stocks; the one bore yellow fruit, the other purple—but each grape was a Mirabelle plum or a damson!

On the twigs of a miniature oak, on which several rebellious acorns were obstinately forming, one beheld walnuts and cherries rubbing shoulders. One of these fruits was an abortion: neither "chalk nor cheese" it was forming into a glaucous tumor streaked with pink—a thing monstrous and repellant.

Instead of cones, a fir tree was dotted with chestnuts like shining stars, and, moreover, it flaunted this strange contrast: the orange—that golden sun of Eastern orchards—and the medlar, which looks like a posthumous fruit of a tree that has died of cold!

Not far away there was a throng of still more fully developed miracles. Flora was elbowing Pomona, as the good Demoustier would have phrased it. Most of the plants that formed this crowd were strange to me, and I only remember the commoner ones, those that anybody knows the list of. I can still see an astounding willow which bore hortensias and peonies, peaches and strawberries. But the prettiest of all those hybrids was perhaps a rose tree with ox-eyes for flowers and crab-apples for fruit.

In the center of the rotunda a bush showed a mingling of leaves so dissimilar as those of the holly, the lime and the poplar. Having pressed them apart I satisfied myself that they issued all three from a single stem.

It was the triumph of grafting—a science that Lerne had for fifteen years been pushing to the verge of the miraculous, so far indeed that the results presented a somewhat disquieting spectacle. "When man sets his hand to Life, he makes monsters." A kind of uneasiness troubled me.

"What right has one to upset Creation?" I said to myself. "Should one turn the ancient laws topsy-turvy? Can one play this sacrilegious game without high treason against Nature? If only those artificial things had been in good taste! But, devoid of real novelty, they were merely curious mixtures, a sort of vegetable chimeras, floral Fauns, half this and half that.

On my honor, graceful or not, this kind of work is impious, and that's the long and the short of it."

Be that as it may, the Professor had toiled most laboriously to bring his work to so successful an issue. The collection vouched for that, and there were other signs that recalled the savant's industry: on a table I perceived rows of bottles and an array of grafting-tools and gardening implements which glittered like surgical instruments. This discovery sent me back to the flowers, and looking into the matter I became aware of all their wretchedness.

They were plastered with various sorts of gum, bandaged and full of gashes which were like wounds, out of which oozed a suspicious juice.

There was a wound in the bark of the pear-bearing orange tree that formed an eye which was slowly shedding tears.

I was becoming quite nervous. Would one have believed it? I was assailed by a ridiculous anguish as I looked at the oak-tree (which had had an operation) because I fancied the cherries looked like drops of blood...! Flop! flop! Two ripe ones fell at my feet like the first drops of a thunder-storm.

I was no longer possessed of the calm necessary for reading the labels. They merely told me a few dates—and the fact that Lerne had covered them with Franco-German terms which had originally been illegible, and were rendered more so by erasures.

With my ears on the alert, and with my brow in my hands, I had to take a moment's respite in order to gather my wits together, and then I opened the door of the right wing.

A little nave, as it were, stretched out before me. Its glass vault filtered the daylight and attenuated it to a bluish and refreshingly cool half-light. My steps rang out on the flagstones.

In this chamber there gleamed three aquariums, three tanks of glass, so pure that the water seemed to be standing of itself in three geometrical blocks.

The aquariums on the two sides of the hall held marine plants which did not seem to differ much one from the other. However, the rotunda had taught me with what method Lerne classified everything, and I could not believe that he had separated into two tanks things absolutely identical. So I watched the sea-weeds attentively.

Their tufts, on both sides of the place, formed the same submarine landscape. On the right, as on the left, arborescences of every color had fixed their rigid and bifurcated stems on the rocks; the sandy bottom was sprinkled with stars like edelweiss, and here and there sprung up sheaves of chalky rods, at the end of each of which a sort of fleshy chrysanthemum unfolded itself like a yellow or a violet flower. I cannot describe the host of other corollæ; they often resembled oily calices of wax or of gelatine; most of them showed an indefinable color in a vague outline, and sometimes they had no edges and were mere nuances in the midst of the water.

Bubbles escaped in thousands from an inside tap, and their tumultuous pearls raced madly along the foliage before they rose to burst on the surface. One would have thought, seeing them, that that aquatic garden had always to be drenched with air.

Recalling my schoolboy memories I grasped that the two sets of flowering things—differing merely in detail—were exclusively composed of polypi, those ambiguous creatures, such as coral or sponge, which the naturalist interpolates between vegetables and animals.

Their peculiar ambiguity is never devoid of interest. I tapped the left-hand trough.

Immediately an unexpected thing moved before me swimming by means of contraction; it was like an opaline Venetian goblet which had remained malleable; a second crossed over the first; they were two jelly-fish. Meanwhile the tapping of my fingers had set other things moving. The yellow and purple tufts of the anemones went back into their calcareous sheaths, then rhythmically unfolding, emerged again; the rays of the star-fish and sea-urchins stirred lazily; grays and reds and saffrons swayed about, and, as if under the influence of an eddy the whole aquarium became alive.

I tapped on the right-hand trough. Nothing budged.

This was proof positive; this separation of the polypi into two receptacles gave me a clearer understanding of the connection which, joining the animal and the vegetable, makes man akin to the blade of grass. At this meeting-place of the two organized kingdoms, the creatures on the left—active—were at the foot of their scale, and those on the right—inactive—at the top of theirs; the former were on the way to becoming beasts, the latter had finished being plants.

Thus, the gulf which seems to separate those two extreme poles in the world is reduced, as far as structure goes, to slight divergences, almost invisible—a less striking difference than that between the wolf and the fox which are, however, brothers.

Now, this infinitesimal difference in organization which Science, however, regards as unsurmountable, since it separates inertia from spontaneous movement—this difference Lerne had bridged! In the basin at the end of the room, the two species were grafted on to one another. I noted there a gelatinous sort of leaf of the immobile order, grafted on to a mobile stem, and now moving about too. The grafts adopted the condition of the plant into which they were inserted; penetrated with a life-giving juice, their indifference changed to animation, and the activity of the other was paralyzed through sucking in the ankylosis.

I would willingly have passed in review the various applications of this principle; but a medusa tied with a hundred knots to some seaweed or other struggled violently in its mossy net, and I turned away in disgust.

This last stage in grafting in spite of difficulties completed the profanation in my eyes, and I looked away into the blue shadow for less disagreeable sights.

The Professor's apparatus stood ready for him. There was a whole chemist's shop on a dresser. Four tables with clear glass tops alternated with the aquariums, and bore on them an arsenal of knives, pincers and tweezers.

No! Lerne had no right to do this! It was as infamous as a butchery! More so indeed! And his odious performances on virgin Nature offered at one and the same time the horror of a murder and the ignominy of a violation!

As I was yielding to this righteous indignation, a noise arose. Some one was knocking.

Ah! my hell beyond the grave will be to hear that little insignificant tapping. In a flash I felt every nerve in my body. Some one was knocking!

In a bound I was in the rotunda, and my face must have been terrible to see, for instinctively the dread of an adversary made me assume a look of ferocity.

Nobody on the doorstep—nobody in the park—I went in again.

The noise began once more. It was coming from the yet unexplored wing. Losing my head, I dashed towards it without realizing my rashness, or the risk of finding myself face to face with the danger, and so excited, that I banged my head against the door, as I opened it with a violent pull.

Nervous exhaustion had brought me down to this condition of weakness. And I ask myself to-day whether it had not to some extent given me hallucinations and made me fancy things to be more bizarre than they really were.

An intense light flooded the third hall and helped me at once to recover my assurance. On a dresser there was a cage upside down which was knocking about with a rat inside it, as in a prison. When the rat jumped, the cage jumped; hence the noise. At the sight of me, the rodent became quiet. I attached no importance to this little episode.

This place, which was less orderly than the others, looked like an ill-kept hothouse. But towels stained with blood and thrown on the ground, lancets lying anyhow among half empty test-tubes, all this told of recent work and might serve as an excuse for the confusion.

I began my investigation.

The first two witnesses to appear did not give me much information. These were some very humble plants in their china pots. Their names in um or us have gone from my memory, a thing I deplore, for they would give my tale more authoritativeness, and more resonance. But who, at the mention of their ordinary names, could fail to represent to himself a tuft of plantain and a tuft of hare's-ear?

The former was, it is true, of an exceptionally long and supple sort. As for the latter, it had nothing distinctive about it, and, like its fellows, it conscientiously counterfeited a dozen great ear-lobes. On two of its hairy, silvery leaves and on one of the twigs of the plantain below it, a bandage showed like a bracelet of white cloth which tar (apparently) stained brown.

I sighed a sigh of relief. "Good," said I to myself, "Lerne has inoculated them. This is only a repetition of what I have already seen, or rather an early, timid and simple essay, a stage on the road to the rotunda, as it is a stage on the way to the atrocities of the aquarium. I might have begun here, gone on to the central garden of Eden, and finished off by the polypi. Thank God, I have seen the worst."

So ran my thoughts, when the twig of the plantain twisted about like a worm!

At the same time a mass of shining gray gave a jump which betrayed its presence behind the dresser. There lay in the midst of a pool of blood a rabbit with silvery fur. It had just expired, and had nothing in the way of ears but two bleeding holes.

The presentiment of the reality made me break out into a sweat. It was then I touched the hairy plant. Having felt the two grafted leaves like ears, I perceived they were hot and quivering.

A recoil sent me up against the dresser. My hand stiff with disgust tried to shake off the feeling of that contact as it would that of a hideous spider; it knocked violently against the rat's cage, which fell.

At once the rat bounded towards the middle of its cage, biting and rolling about with mad fury ... and my staring eyes went continually from the plantain to the animal, from the twig quivering like a thin black snake to the rat which had no tail.

Its wound had healed, but the poor beast bore traces of another experiment which it dragged about in its somersaults—a sort of loosened girdle, which still, however, kept fixed in its place a piece of greenery that had been inserted into its slashed flank!

This growth seemed to me to have withered. So Lerne was mounting the scale of Being. He was now grafting together the higher animals and all kinds of plants! Infamous and great, my uncle inspired me with disgust and admiration, such as one might feel for a maleficient deity.

His works, however, seemed to me less estimable than repulsive, and I had to do violence to myself to force myself to prolong my visit.

It was worth it, even if it was merely a figment of the brain. What remained for me to learn surpasses the nightmare of a madman. Frightful, assuredly, but comic too in a way—grotesque, sinister.

Which of the sufferers inspired most horror? The guinea-pig, the frog or the trees?

The guinea-pig, perhaps was the least extraordinary. Its pelt may have been green only as the result of the green reflection from all those plants. That _may_ be so.

But the frog! But the trees! What was one to think of them?

The frog was green as grass and had all its four legs forced into the soil, planted in the middle of a pot like a vegetable with four roots, its eyelids closed, its aspect dull and mournful.

As for the date trees—at first they had given no sign of motion, and I am certain there was no wind blowing—then, when they did move, it was in all directions. Their leaves swayed very gently—I thought I heard something, but I could not swear to it—yes, the trees swayed and came closer at every moment; suddenly they gripped one another with all their green fingers and embraced convulsively. Was it in wrath or in lust? For battle or for love? I know not. The gestures are much alike.

Beside the frog a vase of white porcelain was full of a colorless liquid in which was steeped a Pravoz syringe. A similar vase and syringe had been placed near the trees, but here the liquid was brown and curdling. I concluded that they were sap and blood.

The date trees had let go of each other, and my trembling hand advanced towards them. I could feel, under the soft warm bark pulse-beats that made it rise and fall with rhythmical cadence.

Since then I have said to myself that one may feel ones own pulse when feeling that of others, and I was doubtless feverish; but at the moment could I doubt my senses?... Besides, what follows in no wise impeaches my lucidity then; it would on the contrary plead in its favor. I do not know whether intensity of recollection in a doubtful case of hallucination is an argument for or against a morbid state; but at any rate I remember very intensely the picture of those monstrosities rising out of the medley of linen wrappings and bottles among the scattered instruments of steel.

Was there nothing more to see? I rummaged in the corners—no, nothing more. I had followed step by step my uncle's work and in the rational order of their ascending scale.

I got back to the château without let or hindrance and regained my bedroom. There the hectic vigor which had been supporting me quite failed me. Vainly I tried, as I undressed, to recapitulate my campaign. It was already assuming the appearance of a bad dream and I no longer believed in it. Could the vegetable kingdom really mingle with the animal? What an absurdity! If plant-polypi are almost animal-polypi, what can an insect and a leaf, for example, have in common? Then I felt a sharp pain in the thumb of my right hand: a little white pustle ringed with pink was budding there. In my journey through the woods something had stung me. But I was unable to say whether it was the vengeance of a nettle or of an ant. This made me feel the possibilities of things, and that I had not to accept them as having been realized by my uncle. My reflections were as follows:—

"To sum up, Lerne has tried to amalgamate vegetables and animals, and to make them exchange their vitalities. His methods, judiciously progressive, have succeeded. But are they aims in themselves, or only a means to something else? What is he trying to reach? I cannot see how those experiments can have practical applications that a financier might exploit. So, they are not ends in themselves. It seems to me that they tend to something more perfect which I can vaguely divine without fully perceiving. My head is full of woolly headache—Come, let me see!... Perhaps the Professor is carrying on at the same time other researches converging to the same point as these, a knowledge of which would make the final object clear. Come, come! Logic, logic. On the one hand.... Oh, Lord I am tired—On the one hand I have seen vegetables grafted together, on the other hand my uncle has begun mixing up plants and beasts ... ah, I give it up."

My exhausted mind refused to reason any more. I saw in a confused way that in his study of grafting he had neglected a whole branch of the subject, or at least that the hothouse was not its theater. My eyelids grew heavy. The more I tried to induce or deduce the more I got confused. The apparition of the preceding night, the gray buildings, and Emma came to aggravate my distraught condition with anxiety, curiosity and desire. In short, never had a feather pillow been the haunt of such a welter of ideas.

A riddle!

Yes, indeed, a riddle! And yet, though the sphinxes were all round me, through the dim vapor which was now less thick I clearly distinguished them. And as one of them had a pleasing face and a youthful figure, I fell asleep smiling.

# CHAPTER IV

## HOT AND COLD

Qui dort dîne. My slumber lasted till the next morning.

And yet I never rested so ill. The bruised feeling caused by a day spent in a motor-car came over my loin-muscles, and for long I felt in them the ricochets of ghostly jolts and the twists of spectral skids. Then I was visited by dreams in which a world of miracle came to life. Brocéliande, the Shakespearean forest, began to move; in the press of it trees walked along arm in arm; a birch tree which looked like a lance made me a speech in German, and I could hardly hear it, for many of the flowers were singing, plants yelped insistently, and great trees every now and then howled aloud.

On my awakening, I remembered this hullabaloo with a phonographic exactitude—so much so, that I was alarmed about it, and I was angry with myself for not having made a full examination of the conservatory; a less hasty and calmer study of it would doubtless have enlightened me. I severely condemned my undue haste and my nervous condition of the day before. But why not make up for it? Perhaps it was not too late?

With my hands behind my back, and a cigarette between my lips, with no particular aim in my steps, I passed in front of the conservatory, as if I were merely taking a stroll.

It was locked.

So, I had missed the one chance of learning the truth, yes, I felt, the one and only chance. Oh, donkey, donkey!

In order not to arouse suspicion, I had passed the forbidden place without pausing, and now an avenue led me towards the gray buildings. Through the grass which covered it, a beaten path bore witness to frequent passings to and fro.

After following the track for some time, I saw my uncle coming to meet me. No doubt he had been on the watch for my coming out. He was quite cheery. His discolored countenance, when he smiled, was now like his young face of long ago. This affable expression restored my equanimity. My escapade had passed unperceived.

"Well, my boy," said he in almost a friendly way, "I bet you are of my way of thinking. It is not a cheerful place. You will soon be weary of your sentimental sojourn at the bottom of this stewpan!"

"Oh, uncle, I have always loved Fonval, not for the scenery, but as a venerable friend, an ancestor, if you like. It is one of the family. I have often played, you know, on its lawns and among the branches of its trees; it's a godfather that has dandled me on its knee—like—like you, uncle."

"Yes, yes," said Lerne evasively. "All the same you will soon have had enough of it."

"Not at all. The park of Fonval is my earthly paradise."

"There you are right. It's just that," he said laughingly, "the forbidden tree grows in its inclosure. Every hour you will come up against the Tree of Life, and the Tree of Knowledge which you must not touch. It's dangerous. In your position I should go out for a run in your mechanical carriage. Oh, if Adam had only had a mechanical carriage!"

"But, uncle, there is the labyrinth!"

"Oh," cried the Professor gayly, "I'll accompany you and guide you. Besides I am anxious to see one of those what d'-you-call-ems working."

"Automobile, uncle."

"Ah, yes, automobile," and his Teutonic accent gave the word, which is a slow-moving one as it is, an amplitude, a weight, a monumental immobility.

We were going side by side towards the coach-house. There was no denying that my uncle had made up his mind to endure my intrusion with courage. Nevertheless his persistent good temper only vexed me. My projects of indiscretion seemed less legitimate to me. Perhaps I should have abandoned them altogether at that moment, had not my desire for Emma driven me to wish ill to her despotic jailor. Besides, was he sincere? And was it not merely to incite me to keep my plighted word that he said to me on arriving at the improvised garage:

"Nicolas, I have reflected a great deal. I really do think you might be very useful to us in the future, and I desire your further acquaintance. Since you want to remain here for some days, we shall often have talks. In the mornings I do not work much; we shall employ them in going about either on foot, or in your car, and in conversation. But don't forget your promises."

I nodded assent. "After all," thought I, "it really seems as if he wanted one day to publish the solution to the problem. Why should it not be legitimate enough, though the operations that are to procure it are not so? It's them he wishes to hide until the result comes; he expects the éclat of the latter to excuse the barbarity of the former and to obtain his pardon—if only the end does not betray the means, and the means can remain forever unknown. On the other hand, might Lerne not be afraid of competition? Why not?"

I was ruminating on all this as I emptied a little tin of petrol into the tank of my excellent car, a tin which propitious Chance had allowed me to find in the boot.

Lerne got in beside me. He pointed out to me a straight road that skirted a cliff of the defile, a surreptitious cross-road ingeniously concealed. I was astonished at first that my uncle should have pointed out this short cut to me, but, after all, was he not showing me how to get away, and was not this au fond what he most desired?

Oh, the dear uncle! He must have lived a very secluded or very absorbed life, for he was pathetically ignorant of all that concerns motor-cars. His was the sort of ignorance savants have with regard to sciences in which they are not specialists. My physiologist was not strong on the subject of mechanics. He hardly suspected the principle of this docile, supple, silent and speedy engine of locomotion which roused his enthusiasm.

At the edge of the forest:

"Let us stop here, please," said he. "You must explain this machine to me. This is where I usually end my walks. I am an old eccentric. You shall go on by yourself afterwards, if you like."

I began my demonstration, and I perceived that the hooter, only slightly damaged, could be repaired in a turn of the hand. Two screws and a piece of wire restored its deafening power. Lerne, at the sound of it, beamed with ingenuous delight. I went on with my lecture, and as I talked, my uncle listened to me with increasing attention.

In truth the thing deserved attentive interest. During the preceding three years, if motor engines had but little changed in the essentials of their structure and in that of their principal organs, fittings on the other hand had progressed, and the materials employed were employed more judiciously. Thus, in the construction of my car, whose only woodwork was the racing-seats, no wood had been employed. My 80 horse-power affair formed a little luxurious and neatly furnished workshop all of cast iron and steel, of copper and aluminum. The great invention of the day had been applied to it—I mean that it did not rest on four pneumatic tires, but on spring-wheels which were wonderfully elastic. Nowadays that seems quite a matter of course; but a year ago my iron fellies caused much surprise.

But the most remarkable thing about my 234 XY, when you come to think of it, was, I think, that improvement which engineers obtained so slowly that one did not see it growing day by day—I mean its automatism.

The first horseless machine was encumbered with levers, pedals, handles and wheels necessary for its guidance, and with taps and grease-valves to turn, which were indispensable for the functioning of the engine. Now, each generation of motor-cars has dispensed with these more and more completely. One by one, almost all those handles have disappeared which require the incessant intervention of man. In our days, by means of its organs which have become automatic, the mechanism controls the mechanism. A chauffeur is no more than a pilot; once going, his machine keeps up its own energy; once awake, it will only fall asleep again at the word of command. In short, as Lerne bade me note, the modern motor-car enjoys properties that a spinal cord might confer; it enjoys instinct and reflex actions. Spontaneous movements take place in it along with the voluntary movements caused by the intelligence of the driver, who becomes as it were the brain of the vehicle. It is from this intelligence that the orders for definite actions go, transmitted by the metallic nerves to the steel muscles.

"Moreover," said my uncle, "the resemblance between this machine and the body of a vertebrate animal is striking."

Here Lerne was entering his own domain. I lent an attentive ear, and he went on:

"We have here the nervous and muscular systems represented by the striker-rods, the driving-gear and the cranks. And the châssis, Nicolas, what is it but the skeleton into which the tenants insert themselves like tendons? Blood, the vital element, circulates in those copper arteries in the form of petrol. The carburetor breathes; it's a lung; instead of combining air with blood, it mixes it with the vapor of the petrol, that's all! This hood resembles a thorax in which life beats rhythmically—our joints move in the synovia as those swivel-joints in oil. Under the shelter of the resisting skin of the case is the tank, a stomach that grows hungry and is replenished. Here, phosphorescent like those of cats, but as yet void of sight, are eyes, its lamps; its voice is the hooter; and—but I need not go into further details. In a word, Nicolas, the only thing wanting to your car is brain, which you sometimes supply; having that it would become a great deaf beast, blind, insensitive and sterile, without the sense of taste or of smell."

"A regular collection of infirmities," I said, bursting into a loud laugh.

"Hum!" rejoined Lerne, "in other respects the motor-car is better off than we. Think how the water cools it; what a remedy against fever! And then what a time the engine can last, if it is wisely used! It can be mended indefinitely—it can always be cured; have you not just restored speech to its maw? You could replace an eye just as easily!"

The Professor was getting excited:

"It's a powerful and terrible body," he cried, "but a body that allows itself to be clothed—it has armor which increases the power of the wearer beyond all expectation, a cuirass that multiplies its force and speed. Why, you inside it are like the Maritans of Mr. Wells in their tripod cylinders! You are nothing but the brain of an artificial monster that it makes one giddy to think of."

"All machines are like that, uncle."

"No. Not so completely. But for the form (which no animal resembles of course) the automobile is the most congruous automaton ever contrived.

It is more made in our image than the best mannikin wound up by a key, the most human of puppets. For under their anthropomorphic envelope those mannikins hide a mere roasting-jack organism, which one would not compare with the anatomy of a snail. Whereas here...."

He drew back a step and regarded my car with a look of tenderness:

"What a superb creature," he exclaimed, "and how great is man!"

"Yes," said I to myself, "there is a deal more beauty in a thing we create, than in all your sinister joining of flesh and wood that are both from of old. But it's not bad on your part to have admitted it."

Though it was late, I went on to Grey-l'Abbaye to replenish my stock of petrol, and though he was a creature of routine, Lerne, infatuated with automobilism, passed beyond the traditional limit of his walks and insisted on accompanying me.

Then we resumed the way to Fonval. My uncle, with all the ardor of a neophyte, bent over the bonnet in order to listen to the pulsations within the metal frame, then he took to pieces one of the oil-valves. All the time he kept questioning me, and I had to inform him of the smallest details of my car, details which he assimilated with an incredible accuracy.

"I say, Nicolas, sound the hooter, will you? Now—go slow—stop—start again—quicker—that will do—put on the brake—back now—stop—it's colossal!"

He was laughing. His cloudy face seemed almost beautified. Seeing us one would have said we were excellent friends. In fact we were so then perhaps. And I fancied that perhaps, thanks to my "two-seater," Lerne might one day confide in me.

He preserved this gayety till our return to the château; the proximity of the mysterious workshop did not affect it; it only disappeared in the dining room. Then suddenly Lerne's brow darkened. Emma had just come in. And the husband of my aunt Lidivine seemed to have effaced himself with my uncle's smile, only an irritable old savant remaining between his two guests. I then felt how little his future discoveries mattered in comparison with this woman, and that he wanted to acquire glory and wealth only in order to keep the charming girl by his side.

Assuredly he loved her just as I did, and with the same fierce desire.

Barbe came and went as she waited on us more or less anyhow. We were silent. I avoided looking at Emma, being persuaded that my looks would have resembled kisses and that my uncle would have divined them.

She, now quite at her ease, pretended indifference; and with her chin in her hands, her elbows on the table, her bare arms showing out of her short sleeves, she gazed through the windows at the meadows whose inhabitants were lowing.

I should have liked to gaze at the same sight as my bien-aimée; this distant and sentimental communion would have satisfied one; but unluckily the meadows were not visible from where I sat, and my eyes wandered idly about, none the less noting the whiteness of her bare arms and the unwonted heaving of her bodice.

As I was interpreting this unwonted emotion on her part in my favor, Lerne, hostile and taciturn, broke up the party. He ordered Emma off to her room and giving me a book bade me go and read in the shade of the forest.

I had but to obey. "Bah," I said to myself, "in spite of his exhortations, he is more to be pitied than I am."

The happenings of that night cooled my pity most notably.

The incident troubled me all the more that it did nothing to lighten the darkness of the mystery; in itself it seemed incomprehensible. This is what it was:

I had peacefully fallen asleep with my mind dwelling on Emma, and the delightful hope she inspired; but sleep instead of bringing me pleasant dreams, brought back the absurdities of the preceding night, the moaning and barking plants. The intensity of the sound kept increasing in my dream, and at last it became so acute, so real, that I suddenly woke up.

Sweat was drenching my body and my hot sheets. The echo of a recent cry was just dying on my tympanum. It was not the first time I heard it. No—in the labyrinth I had heard it before, that cry, far away in the direction of Fonval.

I raised myself on my hands. A ray of moonlight lit my room. I could hear nothing. Only from the old-fashioned clock came any sound—that of Time's sickle. My head fell back on the pillow.

Then suddenly, with a shuddering of my whole being, I buried myself in the blankets with my fingers in my ears. The sinister howling was rising from the park into the night, a sinister, unearthly howling. It was indeed that which I had heard in my nightmare; my dream had mingled with reality.

With a superhuman effort I arose, and it was then that I heard yelpings—a sort of stifled yelpings, very much stifled.

Well, after all, it might all be proceeding from a dog's throat, hang it!

Nothing to be seen from the window on the garden side except the plane tree and the other trees drowsing in the moonlight.

Then the howling began again on the left, and from the other window I saw what seemed to me for a moment to explain everything.

Some distance away a starved-looking dog was standing with its back towards me. It was a huge animal, and it had laid its front paws on the closed shutters of my former bedroom, and every now and then uttered a loud long wail. The other barkings—the stifled ones—replied to him from the inside of the house; but were they really yelps? Had my ears deceived me? It sounded more like the voice of a man trying to imitate the voice of a dog. The more I listened, the more that conclusion forced itself on me. Yes, certainly there could be no mistake; how could I have hesitated? It was quite clear—some practical joker in my bedroom was amusing himself with teasing the poor brute.

And he succeeded in doing so; for the animal gave signs of increasing exasperation. He modulated his howling in the most extraordinary manner, making it sound like a cry of despair. Finally he scratched the shutters with rage and bit them. I heard the crackling of the wood between his jaws.

Suddenly the beast became motionless, its hair bristling. There was a brusque and violent outburst in that room. I recognized my uncle's voice but could not catch the meaning of his reprimand. Immediately the joker was silent. But—and how to account for this amazing circumstance?—the dog whose frenzy should have been appeased, was now beside itself; its backbone bristled up like that of a wild boar. Growling, it began to follow the wall of the château, till it reached the main door.

Just as it reached it, Lerne opened it.

Fortunately for me I had, in caution, not raised my window curtain. His first look was towards my window.

In a low voice, with restrained wrath, the Professor lectured the dog, but he did not come forward, and I perceived he was afraid of it. The other came nearer, growling, with its eyes flashing from under its great brow. Lerne then spoke aloud:

"To your kennel, you dirty brute!" (Then came some words in a foreign tongue.) "Get away," he went on in French; and as the animal still came on—"Do you want me to knock your brains out? Eh?"

My uncle seemed to be losing his wits. The moon heightened his pallor. "He'll be torn to bits," I said to myself, "he has not even a riding-switch."

"Go back, Nell, go back."

Nell? So it was the St. Bernard bitch belonging to the Scot.

And then came a stream of foreign words which to my complete astonishment made me realize that my uncle knew English.

His invectives resounded in the silence of the night.

The dog gathered itself together; it was just going to spring when Lerne, at the end of his resources, threatened it with a revolver and with the other hand pointed out the way he wanted the beast to go.

Now, it has happened to me, when out shooting, to see a dog run away when a gun is leveled at it; he knows its deadly power. That this should happen in presence of a pistol seemed to me decidedly less ordinary. Had Nell already experienced the effect of the weapon? That was a plausible theory; but I fancied that she had understood the English—English being Macbeth's tongue—rather than my uncle's revolver.

She calmed down, as at the voice of Orpheus, cowered and with her tail between her legs, made for the gray buildings which Lerne was pointing out to her. He ran after the hound, and the darkness swallowed them.

In my clock the imperishable Harvester mowed down several minutes.

In the distance a door banged noisily. Then Lerne came in again.

That was all.

So there were at Fonval two beings whose existence had till then been unsuspected by me; Nell, whose pitiful appearance hardly showed her to be happy, Nell, abandoned doubtless by her master in a hasty flight—and the practical joker. For this latter could not, in reason, be either of the two women or one of the Germans; the nature of the joke betrayed its author's age. Only a child could divert itself at the expense of a dog. But nobody to my knowledge lodged in that wing.

"Ah," Lerne had said to me, "I am using your room." Who, then, lived in it?

I was determined to find out somehow. If the hidden presence of Nell in the gray buildings invested them with a new interest, mysterious as they already were, the closed rooms of the château became yet another center of attraction.

At last my objectives were clearing.

And as the prospect of hunting down the secret made me quiver with excitement, a presentiment warned me that I should do well to pursue it to the death, and so defy Lerne's first command before breaking the second.

"Let me find out first what it is all about," said my conscience; "there is something wrong. After that, I can attend to the baggage in peace."

Why did I not follow my own advice? But conscience speaks in a very low voice, and who can hear it when passion begins to blare?

# CHAPTER V
## "THE MADMAN"

A week later on, I was in ambush behind the door of my former bedroom—the yellow one—with my eye to the keyhole.

Oh! it was not easy, or it did not appear so. Never had the left wing of Fonval been so jealously closed, even in the days when the monks had been cloistered there.

How had I got in there? In the simplest manner possible.

The Yellow Room is reached by the central hall—where every one could walk if he liked—by a series of three rooms. The hall joins on to the drawing-room, then comes the billiard-room, which opens into the boudoir, and finally this boudoir opens, on the right, into the Yellow Room, which lies back towards the park.

Now, on this day, before profiting by an increased freedom, I tried, one by one, in the lock, keys which I had stolen from other doors here and there. I had no confidence. Suddenly the lock yielded. I opened the door, and I saw in the half light made by the closed shutters, the whole suite of rooms.

I recognized as I went from threshold to threshold the special odor of each—each a little more musty than in the old days—the sort of odors that the Past would exhale, if one could travel in its dust.

I followed on the tips of my toes a track on which many boots had left their mud—now dry. A mouse ran over the drawing-room carpet. On the billiard-table, the ivory balls—red and white—formed an isosceles triangle. Mentally I calculated the stroke, the amount of screw I should put on, and the place where I should hit the second ball, then I found myself in the boudoir itself. The clock, which had stopped, pointed to twelve. I felt myself very receptive. But, hardly had I had the leisure to see the shut door of the Yellow Room, than a sound brought me back hurriedly into the hall.

It was no jesting matter. Lerne worked in the gray buildings, but he knew that I was in the château, and on such occasions, it was his custom to come in suddenly to watch me. It seemed to me prudent to put off the enterprise.

An hour's liberty was indispensable to me, so I evolved the following stratagem:

The next day I went in my car to Grey-l'Abbaye, and I there bought several articles of toilet, and hid them in a bush in the forest, not far from the Park.

On the day after that, after lunch, Emma heard me say:

"I am going to Grey this afternoon. I am going to get some articles I need. If I cannot get them there, I shall push on to Nanthel. Have you any commissions to give me?"

Fortunately, they had none, otherwise everything would have come to grief.

By this means I could go out for a quarter-of-an-hour, and bring in my purchases from the bush, as if I had gone to make them in the village.

Now, one might reckon on the journey from Fonval to Grey and back taking about an hour-and-a-quarter, so I had an hour at my disposal.

I go out, leave my car in the thicket not far from the hiding-place in the bushes, then come into the garden again over the wall. The ivy on one side, and the trellis on the other, made it easier. Keeping close to the castle wall, I reached the hall.

And now, I am in the drawing-room, with the door carefully shut behind me. In case I might need to make a dash, however, I thought it prudent not to turn the key, and now I am spying, with my eye to the lock of the yellow chamber.

The keyhole was a large one. It made a sort of loop-hole through which a keen air was blowing—and what do I see?

The room was dark and cut into layers by the shutters. A slanting ray seemed to be supporting the window with its column, and the motes of dust were dancing about in it as the worlds dance about in space.

On the carpet the laths of the shutters projected their lines. Here was a den! A gypsy lair! Here and there, clothes on the ground. A plate with scraps, and near it a piece of filth. One would have said it was a hermit's haunt.

Ah! and what was that which moved on the bed? There he is, the recluse! It's a man! He was lying face downwards amongst the disorder of the bolster and the quilt, with his head leaning on his arms. He had on only a nightshirt and trousers. His beard was of several weeks' growth, and, like his hair, which was rather short, was almost of a whitish-yellow.

Ever since that cry the other night, my head had been full of whimsies. No, I had never seen that puffy, dirty face—that podgy body.

His eyes seemed kindly enough—stupid, but good and endearing. Um! What a curious indifference in his face! He must be a lazy chap, though.

The prisoner was snoozing, badly, it seemed. The flies were annoying him. He drives them away with a sudden clumsy gesture of his hand. His indolent eye follows their flight between his snoozes, and sometimes, seized with a fit of anger, and making his lips smack together with a sudden movement of his head, he tries to snap up the insects that irritate him so as they pass by.

The madman! There is a madman in my uncle's house!! Who could he be? My eyelids touched the keyhole. My eye became frozen. The other one, taking its turn of duty, is rather short-sighted. I saw very badly. My line of sight was rather narrow. Good God! I have hit the door and made a noise. The madman has jumped up! How small he is! Hallo! here he is coming towards me! Suppose I were to open the door? Ah! Now he is throwing himself on the floor and sniffing and growling. Poor fellow! It is a sad sight.

He had guessed nothing. Crouching in the track of the sunray, and all striped with the shadow of the shutters, I could more easily examine him.

His hands and face were spotted with little rosy stains, like old scratches. One would have said that he had been fighting.

Ah! but this is graver. A long purple scar goes under his hair, from one temple to the other, round the back of his head. It is very likely the scar of a wound.

The poor fellow has been ill-treated. Lerne has made him undergo some horrible treatment, or he is wreaking some vengeance on him. Oh! the brute!

Immediately an association of ideas worked in my brain. I remembered the Indian profile of my uncle, the unusual locks of Emma,—those of the madman which are so yellow, and the green fleece of the rat. Can Lerne be trying to graft hairy scalps on bald scalps? Can that be the enterprise?—and immediately I see that my idea is absurd. Nothing corroborates it, and then (this is a clinching argument) the madman has not been scalped, as in that case his scar would have described a complete circle. Why should he not have gone mad simply through a fall on the back of his head? At any rate, he is not a dangerous lunatic. He is harmless. He has rather a nice expression. His eyes now shine with a sort of intelligence. I am sure if I questioned him gently he would answer. Suppose I tried.

Only a bolt closed the door on my side. I drew it deliberately, but before I got into the Yellow Room, the recluse dashed forward, head downwards—passed between my legs, knocked me down, and then escaped, with those dog's yelps which the other night had made me take him for a practical joker.

I was disconcerted by his agility. How could he make a fool of me that way? And what a strange idea, that of running between my legs!

In spite of the suddenness of the adventure, just as quickly as he made me fall, I got on my legs again, dazed and astonished. Here is a lunatic let loose—a madman who will ruin me! "Oh! Nicolas, my boy, you are done for, done for! There is not the shadow of a doubt about it. Would it not be better to take French leave than chase the fugitive? What good can it do now? Ah! But Emma and the secret! Oh, damn it all! Let's try and catch him!" and I am after the Unknown.

I hope he won't go near the gray buildings. No, thank goodness, he is taking the opposite direction! None the less, anybody can see us.

The Deserter goes gamboling along in high spirits, and plunges in the wood. Thank heaven, the creature is no longer barking, and that is always something. Is that somebody? No, it is a statue. I must gain on him as soon as possible. If he only takes the wrong turn, we shall be spotted, and it is all up with me. How cheerful he seems, the brute! Curse him! If he goes on in this line, we shall be round the Park, and the chase will pass under the front of the gray buildings—under the very windows of Lerne.

A blessing on the trees which still hide us. Quick.... That drawing-room door which I have left open! Quick! Quick....

But the fellow did not know he was being chased. He did not look behind him. His bare feet were hurting him and keeping him back. I am gaining on him....

He has stopped and is sniffing the breeze; now he is off again; but I have got nearer. He has jumped into the bushes on the left, towards the cliff—so do I. I am only ten yards off, now. He dashes through the brambles without heeding their thorns. I follow in his wake. The branches are lashing at him, and the thorns are hurting him. He is moaning. Well, why does not he thrust them aside? He could easily avoid their clutches. The cliffs are not far away. Now we are making straight for them. On my honor! My quarry seems to know perfectly well where it is going. I see his back now and again. I must track him by the crackling of the branches.

At last I see his narrow head again, against the rocky path. Silently I glide up. Another second, and I shall be upon him, but an unexpected action of his makes me pause at the edge of the clear space which encircles me, and of which the cliff forms one side.

He is on his knees, scratching furiously at the soil. The task tortures his nails, so that he whines as he did a moment ago amongst the thorns of the hawthorn and the bramble.

The earth flies from behind him up to me; his rigid hands working with force and rapid motion. He digs away, groaning with pain, then, ever and anon, plunges his nose into the hole as deeply as he can, snorts, shaking his head, and resumes his task.

The scar is now fully visible to me, it is like a livid crown. Oh! I do not mind his madness. Now's the time. Jump on him, and carry him off!

I come out of the thicket stealthily. Hallo! somebody has already been digging here! A heap of earth, which has become gray, shows that my yellow-haired gentleman is only resuming some old bit of work. Well! Well!

I bend my legs and get ready to jump.

The man then utters a grunt of pleasure, and what do I see in the hole he has made—an old shoe that he has just unearthed! Ah! poor humanity!

I jumped. I have got him, the rascal. Good Lord! he turns round and thrusts me away, but I shall not leave go. It is queer how awkward he is with his hands.

Ah! would you bite, you devil!

I grasp him hard enough to break his bones. He has never done any wrestling, that is clear, but I have not got the better of him yet. Ah! I have made a wrong step! it is the hole....

I am walking on the old boot. Horror! There is something in it—something which is fastening it to the ground. I am beginning to pant. "Nothing fits a foot like a shoe."

I must have done with this. The moments are golden.

Each clasping the other, my adversary and I are face to face, in front of the rock, gasping—equally matched.... Ah! an idea. I opened my eyes terribly wide, as if it were a matter of subduing a child, or a beast. I put on the dominating look of a master, whereupon, the other let go of his hold, quite tamed, and repentant—and if he is not licking my hands in token of obedience!

Ah, well! Come along.

I drag him away. The shoe is an elastic one, and stands up with its toe in the air. It has not that lamentable look of worn-out shoes that have been thrown away on the road, but it is more repulsive. What fixes it on the ground is deep in the soil. One can only see the end of a bit of knitting. Can it be a sock?

Trot along, my friend!

My companion remains docile, thanks to my masterful glances, and we run as hard as we can.

Good Heavens! What will have happened in the castle during this expedition?

Nothing whatever had happened, as a matter of fact.

But, as we got into the hall, I heard Emma and Barbe talking on the floor above. They were beginning to come down the stairs, when the drawing-room door shutting, as we went in, ended my alarms—only to give me new ones.

How, now that the poor lunatic was back in his room, how was I to get out without being observed by one or other of the women?

Stealthily creeping back on tiptoe to the drawing-room, I listened, with my ear to the panel, to distinguish in which direction the two intruders were moving, but suddenly I recoiled into the middle of the room, demented, looking for shelter of some kind, such as a screen, and gasping like a drowning man....

A key was rattling in the lock. Was it my key, left in the door, and stolen during my absence? Not at all. Here is my key, in my waistcoat pocket! I put it there, when I first came in.

Well, then, what could it be?

The verdigrised handle slowly turned. They were coming in. Who? The Germans? Lerne?

Emma! Well, she could only see an empty room. One of the great damask curtains stirred, perhaps, but she did not remark it.

Barbe stood behind her. The girl was saying softly: "Stay in there and watch the garden. Do what you did the other day: that was all right. As soon as the old man comes out of the Laboratory, warn me by coughing."

"It is not he who worries me," replied Barbe, obviously afraid. "He is quite easy in his mind at this moment, I assure you. We shall not see him before night, but as for that Nicolas, that is another pair of shoes. He is coming on!"

So the gray buildings were called the Laboratory, and it was for using that word that the Professor had silenced the servant with a slap. I was beginning to know more.

Emma went on in an irritated tone:

"I tell you again, there is no danger. It is not the first time, is it?"

"Ah! but that Nicolas was not there."

"Come, do what I tell you."

Not quite resigned, Barbe went off to keep watch. Emma remained for a few instants listening.

Beautiful! Oh, she was beautiful! Like the very demon of unlawful love, and yet she was but an outline against the shining rectangle of the door—a motionless shadow, but a shadow as supple as a movement. For Emma in repose, always seemed as if she had paused in the middle of a dance, and was even continuing it through some strange spell, so completely did the sight of her make a harmony—that harmony of the wanton bayaderes, whose only miming is love-making, and who cannot move in their undulating, quivering motions, without shaking their locks, nor make the least little gesture without a suggestion of voluptuousness.

Life was boiling in my veins! My senses whirled. It was like a tide of passion rising from out the depths of the ages.

Emma! In the madman's room! Heavens! With that brute! The wretched girl! I could have killed her.

You will say that I did not know anything, that my suspicions were groundless.

Ah, then, you do not know that impulsive gait, that sly and hungry look of women who are going stealthily to a sweetheart.

It maddened me. The pretty girl, as she hastened to this ignoble scene, brushed the curtain with the swish of her skirt. I stood before her barring the path.

She gave a gasp of terror. I thought she was going to faint. Barbe showed her great round eyes, and fled in panic. Then, like a fool, I gave the reason for my exploit.

"Why are you going to that madman's room?" My words sounded artificial, broken.

"Tell me—Why? In God's name, tell me?"

I had flung myself upon her, and twisted her wrists. She gave a humble moan of complaint, and swayed in my grasp.

I squeezed the soft, firm flesh of her arms, as if I were throttling two doves, and bending over her agonized eyes, I said:

"Well, tell me why?"

She looked me up and down in defiance, and then said:

"Well, what about it? You know perfectly well that Macbeth was my lover. Lerne gave you to understand that in my presence on the day of your arrival."

"Is that Macbeth—that madman?"

Emma did not reply, but her astonishment informed me that I had made another mistake in showing my ignorance.

"Have I not the right to love him?" she went on. "Do you think you are going to prevent me?"

I shook her arms as if they were bell-ropes.

"Do you still love him?"

"More than ever—do you understand?"

"But he is a brute beast."

"There are madmen who think they are gods. He sometimes imagines he is a dog. His lunacy is, perhaps, therefore less grave, and after all...."

She smiled mysteriously. One would have said that she wanted to drive me wild.

Then followed a scene I dare not describe.

WELL, BARBE MADE AN UNTIMELY, BUT FORTUNATE ENTRANCE, COUGHING AS loudly as she could.

"Here is Monsieur coming." Emma dashed from my arms. Lerne was terrorizing her once more. "Off with you! Make haste," she said. "If he knew, you would be done for, and I, too, most likely. Oh, do go! Go, my little duck! Lerne sticks at nothing."

I felt she was speaking the truth, for her dear cold hands were shivering in mine, and her mouth was stuttering with terror.

STILL UNDER THE EXCITEMENT OF AN IMBECILE HAPPINESS, WHICH INCREASED my strength and agility tenfold, I climbed the trellis, hand over fist, and jumped down on the other side of the wall.

I found my car in its garage of greenery. I piled in my parcels as fast as I could. I was ridiculously happy. Emma should be mine, and what a mistress she would make!—a woman who had not recoiled before the duty of bringing to a friend, now become a repulsive thing, the consolation of her visits.

But now it was I who was favored, I was sure of that. How could that Macbeth love her? Nonsense! She had lied to me merely to rouse my passions. She merely had pity on him.

But now, when I came to think of it, how had madness come upon the Scot, and why was Lerne keeping it secret? My uncle maintained that Macbeth had gone away. Then why did he keep poor Nell in prison? I understood her sorrow at the window, and her rancor against the Professor. Some drama had taken place in her prison, in which Lerne, Emma and Macbeth were the personages—a drama which was the result of some grievous fault, indeed, no doubt; but what was the drama? I should soon find out. A woman has no secrets from her lover, and that is what I was going to be.

My joy generally manifests itself in the form of a song. If I remember rightly, I hummed the air of a Spanish dance as I went along, and I only interrupted it suddenly because the remembrance of the old shoe, now full of sinister meaning intruded on my reflections, as the Red Death rises menacing in the midst of a ball.

Instantly my cheerfulness drooped. The sun went down in the depth of my thoughts. All things became dark, suspicious and threatening. There was a great revulsion within me, the most dreadful guesses appeared certainties and even the image of Emma faded away.

A prey to the terrors of the unknown, I re-entered that dungeon-castle and that garden-tomb, where the beautiful Demon awaited me, standing between a madman and a corpse.

# CHAPTER VI

## NELL—THE ST. BERNARD

Some days passed without any event which could satisfy either my love or my curiosity. Had Lerne grown suspicious of me, and contrived to have all my time taken up?

In the morning, he would invite me to accompany him—one day on foot, and another in the motor-car. During those outings we would talk at random of scientific matters, and he would question me as if he really wished to judge of my capabilities.

With the motor-car we used to cover much ground. In our walks, my uncle usually took the road which led straight to Grey. He would often stop, the better to hold forth, and never went beyond the skirts of the wood. Often in the midst of a dissertation or a jest, after we had started walking or driving, Lerne would suddenly go back, distrusting the people he had left at Fonval.

He also organized my afternoons for me; sometimes I was charged with a message for the town or the village, sometimes forced to go off by myself on some errand. I had either to fill up my tank without question, or put on my walking boots.

Lerne always watched me go, and at nightfall, standing on his doorstep, he exacted from me an account of my day. As the case might be, I had either to give a report of what I had done, or describe places.

Now, my uncle was not, as a rule, familiar with places, it is true, but I could not tell which ones, and so any made-up story would have been dangerous. I therefore conscientiously explored the forest and the countryside from dawn to dusk.

And yet, I should have liked to go to Emma's room. I had calculated its place in the topography of the castle by the number of windows which were, or were not shut, and I knew them all thoroughly.

The whole left wing always remained closed. In the right wing, the ground floor, and, of the six bedrooms above, only three remained open for daily use. Mine was in the projecting part of the building, and, at the other end, the room of my Aunt Lidivine opened on the central corridor, and communicated with Lerne's, so that Emma must have succeeded my aunt in my aunt's own bed. The very thought of it maddened me, and I waited impatiently for the opportunity I sought.

But the Professor was keeping watch!

Under his pitiless tyranny, I saw Mlle. Bourdichet only at meal-times. We both put on a detached air. I now ventured to look at her, but I did not dare to speak to her. She persisted in a most absolute silence, so much so, that, in absence of conversation, I had to judge of her nature by her bearing, but I must admit that, however gross may be the human functions of feeding oneself on dead beasts and withered plants, there are two methods of eating. This lady thought nothing of taking the chicken bone, or cutlet bone in her fingers, and every time she gave herself up to this pleasure, I fancied I should hear her say, "My little duck," in her plebeian voice.

Between Emma and me, Lerne fidgeted about. He crumbled the bread, and dallied with his fork, and suppressed anger would make him bring down his fist on the cloth till the cups and glasses rattled.

One day, by mischance, my foot knocked against him. The Doctor suspected this innocent foot of light behavior. He attributed to it telegraphic intentions, and, persuaded that it had communicated through its toe some pedestrian and stealthy love-sign, he decreed at once that Mlle. Bourdichet was feeling unwell, and would thenceforth take her meals in her own room.

So two passions occupied my thoughts—hatred of Lerne, and love of Emma, and I resolved on the most audacious plans to satisfy them both. It so happened that on that very day, my uncle said to me suddenly that he wanted to take me in the car to Nanthel, where he had business. I fancied I saw a chance of escape from his vigilance.

The next day was a Sunday, and Grey was celebrating the Feast of its Patron Saint. I should know how to profit by that!

"With pleasure, Uncle," I said. "We shall start in the car, barring accidents."

"I should prefer to go in the car to Grey, and then take the train to Nanthel. That will be the surest way."

That suited my book admirably.

"Very well, uncle."

"The train starts from Grey at 8 o'clock. We shall come back by the 5.13. There is none before that."

ON ARRIVING AT THE VILLAGE, WE HEARD A NOISE OF BUSTLE, WITH, EVERY now and again, the lowing of cattle. A horse neighed, and some sheep were bleating.

I had some difficulty in making my way across the Square of Grey-l'Abbaye, which had now been turned into a Fair, and was swarming with a good-tempered and slow-moving crowd.

In the spaces between the shooting galleries, and other shabby booths, they had inclosed the cattle which were for sale. Rough hands were calculating the weight of udders, were opening jaws by which a beast's age can be read, slipping their hands along their muscles to judge of their condition, and so on.

The horse dealers were talking big, and between two rows of patient peasants, grooms were trotting about heavy cart-horses, and riding-whips were cracking all round.

The first man drunk that day, stumbled up, addressing me as "Citizen."

We went straight on in the semi-silence of this Ardennes Market. The village inn was already full of people, singing, and not yet fighting. The church-bells were ringing their chimes of warning, and in the center of the Square, a little white building, decorated with greenery, showed that the Municipal Band would soon be adding its very simple strains to the hubbub of the fête.

When we got to the station (this was the moment I had chosen to act), I said:

"Uncle, shall I accompany you in your rounds at Nanthel?"

"Certainly not. Why?"

"Well, Uncle, in my dislike for cafés, taverns and public-houses, I shall ask you to leave me here, where I shall wait for you just as easily as in the shop in Nanthel."

My uncle replied:

"But, you are not obliged...."

"To begin with, I find the Grey Festival attracts me. I should like to watch the crowds a little longer. On such a day one gets the liveliest impressions of the manners of a people, and I feel, to-day, that I have the soul of an ethnologist."

My uncle said, "You are joking, or else it is a mere whim."

"In the second place, Uncle, whom could I trust with my car? The inn-keeper? The drunken tenant of a hovel full of clodhoppers in their cups? You surely do not imagine that I am going to leave a car worth twenty-five thousand francs, exposed for nine hours by the clock, to the tricks of a village on the spree! No, no, I prefer to watch my car myself."

My uncle was not convinced of my sincerity. He wished to checkmate the little trick which I might be planning of going back to Fonval, either in my motor-car, or on a borrowed bicycle, with the intention of coming back to Grey in time for the 5.15—and that was just exactly the plan which I had thought of. The accursed savant nearly upset everything.

"You are right," said he coldly, and he set his foot on the ground, and amid the crowd of holiday travelers in their Sunday best, raised the bonnet of the car, and looked at the engine minutely. I felt quite uncomfortable.

My uncle took out his knife—took the carburetor, and slipped some of the pieces into his pocket, and addressed me thus:

"There is your car, brought to a standstill," said he, "but as you might make off in another way, I am going to give you something to do. On my return, you must show me the carburetor, completely restored, and fitted up with pieces of your own make. The blacksmith has not yet shut up his forge—he will lend you an anvil and vise; but he is a fool, and quite unable to help you. There will be enough there to keep you amused until 5.14."

Perceiving that I did not seem to mind, he went on in a constrained tone:

"I must ask your pardon. Please do not doubt that, all this is only to assure your future by protecting the secret of our work. Good-by."

The train carried him off.

I had let him talk without showing any signs of annoyance; and indeed, without feeling any, for, being but a poor chauffeur, detesting grease and scars on my hands, and obliged by my uncle's will to do without a mechanic, I had brought with me, in the boot of my car, several spare pieces, amongst which, was a complete carburetor, ready to be put in its place. Ignorance stood me in better stead than professional skill, so I set to work at once, being in no wise disturbed, and merely anxious about the inmates of Fonval left to their own devices.

Presently, having garaged my car in a clump of trees, I climbed over the park wall, and I should have climbed straight to Emma's room, if a melancholy barking had not sounded in the direction of the gray buildings.

"The laboratory! Nell!" This curious fact of a dog being chained up in a laboratory made me hesitate between the attractiveness of the mystery, and that of Emma; but this time, a sort of instinct of self-preservation aroused by the unknown, and the danger one attributes to it, was bound to carry the day.

I made my way towards the gray buildings. Besides, the Germans would no doubt be there, and their presence would prevent me from dawdling. So it was merely a matter of snatching a few minutes from love-making.

As I passed the Yellow Room, I put my ear to the shutters in order to assure myself that Macbeth was alone. He was so, a circumstance which filled my heart with a vast satisfaction.

Some white clouds were floating in a cold sky. The wind was coming from Grey-l'Abbaye, and brought me through the gorge the monotonous sound of the church bells. Endlessly they repeated the same three notes, thus performing the chime of the Arlésienne. I was gay! To this sacred accompaniment I whistled the melody played by the orchestra, and the juxtaposition of the two was like placing a modern statuette on a Gothic pedestal.

In front of the laboratory, on the other side of the road, there was a wood. I made tacks to reach it, having formed my plan of assault. In the middle of this wood, I used to possess an old friend—a fir tree. Its projecting branches formed a spiral staircase. It completely dominated the buildings. No laboratory could have been better placed, or more accessible, and in the old days I used to play there at being a sailor on the yard-arms.

The tree offered me a perch, rather short, no doubt, but still, well padded. On the upper branches, a relic awaited me, made of cords and rotten planks—the cross-trees! Who would have said that one day I, who used to spy out continents, archipelagoes—phantasies with some likelihood about them—should now be there as a spy for things so fabulously unreal? My glances turned towards the ground.

As I have said, the laboratory was composed of a courtyard between two blocks of buildings. The one on the left was pierced with large bay windows on its one story, and on its ground floor. It seemed to me to be merely two large rooms—one above the other. I only saw the higher one, which was elaborately equipped—an apothecary's cupboard, marble tables covered with bulbs, bottles and retorts, cases (open), sets of polished instruments, and two indescribable pieces of apparatus of glass and nickel, which recalled nothing analogous, except, perhaps, vaguely, the round globes screwed to a stand on which café waiters lay their napkins.

The other block which was beyond my range, looked from the outside like an ordinary dwelling-house, and was evidently the place where the two assistants lodged.

But, what I had taken for a farmyard on the day of my arrival, took up all my attention.

What a miserable farmyard! Its walls were fitted with wire-netted compartments of various sizes, which rose, piled on one another, to an immense height.

In these lodges, each duly labeled, rabbits, guinea-pigs, rats, cats and other animals which I could not distinguish because of the distance, moved about painfully, or remained lying, half-hidden under the straw.

Some litter, however, was jumping about, but I could not perceive the cause. A nest of mice, I presumed.

The last cage on the right served as a hen-house. Contrary to custom, they had locked up the poultry in it.

Everything looked mute and melancholy. Four hens and a cock, of rare breed, were carrying on a more cheerful kind of life, and strutted about cackling on the concrete floor, pecking at it persistently, in the vain hope of discovering corn or worms.

In the middle of the yard there was a large hollow square of gratings. These were the kennels.

Between the two rows of compartments, like philosophers that were both Cynics and Peripatetics, dogs, with a resigned look, walked up and down—ordinary terriers, butcher's lurchers, watch-dogs, bull-terriers, a ruffianly bulldog and mongrel bloodhounds—in fact, a whole pack of coarse, good-for-nothing-but-fidelity beasts.

They were roaming up and down, and gave this courtyard the appearance of the yard of a veterinary hospital. And this is where things took on a somber coloring. Of all those beasts very few seemed healthy. Most of them were wearing bandages—on the back, round the neck, on the back of the head, and more especially round the head. One hardly saw any of them through the grating, which did not wear a piece of white linen rolled up into a cap, hood or turban, and this procession of sorrowful dogs, with their absurd headdresses of linen bandages, and each with a label attached to its neck, was a most funereal sight to see.

Most of those poor wretches were smitten with some infirmity. One would fall on his muzzle at almost every step; another was limping; the head of a third was shaking and quivering like that of a palsied old man. A mastiff stumbled about, whining without apparent reason, and suddenly it would utter a loud death-like howl.

Nell was not there!

I perceived in a shady corner an aviary—silent and with no bird trying its flight. As far as I could make out, the occupants belonged to the commoner families of birds, and there were sparrows in great numbers. The greater portion of them, however, were a white-headed species, but I did not know enough of ornithology to recognize them from such a height.

The smell of carbolic came up to me.

Oh, for the scents of the farmyard, the cooing of pigeons on the moss-clad roofs, the cock's cock-a-doodle-doo, the yelp of the dog tugging at its chain, the squadrons of geese with outspread wings! I kept thinking of you, in the presence of this lazar-house!

A sad farmyard, indeed, with its severe arrangement, and its patients ticketed like the plants in a hothouse.

Suddenly there was a bustling. The dogs went back to their kennels, and the poultry took refuge under a trough. Nothing budged again. The aviary and the cages seemed to contain nothing but stuffed beasts.

Karl, the German, with his Kaiser-like mustaches, had come out of the building on the left. He opened one of the compartments, thrust out his hand towards a ball of hair which was curled up in it, and drew out a monkey.

The animal, which was a chimpanzee, struggled. The assistant dragged it off, and disappeared with it by the way he had come. The mastiff gave a long howl.

Then began a bustling in the apparatus-room, and I saw that the three assistants had just come in. They stretched out the gagged monkey on the table, and fastened it solidly down; William thrust something under its nose.

Karl, with a morphia syringe, pricked the chimpanzee's flank, then the tall old man, Johann, approached. He put his golden spectacles straight, with a hand which held a knife, and bent over the patient.

I cannot explain the operation so rapid was it, but in less than no time, the face of the chimpanzee was nothing but a hideous blur of red.

I turned away, sickened with a sense of discomfort—a discomfort caused by seeing blood. At last I turned my face back again. It was too late; the sun was striking on the windows, and I could not see for the dazzle; but in the courtyard, the dogs had left their boxes, and amongst them now Donovan Macbeth's dog Nell was prowling about.

She was coughing. Her hairless skin no longer suggested the fine coat of a St. Bernard. The superb creature was nothing but a great carcass, whose leanness contrasted with the comparative plump shapes of her companions.

Nell, too, wore a bandage on the back of her neck. What had Lerne devised to make her suffer since the night of their adventure? What diabolical invention was he trying upon her?

Nell seemed to be reflecting; her very manner of walking suggested consternation. She held aloof from the other dogs, and when a certain bulldog accosted her in the way of gallantry, she started back with a look so fierce, and a hoarse cry so terrible, that the other hurried off to the depths of its lair, whilst the rest of the pack, put out of countenance, raised their bedizened heads.

The coy Nell went her way.

What was I doing, remaining there! In spite of my haste to shorten this reconnaissance, and betake myself to other pastimes, something held me back—something inexplicable in the behavior of this poor dog.

At this moment, a "quick-step" played by the band at Grey-l'Abbaye, reached Fonval on the wings of the wind. My fingers, of their own accord, beat time on the branches of my observation post, and I perceived that Nell had quickened her walk and was marching in time to the rhythm of the music!

I then remembered that, in talking of Nell, Emma had alluded to her performing-dog tricks. Was this a circus exercise taught by Macbeth to his St. Bernard? It did not seem to me that in the absence of the trainer such a dance could have been executed, and that an auditory sensation could arouse, in the case of an animal, those mechanical movements which have always been _our_ prerogative, and are the result of habits more complex than those of instincts.

The music died away as the wind fell. The dog sat down, raised her eyes, and saw me.

"Good Heavens, she is going to bark and give the alarm...!" Not at all. She looked at me without fear or wrath—with eyes, the memory of which will always be with me—then shaking her great shaggy head, she began to groan gently, making a vague gesture with her paw, then she resumed her round, still murmuring, and casting furtive glances in my direction, as if she desired to make herself understood without drawing the attention of the Germans.

(This, of course, is a mere descriptive phrase, but one might, all the same, have imagined that the creature wanted to speak, so human were the inflections of her moans, which roughly formed a long, guttural and monotonous phrase, in which there always occurred the syllables, "Mabet, Mabet." The whole thing made a gurgling sound, rather like English words badly articulated.)

The entry on the scene of the three assistants put a stop to this curious phenomenon.

They crossed the courtyard, and all the dogs—Nell at the head—slunk to shelter. Wilhelm, as he passed, flung over the grating of the kennel a chunk of meat—the body of the monkey, skinned, the hairy part hanging attached.

It fell heavily. It was dead!

The Germans then went into the building on the right, whose chimney was smoking. Then, one by one, the dogs came and sniffed at the remains of the chimpanzee. The bulldog gave the first bite, and then came the whole pack, growling ferociously.

The muzzles of the lame ones were soon dyed red, as their gnashing teeth tore to bits this pitiful caricature of a child's body. Nell, only, in front of her kennel, with her paws crossed, disdained the feast, and looked at me with her beautiful eyes. I fancied I had discovered why she was so thin.

Upon this, a window opened, through which I perceived a table set for three. The assistants were going to lunch in front of my wood. It was time for me to withdraw.

Here I committed an unpardonable piece of folly. I ought to have set out on my campaign against the old shoe—that was elementary. It appeared to me, wrongly, that I had made a supreme concession to prudence—that an elastic boot has many titles to be considered merely an elastic boot, and not a buried man—not even a buried body; and that, to a generous heart a pretty girl is more important than all knickknacks.

I reviewed all these reasons, with the result that I turned towards the château.

THE BEDROOM OF MY AUNT LIDIVINE NOW SERVED AS A LUMBER-ROOM. ONE would have said it was the wardrobe of a lady of fortune. Several wicker lay-figures covered with extremely elegant toilettes, formed a crowd of armless and headless coquettes. The mantelpiece and tables were like a dressmaker's show-cases, where feathers and ribbons go to make up those tiny or huge contraptions, which only become pretty hats once they are on the head. A battalion of dress shoes were fitted on their trees, and a thousand feminine trifles were heaped up everywhere, in the midst of a delicate and suggestive aroma, which was the one Emma loved.

Poor dear Aunt! I should have preferred your room to have been still further profaned, and that Mlle. Bourdichet had made it hers, rather than to hear laughter in the next one—that of your husband; for this left one no illusions.

On my appearance, Emma and Barbe seemed stupefied. The girl immediately understood, and began to laugh. She was lunching in bed, and with a turn of the wrist, she twisted her flaming Bacchante hair into a knot.

I saw the outline of her arm through the sleeve, and she did not think of closing her nightdress.

A table covered with bottles and brushes had been pushed against the bed.

Barbe, who was serving her mistress, cut huge slices out of a ham. My first thought was that Barbe would be much in my way.

"AND WHAT ABOUT LERNE?" SAID EMMA.

I reassured her. He would only come back at 5 o'clock. I guaranteed that. She gave that little cheerful cluck, which is the sob of joy.

Barbe, who was obviously devoted to her, got so uproariously delighted that her whole person took part in the festival.

It was half past twelve. We had four hours before us. I suggested that that was rather short, but "Let us have lunch, will you, dearie?" said she.

I had nothing better to do for the moment, because of Barbe, and I sat down face to face with her.

# CHAPTER VII
## THUS SPAKE MLLE. BOURDICHET

"Well, my dear," she said, "now that we have got as far as that, it is no use trying not to begin again, but I entreat you, no imprudences—safety first! Lerne, you know, Lerne! Ah, you don't know what dangers there are for you—you above all—you especially!"

I saw that she was brooding over the memory of tragic scenes.

"But what are the dangers?"

"That is just the worst of it, I do not know. I do not understand anything that is happening around. Anything! Anything! Except that Donovan Macbeth went mad because I loved him,—and I love you, too."

"Come, Emma, let us be cool. We are allies now. Between us we shall find out the truth. When did you come to Fonval, and what has happened since?"

And then she told me her adventures. I reproduce them, stringing them together as best I can, to make them clearer, but as a matter of fact, her story was spread over a dialogue in which my questions guided the story-teller, who was ever ready to make digressions, and was loquacious in futilities.

Sometimes as we talked, a noise would interrupt our talk. Emma would sit up in terror of Lerne, and I could not prevent myself shivering, at the sight of her fear, for had there been an eye or an ear at the keyhole, the somber story would have been repeated in my case.

One way or another, I learned from Emma her origin and her early life. It has nothing to do with my story, and might easily be summed up in the phrase "How a foundling became a courtesan!"

Emma showed, during this confession, a sincerity which would have been called cynicism in the case of any one less candid.

With the same frankness, she went on:

"I got to know Lerne years ago. I was fifteen, and at the hospital at Nanthel. I had entered his service as a nurse? No! I had had a fight with my friend Léonie about Alcide, who was my man. Well, I am not ashamed of it! He is superb! He is a Colossus! My dear boy, he could chuck you about like a ball. My belt was too narrow a bracelet for him!

"Well, I got a blow with a knife—a nasty one, too. Just look!"

She flung off the coverlet, and showed me, near her shoulder, a livid triangular scar—the handiwork of the execrable Léonie.

"Yes, you may well kiss it," she went on. "I nearly died of it. Your uncle looked after me, and saved me. I may well say that.

"At that time, your uncle was a fine fellow—not stuck-up. He often spoke to me. I thought that flattering. The head surgeon! Think of that! And he talked so well, too. He gave me long sermons, just as fine as any in Church, about my life: it was bad, I ought to change it, and so on, and so forth. And all this without having the least appearance of being disgusted with me, and so sincerely that I for my part, began to be disgusted with it myself, and not to wish for any more of the gay life, or any more Alcide. Illness, you know, that cools one's blood; and Lerne said to me one fine day, 'You are cured now, and can go away when you like, only it is not enough to have taken a good resolution—you must keep it. Will you come to my house? You shall be the laundry-maid, and you will earn your living far from your old companions, and all on the square, too,' he said.

"All this puzzled me. I said to myself, 'Oh, talk away. That is only a pretty speech to fool me. One does not offer to keep a woman for the love of art.'

"But all the same, Lerne's kindness, his rank, his fame, and a certain kind of niceness in him, made me more grateful, and made it into a sort of affection, do you see, and I accepted his proposal, and all that might follow.

"Well, would you believe it! Not at all! There still was a saint on earth, and that was he. For a whole year he kept away from me.

"I had kept my journey secret, for the idea of Alcide finding me again kept me from sleeping.

"'Oh, do not be afraid,' said Lerne, 'I am no longer the hospital surgeon, I am going to work at research. We are going to live in the country, and nobody will come to seek you there.'

"So that is how I was brought here.

"Ah, you should have seen the château and the park, gardens, servants, carriages, and horses—nothing wanting! I was quite happy.

"When we got here, the workmen were finishing off the additions to the conservatory and the laboratory.

"Lerne kept an eye on their work. He was always joking, and repeating, 'Ah, we are going to work there, we are going to work there,' in the same sort of a tone in which schoolboys shout out, 'Hurrah for the holidays!'

"They fitted up the laboratory. Lots of boxes were put in it, and when all was finished, Lerne set off one morning to Grey in the dog-cart. The avenue was still straight at that time.

"I still see your uncle coming back with the five travelers and the dog which he had gone to get at the station—Donovan Macbeth, Johann, Wilhelm, Karl, Otto Klotz—you remember him—the tall dark fellow with the mustache?—and Nell. The Scot had joined the Germans at Nanthel. I think he must have known them before.

"The assistants put up at the laboratory, and Macbeth slept in a bedroom in the château—Dr. Klotz also.

"Klotz frightened me from the first, and yet he was a strong, handsome chap.

"I could not help asking Lerne where he had picked up that jail-bird! My question amused him very much.

"'Oh, make your mind easy,' he answered. 'You are always imagining you see friends of M. Alcide. Professor Klotz has come from Germany. He is very learned. He is not an assistant, he is a collaborator, and will watch over the work of his three compatriots.'"

"Excuse me, Emma," I said, interrupting her, "did my uncle speak German and English at that time?"

"Not much, I think. He tried every day, but it was not much good. It was only at the end of a year, and all of a sudden, that he managed to speak it fluently. The assistants knew a few French words, and Klotz rather more, as well as a little English.

"As for Macbeth, he only understood his own language.

"Lerne told me that he had agreed to take him at Fonval because the young man's father asked him; he wanted his son to work for a time under Lerne's directions."

"Where was your room, Emma?"

"Near the laboratory. Oh, far away from Macbeth and Klotz!" she added with a smile.

"How did all those men stand towards one another?"

"They seemed good friends, but I do not know if they were really. I fancy that the four Germans were jealous of Macbeth. I saw nasty looks sometimes, but in any case, they can't have hurt Donovan much, because his job was not in the laboratory, but in the château and the conservatory.

"His work at first was to swat up French from books. We used to meet often, because I was always coming and going in the house. He was always polite and respectful, to judge by the signs he made, of course, and I was obliged to be amiable, too.

"Those little bits of politeness, I am afraid, made him and Klotz hate each other; I soon saw that, but they both managed to hide their dislike wonderfully.

"Nell could not hide hers, and never missed a chance of growling at the German, and that was, to my thinking, only the smallest sign that a row was likely, but your uncle—he saw nothing, and I did not want to bother him with my complaints. I did not dare to do so, and on the other hand, I thought it rather good fun to make them jealous.

"All my promises to Lerne to be good could not stop me from being amused at the jealousy of those two, and I do not know what would have been the end of it, when everything changed all of a sudden.

"We had been here a year—that is four years ago now."

"Ah, ha!" I cried.

"What is it?"

"Nothing, nothing!"

"Well, it is four years ago that Donovan Macbeth went off to Scotland for a few weeks' holiday with his people. The day after he had gone, Lerne left me in the morning. 'I am going,' said he, 'to Nanthel with Klotz. We shall stay there a whole day.'

"At night Klotz came back alone. I inquired about Lerne, and he told me that the Professor had heard important news and had to go abroad, and that he would be away for about three weeks.

"'Where is he?' I asked again.

"Klotz hesitated, and at last said, 'He is in Germany. We shall be by ourselves for that time, Emma.'

"He had put his arm round my waist, and was looking into my eyes.

"I could not understand how Lerne could do such a thing—to leave me without warning at the mercy of a stranger.

"'How do you like me?' asked Klotz, pressing me against him.

"I have already told you, Nicolas, that he was big and strong. I felt his muscles tighten like a vise.

"'Well, Emma,' he went on, 'you are going to love me to-day, for you will never see me again.'

"I am not a coward. Between you and me, I have been caressed by hands which had just committed murder. I have been made love to in ways that were like murder. My first lover would have stuck a knife into you as soon as look at you. But Klotz was too awful. I shall never forget how frightened I was.

"I woke up late in the morning. He was gone. I have never seen him again.

"Three weeks passed. Your uncle never wrote; he stayed away longer still.

"He came back without notice. I did not even see him come in. He told me that he had made straight for the laboratory as soon as he got back. I saw him come out about mid-day. I was quite sorry for him, he looked so pale. He was bent double as if he were worried to death. He was walking slowly, as if he were following a hearse.

"What had he been told! What had he done! What trouble was he in?

"I asked him gently. He still spoke with the accent of the country which he had just come from.

"'Emma,' said he, 'I think that you love me?'

"'You know very well that I do, my dear benefactor. I am devoted to you, body and soul.'

"'Do you think that you can love me with real love? Oh,' said he, with a snigger, 'I am no longer a young man, but....'

"What was I to say? I did not know. Lerne knitted his brows.

"He seized my two hands. His eyes were terrible.

"'Now,' cried he, 'no more joking; no more little games, you are mine exclusively. I quite understood what was going on here, and that there were admirers hovering round you. I have got rid of Klotz, and as for Donovan Macbeth, be on your guard. If he does not stop, it is all up with him. Look out!'

"Then, Lerne, having got rid of the servants, took on this poor Barbe as his only domestic, and then he arranged the labyrinth and its roads.

"On the day arranged, Macbeth, in his turn, came back to the château, followed by his dog. He was surprised to see the forest all upside down.

"Lerne went up to him while he was still holding his luggage in his hand, and he quite dumbfounded him by such a violent lecture, and so evil a countenance, that Nell bristled up, put out her claws and began to growl.

"What was bound to happen, happened. Considering the age and position of our host, Macbeth and I should probably have 'respected his roof,' as they say, but it was only a question, now, of deceiving an angry tyrant. And we did.

"Meanwhile, the Professor became more and more absurd and irritable every day. He was living in an extraordinary state of excitement, never going out; working like a horse, genial, perhaps, but certainly ill.

"You ask me why I think so. I will tell you.

"His memory began to fail. He used to get strange fits of forgetfulness, and often asked me about things concerning his own past; he remembered nothing clearly except scientific matters.

"No more joking, that was true, and no more happiness with him!

"For a mere whim, Lerne would swear at me. For a suspicion, he would beat me. Not that I mind hard words or hard blows, but only from some one I love.

"I declared to this worn-out old creature that I had had enough solitude. 'I want to be off,' I said.

"Ah, my dear, if you had seen him. He fell at my knees and embraced them.

"What he said was, 'Remain, my dear Emma, for two years more. Wait until then, and we will go away together, and you shall have the life of a queen. Have patience. I understand you are not made to be in this sort of position, as if in a convent. Take my word for it, I am making a vast fortune for you. Two more years, living like a little bourgeoisie, and then the life of an empress.'

"I was dazzled at the prospect, and remained at Fonval.

"But the years followed one after the other—the term was up, and no luxury yet. However, I waited and trusted, because Lerne was so confident, and so clever.

"'Do not be downhearted,' he said, 'we are getting on. All shall happen as I prophesy. You shall have millions,' and to cheer me up, he ordered for me, from Paris, every season, gowns and hats of all sorts, and many other knickknacks.

"'Learn to wear them,' said he, 'learn your part, and rehearse the future.'

"I lived three years in this way. About this time Lerne's great voyage to America took place. It lasted two months, for which time, your uncle had sent Macbeth back to his family, by way of a holiday.

"They came back on the same day.

"I think that the Professor and he had agreed to meet at Dieppe. Lerne was gloomy and angry. 'You will have to wait a bit yet, Emma,' he said.

"'What is the matter?' I said. 'Isn't it coming off?'

"'They think that my inventions are not perfect enough; but there is nothing to be afraid of. I shall find what I want yet.'

"He resumed his researches in the laboratory."

ONCE MORE, I INTERRUPTED EMMA'S NARRATIVE.

"Excuse me," I said, "did Macbeth work also in the laboratory at that time?"

"Never! Lerne gave him jobs to do in the hothouse, where he kept my poor friend a prisoner.

"Poor Donovan, he would have done better to have remained over yonder. It was for my sake that he came back from Scotland, and he tried to make me understand that in his jargon.

"'For you, for you,' was all he could manage to say.

"For me! Good heavens, what had he become 'for me' a few weeks later!

"Now listen! Here is where the madness comes in.

"That winter it was snowing. Lerne was taking a nap in the armchair in the little drawing-room—at least he was pretending to have a nap.

"Donovan gave me a glance. Pretending to go out to have a walk in the snow, which was falling, he went out by the hall. I heard him whistling a tune outside. He moved away. I went back to the dining-room to help the maid clear the table. Donovan joined me there, by the door opposite to that of the little drawing-room which we left open so that we could hear Lerne's movements.

"He flung his arms round me. I embraced him. We had a silent kiss.

"Suddenly Donovan went green. I followed his looks. The door of the little drawing-room has a glass panel, and in that dim mirror, I saw Lerne's eyes watching us.

"Then he was upon us. My knees gave under me. Macbeth is a little man. Lerne flung him to the ground. They struggle. Blood flows. Your uncle uses his feet and teeth and nails ferociously.

"I scream and tear at his clothes. Suddenly he picks himself up. Macbeth is in a faint, and then, Lerne gives a wild laugh, flings him over his shoulder, and carries him off to the laboratory.

"I keep shouting, and then I had a sudden idea.

"'Nell, Nell!' I cried.

"The dog came up. I pointed out the group to her, and she dashed off at the moment when Lerne was disappearing behind the trees with his burden. She disappeared also.

"I listen. She barks, and suddenly I can distinguish nothing more than the rustle of the snow.

"Lerne dragged me about by the hair. It required all my belief in his promise, and all his assurance of a glorious future, to stop me from running away that very day.

"But, having caught me deceiving him, he only loved me the more ardently.

"Days passed. I hardly dared hope that Macbeth had got off as easily as Klotz—and been sent away. Neither he nor his dog appeared again.

"At last the Professor ordered me to get ready the Yellow Room for the Scot.

"'Is he alive, then?' I asked without reflection.

"'Only half,' said Lerne, 'he is mad. This is the sad result of your folly, Emma. First of all he thought himself God Almighty, then the Tower of London. At present he thinks he's a dog. To-morrow he will suffer from some other delusion, no doubt.'

"'What have you done to him?' I cried out.

"'Little girl,' said the Professor, 'nothing has been done to him, just you remember that, and bite your tongue if you ever think of gossiping. When I carried off Macbeth after our struggle in the dining-room, it was so that I might look after him. You saw he fainted. He injured his head badly in his fall. That caused a lesion, and then madness. That was all, you understand?'

"I said nothing more, because I was certain that if your uncle had not put an end to Donovan, his only motive was fear of the family, and the law.

"That evening they brought him back to the château—his head all wrapped in bandages. He did not recognize me.

"I still loved him, and I visited him secretly.

"He got better quickly. Being shut up made him put on fat. The Macbeth of the photograph, and the Macbeth of the Yellow Room, became very unlike each other, so much so, that you did not recognize him at first."

"But tell me—you do not know anything about Klotz? What did my uncle do with him? You said a moment ago he had been sent away."

"I was always certain he had been sent away. His behavior when he left, and that of Lerne when he came back from Germany, made me feel sure of it."

"Has he a family?"

"I think he is an orphan, and a bachelor."

"How long did Macbeth remain in the laboratory?"

"About three weeks or a month."

"Was his hair always fair, before this happened?" I asked, still riding my hobby-horse.

She said, "Certainly, what an idea!"

"And what did they do with Nell?"

"The day after the quarrel, I heard her howling loudly, no doubt because they had separated her from her master.

"According to your uncle, whom I asked about it, she was with other dogs, in a kennel. 'Her right place,' added Lerne. She got out of it the other night—perhaps you heard her.

"Poor Nell, how quickly she found out Macbeth was gone. She often howls at night-time. Her life is not happy."

"Tell me the end of it," I said. "What is at the bottom of it? What is the truth? Do you believe in the madness which resulted from the fall?"

"How do I know? It is possible, but I suspect the laboratory contains horrible things, the very sight of which would drive any one mad. Donovan had never been in it. He must have seen some ghastly things."

I then remembered the chimpanzee, and the horrible impression its death had made upon me. Emma might be right. The incident of the monkey strongly supported her hypothesis, but instead of trying to find the answer to each riddle in detail, should I not have gone back four years, to that critical moment when so many problems had started? Should I not have studied closely the mysterious period when so many doors had closed, in order to find the key which should open them all?

A LITTLE FOOT PEEPED FROM THE COVERLET, AND LAY, WHITE AND PINK, ON the pale yellow cover; it was smooth, and like a strange jewel in its case.

"Good gracious, my dear, can you really walk with that pretty little thing, with its nails polished like Japanese corals—this living ticklish jewel—that a mustache drives away."

The little foot went back into its cover, but however dainty and tender and quick it was, it recalled another one to me by contrast—the one in the forest clearing—that sinister thing, which I now felt sure was a piece of dead flesh in the old shoe.

Suddenly it seemed to me that I was wandering alone in a night full of ambushes.

"Emma, suppose we run away!"

She shook her Mænad's locks, and refused.

"Donovan proposed that to me. No, Lerne has promised me I shall be rich; besides, on the day you arrived, he swore he would kill me if I deceived him, or tried to escape. I found out long ago that he could fulfill his first threat, and I know now that he could carry out the second."

"That is true. When he introduced us to one another, you had the shadow of death in your eyes."

"Now," she went on, "we can hide our love, but we could not hide our running away. No, no, let us stop where we are, and keep our eyes open. Let us be careful."

Half-past four was striking on the clock when I left my mistress, in order to return to Grey-l'Abbaye.

# CHAPTER VIII

## RASHNESS

I made my way as fast as I could back to Grey. The fête was in full swing, and the crowd of merry-makers received me with impertinent remarks and jokes.

Five by the station clock! I profited by the time at my disposal to arrange things a little, so that my uncle might the more easily fall into the snare which he had spread with his own hands when he set me the task of repairing part of the machine of which I had a duplicate.

Having put on my blue overalls, dirtied my hands and face, taken out my tool-box, and turned everything in it upside down, I slightly dented the new carburetor, with light taps of a hammer, and dirtied it with blacklead. With a few scrapes of a file I succeeded in giving it the sort of rough look of a newly forged piece of metal.

The train came in. When Lerne touched my shoulder, I was endeavoring, with a great show of effort to screw up a nut which was already perfectly tight.

"Nicolas!"

I turned towards my uncle a face like a coal-heaver's, putting on as harsh an expression as I could.

"I have just finished," I muttered; "that was a nice trick of yours, getting people to work all for nothing."

"Does it work all right again?"

"Oh, yes! I have just tried. You can see the engine is smoking."

"Do you want the bits I carried away put back into the carburetor?"

"Oh, no! keep them as a remembrance of this happy day, uncle. Come, let us get in, I have had enough of standing about here."

Frédéric Lerne was annoyed.

"You do not mind, Nicolas, do you?"

"Oh no, uncle, I do not mind."

"I have my reasons, you know. Later on...."

"All right, if you knew me, however, you would not have been so much on your guard, but our agreement justifies all you did. I should have had no right to complain."

He made a vague, evasive gesture.

"You are not angry, that is the main point. You understand how things are, don't you?"

Evidently Lerne was afraid he had vexed me, and that, as a result of my annoyance, I might disclose the existence of important secrets at Fonval, even though I might not be able to inform the right people of their nature.

Weighing all the facts of the case, I felt that my presence as a stranger, free to depart when I liked, must have been a subject for constant alarm for my uncle. It seemed to me that in his place, had I been obliged to receive a third party because of his relationship with me, I should assuredly have preferred to make him my accomplice as soon as possible, so as to insure his discretion.

"After all," thought I to myself, "why has my uncle not thought of it? Before the uncertain, and perhaps illusory date when Lerne is to initiate me, he will have to pass through a long period of torment while he exercises over me the double vigilance of an analyst and a police-officer.

"Suppose I were to anticipate his project? He would doubtless gladly hasten to give the information which is as sacred as a secret of the confessional, and which would unite the master and the pupil in the same plot.

"I do not see why he should take my advances badly, for in either of the two possible eventualities, that is, whether Lerne's promises to initiate me into his enterprise are made in good faith or not, the situation to-day has only two issues—either my departure, with its threat of revelation, or my connivance.

"Now, Emma and the mystery tie me to the château, so I shall not go; there remains, therefore, a pretended complicity which would, moreover, have the advantage of allowing me to solve the puzzle—and who except Lerne could reveal it to my eyes, since Emma knows nothing about it, and since each solved problem, if I investigated it by myself, would only leave another one to follow?

"A sage diplomacy might certainly persuade my uncle to make speedy revelations; that is what he wants to do, but how to bring him to do it?

"What I must do is to insinuate that his secrets, however criminal they may be, do not terrify me, so that I shall have to pose as a man of resolution, who does not shrink from contact with crimes, and would not think of denouncing them, because, if need were, he would commit them himself. Yes, that's it!

"But how to hit on a crime which Lerne might perpetrate, and which I might say is natural and harmless, and one which I would commit on the first occasion myself?

"Good heavens, Nicolas! Yes, his own wicked deeds! Tell him that you know one of the worst things he has done, and that you not only approve of it, but of others of the same sort, and that you are ready to help him in the matter. Then, after such a declaration, he will unbosom himself, and you will learn everything, with the intention of using this confidence, dictated by mere self-interest for your own ends. But let me be cunning. I shall only speak to my uncle when he is in a pleasant humor, and provided the evidence of the old shoe is not too damning."

So I reasoned, as I took Lerne back to Fonval, but after my stormy afternoon, my ideas were not very brilliant.

Under the influence of my environment, I brooded over Lerne's unproven crimes and I imagined them to be detestable and innumerable. I forgot that his work, carried on with such secrecy, and secure from risk of imitation, might well have an industrial aim. In my impatience to satisfy my curiosity and by reason of my exhaustion, this strategy seemed to me a brilliant idea.

I underrated the enormity of the fictitious avowal I should have to make before getting anything in exchange.

Further reflection would have indicated the danger to me, but adverse fortune would have it that my uncle, satisfied by my answer, and seeing me take things so well, affected the most surprising joviality. Never would an opportunity more suitable to my designs present itself, so I thoughtlessly seized it.

ACCORDING TO HIS CUSTOM, MY UNCLE WAXED ENTHUSIASTIC OVER THE CAR, and made me maneuver as I went through the labyrinth, and it was while twisting and turning about that I had been deliberating in the manner described.

"Marvelous, Nicolas, I tell you again, it is prodigious, this automobile! An animal—a real organized animal, and perhaps the least imperfect of all, and who knows to what pitch progress may lift it! A spark of life in it! A little more spontaneity! A touch of brain, and behold the most beautiful creature in the world! Yes, more beautiful than we are, perhaps, for remember what I told you—it is perfectible, and undying—two qualities of which the physical being of man is pitifully devoid.

"Our whole body renews itself almost entirely, Nicolas. Your hair!" (Why the devil was he always talking of hair?) Your hair is not the same as it was last year, for example. It comes up again, less brown, and older, and in smaller numbers, whereas the automobile changes its parts at will, and get young again each time, with a new heart, and new brains which have more cunning than the original parts.

"So that in a thousand years a motor-car, which never ceases to improve, will be as young as it is to-day, if it has been put to rights at the proper time, bit by bit.

"And do not tell me that it will not be the same car, since all its parts shall have been replaced. If you made that objection, Nicolas, what would you think about man, who, during this race to death, that he calls life, is submitting to just as ridiculous transformations, but all in the nature of decay.

"So that we must come to this strange conclusion—the man who dies old, is no longer he who was born. He who has just been born, and must succumb later on, will not die, at least, he will not die all at once, but progressively, scattered to the four winds of heaven in organic dust, during which long phase another being forms itself slowly in that place which is the place of the body.

"This other one, whose birth is imperceptible, develops in each one of us, without our knowledge, as the first one crumbles away. It supplants this latter day by day, and it is modified continually by the death and renewal of myriads of cells, of which he is himself the sum total. He it is who will be seen to die.

"I tell you, Nicolas, if the motor-car were by some miracle to become independent, man might pack his trunks. His era would be near its end. Compared with him, the motor-car would be queen of the world, as before him reigned the mammoth."

"Yes, but this sovereign queen would always be dependent upon the mind of man."

"That is a fine argument. Are we not the slaves of the animals, and even the plants which unceasingly rebuild our bodies with their flesh and their pulp?"

My uncle was so pleased with his paradoxes, that he shouted them out, and fidgeted about in his seat, and sawed the air in a frenzy, as if he were seizing ideas in armfuls.

"My dear nephew, what a splendid idea it was of yours to bring this car! It does buck me up wonderfully. I must learn how to drive the beast. I shall be the mahout of this fierce mammoth. Eh! Eh! Ah! Ha!"

At the moment of this outburst of hilarity, I was just finishing my reasoning, and it was the outburst which caused me to make my attack— and to commit my imprudence.

"How amusing you are, uncle! Your gayety cheers me up. I recognize you again. Why aren't you always like this, and why do you distrust me— me, who, on the contrary—deserve all your confidence?"

"But," said Lerne, "you know quite well I will give it to you when the time has come. I have quite decided on that."

"Why not at once, uncle?"

And I plunged bald-headed into my folly. "Are we not made of the same stuff, you and I? You don't know me! Nothing can astonish me, and I know more than you think! Yes, uncle, I share your opinions and admire your acts."

Lerne, somewhat surprised, began to laugh.

"What do you know about it?"

"What I know is that one cannot trust to the law. One has to look after one's own affairs. If some one happens to cross your path, the best way is to get rid of him yourself, and such a removal, if it is illegal, becomes legitimate. A chance incident has confirmed me in this.

"In short, uncle, if my name were Frédéric Lerne, Mr. Macbeth would not be living so comfortably. You do not know me, I tell you."

By the Professor's voice, when next he spoke, I perceived I had committed a blunder. He defended himself in a voice which, I observed, betrayed great weariness.

"Hallo!" said he, "this is something new. What an idea! Are you really as unprincipled as you make out? Well, so much the worse. As for me, I am not tarred with that brush, nephew. Macbeth is mad, but I had nothing to do with it. It is a pity you saw him. It is an ugly sight. The poor creature! I had to put him away. What nonsense, Nicolas! What are you going to invent next? It is a good thing, however, you have spoken to me about it. It has opened my eyes. Appearances are indeed against me. I was awaiting till the patient got better, before telling his people what had happened, so that they might be less affected by a misfortune whose signs were less obvious; but no, this timorous policy is too dangerous. My own safety requires that at the risk of hurting their feelings more, I must inform them. I shall write to them no later than to-night to come and fetch him. Poor Donovan! His departure will, I hope, disprove your suspicion, but you have disappointed me very much, Nicolas."

I was greatly confused. Had I made a mistake, or had Emma lied to me? Or else, did Lerne want to lull my suspicions? However, it was, I had committed a great piece of stupidity, and Lerne, whether innocent or criminal, would bear me a grudge for having accused him falsely or otherwise.

I was defeated. All I had gained was a fresh doubt—this time in regard to Emma.

"In any case, uncle, I swear to you that it was only by chance that I discovered Macbeth."

"If chance leads you to discover other reasons for maligning me," replied Lerne harshly, "do not fail to inform me of it. I shall clear myself immediately. Anyhow, the strict observance of your word will prevent you from helping any chance which should favor your meeting with madmen ... or madwomen!"

We had arrived at Fonval.

"Nicolas," said Lerne, in a gentler tone, "I have a great liking for you. I wish you well. Obey me, my lad."

"Ah, he wants to soft-sawder me," I thought to myself. "He is paying court to me now. Look out!"

"Obey me," he went on, with honeyed sweetness, "and show by your reserve that you are already my ally; intelligent as you are, you must surely understand this fine point. The day is not far off, unless I am mistaken, when I shall be able to tell you about everything. You shall then see the magnificent things that I have dreamt of, and of which I destine a share for you."

"Meanwhile, since you know about Macbeth's absence—come, here is a sign of the good faith I ask of you. Come with me and visit him. We shall decide if he is strong enough to stand a railway journey, and the crossing."

After a short hesitation I followed him into the yellow drawing-room.

THE MADMAN AT THE SIGHT OF HIM HUMPED HIS BACK, AND GROWLING RE-coiled into a corner with a look of terror and a revengeful gleam in his eye.

Lerne thrust me in before him—I was afraid he meant to shut me in.

"Take hold of his hands and bring him into the middle of the room."

Donovan allowed me to touch him. The Doctor examined him thoroughly, but obviously the scar attracted his greatest attention. In my opinion, the rest of the inspection was merely a sham for my benefit.

The scar—it was an incised crown that almost disappeared under the long hair; a wound that went round the back of the head. What possible fall could have caused it?

"His health is excellent," said my uncle. "You see, Nicolas, he was violent at first, and hurt himself badly all over. In a fortnight, it will all have disappeared. He can be taken away. The consultation is at an end. So you advise me to get rid of him as soon as possible, Nicolas? Tell me your opinion, I attach value to it."

I congratulated him on his resolution, although so much kindliness kept me on the alert.

Lerne gave a sigh. "You are right! The world is so evil-minded. I am going to write immediately. Will you take my letter to the post at Grey? It will be ready in ten minutes."

My nerves relaxed. I had asked myself as I came into the _château_ if I should ever come out again, and sometimes, even now the demon of unhealthy dreams shows me the madman's room as a dungeon.

The old rascal was really showing himself paternal and benevolent; though he could dispose of my liberty and imprison me, he sent me for a run in the fields, which might have ended in a flight.

Was a freedom, granted so readily, worth profiting by? I wasn't such a fool! I would not make use of it.

WHILST LERNE WAS WRITING HIS LETTER TO THE MACBETHS, I WENT FOR A stroll in the park, and I there witnessed an incident which made the strangest possible impression upon me.

As has been seen, fortune made ceaseless sport of me. She jerked me like a marionette—first towards calm, and then towards trouble. This time she used a trivial cause to upset my mind. Had I been feeling more at ease, I should not have interpreted what was perhaps only a freak of nature, as so great a mystery, but marvels were in the air. I felt them everywhere, and this phrase was always sounding in my ears:

"Since the night of my arrival, there were certain things outside which should not have been there."

Those that I saw in the park that day—and which I insist would not have astounded any ordinary person as they did me—seemed to me to fill up a gap in my evidence with regard to the Lerne question.

It brought that study, so to speak, to a close. It was very indistinct. I caught a glimpse of a solution of all the problems—an abominable one—but my ideas were not precise enough to express it to myself. For the space of a second, however, they were of unimaginable violence, and if I shrugged my shoulders after the little scene which inspired them, I must admit that they caused me agony. This is what it was: Intending to spend my ten minutes in having a look at the old shoe, I was going down an avenue where the evening dew was already moistening the high grass. The night was beginning to fill the underwood. One heard the chirping of sparrows growing less and less frequent. I think it was about half-past six. The bull bellowed. As I rounded the paddock I could only count four animals there—Pasiphaë was no longer walking about there in the half-mourning of her pied robe, but that is a matter of no interest.

I was walking slowly on, when a tornado of whistling, mingled with little cries—a mass of shrill squeakings, if I may so say, made me pause.

The grass was stirring. I approached noiselessly, stretching out my neck.

A duel was going on there: one of those countless combats which make each cart-rut an abyss of death, in order that one of the combatants may feed on the other.

It was a little bird and a serpent.

The serpent was a rather imposing viper, whose triangular head was marked with a white stigma of the same shape.

The bird looked like a black-headed wren, with this essential difference, however, that its head was white. A variety, doubtless, from the aviary, which I should be able to describe less awkwardly if I were better versed in natural history.

The two combatants were face to face—one approaching the other.

Imagine my bewilderment! It was the wren which was forcing the serpent to recoil! It advanced in little quick jumps, without a quiver of its wings, and as if hypnotizing its enemy. Its fixed eye had the magnetic gleam of a dog's when it points, and the helpless viper was recoiling before it, fascinated by its implacable looks, whilst terror was wringing half-suppressed whistlings from its throat.

"Deuce take it," I said to myself, "is the world upside down, or is my mind topsy-turvy?"

I then made the mistake of drawing too near the scene in order to witness its denouement, and this made a change. The wren saw me and flew away, and its enemy gliding off into the grass left the trace of its passage there in zigzags.

Already the ridiculous and exaggerated anguish which had frozen me was dissipated. I took myself severely to task. "I must be half blind! It is merely an example of maternal love—nothing else. The heroic little bird is merely defending its nest. One does not realize the love of mothers. What a fool I have been!"

"Hallo! Hallo!" My uncle was hailing me. I retraced my steps, but this incident haunted my mind. In spite of my assurance that there was nothing extraordinary in it, I did not speak about it to Lerne.

The Professor looked cheerful. He wore the smiling expression of a man who had just taken a great resolution, and is much pleased at it. He was standing before the principal door of the château, the letter in his hand, and looking at the boot-scraper with interest.

My presence not having interrupted his fit of absent-mindedness, I thought it would be enlightening to look at the scraper, too. It was a sharp blade, mortized into the wall, and generous use by many soles had curved it into the shape of a sickle.

I presume that Lerne, in his meditation, was looking at that knife without seeing it. Indeed, he seemed suddenly to wake up.

"Here, Nicolas, here is the letter! Pardon the trouble I am giving you."

"Oh, uncle, I am used to it! Chauffeurs are messengers despite themselves. Presuming on the pleasure which rolling along without any aim is supposed to give them, many a lady asks them to roll along for something, and to cart away many lots of very urgent and heavy parcels. Our sport is taxed that way."

"Ah, ha!" says uncle, "you are a good fellow. Off with you, the night is falling!"

I took the sad letter which was to announce Donovan's madness to his parents in Scotland—the blessed letter which was going to send Emma's lover from her.

George Macbeth Esq.,
12, Trafalgar Street,
Glasgow,
(Ecosse).
The writing of the address gave me food for thought.

Only a few vestiges of the former flowing script made it resemble Lerne's handwriting, but most of the letters and the general appearance, denoted a "graphic spirit" the exact opposite of that of long ago. Graphology is never at fault. Its decrees are infallible. The writer of this address had changed altogether.

In his youth, my uncle had given proof of every virtue. What vices were now not his, and how he must hate me, he who had loved me so much!

# CHAPTER IX

## THE AMBUSH

The father of Macbeth came to fetch him without delay, accompanied by his other son. Since Lerne had written to him, nothing new had taken place at Fonval. The mystery went on, and more arrangements were made against my person.

Emma no longer came downstairs; from the little drawing room I heard her busy with her futile amusements in the lay-figure room. Her little sharp heels went tap, tap, tap on the floor above. My nights were sleepless. The harassing idea of Lerne and Emma together kept me awake.

I tried to go out once, to take a walk in the cool of the night, and so weary out my body. All the doors down below were locked.

Ah! Lerne was keeping a good watch on me.

However, the imprudence I had committed in revealing my discovery of Macbeth had no other apparent result than a renewal of his friendship. In our walks which had now become more frequent, he seemed to take more and more pleasure in my society, endeavoring to mitigate the rigor of my spy-haunted life, and thus to keep me at Fonval, whether it was really to train an associate for himself, or merely to guard against the risk of an escape. His attentions annoyed me.

This was the period when, without it seeming to be so, I was more carefully watched than before. My days were filled in a way which I disliked. I was eaten up with impatience, between love on the one hand, and mystery on the other—both forbidden ground for me. Though love for a pretty woman, who was inaccessible, called me in one direction, the mystery also attracted me as imperiously in the other—that mystery which was represented by an old boot.

This filthy elastic-sided boot served as a basis for all the theories which I built up at night, in the hope of calming my jealousy by curiosity. It constituted, indeed, the one clear goal to which my indiscretions could tend.

I had noted that the tool-house stood near the clearing, and that was convenient for any attempt to unearth the boot—and whatever else there might be—but Lerne's displays of affection kept me pitilessly away from the hothouse, the laboratory, Emma, and everything else.

So I ardently longed for something or other new to happen, which should revolutionize our relations, and give me a chance of escaping from the vigilance of my guardians,—a sudden journey of Lerne to Nanthel— an accident, anything from which I could derive some advantage.

This windfall was the arrival of the two Macbeths—father and son.

My uncle having been informed of their arrival by telegram, announced it to me with an outburst of delight.

Why was he so pleased? Had I really enlightened him on the danger of keeping Donovan, ill, away from his family? I found it devilish hard to believe that. And then, that laugh of Lerne's, even though sincere, seemed to have a nasty quality. It could only be caused by his having a chance of playing some dirty trick.

But, whatever the reason was, I showed the same delight as the Professor, and that without any guile, for I had every good ground for it.

THEY ARRIVED ONE MORNING IN A TRAP, HIRED AT GREY, AND DRIVEN BY Karl. They resembled one another, and both resembled Donovan of the photograph. They were tall, pale and impassive.

Lerne introduced me with perfect ease of manner. They shook hands with me coldly, with the same glove-clad gesture. One would have said that they had put gloves over their souls.

Having been ushered into the little drawing room, they sat down without a word.

With his three assistants present, Lerne began a long speech in English, full of movement, illustrated by mimic gestures, and very emotional.

At a certain point in his story, he pretended to tumble back like somebody who had slipped. Then, taking the two men by the arm, he led them to the central door of the château, near the park.

There he pointed out to them the scraper, shaped like a sickle and then, once more went through the tumbling farce. No doubt he was explaining to them that Donovan had been wounded by the curved blade which cut his head when he fell backwards.

Good Lord! this was something new!

We went back to the drawing room. My uncle finished his speech with wiping his eyes, and the three Germans tried to do a little sniffling to indicate a need for weeping violently suppressed.

The Macbeths, father and son, never budged; they gave no sign either of grief or impatience.

At length, Karl, Johann and Wilhelm went out of the room on an order from Lerne, and brought in Donovan, clean-shaven, with his hair greased and parted at the side, and the appearance of a very fashionable young blade, although his traveling suit, somewhat worn, dragged on the buttons at the all-too narrow collar, sending the blood into his big good-natured face. His hair almost hid the scar.

At the sight of his father and brother the madman's eye gleamed with genuine happiness, and a smile lit up that face which had seemed so apathetic, with affectionate kindness.

I thought that he was restored to reason—but he knelt down at the feet of his relations and began to lick their hands, barking inarticulately!

His brother could not get anything else out of him. His father failed also, whereupon the Macbeths prepared to take leave of Lerne.

My uncle spoke to them. I grasped that they were declining some invitation or other to lunch. The other did not insist, and everybody went out.

Wilhelm put Donovan's trunk on the box of the carriage.

"Nicolas," said Lerne to me, "I am taking these gentlemen as far as the train. You will remain here with Johann and Wilhelm. Karl will come with me. I leave the house in your charge," said he, in a jovial tone, and he gave me a frank handshake.

Was my uncle making a fool of me? Not much chance of being master of a house when there were two such watchers there.

They got into the trap, Karl and the trunk in front, Lerne, the madman and the two Macbeths behind.

No sooner had the door slammed, than Donovan rose all at once, with a face of terror, as if he had heard Death sharpening his scythe.

A long howl, quite distinct from all others rose from the laboratory. The madman pointed in that direction, and replied to Nell with a long-drawn bestial cry, the horror of which made us all turn pale.

We awaited the end of it, as if for a deliverance.

Lerne, with his imperious eye, and harsh speech, gave orders, "Vorwärts, Karl, vorwärts," and without any consideration, he thrust down his pupil, with a blow, on the seat.

The carriage moved off.

The madman, sitting close to his brother, looked at him wildly, as if he were the victim of some misfortune he could not understand.

The dreadful mystery was on me again. It was around me, coming nearer and nearer. This time I had felt the touch of its wings.

Far away, the howlings were redoubled, then the elder Macbeth exclaimed, "Nell, where is Nell?" And my uncle replied, "Alas, Nell is dead."

"Poor Nell!" said Mr. Macbeth.

Duffer as I was, I knew enough English to translate this school-book dialogue. Lerne's lie made me indignant. To think of his daring to say that Nell was dead, and that that was not her voice! What a piece of villainy! Ah! why did I not shout out to this phlegmatic couple, "Stop, you are being fooled! There is something strange and terrible here!"

Yes, but I did not know what it was, and the Macbeths would have taken me for another madman.

Meanwhile, the hired horse trotted along towards the gate, where Barbe stood ready to shut it.

Donovan had sat down again, in front of them. The Macbeths, father and son, maintained their stiff dignity, but as the carriage turned at the gate, I saw the father's back suddenly bend and quiver more than could have been explained by the jolting over the stones.

Then the old cracking halves of the gate closed again.

I am sure that the brother Macbeth broke into sobs not much later.

JOHANN AND WILHELM DEPARTED. WERE THEY GOING TO RELIEVE ME OF THEIR company? I tracked them along the park as far as the laboratory. Nell was continuing her lamentations. They probably wanted to silence her, and, in fact, her howls ceased as soon as the assistants got into the yard.

But my fears were groundless. Instead of going up to the château to lock me in, the black-guards, having lighted cigars coolly sat down for an obvious siesta.

Through an open window of their block, I could see them in their shirt sleeves, smoking like chimneys, and rocking in their rocking-chairs.

When I had assured myself of their intentions, without asking myself whether they were acting thus against Lerne's orders, or with his consent, and a thousand miles from thinking that, as they puffed away at the open window, they were carrying out his instructions point by point, I betook myself to the tool-house.

Soon I was digging at the ground round the old shoe. I may now say, "round the foot."

With its point upwards, it stood up at the bottom of a hole where Donovan's nails still showed their marks, among less recent scratches. When one examined these latter, which had been made by strong and powerful paws, the only possible conclusion was that the first digger must have been a dog of large size—apparently Nell, at the time when she wandered about the park in complete freedom.

A leg was attached to this foot, and only lightly covered with earth. I clung to the possibility of some anatomical _débris_, but without much conviction. A hairy body followed the leg—a whole corpse, hardly clothed, and far advanced in decomposition!

It had been buried aslant—the head, lower down than the feet, still remained buried. It was with a trembling spade that I uncovered the chin, whiskers that were almost blue, then a thick mustache—finally a face.

I now knew what fate had overtaken all the personages who were grouped in the photograph.... Otto Klotz, half unburied, with his head in the earth, was lying there before me!

I identified him without any hesitation. It was quite unnecessary to uncover him completely—on the contrary, it was best to fill in the hole, so as to leave no traces of my escapade.

However, all of a sudden, I seized the pick in frenzy, and began digging away by the side of the dead man. Here rose up a bone like a white and spongy mushroom. Were there other things buried there? Oh!!

I dug and dug. I was in a fever. White spots flickered before my eyes, and it seemed to me that tongues of fire were raining on my maddened eye like a pentecostal deluge.

I dug and dug, and uncovered a whole cemetery, but thank God! a cemetery of animals—some, mere skeletons, others, with their feathers or fur—dry or oozy! Guinea-pigs, rabbits, dogs, cats—sometimes whole, sometimes in bits, the rest of which had gone to feed the pack. The leg of a horse! Ah, dear Biribi, it was yours; and under a layer of earth which had been recently stirred, bits of butcher's meat wrapped up in a dappled skin—the remains of Pasiphaë!

A fetid stench choked me. Exhausted, I leaned over my filthy pick, in the midst of the charnel-house. The sweat which poured from me, stung my eyes. I was gasping for breath.

At that moment, my eyes lighted, by chance, on a skull—that of a cat. Immediately I picked it up. It was a regular pipe's bowl! That is to say, a great circular hole took the place of the crown.

I then took up another—a rabbit's, if I remember rightly. Here too, was the same peculiarity.

Four—sixteen other skulls, each showing its gaping hole, but with some differences in its position.

Here and there the bony tops of skulls strewed the clearing with their large or tiny cups—some deep—some flat.

One would have said that all those creatures had been massacred in a scientific hecatomb—a carefully reasoned-out sacrifice.

Suddenly, an atrocious idea seized me. I bent down over the dead man, and succeeded in getting the mud off his head. Nothing abnormal in front. His hair was closely cropped, but behind, encircling the whole occiput, like Macbeth's scar, from one temple to the other, a horrible cut laid bare the broken brain.

Lerne had killed Klotz! He had suppressed him because of Emma, in the same way that he knocked the life out of animals and fowls, when he had exhausted their power of enduring his experiments. It was a surgical crime. I now imagined I had probed the mystery to the bottom.

I thought to myself, "Macbeth's madness comes from this, that Lerne missed his blow. The poor doomed creature saw a dreadful death coming on him. But why should my uncle have missed him? Perhaps in his blind fury, he suddenly saw clear, and feared reprisals from the Macbeth family."

As for Klotz, he was an orphan and a bachelor, as Emma assured me, so there he is! and the same fate awaits me—awaits her, perhaps, if we are found together!

"Oh, to flee, to flee, she and I together, to flee, it's the only reasonable plan, and opportunity favors us! Will it ever occur again?"

We must make for the station, through the forest, in order to avoid Lerne and Karl, who are coming by the road. But the labyrinth!—Perhaps it would be better to use the motor-car and pass over their bodies. I do not know, we shall see!

Shall I be in time? Quick, for God's sake, quick!

I ran panting, striving to outstrip the light, swift, unseen feet of Death.

I ran, twice falling and twice picking myself up, and gasping with the fear of that Pursuer.

The château! No Lerne yet! His felt hat was not hanging on its usual peg in the hall. I had won the first lap. The second was to get us away, without return. I dashed up the staircase, crossed the landing, went through the dressing-room at a bound, and burst into Emma's room.

"Let us begone," I blurted out. "Come, sweetheart, come, I will explain all. There is murder being done at Fonval!"

"What's the matter? What is it?"

She remained rigid in the presence of my excitement, standing stiffly up.

"How white you are. Don't be afraid."

Then, and then only, I perceived that terror possessed her, and that with frightened eyes, and bloodless lips, her poor dead face was signing to me to be silent, and announcing the imminence of a great danger, close at hand, too close for her to be able to warn me of it with a gesture or a sound, without the watchful enemy taking revenge upon her.

And yet, nothing happened. I took in the whole peaceful chamber at a glance. Everything in it seemed to me mysterious. The air itself was a hostile fluid—an unbreathable ocean in which I was sinking.

I felt a terror of what might happen behind me. I waited some legendary apparition.

And it was more terrible, this apparition, than the sudden appearance of Mephistopheles. _For it was Lerne calmly coming out of a wardrobe!_

"You have kept us waiting, Nicolas," he said. I was thunder-struck. Emma sank on the ground foaming at the mouth, and twisting about under the furniture.

"Jetzt!" cried the professor.

A rustle of dresses in the next room—I heard the lay-figures fall. Wilhelm and Johann flung themselves on me.

Bound! Caught! Lost! And the terror of torture made me a coward.

"Uncle," I entreated, "kill me at once, I beg you. No torture! A revolver; the dagger—poison! Anything you like, uncle, but no torture!"

Lerne sniggered, as he flipped Emma's cheeks with a wet towel.

I felt myself going mad. Who knows if Macbeth's reason had not gone in a moment like this! Macbeth! Klotz!

The hallucination made me feel a sharp pain, which pierced my skull from temple to temple.

The assistants took me downstairs, Johann at my head—Wilhelm at my feet.

Were they simply going to put me away in a locked room!

A nephew, damn it all, is not to be slaughtered like a chicken!

They took their way to the laboratory.

In my fainting condition, my whole life, day by day, passed before me in the moment of a heart's beat.

The Professor joined us. We went past the Germans' block, and along beside the courtyard wall. Lerne opened a door on the ground floor of the left wing, and I was laid out under the operating theater, in a sort of wash-house that was as bare as a sepulcher, and all inlaid with white tiles.

A curtain of thick cloth hanging from a rod on rings, separated it into two compartments of equal size.

Its atmosphere was that of a chemist's shop. There was plenty of light in it.

They had set up against the wall a little truckle-bed, which Lerne pointed out to me saying, "Your bed has been ready for you for some time, Nicolas."

Then my uncle gave some instructions to the Germans, in their native language. The two assistants having unbound me, undressed me. Resistance was useless.

A few minutes later I was comfortably lying in bed, with sheets up to my chin, and tucked in. Johann alone watched over me, sitting astride on a stool, the only ornament of this austere place.

The curtain drawn aside let me see another folding door—the door into the courtyard.

In front of me,—through the bay window, I saw my old friend the fir tree.

My sadness increased. My mouth had a bad flavor in it, as if it had already tasted its approaching decomposition.

"Oh, to think that in a short time some filthy chemistry would be a prelude to that!"

Johann toyed with a revolver, and aimed it at me every now and again, much pleased with his excellent joke.

I turned round towards the wall, and that caused me to discover an inscription engraved in uncouth letters on the varnish of the tiling, made by the help, at least so I thought, of the jewel in a ring:

"Good-by, for ever, my dear father; Donovan."

The unhappy man. He also had been laid on this bed—Klotz also, and who could prove that my uncle had made only those two his victims before me; but I cared very little.

The day sank into night. There was a rapid coming and going above us. At night this slackened and ceased. Then Karl, who had come back from Grey-l'Abbaye, relieved Johann of his post.

Almost immediately afterwards, Lerne had me plunged into a bath, and forced a bitter liquid down my throat. I recognized sulphate of magnesia. No doubt they were going to cut me up. These were forerunners of an operation. No one is ignorant of that now, in this age of appendicitis. It would be on the next day.

What were they going to try on my body before killing it!

I was alone with Karl!

I was hungry!

Not far from me a murmur arose from the wretched poultry-yard. There was a faint sound of stirred straw; timid cackling, strange barks. The beasts began to moan.

Night!

Lerne came in. I was in a state of wild agitation. He felt my pulse. "Are you happy?" he asked me.

"Brute!" I replied.

"Very well, I shall administer a sedative." He offered it to me, and I drank it. It stank of chloral.

Once more I am alone with Karl.

Songs of toads, light of stars, dawning of the moon, uprising of its red disc. Mystic assumption of the luminary from star to star. All the beauty of night....

Then a forgotten prayer—the petition of a little child—went up from my distress towards the paradise which yesterday seemed a myth, and now was a certainty. How had I ever doubted its existence?

And the moon wandered in the firmament like an aureole in search of a brow.

It was long since my eyelids had closed on tears. I fell into drowsy delirium. The buzzing in my ears became a hubbub. (There are certain noises almost imperceptible, which seem like the thunder of cataclysms far away.)

They were heaping up straw. That poultry-yard is exasperating. The bull was bellowing. I even had an illusion that it was bellowing louder and louder.

Did they bring it in every evening, along with the cows, into the stall of that strange farm?

Good Lord, what a row!

It was while my mind was wandering in that way, under the influence of the drug, that, condemned to death, or destined for madness, I fell into a heavy and artificial sleep, which lasted till the morning.

Some one touched me on the shoulder. Lerne, in a white overall was standing near the bed. The murder idea had sprung up again instantaneously and clearly in me.

"What o'clock is it? Am I to die, or is your business over?"

"Patience, nephew. Nothing has begun yet."

"What are you going to do with me? Are you going to inoculate me with plague, tuberculosis, cholera? Tell me, uncle."

"No!"

"What then?"

"Come, come, no nonsense," he said.

He withdrew, and revealed an operating table, which, lying on narrow supports like an open bier, had the appearance of a rack.

All the sets of instruments and the crowd of bottles shone in the light of the rising sun. Antiseptic dressings lay on a little table in a woolly cloud.

The two nickel-plated spheres on their supports, showed round, like divers' helmets. A spirit lamp was burning under them. I nearly fainted with horror. At the side behind the curtain something was going on. A penetrating odor of ether came from it.

The secret, the secret always!

"What's behind that?" I cried.

From between the wall and the curtain Karl and Wilhelm appeared, leaving the room which had thus been contrived on the other side of the compartment. They also had put on white overalls, though they were only assistants, but Lerne had seized something, and I felt, on the back of my neck, the chill touch of steel.

I uttered a cry.

"Idiot!" said my uncle, "it's a clipper."

He cut my hair, and shaved my hairy scalp close. At every touch of the razor I thought I felt the edge in my flesh.

After that, they soaked my skull again, dried it, and the Professor, by means of a soft pencil and calipers, covered my baldness with cabalistic lines.

"Take off your shirt," he said to me. "Take care, do not spoil my diagrams."

"Stretch yourself out on that, now."

They helped me to haul myself up on the table, to which they bound me fast, with my arms under the bier.

Where was Johann?

Karl, without any warning, put a sort of muzzle over me. An odor of ether penetrated my lungs.

"Why not chloroform?" I said to myself.

Lerne recommended as follows:

"Breathe deeply and regularly—it is for your own good. Breathe!"

I obeyed.

There is a syringe with a sharp-pointed nozzle in my uncle's hand.

Hallo! he has pricked my neck with it!

I moved my jaws, my tongue and lips feeling like lead.

"Wait, I am not sleeping yet. What is this virus?"

"Morphia," said the Professor simply.

The anesthetic was gaining on me. Another prick, on the shoulder—this time very sharp.

"I am not sleeping! Good heavens, wait! I am not sleeping."

"That is what I wanted to know," growled my executioner.

For some moments a consolation had been assuaging my torture. Did not the cranial preparations seem to show that they were going to slaughter me without delay? And yet Macbeth had survived his trepanning.

I seemed to get far away inside myself. Silvery bells gayly rang a celestial chime, which I have never been able to remember, though it seemed to me unforgettable.

Another prick on the shoulder, which I hardly felt. I wished to say again that I was not sleeping. Vain effort! My words sounded dully submerged in the depths of an invading sea. They were held lifeless, and I alone could make them out.

The rings glide along the curtain rod, and without suffering, on the threshold of this artificial Nirvana, this is what I seemed to perceive.

Lerne makes a long incision from the right temple to the left, round the occiput—an incomplete scalping, and he brings down all the strips of flesh in front of my face, making my forehead like a shambles. From in front, one must see me with the bleeding and jumbled head which I remembered on the monkey.

"Help, I am not sleeping!"

But I cannot hear my cries for the jangling of the silver bells. To begin with, they are too far down under the sea, and now the sound of the bells is deafening, like great church bells chiming with a formidable din, and it is now I who plunge into the ocean of ether.

Am I living, or am I not? I am a dead man who is conscious of being dead....

Even more so....

Nothingness!—

# CHAPTER X
## THE CIRCEEAN OPERATION

I opened my eyes on thick darkness in a place where there was neither noise nor smell.

I wanted to say once more, "Do not begin, I am still awake," but no word sounded.

The delirium of the night was being prolonged. It seemed to me that the bellowing had got nearer, so much so, indeed, that I seemed to hear it in myself. I could not manage to master my ridiculous senses. I kept quiet.

Then there grew in me the assurance that the mysterious business was at an end.

Gradually the darkness lightened. Unconsciousness was coming to an end.

As my blindness got better, smells and sounds, ever in greater number, were like a welcomed crowd coming towards me.

"Oh, happiness, to remain thus—thus for ever!"

But this inverse death struggle came ever on in spite of me, and life seized me once more.

However, objects, though now distinct, remained shapeless, without perspective, and curiously colored.

My vision embraced a wide space—a field vaster than before. I remembered that the influence of certain anesthetics on the dilatation of the pupil, a phenomenon which no doubt brought on these disturbances of sight.

I noted, however, without very much difficulty, that they had lifted me from the table, and laid me on the ground, on the other side of the room, and in spite of my eye, which functioned like a distorting lens, I succeeded in recognizing the situation.

The curtain was no longer drawn.

Lerne and his assistants, grouped round the operating table, were busy about something which their grouping hid from me—probably the cleaning of instruments.

Through the wide-opened door, one could see the park, and hardly twenty yards away, a corner of the paddock, where the cows were ruminating and lowing.

Only, I might have imagined myself transported into the most revolutionary picture of the impressionist school. The azure of the sky, without losing its limpid depths, had changed into a fine orange dye. The paddocks—the trees—instead of being green seemed to me to be red. The buttercups of the meadow, starred vermilion grass with violets.

Everything had changed color, except, however, the black and white things. The dark trousers of the four men obstinately remained as before, as also their overalls, but those white overalls were marked with green stains.

Green stains were also shining on the ground, and what could this liquid be except blood, and what was there astonishing in its appearing green, since greenery gave me the sense of red?

This liquid exhaled a pungent smell, which would have driven me far away, if I had been capable of budging, and yet, the smell was not that which I had been accustomed to associate with blood.

I had never smelt it, any more than those other perfumes, or any more than my ears remembered having heard sounds like these.

It was strange that the aberration of my senses had not been dissipated along with the vapors of the ether. I endeavored to fight against this feeling of numbness. No use! They had stretched me out on a litter of straw, of purple straw.

The operators kept their backs turned to me, except Johann.

Every now and again, Lerne flung into the basin cotton-wool stained with green blood....

Johann was the first to perceive my awaking, and he told the Professor of it. There was then a movement of general curiosity with regard to me, which, breaking up the group, allowed me to see an absolutely naked man bound to the table, with his hands under it—motionless and white, the color of wax, like a corpse, the blackness of his mustache making the paleness still paler, and his head, enveloped in bandages bedabbled with spurts of green.

His breast rose rhythmically. He was breathing in the air with all his lungs, his nostrils quivering with each inhalation. This man—it took me some time to accept it—was myself_.

When I was certain that no mirror was giving me back my own image, which was an easy matter to settle, it came into my mind that Lerne had doubled my being, and that now I was two....

Or else, was I not dreaming?

No, assuredly not, but up to now the adventure had not got beyond the bizarre stage. I was neither dead nor mad, and the evidence of this cheered me mightily.

(Protest as one may against the conviction which I felt of possessing all my reason, the future was to confirm this rash judgment.)

The man on the operating-table shook his head. Wilhelm had unfastened him, and I beheld my other self awaking to a faint-like condition.

Opening eyes like those of a blind man, he waggled his head about with an idiotic air, stroked the edges of the table and sat up.

He did not look at all well. I could not accept the idea that my double should behave so like a brute beast.

They laid the patient in the little truckle-bed. He allowed himself to be patted; but soon he was convulsed with painful vomiting proving beyond doubt the total absence of communication between him and me, since I suffered in no wise from his troubles, except mentally, and through the effect of a feeling of compassion, which was very natural, towards a gentleman who was so very like myself.

Like! Was that only a replica of my body, or was it really my body?

Bosh! Absurd! I could feel, see and hear—very badly, it is true, but enough in any case to convince myself that I possessed a nose, eyes and ears.

I made an effort, and cords cut into my limbs, so I had flesh—flabby and benumbed, but still flesh. My body was here, and not there.

The Professor announced that he was going to unbind me. The hempen thongs were undone. I rose with one shake, and a complex impression spread terror into my soul and made it sink.

Good Heavens! how heavy I was, and how short. I wished to look at myself, and there was nothing below my head, and as I bent it more, with great trouble, I saw, instead of my feet, two cloven hoofs which ended black and knotty legs covered with thick hair!

A cry arose in my throat!...

And it was that nocturnal bellowing which broke out in my mouth, making the house shake, and echoing far away amongst the inaccessible rocks.

"Hold your tongue, Jupiter," said Lerne, "you are annoying poor Nicolas there, who needs rest," and he pointed out my body, which had raised itself in alarm on the bed.

So I was the black bull! Lerne, that loathsome magician had changed me into a beast!

He abandoned himself to brutal enjoyment. The three servile ruffians held their sides and guffawed, and my ox's eyes learned to weep.

"Well," said the sorcerer, as if replying to the rush of my thoughts. "Well, yes, you are Jupiter, but you have a right to ask me more."

"Here is your birth certificate. You were born in Spain, in a celebrated _ganaderia_, and you come from famous parents, whose male posterity falls gloriously with a sword at their throat, on the sand of the bull-rings. I rescued you from the bandarillos of the toreadors, your pedigree suiting my purpose, and paid a high price for you—you and the cows. You cost me two thousand piastres, exclusive of carriage.

"You were born five years and two months ago, so you can live as long again—no more; if we let you die of old age.

"To sum up, I bought you in order to try some experiments on your organism. This is only the first one." My facetious relative was seized with an attack of uncontrollable laughter. When he had exhausted his superfluous gayety, he went on:

"Ah, ha! Nicolas! you are all right aren't you? You are not at all uncomfortable? I am sure your curiosity, you son of woman, your infernal curiosity, must be keeping you up and I bet that you are less annoyed than interested. Come! I am a kindly chap, and since you are discreet now, my dear ward, listen to the information which you desire.

"Did I not say to you, 'The time is drawing near when you shall know all?' Nicolas, you are now going to know all, and indeed it would not please me to pass as a devil—a miracle-monger, or a sorcerer. I am neither Belphegor, nor Moses, nor Merlin—I am just Lerne, tout court! My power does not come from the outside, it is my own, and I am proud of it. It is my science. All that one could say by way of correction, is, that it is the science of humanity, which I have continued in my day, and of which I am the most advanced pioneer and chief master.

"But, do not let us be conceited! Do the bandages stop up your ears? Can you hear me?"

I made a sign with my head.

"Well, listen, then, and do not roll your eyes about—all will be explained."

Good Lord! we are not in Wonderland.

The assistants were cleaning and arranging the instruments. My body was asleep and snoring.

Lerne dragged his stool up beside me, and sat down, with his mouth on a level with my ear, and discoursed in the following terms:

"To begin with, my nephew, I was wrong a moment ago, in calling you 'Jupiter.' To use words in an exact way, I have not metamorphosed you into a bull, and you are still Nicolas Vermont, for the name denotes, above all, the personality which is the soul and not the body.

"As, on the one hand, you have kept your soul, and as, on the other, the soul has its seat in the brain, it is easy for you to argue by induction, in the presence of those surgical instruments, that I have just exchanged Jupiter's brain with yours and that it now lives in your cast-off body.

"You will probably say, Nicolas, that it is a disgusting pleasantry on my part!

"You do not divine either the supreme object of my studies, nor the series of ideas which has inspired them, and yet, from this logical series is derived this little pleasantry derived from Ovid; but it is possible that it means nothing to you, for I have only gone in for this by the way.

"We will call it, if you like, a workshop joke!

"No, my ultimate aim does not reveal itself in this form—a funny and malicious one, you will admit, but puerile, without any results social or industrial that can be exploited.

"My aim is the 'introversion' of human personalities, which I have endeavored to achieve, in the first place, by the interchange of brains.

"You know my inveterate passion for flowers! I have always cultivated them with the utmost enthusiasm. My earlier life was absorbed by my profession, which was interrupted only on Sundays with this recreation—a day's gardening.

"Well, the hobby influenced my profession. Grafting influenced my surgery, and in the hospital I was inclined to give myself up more especially to animal grafting. I became a specialist in that, and grew fond of it, finding in my clinics the enthusiasm of the hothouse.

"Even in the beginning I had dimly foreseen a point of contact between animal and vegetable grafts—a hyphen which my logically conducted labors made clear some time ago.... I will return to that.

"When I took up animal grafting with enthusiasm, this branch of surgery was languishing. In fact, ever since the Hindoos of antiquity, who were the first grafters, it had remained stationary.

"But perhaps you forget its underlying principles. That doesn't matter. Learn them afresh. They are based, Nicolas, on this fact, that animal tissues possess, each of them, a personal vitality, and that the body of an animal is only the milieu adapted to the life of those tissues—a milieu from which they may be removed, and live for a more or less long time.

"1. Don't the nails and the hair grow after death? You are not ignorant of that. They survive.

"2. A man who has been dead for fifty-four hours, and has left no descendants, still fulfills the chief condition for remedying that. Unfortunately, other essential faculties are wanting. But I will pass on.

"3. In certain conditions of humidity, oxygenation and heat, scientists have been able to keep a rat's tail, which had been cut off, alive for seven days; an amputated finger, for four hours. At the end of those periods they were dead, but if during those seven days or those four hours, they had been cleverly glued on again, they would have continued to live.

"This is the procedure employed by the Hindoos, who thus restored to their places reintegrated noses that had been cut off by way of punishment, or if those appanages had been burnt, they replaced them by noses made of flesh and skin, taken, my dear Nicolas, from another part of the anatomy of the man who had been punished.

"The operation thus effected goes into the first category of animal grafting, and consists in transplanting a part of the individual to himself.

"The second consists of joining together two animals, by two wounds which coalesce. One can then cut off from first, the fragment of his person nearest the point of junction, which thereafter will live upon the second.

"The third consists of transplanting, without any attachment, a part of one animal to another animal, always in such a way that it preserves its own life. That is the most elegant way of the three, and the one which has attracted me.

"The operation was regarded as a ticklish one, for many reasons, the principal one of which is, that a grafting is less likely to succeed the further removed the two subjects are from one another in the scale of relationship.

"Grafting succeeds when it is done on the same animal; less well from father to son, and worse and worse from brother to brother, from cousin to cousin, from Frenchman to Spaniard, man to woman, and child to old man.

"When I came on the scene, the exchange I am talking about always came to naught in different zoölogical families, and more so still in the case of genera and species.

"However, some experiments are an exception to this—experiments on which I have based my own, wishing to accomplish the greater thing, before successfully accomplishing the lesser, and to graft a fish on a bird before dealing with humanity alone. I say a few experiments.

"1. Wiesmann tore from his arm a canary's feather, which he had transplanted into it a month before, and which left a little bleeding wound.

"2. Baronio has grafted the wing of a canary, and the tail of a rat on the comb of a cock.

"This was not much, but Nature herself encouraged me.

"3. Birds cross without any shame, and produce numerous hybrids, which bear witness to the possibility of fusion between species.

"4. Then, getting further away from man, vegetables have considerable plastic force.

"Such, reduced to its simplest expression, is the summary of the situation in the presence of which I found myself, and on which I staked all.

"I came here to work more comfortably, and almost immediately I performed remarkable operations, which became very famous. One more especially. I wonder if you remember it?

"X, the Pickle-King, the American millionaire, had only one ear, and desired to have a pair of them. A poor devil sold him one of his for five thousand dollars. I performed the little ceremony. The grafted ear only died with X two years later, when he succumbed to indigestion.

"It was then, when the world was applauding my triumph, and just as the very moment when love, having come on the scene, was urging me to make money, in order that Emma should live a life of luxury—it was just then that I conceived my great idea, which proceeded from this reasoning:

"If a millionaire, dissatisfied with his physique, pays five thousand dollars for the pleasure of embellishing it a little, what would he not give for changing it altogether, and acquire a new body for his ego, for his brain—a covering full of grace, vigor and youth, in place of an old sickly and repulsive casing!

"On the other hand, how many beggars I know would give up their magnificent anatomy for a few years of jollification!

"And observe, Nicolas, this purchase of a young body would not only furnish advantages of suppleness, warmth and endurance, but also the enormous advantage that in a youthful milieu, the transferred organs are rejuvenated.

"Oh! I am not the first to advance this theory, and Paul Bert, admitted the possibility of grafting an organ on several consecutive bodies, as each of these latter grow old, so that by a series of rejuvenations, he foresaw that one might make the same stomach, the same brain _live indefinitely—as an integral part of successive constitutions. This was tantamount to declaring that a personality can live indefinitely, by a series of incarnations, in a journey through different carcasses, each discarded at the proper moment.

"The discovery to be made surpassed my hopes. I was not only pursuing the choice of a pleasing outward appearance—I had my hand on the secret of IMMORTALITY!

"The brain being the seat of the ego (for you know that the spinal cord is only a transmitter, and a center of reflexes), the only question was ability to graft.

"Certainly the ear is one thing and the brain another and yet this difference is only a question of the degrees which separate:

"1. Cartilaginous matter from the nerve matter, and

"2. The accessory from the principal organ.

"Logic backed up my conviction, and my reasoning was based on famous premises officially verified.

"1. Besides their grafts of mucous membrane, skin, etc., in 1861, Phillippeaux and Vulpian replaced the nerve matter in an optic nerve.

"2. In 1880, Gluck exchanged a few centimeters of sciatic nerve in a hen for a rabbit's nerves.

"3. In 1890, Thompson removed a few cubic centimeters of brain from dogs and cats, and into the cavity thus obtained, introduced the same quantity of cerebral substance taken from dogs and cats, _or from different species_. Here we have passed from cartilage to nerve, and from ear to fragment of brain.

"Let us now turn to the difficulty of the second order:

"1. Gardeners often graft whole organisms.

"2. Besides fingers, tails and paws, Phillippeaux and Mantegazza grafted rather important organs—spleens, stomachs and tongues. They made a hen into a cock as a joke, they even tried to graft the pancreas and the thyroid.

"3. Carrel and Guthrey, in 1905, in New York, came to believe that they can substitute the veins of the arteries of animals for those of man. We have bridged the distance between the accessory and the principal.

"4. Finally, Mantegazza maintained that he had grafted spinal cords and _brains_ of frogs!

"These examples were ample proof that my projects were realizable, so I said to myself I would realize them.

"I began my task. An obstacle was in the way!

"It being impracticable to employ an 'attachment,' it resulted that the body and the brain, once separated, perished, one or other, or both, before having been placed in contact with their new companions.

"But here again facts gave me courage. So far as the body is concerned:

"1. An animal can live quite well with one cerebral lobe. You saw a pigeon circling round, which has been deprived of three-fourths of its brain!

"2. Often decapitated ducks fly for a hundred yards from the block on which their severed head remains.

"3. A locust lived for fifteen days without a head—fifteen!

"That is an experiment duly attested.

"So far as the severed organ is concerned, there were these certified cases.

"This persuaded me that the brain and the body, if properly treated, would be able to live, each independently, for the few minutes of separation which the work requires. However that may be, the necessary slowness of trepanning induced me as a rule to exchange not brains, but heads, having learned from Brown Séquard that a dog's head injected with oxygenated blood, had survived decapitation a quarter-of-an-hour.

"From this period date heteroclite creatures—a donkey with a horse's head—a goat with a stag's head—which I should like to have preserved, because the beasts which composed them were somewhat distant from one another, although they belonged to the same family—a distance which I have never been able to increase by this means.

"Alas! on the night of your arrival, Wilhelm left the doors open, and those monsters, worthy of Dr. Moreau, escaped, with many other subjects which were under observation. You may boast of having come into Fonval like a bull into a china shop!

"I resume; but in order to avoid exhausting the attention of a convalescent, I shall pass over, as far as details are concerned, the abandonment of this method, the discovery of the Lerne trepanner with an ultra-rapid-circular-saw, that of the brain-preserving globes or artificial meninges, that of the ointment for joining nerves, the recognized efficacy of the injection of morphia, approved of by Broca, for contracting the blood vessels, and so diminishing the loss of blood, the generally accepted employment of ether as an anesthetic, the manipulation of brains for the purpose of fitting them exactly to skulls, etc., etc.

"Thanks to all that, I exchanged the personalities of a—ah, I can never remember that word—squirrel and a wood-pigeon. That wasn't bad! Then that of a wren and a viper. Then that of a carp and a blackbird—hot blood and cold blood. It was perfect!

"In face of these prodigies, my aim, that of human substitution was mere child's play.

"At this juncture Karl and Wilhelm volunteered to submit themselves to the convincing test. It was quite epic. Otto Klotz had left me. Hum! Macbeth was not to be trusted! I operated alone, with the help of Johann and automatic machines.

"Success! ah! what fine fellows! Who would have imagined that whole bodies had been amputated? and yet, each of them, ever since that day, lives in the carnal abode of his friend. Look!"

He summoned his assistants, and raising their hair, showed the violet colored scar.

The two Germans smiled at one another, and I could not prevent myself from admiring them.

Lerne went on:

"My fortune, then, was made, and at one stroke, I was assuring my own and Emma's happiness, and her love, which is my most inestimable possession, Nicolas.

"But the discovery, one certain, had to be applied.

"To tell the truth, one dark spot worried me. I mean the influence of the moral side on the physical and vice versa.

"At the end of a few months my patients became modified. If I had endowed their body with a mentality finer than before, the latter ruined the former, and I have seen, amongst others, pigs with a dog's brain become ill and thin, and die soon.

"On the other hand, intellects coarser than their predecessors, allow themselves to be overcome by the corporal part, and the composite animal then becomes stupider and fatter. That is an invariable rule.

"Sometimes, also, the imperious flesh refashions the mind according to the instincts of brutal matter.

"One of my wolves, my dear nephew, installed cruelty in the brain of a sheep! But this drawback was bound, was it not, in the case of my future clients—men—to reduce itself to slight indifferences of health and character? It was not worth thinking about, and it did not give me any pause.

"Not caring to leave Macbeth with Emma, I sent him off to Scotland, and I set out towards America—the land of audacity, of millions, and of the grafted ear—as it seemed to me the best soil to cultivate.

"That was two years ago.

"The day after my landing, I had thirty-five ruffians at my disposal, who were resolved to part with an impeccable bodily constitution, for the benefit of any thirty-five millionaires I should get to know, teach and convince.

"Check!

"I began with the most dreadful ones, and the most unhealthy.

"Some called me a madman and showed me the door. Others got angry, looking me majestically up and down with displeasure in their eyes, thrusting out very consumptive chests or flabby thoraxes; or they drew themselves to their full height on their twisted legs and expressed astonishment that anybody should think them ugly.

"Those who were dying were sure they would get well—surer than that they would not collapse under the ether.

"Some showed fear. 'It was tempting Providence!' They stood aloof from me as from the Devil, and some of them would have sprinkled me with Holy Water.

"It was no use my declaring, in answer to them, that man is modified more completely in the course of his life than they would change under my lancet, and that religious doctrine has traveled some way since 1670, when that Russian was excommunicated, for having had his skull mended with a piece of a dog's bone.

"It was no use.

"Many sententiously remarked, 'One knows what one has got—one does not know what one is getting.'

"Would you believe it! The women nearly saved me! Crowds of them aspired to become men. Fortunately, my black-guards—except one or two—categorically refused to adopt the female sex.

"In despair, I dangled before them the attractive prospect of a life prolonged indefinitely, resuming its course at each new incarnation.

"'Life, replied the three-score-years-and-tenners, is already too long, as God has limited it. We desire nothing more than to die.'

"'But I shall restore to you all your desires, at the same time as your youth.'

"'Thank you, the fate of desires is to remain ungratified!'

"Amongst adults I often received this reply:

"'The charm of acquired experience is worth preserving from all things that might lessen that experience, and let us not risk diminishing it through the inexperienced rashness of adolescent blood.'

"There were some, however, who were ready to imitate Faust, and sign the pact of youth, but all these Nabobs I sounded offered me the same objection—the danger of the operation—the folly of risking life in the desire to prolong life.

"To tell you the truth, Nicolas, the only people who allow themselves to be operated on without any qualms, are young people at the point of death, and aware of their state.

"Understanding the necessity of overcoming the danger they apprehended, I felt ready for new researches—but greatly disillusioned, thenceforward knowing that even were these rewarded by a second discovery, my clients would be few, but also aware that they would be sufficient to secure me my fortune and happiness. But all this was deferred till the Greek Calends.

"I came back to Fonval—bitter, silent, and with rage in my heart.

"Emma and Donovan could not have found a more implacable judge. I surprised them. I took my revenge. You have guessed it, have you not? Yesterday, the two Macbeths carried off the brain of Nell, and the soul of Donovan is lodged in the body of the St. Bernard!

"The same punishment awaited both of you for the same fault. Solomon could not have better judged, nor Circe have better carried the sentence into execution.

"Now, look here, nephew! I have worked at what, but for your intru-sion, and my need for watching your acts, would in a few days, have been the beginning of the interchange of personalities without surgical inter-vention.

"I was wise enough, you see, not to give up my vegetable grafting. I had even carried all its developments very far, and this training, supplemented by my zoölogical experiments, constitutes almost the whole curriculum of grafting.

"It was the combination of this science with other sciences, which revealed the probable solution to me.

"People never generalize enough, Nicolas! Devoted to interminable subdivision, fanatical about the infinitely little, which is always becoming infinitely less, we have a mania for analysis. We live with our eyes glued to microscopes. In half our investigations we should employ another instrument to show things as wholes—an apparatus of optical synthesis—a synoptic telescope, or if you prefer to call it so, a megaloscope.

"I foresee a colossal discovery! And to think that but for Emma, I should have disdained financial rewards and never aspired to wealth! So that love caused ambition, and ambition brought glory!

"Apropos of this, nephew, you very nearly put on the features of Professor Lerne! Yes, she adored you with such a fine ardor, nephew, that I thought of disguising my appearance by assuming with your features, in order to be loved in your place....

"That would have been the very best revenge, and very piquant, but I have still need, for some time, of my antique and awkward carcass. Later on we shall see about getting rid of this old trumpery frame. Is not your captivating appearance always at my disposal?"

At those sarcastic words, my weeping was redoubled.

My uncle went on, affecting consideration for me.

"Ah! I am abusing your courage, my dear patient. Have a rest. The satisfaction of your curiosity will give you, I hope, a refreshing sleep.

"Ah! I was forgetting! Do not be astonished if the world appears to you other than it was.... Amongst other novelties, things must be seen by you as flat as in a photograph. That is because you look at things only with one eye at a time, so that one might say—using the terms jocularly, that many animals are only double one-eyed things. Their sight is not stereoscopic. Other eyes—other phenomena.

"New ear-drums, other sounds, and so on!

"Amongst men, themselves, each one has his manner of appreciating things. Habit teaches us, for example, that we must call a certain color red, but a man who calls it red receives from it a green impression—that is a common occurrence, and another, an impression of olive or dark blue.

"Well, good-night!"

No, my curiosity was not satisfied, but I realized that that was so without being able to fix the points which my uncle had not made clear, for my awful experience overwhelmed me with anguish, and the Circeean operation left me impregnated with ether, whose penetrating vapors upset in me the man's understanding and the bull's stomach

# CHAPTER XI
## IN THE PADDOCK

During the eight days of my convalescence in the laboratory, nursed and kept quiet, and treated with drugs, I underwent the alternation of great sorrows; fits of despair each followed by a collapse. Every time I slept I thought I had dreamt this calamity.

Now, it must be observed that the sensations at my awakening confirmed me in this error, which was, however, immediately dissipated.

It is well known that those who have had a limb amputated, suffer a great deal, and refer their suffering to the extreme periphery of the severed nerves, that is to say, to the limb which they have lost, and which they think they still possess.

The severed limb, or arm, hurts them. If one reflects that I had had my whole body cut off, one will understand that I suffered in all its parts—in my distant hands, in my human feet; and that this pain seemed proof positive of the possession of that of which I had been deprived.

This phenomenon grew gradually less distinct, and finally disappeared.

Grief went from me less quickly. Those who have entertained others with the recital of tricks of this sort—Homer, Ovid, Apuleius, and Perrault, did not know what tragedies their fictions would become, once they became realities.

What a drama there is really in Lucian's "Ass"! What a martyrdom for me this week of dieting and enforced inaction!

Dead to humanity, I awaited with terror the tortures of vivisection, or the premature old age which would be the end of everything, before five years were out.

In spite of my despair, I got well. Lerne having ascertained this, I was turned out into the paddock.

Europa, Athor, and Io gamboled in front of me. Many long days were to pass before I could make them accustomed to me. Long days, and all a man's cunning employed in the task.

A good bout of kicking finally subjugated them.

This incident would be a fit theme for deep philosophizing, and I should succumb to the temptation to hold forth, were it not that such dissertations are an awkward interruption of the course of a story.

For the time being, annoyed at the welcome with which the three horned ladies received me, and only desiring their favors with the ardor of a valetudinarian, I began peacefully to browse on the grass of the meadow.

Here begins the most interesting period—that of my observations on my new condition. They occupied me so completely, that I began to consider the bull's body as a moveable dwelling—an exile's home, no doubt, but an unexplored, bewildering place, full of surprises, from which chance would perhaps deliver me—for as soon as a place is merely not unpleasing, one immediately feels the risk of being driven from it.

As long as this accommodation of my man's mind to the organs of the beast lasted, I was really fairly happy.

The fact was that a new world was just being revealed to me, together with the taste of the simple herbs on which I was feeding. Just as my eyes, my ears and my muzzle sent to my brain visions, sounds, and smells hitherto unimagined, my tongue with its strange papillæ was bound to afford me very original sensations of taste.

Simple herbs gave a savor of which human palates have no idea. The cuisine of the epicure cannot possibly give them as much pleasure with twelve courses, as a bull gets in a small meadow.

I could not refrain from comparing the taste of my fodder with that of my former food. There is more difference between lucern and clover than between a fried sole and a rib of venison with sauce chasseud.

Plants have all sorts of tastes for the mouth of a graminivorous animal.

The buttercup is rather insipid, the thistle rather peppery, but nothing equals fragrant and many-flavored hay. Pastures are a continually spread feast to which hunger impels their denizens to devote themselves.

The water of the trough changed in taste, according to the time and the weather. At one time acidulous—at another time salt or sweet. Light in the morning, and syrupy in the evening.

I cannot describe the delight of drinking it, and I think that the lamented Olympians, in their vindictive and jocular testimentary disposition, leaving men only the power of laughter, left as a legacy to other animals the tasting of ambrosia in the grass of the lawns and the drinking of nectar at every fountain.

I was initiated into the delights of chewing the cud, and I understood the placid moods of those grave epicures, the oxen, during the activity of their four stomachs, when, with the scents of the fields, a whole pastoral symphony fills their nostrils.

By dint of experimenting with my senses, and testing my faculties, I obtained strange impressions. The best memory that remains to me is that of my muzzle—that tactile center—that invaluable and subtle touchstone of good and bad grains—that warner of an enemy's approach—that pilot and councilor—that sort of authoritative and dogmatic consciousness—that oracle of yes and no, which never fails, and is always obeyed.

It is a question if the god Jupiter, when he put on the form of a bull, for the benefit of the Princess Europa, was not more charmed by his muzzle, than with all the rest of that scandalous escapade.

It was wise of me to establish these facts straight away, for soon, as my health failed, I lost the calm, without which accuracy of observation is impossible, as well as the desire to continue them. I suffered from attacks of headache, colds, toothache—the whole sequence of indispositions which citizens of the twentieth century are heirs to.

I grew thin. Dismal ideas haunted me.

The cause of it was, first, the predominance of the soul over the body, which my uncle had mentioned, and secondly, two incidents which immediately aggravated my malady.

After a disappearance, due, I presume to an illness following on her great fright, I saw Emma again.

Without feeling any emotion, I saw her at the windows of her room, then at those of the ground floor, and finally outside. She came out every day, leaning on the servant's arm, and went round the park, avoiding the laboratory, where Lerne and his assistants were steadily working.

I had expected features less drawn, and eyes less red.

She walked along slowly—pale, and with fixed eyes—displaying to the sun her moonlight complexion, and eyes like those one opens on the night.

A pathetic widow, she let one see, with a certain nobility, the revolt of her love in its mourning, and the keenness of her regrets.

So, she still loved me, and not seeing me any more, supposed my fate to have been that which she imagined for Klotz, and not the destiny of Macbeth (which, however, she had misapprehended). In her thought, I could only be dead, or a fugitive. The real truth escaped her.

Each day, with greater affection, I followed her on her walks, as long as I could. Separated from her by barbed wire, I attempted mimicry and words, but Emma was afraid of the bull—its little leaps, and its lowing. She understood nothing, any more than I had understood about Donovan from the capers of the dog.

Sometimes, when in my attempts to make too human a gesture I stumbled in my quadrupedal way, the girl was amused at it, and I found myself stumbling intentionally, in order to see her smile.

Thus love by degrees resumed its torturing sway.

It could not return unaccompanied by jealousy, and the latter also hastened the progress of my languor.

It was jealousy, but attended with an extraordinary sentiment!

There stood between the paddock and the pond that hexagonal summerhouse which had been the Giant Briareus.

Lerne inflicted on me the annoyance of lodging my former body in it. I saw his assistants bring in some elementary furniture, and then the creature itself—and ever since that day, there he was, with his forehead glued to the windows, and stupidly watching me.

His hair was growing again. His beard was sprouting. Now heavy and chubby, his person was bursting through his clothes.

His eye—that almond eye, of which I had been so proud—was now becoming a round ox's eye.

The man with the bull's brain was assuming the expression which I had remarked in Donovan, but more bestial still, and less good-natured.

My poor body had reserved the habit of certain familiar gestures. An incorrigible trick made it shrug its shoulders now and then, so that the wretched creature seemed to be laughing at me from the windows of the summerhouse.

He often would shout out in the dusk of evening.

My beautiful baritone voice was distorted into discordant clamors—into the yells of a gorilla.

Then, in the laboratory, Macbeth would howl, with his poor canine throat, and the irresistible need of making my own lamentations heard, filled the valley of Fonval with the sounds of a monstrous trio.

Emma perceived that the summerhouse was inhabited. That day she and Barbe were walking round the paddock. I had, as usual, accompanied them to a certain little wood which was crossed by the road, and I awaited them at the entrance of that avenue where the doves were cooing.

They came out of it and then they suddenly paused.

Emma was transfigured. She had taken on that animated expression which I knew of old—quivering nostrils—eyes half shut, and her bosom heaving. She pressed Barbe's arm.

"Nicolas," she murmured, "Nicolas. There, there! Do you see nothing?"

And whilst amongst the leafage the turtle-doves faintly cooed, Emma pointed out to Barbe the creature in the summerhouse, behind his window.

Having assured herself that she was not seen from the laboratory, Emma made some signals, and flung kisses. The creature had excellent reasons for not understanding anything, but opened his round eyes, dropped his jaw, and turned my former integument which I now so greatly regretted into a type of perfect imbecility.

"Mad," said Emma, "he, too! Lerne has made him mad, like Macbeth."

Then the kind-hearted girl sobbed with all her heart, and I felt anger rising in me.

"Now, remember," said the servant, "above all things, do not go near that summerhouse, it is overlooked on all sides."

The other shook her beautiful locks, dried her tears, and lying down on the grass in the attitude of a sphinx, with her head in her hands, and her body curved, she gazed, for a long time affectionately, on that young figure whom she had loved so much.

The brute beast seemed to take more interest in this pose than in her former gestures.

A scene like this went beyond the bounds of the grotesque and horrible. That woman in love with my form—the form in which I no longer lived! That woman whom I adored, in love with a beast! How to accept such a thing with equanimity?

My anger exploded. This was the first time that I experienced the domination of my ardent bodily constitution. Mad with rage, blowing and snorting and foaming, I dashed over the meadow in all directions, and tore at the ground with my horns and hoofs, in the wild desire to kill somebody no matter whom.

From that time on, hatred poisoned my daydreams—ferocious hatred against this supernatural brute—this ridiculous Minotaur who turned all the forest of Brocéliande with its forest labyrinth into a comical Crete.

I cursed that body which had been stolen from me. I was jealous of it, and often when Jupiter—I and I—Jupiter looked at one another, both victims of our cast-off bodies, fury seized me once more. I charged about wildly, bellowing like a bull in the ring, with my tail in the air—my nostrils smoking—my head down, ready for murder, and desiring it as one longs for love in the springtime.

The cows warded me off as best they could. All the beasts feared the mad bull. One day, Lerne, passing that way, took to his heels.

Life weighed heavily on me. I had exhausted all the pleasures of observation, and my new dwelling-place only occasioned me distress and repugnance.

I got thinner and thinner. The pasturage lost its savor. The spring was tasteless, and the company of the heifers became odious to me.

On the other hand, old desires imposed themselves on me like morbid whims—a desire to eat meat, and quaintest of all, the craving to smoke!

But other considerations were not so laughable. Fear of the laboratory made me tremble every time that an assistant came near the paddock, and I could not sleep for fear lest I should be bound during the night.

And that was not all! I was haunted by the conviction that my ox's brain would go mad. My attacks of uncontrollable wrath might bring on madness, and they became more frequent, for the conduct of Emma was not calculated to mitigate them.

Can the face of a savage murderer be the face of love, and can one be astonished that so many sweethearts close their eyes when the god kisses them?

So Emma looked with pleasure at the hideous Minotaur, and did not perceive Lerne, who was on the watch, laughing in his sleeves at her mistake.

Yes, laughing, but in the philosophical way, in order not to weep! My uncle was obviously suffering. He seemed to have grasped that Emma would never love him, and the Professor took his disillusionment ill.

He was growing old, and killing himself with work.

On the terrace of the laboratory and on the roof of the _château_, some machines had been installed whose handling interested me very much. They were surmounted with characteristic antennæ, and as electric bells were continually ringing in the recesses of the two buildings, my opinion was that they had been transformed into wireless telegraphy and telephone stations.

One morning Lerne made a little boat dart about on the pond—a toy torpedo-boat. He directed it from the shore with the help of an apparatus, which also was fitted with feelers.

Tele-mechanics—it was certain! The Professor was studying how to make communications at a distance without any tangible intermediary. Was this a new method for the introversion of personalities? Perhaps it was.

I lost interest in the matter. A happy issue out of my afflictions now seemed to me an impossible miracle. I should never learn this future discovery, nor all the secrets which were a blot on the past of my uncle and his companions.

It was, however, by meditating on those last mysteries, that I beguiled the torturing insomnia of my nights, and my idleness by day, but I could make nothing of it. It may be the case, indeed, that my mind was dulled, for there were, amongst the daily occurrences which I have just narrated, some that it could not retain—to which some confidences on Lerne's part gave capital significance, and the rational examination of which would have made me hope for deliverance.

And so, about mid-September, this deliverance was brought about without my having guessed anything, and in the following circumstances:

For some time past the friendship of the Minotaur and Emma had grown stronger. The monster, now accustomed to my body, began to make gestures.

One afternoon, while I was endeavoring to see my mistress through the bushes where she was watching the false Nicolas, there was a sudden noise of smashed and falling glass.

The Minotaur had dashed through the window of the summerhouse! Without in the least heeding my unfortunate body, he dashed up, cut, slashed, and bleeding, with roars of fury.

Emma shrieked, and tried to make off, but the creature had disappeared into the little wood.

I then heard behind me the noise of people running. At the sound of the broken windows, Lerne and his assistants had come out of the laboratory. They had seen the escape, and were making at full speed for the fatal wood.

Unfortunately, the assistants were afraid of my proximity, and the détour which they were making to avoid me, outside the paddock, would delay them.

Lerne had boldly taken a short cut, climbed over the wire, and was hurrying to the middle of the enclosure, with his coat torn by the artificial thorns.

Alas! he was old and slow! They would arrive—all of them, too late!

I dashed at the frail barrier, broke it down, and smashed and crashed through it, in spite of the little chevaux de frise which lacerated my skin.

I was over the wall of greenery in a moment, at a jump. The sun, through the vault of leaves, was dappling the underwood with its rays, and there, on the edge of the forest road I saw Emma lying—the Minotaur gloating over her.

I had no leisure for a longer look. In a moment, all my maddened blood was in my head, and goaded by an indomitable wrath I dashed ahead with my horns down.

I struck something which fell. I trod it under my four hoofs, and with my back to my victim, I kicked, and kicked, and kicked!

Suddenly the voice of my uncle, gasped:

"Hallo! hallo! hallo! you are killing yourself!"

My madness vanished—the stars went out, and everything reappeared.

The beautiful girl, awaking, blinked her eyes, without understanding anything.

The assistants watched me, each behind a tree, and Lerne, leaning over my form, which was inert and dislocated, raised its head, in which a large hole was bleeding, and it was I! I! who had committed the mad act of injuring myself!

The Professor, who was feeling the victim all over, gave us his diagnosis:

"One arm dislocated, three ribs broken, fracture of the left clavicle and tibia. One recovers from that, but the kick on the head—Ah! that's more serious. Hm! the brain is beaten to a pulp—it is destroyed—all will be over in half-an-hour. Finita la Commedia!"

I had to put my shoulder up against a tree, to save myself from falling. So my body, my country of countries, was going to die! It was all over! Now, for ever banished from my ruined dwelling. I had destroyed the first condition of my deliverance. It was all over. Lerne himself could do nothing; he had admitted as much. In half an hour all would be over!

But this brain! Perhaps he could.... Yes, he could do anything! Yes!

I drew near him. It was my last chance.

My uncle, who had turned to the girl, was speaking with grief in his voice.

"How you must have loved him, to love him still in his pitiable condition. My dear Emma, am I so little lovable, that you prefer such a wreck to me?"

Emma was weeping in her hands. How she must love him, looking turn by turn at the Professor, the dying creature and at me. How she must love him!

For the last few moments I had been dancing about with a sort of little steps, and more or less musical sounds, which were meant to translate my thought. My uncle pursued the train of his.

Without remarking that his cloudy brow must be hiding some stormy conflict of interests and passions, and dominated by the imminence of a catastrophe which he alone could ward off, I redoubled entreaties.

"Yes, I understand your desire, Nicolas," said my uncle. "You want to give back your brain to its former envelope, which would thus be saved, since you have made Jupiter's brain an impossibility. Well, so be it!"

"Oh, save him, save him," cried Emma, who had only grasped that one word. "Save him! I swear to you, Frédéric, I swear never to see him again."

"Enough, enough," said Lerne. "On the contrary you must love him with all your strength. I no longer wish to grieve you. Why struggle against destiny?"

He summoned his assistants, and gave them some brief orders. Karl and Wilhelm seized the Minotaur, who was moaning.

Johann had set off to make preparations, as hard as he could.

"Schnell, schnell!" said the Professor, and he added, "Quick, Nicolas, follow us!"

I obeyed, my mind half filled with the joy at recovering my body, and half filled with fear lest it should die before the operation.

The operation was a great success.

However, deprived of the attentions which should have preceded the administration of the anesthetic, and which the urgency of the case did not allow them to give us, I lived an instructive but painful dream under the influence of ether.

It lasted, perhaps a quarter of a second—just enough to let me feel the tooth of some scratchy saw, or the edge of some badly sharpened lancet.

The sunset was filling the wash-house with a rosy half-light. Through my lowered eyelids I perceived my mustache.

This was the resurrection of Nicolas Vermont.

It was also the end of Jupiter. They were carving up, at the end of the room, that black mass in which I had sojourned.

In the courtyard the dogs were quarreling for the first bits that Johann had flung to them. My bones were aching.

Lerne was watching by my side. He was quite joyful, as well he might be. Was he not at peace with his conscience? Had he not atoned for his wrongs to me? How could I feel rancor towards him? It even seemed to me that I owed him a certain debt of gratitude.

So true is it, that nothing seems so great a benefit as the reparation of a wrong done.

# CHAPTER XII
## LERNE CHANGES HIS METHOD OF ATTACK

When I was in the black hide of the bull, I had sworn to myself, if my original shape were ever restored to me, to flee away at once, with or without Emma; and yet the autumn was growing old, and I had not yet left Fonval.

The fact was, my treatment was now the exact reverse of what it had been. To begin with, I disposed of my time as I liked.

The first use that I made of that liberty was to go to the shambles in the forest-clearing, and there efface all traces of my visit. A favoring god had _not_ decreed that during the time I had lived a bucolic life in the meadow, somebody should come there, and the assistants should remark the violation of the sepulcher.

Either they had changed their cemetery, or my uncle no longer dissected anything, except tiny creatures, of which the dogs left no trace, or else experiments in animâ vili were completely abandoned.

Let me say that I proved to my satisfaction a detail which lifted a great weight from my heart. I had been afraid that the soul of the unhappy Klotz had been transferred into some animal carefully kept in hiding; but his remains themselves, although marvelously recalling Baudelaire's famous poem, refuted me. The brain of the dead man, marked as it was with numerous and deep sinuosities, still visible, whilst bearing witness to his humanity, was proof of a murder pure and simple, thank Heaven!

So I enjoyed a large measure of freedom, and besides, an affectionate and repentant Lerne had shown himself at my bedside while I was convalescent. Oh, not the Lerne of long ago, the companion of my Aunt Lidivine; no, but he was no longer the grim and bloodthirsty host, who had received me in the manner in which one shows people the door.

When he saw me up and about, my uncle brought Emma in, and said to her in my presence, that I was cured of a passing touch of lunacy, and that she might now adore me as much as she liked.

"For my part," he continued, "I give up emotions no longer suitable to my age. You shall have Emma. All I ask of you is not to leave me. A sudden solitude would increase my distress, which you can easily understand, and which both of you will pardon. This distress will pass. Work will get the better of it. Do not be afraid, my dear; the chief part of my profit shall be for you! Nothing has been changed with regard to that, and Nicolas shall be mentioned in the partnership deed and in my will. You may love one another in peace."

With these words he went off to his electrical machines.

Emma showed no astonishment at anything. Trustful and simpleminded, she had accepted my uncle's speech with a clapping of hands.

I, knowing him to be an actor, might have told myself that he was feigning kindness, in order to keep me in the house; that either he was afraid of what I might reveal or that he was hatching some new project; but the two Circeean operations had rather troubled my memory and my reasoning powers.

"Why," said I to myself, "why doubt this man, who has, of his own free will, rescued me from the most awful position? He perseveres in the good way, and all is for the best."

At the sight of my laborious and domesticated Professor, who could have believed in his victims, and in a trap which he had laid for me, in the assassination of Klotz, in the distress of Nell? She never ceased her howlings to the stars, suffering from the troubles which I had endured; for she was still there, and it puzzled me that Lerne should continue the punishment of a fault which must appear much less now that Emma no longer interested him.

I resolved to confide in my uncle.

"Nicolas," he said, "you have put your finger on my greatest anxiety, but what is to be done? In order to reëstablish the right order of things in this affair, it is absolutely necessary that the body of Macbeth should come back here. By what stratagem are we to persuade his father to send him back? Try to find one. Help me. I promise to act without delay as soon as one or the other of us has found a solution."

This reply had dissipated my last feelings of dislike. I did not ask myself why Lerne had metamorphosed himself so as to give in so easily and quickly.

My belief was that the Professor had at last been restored to wisdom; and in default of the other virtues, which would no doubt appear in due order, his rectitude of long ago seemed to me to be born again, rectitude which was as great as the erudition which had never abandoned him, and as evident as _it_ was.

And Lerne's erudition was almost inexhaustible. Each day I was more and more convinced of it.

We resumed our walks, and he profited by them to discourse learnedly about everything we came across—a leaf led him on to botany, entomology was suggested by a beetle; a drop of rain let loose upon my admiration a deluge of chemistry, and when we had got to the edge of the forest, I had heard from Lerne's lips the lecturing of a whole collegeful of dons.

But, it was there, at the edge of the woods and fields that one should have seen him. After the last tree had been passed, he never failed to stop, hauled himself up to the top of a boundary stone, and held forth concerning the Universe, in presence of the plains and the heavens.

He described things so ingeniously, that one could believe one saw Nature unfold and open to the very depths of the earth, and to the very ends of Infinity.

His words knew equally well how to dig into the hills to lay bare the strata of the soil, as to bring near to us, the better to discourse about them, the invisible planets.

He knew how to analyze the vapor of the clouds, as well as to show the origin of the cold wind—to evoke prehistoric landscapes, and to prove in the same way the unending future of the countryside.

He roamed in spirit with his eyes over the immense panorama, from the hut near at hand, to those wide horizons—the distant tints of blue.

In a few words each thing was defined, explained, and illuminated by commentary, and as he made sweeping gestures to every point of the compass, to draw attention now to a river, and now to a steeple, his outspread arms seemed to lengthen into rays, like those of a lighthouse, which sheds its long protecting beams over the countryside.

The return to Fonval usually took place in less scientific circumstances. My uncle continued his speculations which he would keep to himself, assuming them, I suppose, to be too abstruse for my intelligence, and he hummed as he went along, his favorite air, which I suppose he had learnt from one of his assistants, "Rum fil dum."

Once we got back, he hastened to the laboratory, or the hothouse.

We varied these walks with expeditions in the motor-car, and then my uncle put himself astride another hobby-horse. He classed my vehicle in its rank amongst animal categories, showed the creatures of to-day, of yesterday, and of to-morrow, among which, no doubt, the automobile would take its place, and this prophecy finished up with a warm panegyric of my 80 h. p.

He wanted to learn how to drive the engine. It was an easy business. In three lessons I made him a past master. He always drove now, and I did not complain, as ever since the two severings and two re-joinings of the optic nerves, any long strain tired my eyes.

My left ear had not yet recovered all the sensibility one could have wished, but I did not dare to talk about it to Lerne for fear of adding one more to the many remorseful thoughts that seemed to haunt him.

It was at the end of one of those pleasure trips that I happened, in cleaning my car—a thing I had to do myself—to find between the back and the cushion of Lerne's seat, a little note-book which had slipped from his pocket. I put it away in mine, with the intention of restoring it to him.

My curiosity got the better of me. On regaining my room, and without rejoining the Professor, I examined my find. It was a diary crammed full of rapid notes and figures sketched in pencil. It resembled the daily record of some research—a laboratory journal.

The figures conveyed no meaning to my eyes. The text was composed mainly of German terms (more especially) and French ones, too. The terms seemed to be chosen in either language, as inspiration directed. The ensemble did not have any meaning for me. However, I discovered a piece of less chaotic literature dated the day before, in which I thought I could recognize a résumé of the preceding pages; and the fact of my understanding some French words, and the sense which they assumed (once they were put together) awoke in me both an inveterate detective and a new-born linguist.

Among such words were the following substantives, connected by German words: "transmission of thought," "electricity," "brains," "batteries."

With the help of a dictionary which I stole from my uncle's room, I deciphered this sort of cryptogram, in which, fortunately, the same expressions frequently recurred. Here is a translation of it—I give it for what it is worth, unfitted as I am for this task, and driven to haste as I was by the necessity of restoring the note-book as soon as possible:

"Conclusions dated the 30th: Aim pursued: Exchange of personalities without exchange of brains.... Basis of research: Ancient experiments have proved that everybody possesses a soul; for the soul and the life are inseparable, and all organisms, between their birth and death, enjoy a more or less developed soul according as they are higher or lower in the scale of existence. Thus, from man to moss, passing through the polypi, each living being has its own soul. Do not plants sleep, breathe and digest? Why should they not think?

"This proves that there is a soul where there is no brain.

"So the soul and the brain are independent of one another.

"Consequently, souls can be exchanged with one another without the brains being exchanged....

"EXPERIMENTS IN TRANSMISSION."

"Thought is the electricity of which our brains are the batteries or the accumulators—I do not know yet; but what is certain, is that the transmission of the mental fluid takes place in a manner analogous to that of the electric fluid.

"The experiment of the 4th proves that thought is transmitted by conductors. That of the 10th, that it is transmitted without conductors, on the ether waves.

"Subsequent experiments have shown a weak spot which I now set down.

"A soul which is projected into an organism unknown to this latter, compresses, so to speak, a soul which is there, without being able to expel it; the projected soul—the soul which has broken loose from the body—is itself kept bound to its organism by a sort of inexplicable mental 'attachment,' which nothing up till now has been able to cut.

"If the two beings are consenting, the reciprocal transmission fails for the same reason. The major part of each soul re-installs itself perfectly well in the organism of its partner, but the troublesome mental 'attachment' prevents each of them from completely quitting the body from which it is striving to detach itself.

"The simpler the recipient organism is relatively to the transmitting organism, the more soul can this latter project into a receptacle, which contains so little of it in the beginning, and the thinner, so to speak, becomes the 'attachment' which keeps fast the mind in the transmitting body, but it always exists.

"On the 20th I projected myself, mentally, inside Johann—on the 22nd I invaded a cat, on the 24th an ash tree.

"Access has become easier and easier, and the invasion more and more complete, but the 'attachment' remains.

"I thought the experiment would succeed on a corpse because there was no fluid to encumber the receptacle to be filled. I had not reflected that death is not compatible with a soul—that inseparable companion of life itself. I did not get any results, and the sensation is abominable.

"THEORETICALLY, IN ORDER THAT THE 'ATTACHMENT' SHOULD BE SUPPRESSED, what is required? A receiving organism, which should have no soul at all (in order that one may lodge one's own entirely), and yet which should not be dead, and in other terms, an organized life which has never lived. That is impossible.

"So, in practice, our efforts must tend to the suppression of the 'attachment' by means of artifices, which I do not yet perceive....

"Not but what the experiments of this period have yielded curious results, since we have arrived at the following demonstrable conclusions:

"(1) The human brain can discharge itself almost entirely into a plant.

"(2) From man to man, _with mutual consent_, the passage of personality is accomplished very completely (except for 'attachment'), which makes those souls, as it were, sister souls—Siamese mentalities.

"(3) From man to man, _without mutual consent_, the compression of the receiving soul (under pressure by the other) produces, in spite of the imperfection of the process, a partial and momentary incarnation of the transmitting individual.

"A very interesting incarnation this, for it satisfies some of those desiderata, all of which I shall satisfy if I attain the aim at which I am driving.

"It seems to me unattainable."

SO THIS IS THE RESULT OF THE STUDIES WHICH MY UNCLE HAD BEEN SO ARdently lauding!

The theory was disconcerting. I ought to have been astounded by it; for there was revealed a tendency towards spiritualist doctrine—very strange in the case of a materialist like Lerne—and the new doctrine appeared in the light of a phantasmagoria, which would have made many eyes open wide behind learned spectacles, erudite pince-nez, and pedantic monocles.

As for me, I did not discover all the subjects of wonder at first sight, being still, at that time, somewhat unwell, and I did not perceive that I had translated a Franco-German mene mene tekel upharsin destined for me!

My attention was concentrated upon these facts—that the _organized being which had never lived, did not exist, and that, on the other hand, the Professor was doubtful of being able to suppress the "attachment." So he was foiled. After his former triumphs I expected any miracle from him; only his inability to perform them would have astonished me.

I set off to seek my uncle, in order to give him back his note-book.

Barbe (with her corpulent figure), whom I met, told me that he was walking about in the park. I did not meet him there, but at the edge of the pond I saw Karl and Wilhelm, who were looking at something in the water. Those two black-guards inspired me with aversion, because of their interchanged brains.

Their presence was usually enough to drive me away, but that day, the sight which kept them on the water's edge, drew me to them.

This something they were looking at kept jumping out of the water with a shower of diamond drops; it was a carp. It leaped up, shaking its fins, which beat the air like wings. One would have said that it was trying to fly away. The poor creature really was trying to do so!

I had before me that fish which Lerne had dowered with a blackbird's soul.

The captive bird—a prey in its scaly flesh to the old aspirations of its race, and weary of its watery home—was leaping towards an impossible heaven.

Finally, with a more despairing effort, the creature fell on the shore, with its gills quivering.

Then Wilhelm seized it, and the assistants departed with their booty. They apostrophized it, and amused themselves with it like old ill-conditioned guttersnipes. They were whistling, and imitating the blackbird's song in mockery, and then, by way of a laugh, a great neighing came from their chests, and without knowing it, they reproduced the sound of a horse's trumpet much better than they had that of the winged flute.

I remained dreamily contemplating the pond, that liquid cage in which the enchanted carp had suffered the haunting desire to fly, and the regret for a nest. The liquid mirror, a moment disturbed by the fury of the fish's leaps, would not have reassumed its leaden calm before the creature was dead.

Its martyrdom was going to end in the stewpan. How would that of the other victims finish, the escaped beasts, and Macbeth?

Oh, Macbeth! how to deliver him!

On the water, now becalmed in deep repose, a last ripple was spreading its circles, and the depths of the firmament were reflected in its mirror again. The evening star was shining in the depths of the lake millions of leagues away, but at will, it was possible, on the contrary, to imagine it floating on the surface, and the leaves of the water-lilies, crescents and half-circles, seemed like reflections of the moon at its successive ages, which had remained there, slumbering in that chill water.

Macbeth! I thought once more. Macbeth! What about him?

At this moment there was the sound of a distant bell at the main door. Somebody at this hour of the day! Nobody ever came!...

I retraced my steps to the _château_ at a rapid pace, asking myself for the first time what would happen to Nicolas if the Law descended on Fonval.

Hiding behind the corner of the château, I ventured a glance. Lerne was standing at the door reading a telegram that moment received, and I came out from my hiding-place.

"Here, uncle," said I, "here is a pocket-book. It belongs to you, I think. You left it in the car...."

But the rustling of petticoats made me turn round.

Emma was coming to us, radiant in that sunset, in which her hair seemed, every evening, to gain a new wealth of red light—with a tune sounding on her lips, like a rose between her teeth.

She came straight on, and her gait was that of a dance.

The bell had interested her also. She inquired about the telegram. The Professor did not reply.

"Oh, what's the matter?" said she. "What's the matter, again, mon Dieu?"

"Is it so grave, uncle?" I asked in my turn.

"No," replied Lerne. "Donovan is dead, that's all."

"Poor fellow," said Emma. Then after a silence: "Is it not better to be dead than mad? After all it is the best thing for him. Come, Nicolas, you are not going to put on a face like that! Come!"

And she seized my hand, and dragged me to the château.

Lerne went away in the other direction.

I was prostrated. "Let me alone," I said, "let me alone. Donovan, the poor wretch. Let me alone. You cannot know! Let me alone, I say."

A maddening fear came over me. Leaving Emma I ran after my uncle and joined him at the laboratory. He was talking to Johann, and showing him the telegram. The German disappeared into the house at the very moment that I accosted the Professor.

"Uncle, you have not told him anything, have you? You have not said anything to Johann?"

"Yes, why?"

"Oh, but he will inform the others, and the others will repeat it before Nell! Nell will know it, uncle, that is certain. They will tell her, and Donovan's soul will learn that it no longer has a human body. It must not be! It must not be!"

"There is no danger, Nicolas, I assure you."

"No danger! Those men are scoundrels, I tell you! Let me prevent this catastrophe! Time is passing, let me in, I entreat you! Please, for a second, I entreat you! Damn it all, I will pass!"

The lessons I had learned from the bull stood me in good stead; I charged head first.

My uncle fell back on the grass, and with a blow of my fist I opened the already half open door. At this, Johann, who was on the watch behind it, fell back, bleeding at the nose, and then I penetrated to the courtyard, and decided to take away the dog at any hazard, and never again be separated from it.

The pack slipped into their kennels. I saw Nell immediately. They had given her a kennel apart from the others. Her great starved, hairless, wretched body was lying against the grating.

I called out, "Donovan, Donovan!" She did not budge.

The eyes of the dogs gleamed in the depths of their somber huts, and some of them growled.

"Donovan! Nell!" I had an intuition of the truth. There also the scythe of Death had done its work. Yes, Nell also was cold and stiff. A chain twisted round her neck seemed to have strangled her. I was going to make sure of this, when Lerne and Johann showed themselves at the entrance of the courtyard.

"Villains," I cried, "you have killed her."

"No, on my honor, I swear," declared my uncle. "They found her this morning, exactly as you see."

"Do you think, then, that she did it of her own accord—that she put an end to herself? Oh, what a horrible end!"

"Perhaps," said Lerne. "However, there is another solution, and a more likely one. A supreme convulsion, I think, twisted the chain. The body was sickly. Hydrophobia declared itself some days ago. I hide nothing from you, Nicolas. I am not exculpating myself in any way. You can see that."

"Oh," I cried, in terror, "rabies."

Lerne went on quietly, "It is possible, also, that another reason for this death escapes us. They found the dog at 8 o'clock this morning still warm. The death had taken place an hour before, and," added he, "Macbeth succumbed at 7 o'clock—just at the same instant."

"From what did he die?"

"He died of rabies also."

# CHAPTER XIII
## EXPERIMENTS! HALLUCINATIONS!

Emma, Lerne and I were in the little drawing room after lunch, when the Professor had a sort of fainting-fit.

It was not the first. I had already observed similar signs of breaking health in my uncle, but this one was very clear evidence. I could observe all the details of it, and it was accompanied by curious circumstances; that is why I shall speak about it more particularly.

Any one who saw them and did not know all the facts would have attributed those incidents to intellectual overwork. To tell the truth, my uncle did have spells of overwork. The laboratory, hothouse and château were no longer sufficient for him. He had annexed the park, also, and now Fonval bristled with complicated poles, abnormal masts, and unusual semaphores, and as some trees interfered with the experiments, a gang of woodcutters was sent for, in order to cut them down.

The joy of seeing the possibility of free passage to and fro restored in the grounds consoled me for this sacrilegious destruction. All about the immense workshop of the valley basin one saw the Professor feverishly moving about from one building to another, from a dynamo to a switch, ferociously determined to suppress the fatal "attachment."

Sometimes, however, he had an attack of weakness, as the result of one of those very peculiar fainting-fits which I am describing. It was always whilst he was reflecting profoundly, with his eyes fixed on some object or other, and brain working at high pressure that the attack came, and he collapsed. At such times he became paler and paler, until the color came back into his cheeks by itself, and by degrees.

Those attacks left him limp and without strength. They robbed him of his fine feeling of confidence, and I heard him complain after one of them, and murmur in a tone of discouragement:

"I'll never succeed, never!"

Often had I been on the point of asking him about it. That day I made up my mind to do so.

WE WERE DRINKING OUR COFFEE, LERNE SEATED IN AN ARMCHAIR IN FRONT OF the window, holding his cup in his hand. Our talk was a broken sort of conversation, with longer and longer intervals.

For want of something to talk about, the conversation languished. Gradually it ceased altogether, as a fire goes out for want of fuel.

The clock struck, and one saw the woodcutters going to their work, with their axes over their shoulder. They brought before my mind a picture of ragged lictors going to carry out an execution of trees.

Which amongst my old comrades would perish to-day—this beech, or that chestnut? I saw them from my window, clothed in all the yellows of autumn, from the deepest copper to the palest gold, each showing its dark touch of shade, or its reddish light amongst those various yellows.

The firs were beginning to get black. Leaves were falling here and there as seemed good to themselves, for there was no breeze.

With a spire like that of a cathedral, a poplar colossus with a hoary head dominated the leafage. I had always known it thus—a monumental tree—and the sight of it stirred in me the memories of my childhood.

Suddenly a flight of terror-struck birds escaped from it—two rooks left it, cawing, a squirrel jumped from branch to branch, and took refuge on the neighboring walnut tree.

Some unpleasant creature, climbing into the tree, had doubtless threatened their safety. I could not distinguish it, for a clump of bushes hid all the lower part of the poplar, but with a surprise that was almost pain I saw it quiver from the top to the roots, shake itself once or twice, and slowly sway its branches. One would have said that a breeze had sprung up which blew for it alone.

I thought of the woodcutters, without, however, forming a very precise conception of the part they might be playing in this drama.

"Can my uncle," I said to myself, "have ordered them to execute the poplar—that venerable patriarch—that king of Fonval? That would be too much."

Then, as I was on the point of asking Lerne about the matter, I perceived that he was in one of his fainting-fits.

I satisfied myself of the presence of the distinctive symptoms of his trouble, the immobility—the pallor—the fixed look—and I succeeded in determining what he was looking at with that persistent fixed stare of a somnambulist.

What he was gazing at was the poplar—that _animate tree, whose appearance at the moment was recalling in so terrifying a way the date trees of the hothouse excited by love and battle.

I remembered the note-book. Was there not some appalling analogy between the absence of that man and the life of that tree?

Suddenly an ax smote the trunk with a sound as of low thunder. The poplar quivered, twisted about, and my uncle gave a start. His cup dropping from his hand, was dashed to pieces on the floor, and whilst his cheeks regained their color, he put his hand down quickly to his ankles, as if the ax had struck the man and the tree at the same blow.

Meanwhile, Lerne gradually recovered. I pretended to have observed nothing except his fainting, and I told him that he should look after himself—that those repeated fits would end by killing him. Did he know what caused them?

My uncle gave a sign that he did. Emma came near his chair.... "I know," said he, at last, "cardiac syncope. I am treating myself."

That was not true. The Professor was not treating himself. He was using up his life in the pursuit of his chimera, without more heed for his skin than it if had been an old work-jacket, to be thrown away as soon as the task was over.

Emma advised him to go out.

"The air will do you good," she said.

He went out. We saw him going towards the poplar, smoking his pipe. The blows of the ax fell faster and faster. The tree bent over and fell. Its fall made the sound like an earthquake. The branches hit my uncle but he did not step aside.

And now, robbed of its only campanile, Fonval seemed to have sunk lower than ever into the depths of the valley, and I sought, in the forlorn sky, to fix the place of the tree, which one had already forgotten, and its tall form, which was already legendary.

Lerne came back. He did not seem to know that he had been imprudent. His carelessness made one tremble when one realized that he might be as reckless in the most hazardous experiments—for example, those transfusions of soul about which the note-book spoke.

Was it one of those attempts which I had just witnessed? I meditated about it, with that strange feeling which I had already experienced at Fonval, like that caused by groping about in mysterious darkness.

Were Lerne's fainting-fit and the tragedy of the tree some mysterious coincidence, or had some strange bond united them at the moment of the ax's blow?

Certainly the arrival of the woodcutters at the foot of the poplar would have been enough to cause the flight of the birds, and as for the shuddering, why should the cutter not have produced it by climbing up the other side of the trunk in order to fix the traditional rope?

Once more, the crossways of probability offered me a choice of solutions, like so many roads, but my mind was not acute at the time.

I WAS OFTEN WITH EMMA, BUT AS MUCH AS I LOVED THOSE MEETINGS, I HAD to make up my mind to stop them, for the following unanswerable reason—but for the note-book I might have attributed it to my nervous condition; I should then have called it a pathological consequence of the operations, and Lerne would have fooled me to the end—fortunately I guessed his tactics at the first.

He had confided to me that he was thinking of assuming my shape, in order to be loved in my place. His eagerness to save my mutilated body; the method he had explained in the note-book, and the business of the poplar—all coordinated themselves in my mind. His fainting-fits assumed all the appearance of experiments, in which Lerne, through a sort of hypnotism, flung his soul into other beings.

So now with his eye to the keyhole he watched every move I made, transfusing his ego into my brain, using the power which his unfinished discovery procured him, to put in practice the most astounding substitution of personalities. I shall be told that this very appearance of unlikeliness ought to have weakened the value of my reasoning; but at Fonval, incoherence being the rule, the more absurd an explanation was, the more likely it was to be the right one.

Ah! that eye at the keyhole. It pursued me like that of Jehovah blasting Cain from the top of its triangular peephole! I was never free of it. Emma felt my distress, but she was far from understanding the real cause of it.

Although I am joking now, I had perceived my danger, and my one thought was how to avert it. After long deliberation, I determined to take the only reasonable course—one which I should have taken long before, viz., departure. Departure with Emma, of course, for now nothing in the world would have made me leave to my uncle what I had won.

But Emma was not one of those women whom one can carry off against her will. Would she consent to leave Lerne, and the promised wealth? Assuredly not!

The poor girl did not see this modernized form of fairy-tale going on around her. The glories to come completely occupied her mind. She was both silly and avaricious. To make her follow me I should have to make her believe that she would not be worse off by a penny, and it was only Lerne who could reassure her effectively on that score.

So, what I required was the Professor's consent! Certainly there could be no question of any consent except of one sort; only one wrested from him by constant intimidation would serve the purpose.

I would make play with Macbeth's murder, and Klotz's assassination, and my terrified uncle would speak to Emma as I wanted him to, and I should carry her off, no doubt depriving Mr. Nicolas Vermont of an inheritance (very much eaten into), and Mlle. Bourdichet of (probably quite chimerical) splendors.

My plan was soon arranged in detail.

# CHAPTER XIV

## DEATH AND THE MASK

**B**ut this plan was never carried out. Not that I hesitated to put it into action—I was always determined upon it, and any doubt that came to me about the existence of the danger to be avoided, arose only when all chance of realizing my projects had passed.

As long as they were still possible, on the contrary, I awaited with patience the opportunity of accomplishing them, and I will even admit that my growing terror ceaselessly urged me to have done with it all.

Everywhere danger showed itself to my hallucinated eyes, and all the more perfidiously that there was often nothing to be afraid of.

It was easy to see that it was time for me to leave Fonval and I longed with all my strength to go, but I had resolved to choose the moment when Lerne should listen to my proposal sympathetically, so that thus I might only use my threat as a last resource.

And the moment was long in coming. The discovery would not come to birth. Its failure was undermining the Professor's health. His fainting-fits—or rather his experiments, grew more frequent, and were rapidly weakening him, and his temper suffered in consequence.

Our walks were the one thing which had not lost their power of cheering him up.

He still kept singing "Rum fil dum," stopping every ten yards to utter some scientific truth. But the motor-car, of all things, exerted its magic over the magician, so in spite of the bad result obtained in the same conditions some months before, I had to make up my mind to speak to him during the journey in my 80 h. p., and should have done so—but for the accident.

IT TOOK PLACE IN THE WOODS OF LOURCQ, THREE KILOMETERS THIS SIDE OF Grey, as we were coming back to Fonval from a run to Vouziers.

We were climbing a slight hill at full speed. My uncle was driving. I was going over in my mind the speech which I was going to make, and was repeating to myself for the hundredth time the phrases which I had prepared some time before, while apprehension dried up my tongue. Ever since our setting-out, I had put off the attack on my tyrant from moment to moment—rehearsing the firm tone which would intimidate him. Before each turn in the road I had said to myself, "It is there I shall speak," but we had passed through all the villages, and gone round all the turns in the road, without my being able to articulate a syllable, and now I had hardly ten minutes left!

Well, I should open fire when we got to the top of the incline.

My first phrase was ready at the gates of my memory, and was awaiting expression, when the car lurched alarmingly towards the right, then towards the left, skidding on its two side wheels.

We were going to overturn!

I seized the wheel, and put on all the brake I could, with feet and hands. The car gradually came under control, again slackened its speed, and stopped right at the top of the hill.

Then I looked at Lerne. He was leaning out of his seat, his head nodding from side to side, and his eyes staring vacantly behind his spectacles. One of his arms was hanging down.

A fainting-fit! We had had a narrow escape; so, those fainting-fits were really syncope. What had I been imagining with my silly ideas?

However, my uncle was not coming to. When I took off his mask, I saw that his clean-shaven face was as pale as a wax candle. His ungloved hands too looked as if they were of wax. I took them, and being quite ignorant of medicine, I slapped them vigorously, as one does to actresses, for hysterics.

This form of applause was in the nature of a claque in the repose of the countryside—sonorous and funereal; it greeted the withdrawal of the great charlatan from the stage.

Frédéric Lerne had indeed ceased to live. I perceived it from his chilled fingers—from his livid cheeks, his soulless eye, and his heart, which had stopped beating. The cardiac affectation about which I had been so skeptical, had just put an end to his life, as is the way with those diseases, without any warning.

Stupefaction, and the reaction from the narrow shave I had just had, kept me motionless. So, in a second, there remained nothing of Lerne except food for worms, and a name fit for oblivion!

Nothing! in spite of my hatred for this detestable man, and my relief at knowing that he no longer had power to harm me, I was awestruck by the swift death which had spirited away this monster's intelligence.

Like a puppet deprived of the hand that gave it life, and prostrate on the edge of the stage, Lerne lay stretched out, limp, his arm hanging down, and his funereal Pierrot's face made whiter by Death.

And yet, as the spirit departed from it into the Unknown, the dead body of my uncle seemed to me to grow more beautiful. The soul is so praised in comparison with the flesh, that one is astonished at seeing the latter become beautiful at the departure of the former. I followed the progress of the phenomenon on Lerne's features. The Great Mystery shed the light of a divine serenity over his brow, as if life were a cloud whose passing reveals some strange sun; and thus whilst the countenance took on the hue of white marble, the puppet became a statue.

Tears dimmed my eyes. I took off my hat. If my uncle had perished fifteen years before, in the fullness of happiness and wisdom, that Lerne of long ago could not have been more beautiful to see.

But I could not go on dreaming in this way, keeping up a conversation with a corpse on a frequented road. So I raised him in my arms calmly, deliberately, and placed him on my left; a strap from the grid fixed him firmly in the seat. With his gloves on his hands again, his cap pulled down over his eyes, his spectacles on his nose, he seemed as if asleep.

We set off side by side.

Nobody at Grey noted the stiffness of my neighbor, and I was able to take him back to Fonval, with veneration in my heart for the dead man, and full of pity for this old lover who had suffered so much. I forgot the offenses in the presence of the offender's death. He filled me with a profound respect, I must also say, with an invincible repugnance, which kept me from him in the depths of my seat.

Since our meeting in the middle of the labyrinth on the morning of my arrival, I had not addressed a word to the Germans. I went to seek them in the laboratory, leaving the car and its sepulchral chauffeur in front of the hall door in charge of the servant.

The assistants understood at once, by my gesticulations, that something extraordinary had happened, and followed me. They had that anxious look of criminals who foresee disaster in every trifle. When they were certain what had befallen them, the three accomplices could not hide their dismay and anxiety. They talked together excitedly. Johann was domineering: the two others became obsequious. I awaited their pleasure.

At last they helped me to carry the Professor's body up to his room, and on to the bed.

Emma saw us, gave a cry and fled, while the Germans made off without more ado.

Barbe came, and I left her with my uncle. The stout serving-woman wept a few tears, paying a tribute to Death as a thing in itself, and not to the shade of her master.

She looked at him from the top of her bulky person. Lerne was changing. The nose became pinched—the nails became blue.

"You will have to lay out the body," I said suddenly.

"Leave that to me," replied Barbe. "It is not a cheerful business, but I know all about it."

I turned my back on her and her preparations. Barbe possessed the knowledge of the peasant women, who are all, more or less, midwives and undertakers.

She soon came and announced to me, "It is all done, properly now. Nothing is wanting except Holy Water and the decorations, which I can't find."

Lerne was so white on his white bed, that they mingled together, and resembled an alabaster sarcophagus, with its effigy on it, and both hewn from the same block of marble. My uncle, with his hair carefully parted, had been clothed in a frilled shirt, and a white tie. His pale hands were clasped together, and held a rosary. A crucifix showed like a star on his breast. His knees and feet stood out under the sheets like sharp snowy hills, very far away.

On the night-table, behind the bowl, in which there was no Holy Water, and in which lay useless a sprinkler of withered boxwood, two candles were burning.

Barbe had turned this piece of furniture into a sort of altar, and I scolded her sharply for this piece of absurdity. She replied that that was the "custom," and then shut the shutters.

Shadow's sank into the face of the dead man, thus anticipating the sequel, and creating a premature livor.

"Open the window wide," I said, "let the daylight in, and the songs of the birds, and the scents of the garden."

The servant obeyed me, although it was against the "custom"; then, when she had received her instructions from me for the necessary ceremonies, she left me at my wish.

From the park there came the powerful aroma of dead leaves. It is infinitely sad! One breathes it in, in the way one listens to a funeral hymn. Crows passed cawing, as they caw when they fly in great numbers from a steeple. The approach of evening darkened the day.

I examined the room; for I felt I must look anywhere but at the dead.

Over the writing-desk was a drawing in chalk, which represented my Aunt Lidivine, smiling. It is wrong to make portraits smile! They are destined to see too many sad things, just as Lidivine, in colors, having smiled to see her husband carrying on his illicit amours, smiled again, in the tragic presence of his remains.

The picture was twenty years old, but the chalk powder, which resembles the dust of age, made it look more time-worn. Every day made it darker. It seemed to remove, far away into the past my aunt and her own youth. It displeased me.

I endeavored to interest myself in other things—in the falling dusk—in the early bats—in the knickknacks of the room—in the candles which threw a feeble light with their dancing flames.

The wind rose, and took off my attention for the moment. It streamed moaning through the leafage, and as one heard it groaning in the chimney, one fancied one could hear the passage of Time. With a sudden stronger gust, it put out a candle. The other flickered, and I shut the window quickly.

Suddenly, I was sincere with myself, and no longer sought to be my own dupe. I required to look at the dead man, to keep an eye on his seeming powerlessness; then I lit the lamp and placed Lerne in a flood of light.

Really, he was handsome—very handsome! Nothing remained of the grim physiognomy which I had encountered, after fifteen years of absence—nothing! except, perhaps, a certain irony on the mouth—the shade of a grin.

Had my late uncle still some arrière pensée? Dead, he seemed still to be defying Nature. Dead! he who in his lifetime had set his finger to creation!

And his work appeared to me in all the sublime audacity and criminal boldness, which made him worthy of the pillory, as well as of the pedestal, of the rod of the slave and of the palm of the victor.

Of yore, I knew he was worthy of honor, and I would have taken my oath that he would never have deserved dishonor; but what astounding chance, some five years ago, had befallen, which had made of him the wicked lord of a castle who murdered his guests?

I kept asking myself this, and meanwhile the shades of Klotz and Macbeth seemed to be crying out their torture in the recesses of the moaning chimney.

The gust, turning to a gale, whistled at the loosely fitting doors. The flames of the candles became restless. The curtains rose and fell again, with melancholy motions. The hair of Lerne was blown about, white and feathery. The storm disordered those hairs, and brushed them this way and that, and whilst the spirit hand of the gale sported amongst the long hair, I, transfixed with amazement, bent over the bed, looking at something that appeared and disappeared under the silvery locks—a purple scar, which encircled Lerne's head from temple to temple, the dreadful semi-crown which indicated the Circeean operation! My uncle had been operated on by whom? Otto Klotz, of course!

Light had penetrated the mystery. Its last veil, a winding-sheet, had been torn. All was explained now—all! The sudden metamorphosis of the Professor, coinciding with the disappearance of the principal assistant, with Macbeth's journey, and the eclipse of Lerne; all! The brutal letters, the changed handwriting—my failure to recognize him; the German accent, his failures of memory, and also the violent temper of Klotz—his rashness, and passion for Emma, and then his wicked activities and the crimes committed on Macbeth and on me!

All! All!! All!!!

Calling to mind Emma's account, I was able to reconstitute the history of an unimaginable crime.

Four years before my return to Fonval, Lerne and Otto Klotz returned from Nanthel, where they had passed the day. Lerne was probably in a happy mood. He was going once more to take up his noble studies in grafting, whose only aim was to relieve humanity. But Klotz, being in love with Emma, was hoping to divert those efforts to another object—one of profit—one of lucre—the exchange of brains: doubtless this very idea (which he was not able to carry out at Manheim for want of money), he had already proposed to my uncle, and without any result.

But the assistant had his own Macchiavelian idea. With the help of his three compatriots, warned beforehand, and hidden in the thicket, he struck down the Professor, gagged him, and shut him up in the laboratory—this man, whose wealth and independence—in other words, whose personality—he invaded.

THE NEXT DAY, BEFORE DAWN, HE WENT BACK TO THE LABORATORY, WHERE Lerne, who was being watched, awaited him.

His three accomplices administered anesthetics to both, and placed the brain of Klotz in my uncle's skull.

As for the brain of Lerne, they no doubt contented themselves with placing it as best they might in the skull of Klotz, who was now only a dead body, and they buried it all in haste with the other débris.

So there is Otto Klotz behind the mask, clothed in the appearance he desired, dressed like Lerne, master of Fonval, of Emma and the laboratory—a sort of monk of St. Bernard sheltered in the shell of the being whom he killed.

Emma saw him come out of the laboratory. He entered the château, pale and trembling, upset the usual habits and customs, made the criss-cross roads of the labyrinth, and then, sure of impunity, began his terrible experiments.

Fortunately the body-snatcher had died too soon, without reaping the reward of a robbery of which he was now the victim, since the heart-disease which had just carried off the spirit of Klotz, belonged really to the body of Lerne.

In this manner is the burglar in a house punished when the roof falls in upon him.

I now understand why that mask had resumed the real expression of my uncle. The soul of the German no longer inhabited it, to give it Klotz's expression.

Klotz the murderer of Lerne, and not Lerne the assassin of Klotz! I could not get over it.

That is a confidence which the double person had forgotten to make to me, and vexed at having been his dupe so long, I said to myself, that, had I been living alone with him, I should probably have discovered his imposture, but that the society of people as easily deceived as Emma was, or accomplices like the assistants, whether duped themselves or trying to dupe me, had dragged me into this delusion.

Ah! Aunt Lidivine, thought I, you were right to smile with your lips of chalk. Your Frédéric fell into a villainous trap five years ago, and the mind which has just quitted that form, is not his. Nothing alien any longer remains in it, except a deserted brain—a carnal globe as uninteresting as the liver. So it is your husband whom we are watching; it is the other who has just died, and paid his debt.

At this idea I sobbed heart-broken, in the presence of the strange corpse, but the sardonic grin, left at the time of its flight by the evil soul like a stamp, still checked my emotions.

I effaced it with the tip of my finger, forming the mouth, which was now stiff, and hardly malleable into the shape I wanted.

At the moment, when I was stepping back, the better to judge of the effect, there was a gentle scratching at the door.

"It's I, Nicolas, I, Emma!"

Poor simple girl! Should I tell her the truth? How would she take such a strange turn of destiny? I knew her; having been many times fooled, she would have reproached me with trying to mystify her, so I held my peace.

"Take a rest," said she, in a low tone. "Barbe will take your place."

"No, no," said I, "let me be."

I felt I must keep this vigil by the side of my dead uncle to the end. I had accused him of too many crimes, and I felt the need of asking forgiveness of his memory, and of that of my aunt; and that is why, despite the wild fury of the storm, we conversed all night long—the dead man, the chalk drawing and myself.

After Barbe had come at dawn, I went out into the cool of the morning, which soothes the skin and allays the fever of a long night of watching.

The park in autumn exhaled an odor of decay as of a cemetery. The great wind in the night had piled up all the leaves and my steps rustled in the thick bed. Only one or two could be seen here and there on the skeleton trees, and I could scarce tell whether they were leaves or sparrows.

In a few hours the park had prepared itself for winter. What was going to become of the marvelous hothouse, at the coming of frost? Perhaps I should be able to get into it by reason of that death which had flung the Germans off their guard.

I made my way obliquely in its direction, but what I saw from a distance made me quicken my steps.

The door of the hothouse was open, and smoke escaped from it— acrid and foul—and also made its way through the openings in the glass.

I went in.

The Rotunda, the Aquarium and the third hall, were a picture of confusion. They had pillaged, broken and burned everything. Heaps of filth were accumulated in the middle of the three halls. I there found jumbled together, broken plants, shattered pots, bits of glass and sea anemones, flowers defiled, close to dead beasts.

In short,—three disgusting rubbish heaps, wherein the triple palace beheld the end of its pleasant, moving, or repulsive marvels. Some rags were still burning in a corner. In another, a heap of branches—the most compromising ones—were just hissing embers.

No doubt the assistants had worked feverishly at this task of destruction, in order that no vestige of their labors should remain, and the storm alone had prevented me from hearing them, but it was not likely they had stopped short there in their congenial task.

To make sure of that, I examined the shambles near the cliff. In that gaping ditch there was nothing but bones and carcasses of unimportant animals, some without a skull, others without a head. Klotz was no longer there. Nell was not there.

The sack of the laboratory gave me the impression of a masterpiece. It proved the innate capacity of men in general, and certain nations in particular, for this sort of diversion.

I ransacked the house at will; all the doors banging and clashing as the wind caught them.

In the courtyard there only remained living animals which had not yet undergone any treatment. I did not discover the others till later on, so here there was nothing destroyed. The operating rooms, on the other hand, disclosed an indescribable chaos of broken bottles, the mingled contents of which flooded the tiles with a pool of chemicals. A jumble of books, notes and notebooks, was spread over the holocaust of twisted implements.

Lastly, most of the surgical instruments had been stolen. The villains had fled with the secret of the Circeean operation, and the implements needed for performing it. The building where they had lived, indeed, with its chests and cupboards emptied, its furniture upside-down, proved the flight of the three associates.

# CHAPTER XV

## THE NEW BEAST

Under the influence of an indifference most praiseworthy, in these unfortunate circumstances, the official doctor asked no questions, examined nothing. I told him how my late uncle had died of syncope. He had heard about his heart-disease, and this official doctor gave me the Burial Certificate.

"Dr. Lerne is dead," said he, "and our mission to-day will stop at that, if you please. For the rest, it is not our business to set investigations on foot which might bring us to contradict so eminent a master, and make him die otherwise than he desired."

The funeral took place at Grey-l'Abbaye, without any pomp or spectators, after which I employed ten days in unraveling the affairs of this inconceivable duality; this unparalleled amalgam of assassin and victim: Klotz-Lerne.

During the course of his "phenomenal" existence, that is to say the last four and a half years or so, he had made no testamentary dispositions. This was to me the proof that in spite of his forebodings of his end, death had overtaken him unexpectedly, for no doubt had it been otherwise, he would have done everything to disinherit me.

I found in his desk, at the bottom of the secret drawer, my uncle's Will, as the letter of long ago had told me I should. It appointed me his residuary legatee.

But Klotz-Lerne had charged the estate with a super-abundance of mortgages, and contracted numberless debts.

My first thought was to appeal to the Courts, and then the absurdity of the case struck me, and I perceived all the confusion, which such a substitution of persons could cause to legal minds—those frauds of a kind not provided against by the Code, those false pretenses and all this legacy-hunting, which were a defiance of nature and law alike.

I had to resign myself to all the consequences of an astounding imposture, and not say a word about it, for fear of arousing the worst suspicions.

Everything considered, however, the acceptance of the succession still brought me some profit, and whatever happened, I was resolved to get rid of Fonval, judging that it would, henceforward, be for me but a nest of evil memories.

I went through all the papers. Those of the real Lerne, confirmed his medical honor, and the legitimacy of his researches in grafting in every line. Those of Klotz-Lerne, usually recognizable by the illustrations in the manuscript, and often blackened with German Gothic characters, were carefully examined, and were reduced to ashes, for they were irrefutable witnesses of several crimes, and contained nothing to refute the presumption that a certain Nicolas Vermont, who had been present at Fonval for six months, had been a partner in them.

Under the influence of this same dread, I ransacked the park and outhouses.

That done, I presented the animals to the villagers, and dismissed Barbe.

Then I summoned help. We filled trunks and cases with family treasures, whilst Emma packed her boxes—half annoyed at the loss of her daydream, and half pleased to follow me to Paris.

After the death of Klotz-Lerne, eager to take my place again in the world, and to enjoy once more the comforts of wealth, without passing through the worries of too small a house, I had written to one of my friends, asking him to take a flat for me, a little larger than my bachelor rooms, and suitable for a couple of lovers. His answer delighted us. He had found out a home for us in the Avenue Victor Hugo—a little house built as if to our measure, and furnished exactly to our taste. Servants, recruited by his good offices, awaited us.

All was ready. I sent off a mountain of parcels belonging to Emma along with her trunks.

One morning Maître Pallud, the Notary of Grey, had a final interview with me with regard to the sale of the property. Emma could not keep still. We fixed that very evening for our departure in the car, intending to sleep at Nanthel, in order to be in Paris the next day.

And the hour came for departing from Fonval for ever. I went over the château, which was empty of furniture, and the park, in which there was no leafage. It looked as if the autumn had stripped them both.

The old perfumes still clung to the abandoned rooms, recalling sad memories. Ah! what charm there sometimes is in musty things! One saw on the walls the indelible outline of pictures or mirrors now taken down, sideboards or chiffoniers that had gone, leaving behind patches that looked new against the faded paper, outlines of things magically given by them to the familiar wall, bright spots destined to grow pale, as time went on, just as the memory of the absent.

Some of the rooms seemed made smaller by being emptied, others larger, without any obvious reason.

I went over the house from garret to basement, by the light of the skylight and the gleams of a grating. I explored from attic to cellar, and I did not grow weary of wandering through this scenery of my youth, like a living being haunting a phantom place. Ah! my youth! It alone dwelt in Fonval. I felt that. In spite of their importance, the recent dramas were pale beside it. The bedrooms were duller than ever, and Donovan's and Emma's were no longer anything but my own and my aunt's.

Was I not right to have put up Fonval to auction?

This double feeling accompanied me in my farewells to the park. The paddock became a lawn, and the summerhouse of the Minotaur only recalled Briareus to me.

I made a circuit to the cliff. The clouds were so low that one would have said it was a ceiling of gray wool, laid over a circular crater.

Under this subdued light, which is that of winter, the statues, now bereft of their green togas, showed their concrete, weather-beaten and rain stained, with their noses knocked off, or their chins broken; some of them were crumbling to bits—one with a Bacchante's gesture, was stretching out her arm, the hand of which, carrying a mixing-bowl, only stuck to the wrist by its iron bone, which was dreadful to see. They were going to continue their poses in solitude.

Something wild and savage was already beginning to emerge, but no more than was vaguely perceptible. A hawk was sharpening his beak on the weather-cock of the summerhouse. A weasel crossed the paddock with little quiet jumps.

Unable to make up my mind to depart, I unlocked the door of the château again, then I came back to the park. I heard my movements resounding on the flooring of the corridors and rustling amongst the leaves of the alleys.

The silence was deepening every moment. I felt a certain difficulty in breaking it. It knew well it was going to reign as a master, and as I paused in the midst of the domain, it put forth its almighty power.

There I dreamt a long time—I, the human center of the enormous amphitheater, the center, also, of a Walpurgis dance of thoughts. To my call there came in a whirlwind, the faces of long ago and yesterday— imaginary or real—personages of fairy tales, or truth; they whirled round me in a wild crowd, and made of all the deep valley a maelstrom of remembrance, in which the whole past turned and turned again.

But I had to go away at last, and leave Fonval to the ivy and the spiders.

In front of the coach-house, Emma ready dressed for her journey, was impatiently mounting guard.

I opened the door. The car was standing askew at the end of the old shed. I had not seen it again since the accident, and I did not even remember having housed it. The assistants, no doubt, through some tardy act of courtesy, had got it in somehow.

Heedless of my negligence, the engine roared admirably, the moment the electric contact was made, so I brought out the car as far as the semi-circular terrace, and shut on so many memories a symbolical portal, which closed with a sound like a sob.

Thank Heaven! No more of the awful business of Klotz, but no more, also, of my youthful years. Then it occurred to me that by keeping Fonval I might prolong them.

"We shall stop at Grey, at the Notary's," I said to Emma. "I am not going to sell, I am going to let it."

I plunged on the straight road; the rocky walls seemed to straighten themselves. Emma was prattling.

At first the car hummed cheerfully. However, I was not slow in repenting that I had paid so little attention to it. With a sudden jerk it slowed down; then several more, and its progress was soon no more than a succession of abrupt jumps.

I have said, with regard to this car, that it was the perfection of automatism—pedals and handles reduced to the minimum. Such a machine presents only one drawback. It must be perfectly in order before setting out, for once en route, one has no more influence on it, except to quicken the pace, or to moderate it, but not to fortify it by dosing and repairs.

The prospect of a halt spoiled my good humor.

Meanwhile, the car pursued its jumpy course, and I could not prevent myself laughing.

This manner of advancing recalled to me, in a comical way, the walks I had taken in this very place, with Klotz-Lerne, and the capricious way in which my sham uncle would stop, and then set off again.

Hoping that it was merely a passing indisposition of the machine,— too much oil, for example,—I let the engine run on, and endeavored to find out by the noise it made, which of its functions was defective, and every now and again caused those inequalities of power transmission, which grew more marked at every pause, and some of which were so accentuated, indeed, that we were almost motionless for a second.

My absurd comparison became clearer to me, and that amused me.

"Just like that blackguardly Professor," I said to myself. "It is amusing!"

"What is the matter?" said my fellow-traveler. "You are not looking cheerful."

"I? Nonsense!"

It is a curious thing, but this question had affected me. I should have thought that my face was quite calm. What motive had I not to be easy in my mind? I was annoyed, that was all. I simply was asking myself what organ was suffering in this great body (as the Professor had called it) and not being able to find anything, and it being about to stop altogether, I was annoyed, that was all.

In vain I listened with a carefully trained ear to the explosion, clickings, dull-sounding knocks; no characteristic sound revealed to me the stiffness of valves or cranks.

"I bet it is the clutch which has gone wrong," I cried, "and yet the engine is all right."

And then Emma said, "Oh, Nicholas, do look! Should that thing there move?"

"Ah! I told you so. There, you see!"

She had pointed to the clutch-pedal, which was moving by itself, while the jolts of the car coincided with its motions.

"That was the trouble."

Whilst my eyes were fixed on the pedal, it remained pushed right over.

The car, unclutched, stopped. I was going to get out of it, when it set off again in a most brutal way. The pedal had come back. A certain uneasiness tormented me; it is certain nothing is so annoying as a car that will not work; but all the same, I do not remember ever having been so curiously affected by engine-trouble.

_Suddenly the hooter began to yell of its own accord._ I felt the insurmountable need of saying something or other, but my dumbness redoubled my anxiety.

"It is out of order generally," I said, endeavoring to speak in a casual tone. "We shan't get there before night, my dear."

"WOULD IT NOT BE BETTER TO REPAIR IT IMMEDIATELY?"

"No, I prefer to go on. When one stops one never knows when one will be able to set out again. There will always be time to...."

"Perhaps it will warm up again," but the hooter drowned my hesitating voice with a great clamor, and my fingers clutched hold of the steering-wheel, for when this clamor had died down, it turned to a continuous note which took on rhythm and inflections, and I felt coming through this cadence an air—a marching tune (after all, it was perhaps I who made myself hear it).

This air drew nearer, so to say, became more defined, and after some halting attempts like those of a singer trying his voice, the car resolutely thundered out with its copper throat, "Rum fil dum, fil dum."

At the accent of the German's songs, a horde of suspicions swooped on my uneasy mind. I had an intuition that something fantastic, mysterious, monstrous, had happened. I tried cutting off the petrol. The handle resisted. The brake resisted. A superior force kept them immovable.

Losing my head altogether, I let go the steering-wheel, and took two arms to the diabolical brake. The same result, but the hooter made a gargling sound, and then was silent.

The girl exclaimed angrily, "That's a funny trumpet!"

As for me, I had no desire to laugh. My ideas began to follow one another in a giddy whirl, and my Reason refused to sanction my reasoning.

This metallic car, from which wood, india rubber and leather had been banished—of which no fragment belong to matter at one time alive, was it not an organized body which had never lived? This automatic mechanism—was it not a body capable of reflexes, but a body devoid of intelligence? Was it not in fact—according to the note-book—a possible receptacle of a soul in its totality,—that receptacle which the Professor in his haste had declared to be non-existent?

At the moment of his apparent death, Klotz-Lerne had doubtless indulged in an experiment on the car, recalling that of the poplar tree, but having been absent-minded for some weeks, perhaps he had not foreseen (fatal want of logic), that his soul would slip entirely into that empty receptacle, and that the "attachment" being broken, his human form would be no more than a corpse, into which the laws of his own discovery forbade him to return. Or else, perhaps, weary with pursuing the fortune he could not seize, Klotz-Lerne had acted of his own free will, and committed a sort of suicide, by exchanging the substance of my uncle for that of a machine.

But why should he not have wished, simply and solely, to become the new beast, foretold by him in a moment of eccentricity—the animal of the future—the ruler of creation, which the re-fitting of its organs was to make immortal and infinitely perfectible, according to his lunatical prophecy?

Once more, however sensible this inner discussion with myself was, I would not accept its conclusions. A resemblance in manner between the car and the Professor, a probable hallucination of my sense of hearing, and possibly the way of gripping the lever, should not suffice to prove this absurdity. My distress wanted a more decisive proof. It came without delay.

We were coming to the edge of the forest, to that limit where the dead maniac invariably paused in his walks. I understood that I was going to have the question settled, and at all hazards, I gave Emma warning.

"Hold tight; keep your body back!"

In spite of our precaution, a sudden stop of the car threw us forward.

"What's the matter?" said Emma.

"Nothing, do not worry."

Frankly, I was undecided. What was to be done? To get down would have been perilous. Inside the Klotz-car we were at least out of his reach, and I did not desire to be butted at by him, so I endeavored to get him forward.

As before, no bit of him would obey my orders.

We were in this awkward position, when suddenly I felt the steering-wheel turn round, (levers and foot-breaks working away); and the car, making a wide sweep, faced about, and began to take us back again towards Fonval.

I was luckily able to turn it round again by a sudden movement, but the moment it was set in the right direction, it definitely manifested the wish not to move a wheel forward.

At last Emma perceived that there was something unusual the matter, and she urged me to get down to put this right, but for some moments my terror had been changed into rage.

The hooter laughed!

"He who laughs last, laughs loudest," I cried to myself.

"What is the matter? What is the matter?" said my companion.

Without listening to her, I took from the grid a steel rod, which served me as a defensive weapon, and to the profound stupefaction of Emma, I hit the restive car with it. Then there was an epic scene!

Under the formidable hail of blows, the heavy vehicle behaved like a restive horse—plunged, kicked and bucked. It tried everything to fling us out of the saddle.

"Hold fast!" I said to my companion, and I laid on all the harder.

The engine growled; the hooter yelled with pain, or bellowed with rage. On the sheet-metal of the hood, the blows rained thick and fast, and the thrashing made the woods resound with a fabulous noise.

Suddenly uttering a shrill scream like an elephant, the metallic mastodon gave a bound, executed two or three plunges, and then dashed forward with the speed of lightning.

A runaway!

I was no longer master of the situation. The frenzy of a mad monster ruled our fate. We were almost flying. The 80 h. p. car sped on with the rapidity of a falling body. We could no longer breathe the wild rushing air. Sometimes the hooter gave a strident cry.

We flashed through Grey-l'Abbaye like lightning. Hens and ducks were under our wheels—blood on my glasses. We were going so fast that the brass-plate of Maître Pallud gave me the impression of a golden streak.

On issuing from the village, the Route Nationale hedged us with its plane trees, then the long hill with its slope formed an obstacle to our speed. There, showing signs of weariness, for the first time, the car slackened down, and allowed itself to be managed.

I HAD TO THRASH IT OFTEN, TO MAKE IT BRING US AS FAR AS NANTHEL WHERE we got in late, and without any hitch. As we passed over a gutter, however, the copper mouth uttered an exclamation of pain, and I saw that the jolt had just broken a spring of the off hind wheel.

When we got into the courtyard of the Hotel, I tried to fasten a new spring into the felloe, but did not succeed. My attempts roused such a noise from the hooter, that I had to give up trying to repair the damage; besides it was not very urgent.

I had resolved to finish the journey in a train, and to put my recalcitrant machine in the goods station. The future should decide about its fate. For the moment I put it in the garage amongst the phaëtons, buggies and limousines, but I hastily withdrew, knowing that behind me, the round eyes of its head-lamps were shining with a treacherous look.

As I reflected on all the ins and outs of this astonishing phenomenon, and as I moved away, a phrase in a scientific article which I had once read, and which had struck me, came into my mind, and I was not a little surprised at finding in those words a vague explanation of the marvel, and the promise of happenings no less astonishing.

"It is possible to imagine that there exists an intermediate link between living creatures and inert matter, just as there exist links between animals and vegetables."

THE HOTEL HAD ALL THE OUTWARD SIGNS OF LUXURIOUS COMFORT. A LIFT took me up, and I was taken to our room.

My partner had preceded me. After being a prisoner for so long, she was looking with a sort of eagerness at the street, the people moving about, and the shops, whose glories were being lit up.

Emma could not tear herself away from the spectacle of life, and as she dressed, she turned continually to the window, drawing aside the curtains to behold the spectacle again.

I thought I perceived that she was less affectionate towards me.

My strange conduct in the car had not failed to surprise her. As I had made up my mind not to give any explanation, I had no doubt that she regarded me as a lunatic, hardly cured of his madness.

At dinner, which we took at little private tables lit up by candles, whose soft light was that of a boudoir, Emma, surrounded by men in evening dress, and women in low-necked frocks, made herself conspicuous by her aggressive behavior which was quite out of place. She ogled the men, and looked with a sneer at the women—sometimes admiring and sometimes contemptuous—speaking her approval in a loud voice, and laughing ostentatiously—which caused amusement and astonishment all round us—in the most ridiculous and delicious manner.

She wanted to jabber with everybody there.

I carried her off as soon as I could, but her desire to get back to the life of the world was so ardent, that we had to go immediately to some place of public entertainment.

The theater was shut, and only the Casino was open, and that evening, the entertainment consisted of a wrestling tournament organized in imitation of Paris.

The little Hall was full of counter-jumpers, students and common folk. A cloud was floating in it which was a mixture of all proletarian and lower middle-class tobaccos.

Emma spread herself in her box. A vulgar bit of ragtime proceeding from the shameless orchestra plunged her into ecstasy, and as her ecstasies were not discreet, three hundred pairs of eyes turned round to look at her, attracted by the waving of a fan, and the hat-feathers which also courageously beat time.

Emma smiled and looked at the three hundred pair of eyes.

The wrestling aroused her enthusiasm, and more especially the wrestlers. Those human brutes, whose heads—great jaw, and no brow— seem destined for the sawdust-box of the guillotine aroused the most unseemly excitement in my fair friend.

A hairy, tattooed colossus won. He came to make his bow, and as he did so, awkwardly nodded a myrmidon's head, with two little pig's eyes surmounting his titanic body.

He belonged to the town. His fellow-citizens gave him an ovation. He was given the title of "Bastion of Nanthel," and "Champion of the Ardennes."

Emma rose in her seat, applauding him so loudly and insistently, that she both scandalized and amused the audience.

The Champion threw her a kiss. I felt my face getting red with shame. We returned to the Hotel, exchanging bitter remarks.

Our apartment happened to be above the arch of the main door, where motor-cars kept passing and re-passing until morning, which made me dream of misfortunes and absurdities. My awakening brought me real ones. Emma was gone!

In my astonishment, I endeavored to find plausible reasons for her absence.

I rang for the waiter. He came, and handed me this letter, which I have preserved, and whose criss-crossed paper, bespattered with blots and blobs of ink, I now pin on to my piece of white paper:

"DEAR NICK,

"Pardon me for the pain I am causing you, but it is better that we should part. I found again yesterday, my first lover Alcide, the man I fought with Léonie about. He is the handsome fellow who won the wrestling-match yesterday. I am going off with him. I could not give up that kind of life, except for the sort of money which Lerne promised me. I should have made you unhappy, and should have been unfaithful to you. All the rest amounts to nothing. I want a real man. It is not your fault, and so I hope this will not cause you any pain. Adieu for life.

"EMMA BOURDICHET."

In the presence of so categorical an intimation, couched in jargon almost as barbarous as that of the Law Courts, I could only bow to fate. Moreover, were not those sentiments which Emma was expressing, exactly those which had charmed me in her? Had I not loved in her just that thirst for pleasure which was the cause of her bewitching beauty, and the cause of her infidelity?

I had the energy and wisdom to defer the rest of my reflections until the morrow. They might have brought on weakness in action.

I inquired about the first train for Paris, and sent for a mechanic to undertake to dispatch my 80 h.p. car, or, if you prefer to call it, the Klotz-automobile, to me.

I was soon informed of the man's arrival. Together we went to the garage.

The car had disappeared!

It can easily be imagined that I put the two treasonable acts together, and accused Emma of a secret complicity.

But the Manager of the Hotel, thinking he had to do with audacious thieves, went off to the police-office. He came back, saying that they had found in a little street of the faubourg, a car with the number 234XY, which had been abandoned, as he thought, by thieves, for want of petrol. The tank was empty.

"Ah! just so," said I to myself. Klotz wanted to run away. He forgot about the exhaustion of the petrol, and there he is, paralyzed.

I kept the true version of the incident to myself, and advised the mechanic to push the car to the train, without making the engine go.

"Promise me this," I insisted, "it is very important. My train is due, I must be off. Off you go, and remember, no petrol."

# CHAPTER XVI
## THE WIZARD FINALLY DIES

And now, here I am, in this house in the Avenue Victor Hugo, which I had taken for Emma, and I am alone with my strange memories, since she preferred to sacrifice her intoxicating and lucrative beauty to M. Alcide. Let us say no more about it!

February is beginning. The fire is flaming behind me with the flapping sound of a waving flag.

Since I came back to Paris, having nothing to do, and reading nothing, I write every evening and every morning, at this round table, the story of my singular adventures.

Are they over yet?

The Klotz-automobile is there in the coach-house, in a box which I have specially constructed for it.

In spite of my orders, the Nanthel mechanic put in some petrol, and my new chauffeur and I had the greatest trouble in bringing the human car here, for it was impossible to turn the waste-cocks for emptying the tank.

It began by destroying its successor—a 20 h. p. machine of the latest model. What could I do with this accursed Klotz-car? Sell it? Expose my fellow creatures to its malignity? That would have been a crime. Destroy it and so kill the Professor in his final transformation? That would be murder. So I locked it up.

The box has high oak partitions, and the door is heavily bolted.

But the new beast passed its nights in roaring its threats and chromatic cries of pain, and the neighbors complained.

Then in my presence I had the delinquent hooter taken to pieces. We had extraordinary difficulty in taking out the screws and the bolts, and we found that the apparatus was, so to speak, soldered to the car. We had to tear it off, and as it came away the whole machine quivered.

A yellowish liquid, smelling like petrol, spurted from the wound, and flowed drop by drop from the amputated pieces. I concluded from this that the metal had become organic through the action of the infused life, hence my vain efforts to fix the new spring in the wheel, this operation being a sort of animal grafting, as impracticable as the transplanting of a wooden finger on to a living hand.

Though deprived of power of speech, my prisoner none the less persisted in his nightly outbursts for a week, dashing the battering-ram of its mass against the door. Then suddenly it became silent.

It was a month ago, I think, that the petrol and oil tanks were empty; but, I have forbidden Louis, my mechanic, to go and make sure, and enter the cage of that savage beast.

We have peace now, but Klotz is still there.

LOUIS HAS PUT AN END TO THE PHILOSOPHICAL REMARKS WHICH WERE READY to flow from my pen. He came in suddenly, and he said to me with his eyes starting from his head, "Monsieur, monsieur, come and see the 80 h.p. car."

I did not wait to be told more, but rushed out.

On the staircase the servant confessed to me that he had ventured to open the door of the coach-house, because for some time a bad smell had been coming out of it. Indeed the stench of the courtyard itself was sickening.

Louis exclaimed in a tone almost of admiration:

"That's it. A nice stink, isn't it, sir?" and we entered the box.

So strange did the car look, that at first I could hardly recognize it.

Sunk on its deflated tires, it had lost its shape, as if it had been a car of half-molten wax. The levers were bent over like bars of india rubber. The head lamps were battered and out of shape, and their lenses, bluish and sticky, were like the bleared eyes of the dead.

I saw suspicious stains, which were eating into the aluminium, and holes which were rusting the iron. The steel had become porous, and was crumbling, and the copper had grown spongy like a mushroom.

Lastly, the whole machinery was mottled as with a red or greenish leprosy which was neither rust nor verdigris.

On the ground there was a syrupy disgusting pool all round this repulsive heap of refuse, oozing from it and all streaked with colors suggesting unimaginable horrors.

Strange chemical reactions occurred from time to time which made this putrefying metallic flesh boil with great bursting bubbles, and, in its depths, the mechanism rumbled and gurgled intermittently.

Suddenly in a squashy fall, the steering-wheel collapsed, one end going through the floor, and the other through the hood.

A nameless mess was stirring in there, and the horrible stench of organic decomposition flung me backwards.

I had had time to see worms wriggling about in the dark depths.

"What a filthy machine," said the mechanic.

I tried to make him swallow the idea that vibration sometimes disintegrates metal, and may give rise to molecular modifications like this. He did not seem to believe me, and I, who knew that the truth was stranger still, was forced, in order that he might grasp and accept it, to enlarge on the subject and give him, confidentially, a careful explanation of the whole matter.

Klotz is dead! The car is dead! And so goes to limbo, along with its author, the beautiful theory of an animalized mechanism made immortal by the replacing of parts, and infinitely perfectible!

Giving life means also giving death, and to organize inorganic bodies, means to sooner or later disorganize them.

But, to my surprise, it was not for want of petrol that the fantastic creature died. No, the tank was half full. It was the soul, therefore, which killed it—the human soul, that corrupt soul, which so rapidly wore out the constitutions of animals, more healthy than ours, and soon ruined this pure metallic body.

I ordered the filthy bundle of refuse to be flung away. The drains were to be the tomb of Klotz.

He's dead! He's dead! I'm rid of him. He is dead, and he can never come to life again. In fact, he is dead! His spirit is with the deceased. He can never hurt me again. Ah, ha! DEAD! The filthy brute!

I ought to be happy, but I am not very. Oh, it is not because of Emma. No doubt the "baggage" causes me pain, but that will soon be cured, and to admit that grief is consolable, is already to be consoled from it. My great trouble comes from my recollections. What I have seen and felt harasses me.

The madman Nell! The operation! The Minotaur! I—Jupiter! And so many other horrors.

I dread eyeballs that stare at me, and I lower my eyes in the presence of keyholes. Those are the sources of my trouble, but I also dread the horrible future.

Suppose it were not all finished?

Suppose Klotz's death did not wind up my story?

I do not care about him, as he no longer exists; even if he should come and haunt me in the features of Lerne or a car, I should know that he was only an hallucination of my weak eyes.

He is dead, and I do not care a jot about him, I repeat. It is the three assistants who trouble me. Where are they? What are they doing? That is the question. They possess the Circeean formula, and must be using it for their own profit, in order to indulge in the traffic in personalities.

In spite of his rebuffs, Klotz-Lerne had induced several people to submit to his malevolent surgery, and to exchange their souls for somebody else's. The three Germans are daily adding to the number of those poor creatures who are craving for money, youth or health. There are in the world, unsuspected men and women who are not themselves.

I am no longer certain of anything. Faces seem to be masks. Perhaps I might have known this sooner. There are certain people whose physiognomy reflects a soul the very opposite of their own; people virtuous and honest, who, for a moment, give glimpses of unexpected vices and monstrous passions, which strike terror like a miracle. They have to-day their soul of yesterday.

Sometimes in the eyes of the man who speaks to me there passes a strange flash—an idea which does not belong to him. He will contradict it immediately after expressing it, and he will be the first to be astonished that he could have thought of it.

I know people whose opinions vary day by day, and that is very illogical.

Lastly, there is often an imperious something, which eludes me—a brutal overmastering power thrusting me back into myself, so to speak, and commanding my nerves and muscles—evil actions or words I regret, a cuff or a curse.

I know, I know! Everybody feels those unreflecting movements, and always has felt them, but the reason has become obscure and mysterious to me.

It is called fever, anger, want of thought—just as customs or decorum are called calculation, hypocrisy or diplomacy. This is the way people account for these sudden revelations, which I have noted so often in my fellow-creatures, and which the world says, can only be failures to comply with those great powers, or revolts against them.

Might not the science of a wizard be the real prime cause?

Clearly the mental stage in which I am is exhausting me, and requires treatment. Now, it is kept alive by the obsession of the fateful time I spent at Fonval. That is why, since my return, realizing that I must rid myself of the remembrance of it, I have resolved to test myself by telling the story—not, Good Heavens! with any ambition to write a book, but in the hope that if one put it down on paper, it would get out of my head, and that to put it down would be to drive it away.

That is not the case, far from it. I have just lived it again, and with more reality as I told the story, and some mysterious power or other has sometimes forced me to put in a word or phrase against my own intentions.

I have failed in my aim. I must try to forget this nightmare, and suppress even trifles that might make me think of it.

I must sell Fonval and all the furniture. I must live, live in my own personality—however ridiculous, foolish or extravagant the original may be—independent, and without suggestions, and free—free from memories.

Those abominations, I swear, are now crossing my brain for the last time. I write this down to heighten the solemnity of my oath.

And you, you criminal manuscript, you, who would perpetuate beings and facts when I should refuse to admit that they have existed—into the fire with you, "Dr. Lerne"!

Into the fire...!

**The End**

# WHAT?

*These miniature bicycle-like skates actually required pedaling.*
*What a cool fella, eh?*
*Photo from November 1910.*

# READING BREAK!!!

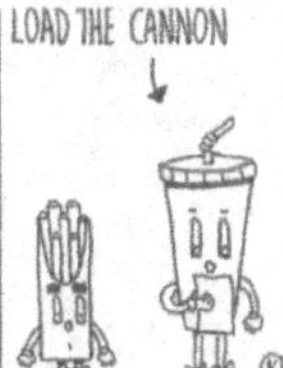

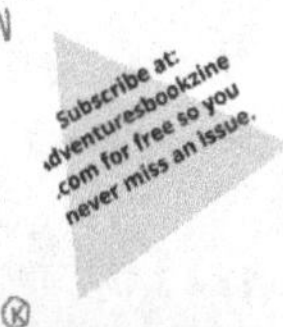




## SUDOKU

(MEDIUM DIFFICULTY; ANSWERS IN BACK OF BOOK)

|   |   |   | 6 | 1 |   |   |   |   |
|---|---|---|---|---|---|---|---|---|
|   | 7 |   |   |   |   |   |   |   |
| 3 |   | 8 | 5 |   |   |   |   |   |
|   | 2 |   |   |   | 8 |   |   | 5 |
|   | 8 |   |   |   |   | 4 |   | 3 |
| 1 |   | 4 |   |   |   |   |   |   |
| 4 |   |   | 2 | 3 | 5 |   |   | 7 |
| 7 |   |   |   | 9 |   |   | 1 |   |
|   |   | 9 |   |   |   |   |   |   |

> "Crisis is the rallying cry
> of the tyrant."
> -James Madison

*Explore the Books at*

# flick-it-books.com
**Small Independant Publishing House**

# R.RIVETER.
AMERICAN ★ HANDMADE

**Want your short
story published in
*Adventures*?**

Email your entire story, with
"Submission" in Subject to:
OffBeatReads@pm.me

# TWAS THE DAY BEFORE CHRISTMAS

## BY KYLE OWENS

*A New Original Story*

*From the author of the Vegas Chantly Mysteries*

Rhonda Miller was asleep in bed with her husband whom was snoring loudly beside her when she was brought awake by the blaring sound of the alarm clock. She reached over to turn it off, but couldn't find it.

Rhonda sleepily rose up and looked in the regular place for the alarm clock on the nightstand beside the lamp, but it wasn't there. Though she could hear it blaring about the room, it sounded muffled and distant. She turned the lamp on then followed the electrical cord that was attached to the clock to where it was under the bed.

She got out of bed then crawled under it and shut the alarm off. She came back out from beneath the bed, leaned her back up against the bed and stared at the clock in her hands.

"How in the world did you get under the bed?"

That's when she heard her husband, Bill, asking for her. "Honey, where did you go?"

"I'm down here."

"Down where?"

"In the floor."

Bill scooted over to the edge of the bed and saw his wife through squinted eyes sitting in the floor holding the alarm clock with her back rested against the side of the bed.

"Why are you in the floor at six o'clock in the morning on Christmas Eve?"

"I had to turn off the alarm clock."

"You couldn't do that from the bed?"

"It was under the bed."

"What was under the bed?"

Rhonda scooted around to face her husband. "The alarm clock was under the bed. Why would it be under the bed?"

Bill stared at her before slowly falling back to sleep.

Rhonda began poking at him. "Bill, honey, you have to get up."

"But I don't want to," said Bill into the pillow sounding like a six-year-old that didn't want to go to school. "It's Christmas Eve. I shouldn't have to work on Christmas Eve."

"But you have to go in today until two."

Bill raised his head off the pillow. "What day of the week is it?"

"Thursday."

He slowly digested this bit of information. "This Thursday or next Thursday?"

"It's this Thursday."

"Do you have to go into work today?"

"No. I'm off until after New Year's. Being a teacher has its advantages."

"It's not fair," Bill said as he rested on his right elbow and rubbed his face with his left hand in an attempt to wake himself up.

"Maybe since its Christmas Eve it won't be too bad. You do get off at two."

"I guess. I better get up."

As soon as Bill started to get out of bed the bedroom door slammed opened and their seven-year-old daughter, Adie, came running inside wearing her *Spongebob Squarepants Pajamas*, jumped onto the bed and straddled Bill.

"Tiger's gone!" she said in a frenzy of fear.

"What?"

"Tiger's gone!" Adie stated again. "I went out to feed him and he's gone!"

"You went out to feed him at this hour?" asked Rhonda.

"Mom, don't scold me now when I'm going through a childhood trauma. We have to find Tiger!"

"I'm sure he's not gotten far," Bill assured her as he dozed back to sleep.

"Did you not shut the door to the kennel?"

"Yes. I know I did. I just know it. I think."

"Well, dogs are crazy people. He's probably around the yard," suggested Rhonda.

"But I looked under the porch and down by the creek and he's not there."

"You've been under the porch this morning?" asked Rhonda.

"I had to try and find him. We have to go look for him," Adie said as she tried to pull Bill out of the bed.

Bill woke up in a bit of a stupor. "Why am I moving?"

"You're going to help me find Tiger."

"I can't go look for him now, baby. I have to go to work."

"But he's out there somewhere lost. If I was lost, would you come looking for me?"

"As soon as I got off from work," kidded Bill as he kissed his daughter on the forehead.

"Maybe I can help you find him," volunteered Rhonda.

Adie looked over at her mother with a confused look on her face. "Why are you in the floor?"

"I wanted to try something new."

Adie stared at her mother for a moment then turned back to her father and began pleading again. "You have to help me find Tiger."

"Honey, I have to go to work now. I'll help you find him when I get back."

"But that'll be too late. Something could have happened to him by then."

Rhonda said, "Uh, yoo hoo- I can help you find him. I don't have to go to work today."

Adie said, "But you can't find him."

"What makes you think that?"

"You'll be too tired from sleeping on the floor all night."

"I didn't sleep on the floor last night."

"Then why are you in the floor now?"

"I had to turn off the alarm clock."

Adie rolled her eyes. "Oh, that clears everything up." She then turned back to her father where she stood up, grabbed his right hand and tried to pull him up out of bed. "Come on, dad. We have to find him."

Rhonda then got up off the floor and pulled Adie off the bed then stood her on the floor. "Here's what we'll do. You'll go get dressed, I'll fix breakfast and see your daddy off to work then you and I will go looking for Tiger. Deal?"

"I don't have time to eat!" shouted Adie. "I have to find Tiger. Would you eat breakfast before you came looking for me if I was lost?"

"Well, it is the most important meal of the day," said Rhonda to which Bill laughed and Adie didn't.

"Now we'll find Tiger," assured Rhonda as she ushered Adie out the door. "Get dressed and I'll hurry and get breakfast ready."

Rhonda turned to Bill. "I guess I'll not be sleeping late this morning."

"Welcome to motherhood," said Bill before he fell asleep and began snoring.

Fifteen minutes later Adie was in her chair at the kitchen table gulping down her cereal in giant spoonsful as Bill leisurely drank his coffee and ate some toast. Rhonda got some orange juice from the refrigerator and sat down across from Bill.

"Slow down, Adie," Rhonda instructed. "You're going to get choked."

"Igghg lrrgh to grbh Tggher," Adie replied with a mouthful of cereal.

"You can't find him if you get choked."

Adie finished her cereal then left the kitchen table in a rush of activity.

Bill looked at Rhonda and asked, "You understood what she just said?"

"She said she had to hurry so she can find Tiger."

"Hmm- mothers are amazing," mused Bill as he finished his last bite of toast and the final sip of coffee.

Rhonda looked at the cereal box. "What kind of prize came in this?"

"Prize?"

"When my father was little, he would always get a prize in his cereal of some sort. He always got the cereal with baseball cards in them. This one doesn't have anything except sugar. Kids are missing out on so much today."

"When my mom was little, they used to get a box of detergent and it would have a six-ounce glass inside."

"That's kind of amazing."

"Of course, on the side of the box it read that the detergent was harmful if swallowed so they put a glass in it so you can drink out of it. I have to admit that sounds like strange marketing to me."

"Well, people were tougher back then. They could eat a whole box of detergent and it wouldn't even faze them."

"True. Well, I guess I better go."

Bill stood up as Rhonda stood up with him. They wrapped their arms around one another as she asked, "Are you sure you got all your Christmas shopping done?"

"I'm sure. I think."

They kissed.

"Ooo, gross," said Adie with an armful of papers, staple gun and a roll of packing tape clutched in her hands.

"Be quiet, mommy's working here."

"Mom, we have to go find Tiger."

"You need to stop worrying about Tiger," Rhonda said. "He'll be back."

"How do you know that?" asked Adie.

"Because we feed him," answered Rhonda. "Dogs always come back to where they can get free food. They're like men."

Bill laughed then kissed his wife again. "I'm off to work. I'll get off at two so depending upon Christmas Eve traffic I should be back between two-thirty and three."

"Okay. Bye."

He walked over to Adie, kissed her on the head then told her, "You'll find Tiger. Your mom is very good at finding things. Don't ask me how I know that. See you this evening."

Bill left and Rhonda turned toward Adie who stood staring at her with an impatient look on her face.

"Okay," said Rhonda. "We'll go looking for Tiger. What do you have in your hands?"

"I made copies of the last photo I took of Tiger so we can hang them up all over town."

Rhonda took one of the copies and looked at it. "Nice photo. Where did you take it at?"

"I took it in the park by the big tree next to the swings after I went to the bathroom in the woods."

"You did what?" asked Rhonda in horror.

"I had to go. If you try and hold it you could pop something. Do you want me to pop something?"

"No," Rhonda said as she stared at all the papers in her daughter's hands. "Just how many of these copies did you make?"

"Until it said we needed a new printer cartridge."

"I just put in a new cartridge yesterday."

"Me and Tiger thank you for it too."

Rhonda looked at the photocopy again when she became shocked at what she saw. "This says a reward of one hundred dollars. Why did you put a reward on it for?"

"That's how the FBI gets information. Don't you ever watch TV?"

"You should have asked before you put the one hundred dollars on here."

"You were busy."

"I would have gotten unbusy for one hundred dollars. Why did you make so many copies for?"

"We have to hang them up all over town. Do you know how big our town is? Well, I know and it's big."

"We don't have to go all over town. We'll just look in the neighborhood. I'm sure he hasn't gotten far."

Adie shook her head in disbelief. "We have to look everywhere. He's my best friend. You know we wouldn't have lost Tiger if you let me keep him in the house."

"I don't want dogs in the house. They make too big of a mess and you have to potty train them and everything."

"That's what dog owners are for. We have to train our dogs to fit into society."

"Dogs are meant to stay outside so they can go to the bathroom outside."

"You potty trained me."

"I apparently didn't do it very well if you're going in the woods down at the park."

Rhonda's cellphone rang to the tune of *Joy to the World*.

"Ah man, we're never going to get out of here to find Tiger," said Adie in frustration.

Rhonda picked the phone up off the table and stared at the screen. "It's your grandmother."

"Tell her we have to go find Tiger."

"That's not going to make your grandmother go away. You'll need a cross and holy water. Hello?"

"Hi, baby."

"Is anything wrong?"

"I was wondering how do you unsend an email?"

"What?"

"How do you unsend an email?"

"You can't. Once you send it then it's done. You can't take it back or unsend it."

There was a moment of silence on the phone. "Hmm- so it's like firing a gun then."

Rhonda was taken aback by her comment. "I guess."

"I'm going to be in for a few interesting days then."

"Listen, mom I have to go. Tiger's missing and I have to go with Adie to look for him now or she's going to tie me up and put me in the closet."

"Okay. I hope you find him."

"I'm sure he hasn't gotten far."

"How are Bill and Adie doing?"

"They're fine. I'll talk to you later."

"Are you doing, okay?"

"Yeah, I'm okay. I'll call you later."

"I'm fine too except for that email thing. Aren't you curious about what it's about?"

Adie began pacing as her mother tried to get off the phone. "Not right now. I'll call you when I get back. Will you be at this number or do I call the prison?"

"I'll not know until this evening."

"Bye, mom. I love you most of the time."

"Same here."

Rhonda hung up the phone, slid it in her pocket and looked at Adie whom looked as if she was about to burst in anger.

"We can go now."

Adie marched outside leaving the door opened as Rhonda got her coat and walked out closing the door behind her.

Adie stood at the SUV when Rhonda came out into the cold overcast morning. Rhonda asked her daughter, "What are you doing?"

"I thought we were going to look for Tiger in the car?"

"We'll just walk around the neighborhood."

"But we can cover more ground by taking the beast."

Adie's statement surprised Rhonda. "The beast?"

"That's what dad calls your SUV."

"It's not a beast. I would call it more of a Mabel."

"Mabel?"

"I had an Aunty Mabel and she was always going out on grand adventures and far away travels."

"Well, I think we should take Aunty Mabel then because she sounds like she would eventually leave the yard so we can find Tiger."

"Mabel needs her rest. Now let's just begin at the beginning."

"I can't begin at the beginning because I don't even know your Aunty Mabel."

"No. Leave Aunty Mabel out of this. Just tell me what you did the last time you saw Tiger."

"I put him in his cage behind the garage."

"It's his kennel. Calling it a cage makes us sound like villains in a Charles Dickens novel."

"It's a cage to Tiger. We're like bad circus people. No wonder he ran away."

"When I was little, I thought about running away to the circus."

"Where you going to be a circus freak?"

Rhonda was startled by her daughter's comment. "No, I wasn't going to be a circus freak. What makes you think that?"

Adie just humped her shoulders and the two of them stood in silence for a moment.

"I wanted to be the tightrope walker, but I was afraid of heights. I was also afraid of clowns, but was very interested in lions. I wonder why I would be afraid of clowns and not lions?"

"Can we get back to my childhood trauma now and deal with yours later?" asked Adie.

"That's fair. Let's go check the kennel."

Adie rolled her eyes. "He's not there, mom. I already checked."

"This is how all detectives begin their cases. They start at the beginning then work their way out into the neighborhood toward the commercial break."

"We're not detectives. Right now, we're barely people."

"What makes you say that?"

"People would be worried more about their lost dog. They wouldn't be standing by a vehicle named after their Aunty talking about their circus fantasies!"

Adie stomped off around to the back of the garage grasping her photocopies, stapler and tape.

Rhonda watched her daughter walk away when she mumbled, "You're supposed to be full of sugar and spice and everything nice."

They arrived behind the garage and the gate to the dog kennel was opened. "Is this

how you found it?" Rhonda asked.

"Yeah, he must have used his nose to push up on this thingy right here or whatever it's called. What's it called?"

"I call it a thingy too. We should get a padlock to put on it so he can't do that."

"How did he learn to do that to start with?"

"Yellow labs are very smart animals. He just watched how we opened it then he started doing it."

"But where would he go?" asked Adie with tears in her eyes.

Rhonda knelt down to try to console her daughter. "We'll find him. You don't have to get this upset about it. Dogs run off all the time. It's in their nature."

"But I don't want to lose him."

"Technically we already have."

"Mom, don't say things like that," said Adie as she tried to keep from crying.

"Don't get upset. I was just trying to lighten the mood. I guess I don't fully understand your attachment to Tiger is all."

"Didn't you have a dog when you were little?"

"No. When I was eight, I asked my parents for a pony. Do you know what they got me?"

"What?"

"A bow and arrow set."

Adie looked at her mother with a confused look on her face. "Why did they get you that for?"

"They're Presbyterian. But they got it for me so I thought I'd try it out. So, I took

the target that was on the back of the box and placed it in the yard then marched off twenty steps, aimed the arrow and let her fly."

"Did you hit the box?"

"I overshot the box by about twenty feet and shot the tire out on the wheel barrow."

"What did you parents say?"

"They said take that bow and arrow set away from her before she kills somebody. Then they took my bow and arrow set away and I never got to play with it again. That was one strange birthday."

"Are we going to look for Tiger now or take you to a psychiatrist to discuss your childhood?"

"A psychiatrist can't help me now; I'm too far gone. Now when you let Tiger out of his pen where does he usually go?"

Adie looked about. "I guess the first thing he does is jump on me then he runs back and forth in the yard like he wants to play. So, I play with him. He has a tennis ball I throw and he runs and gets it then buries it in various places."

"That's where those holes are coming from. I thought we had moles."

"What's a mole?"

"It's like a mouse, but its pronounced mole. They're little blind critters that live under the ground."

"They're blind? That's sad."

"It's how they're made. They burrow underground all the time so they don't need eyes."

"How do they play catch with their dog?"

"They don't have dogs."

"Why not?"

"Because you can't throw a tennis ball underground, it doesn't bounce right. I think we're really getting off track here."

"We've been off track since dad left."

"I kind of get the feeling that you wished your daddy was helping you find Tiger instead of me."

"You think?"

"I can do this. I'm a modern woman. I cook and clean- hmm, maybe I'm not as modern as I want to be."

"But you don't even like Tiger. You were against me getting him to start with.

Daddy was the one that went with me to get him. You kept saying, '*He has to stay outside! I don't want that dog in the house,*'" Adie said in a poor imitation of her mother.

"First of all, I don't talk like that. That's how my mother talks. Secondly- I have to admit that I've grown fond of Tiger. Well, until I found out he's the one digging holes in the yard."

"Are we doing this?"

"Yes. Now which way do you think he may have gone?"

Adie walked around to the front of the house and stood on the sidewalk at the edge of the yard where her mother followed. She gave her mother the copies, tape and stapler. She put her index finger in her mouth to wet it then held it out in front of her and motioned her arm from west to east. She then pointed east and said, "He went that way."

"What makes you think that?"

"In the summer that's the direction the Ice Cream truck comes. Tiger really likes ice cream. Of course, he was younger back then and more carefree."

"We all were. Why did you wet your finger for?"

"That's how I determine where something is that I've lost."

"I'll try that the next time I can't find the alarm clock."

The two of them silently looked east with some apprehension as if they were about to climb Mount Everest in flip flops.

"I guess we go that way then," said Rhonda.

"Well, come on woman," said Adie as she marched off.

"I get to be the mom now," said Rhonda as she reluctantly followed.

`Adie walked up to a telephone pole beside the sidewalk. "This looks like a good place to hang a flyer. Don't you think?"

"It looks as good as any other pole I suppose."

Adie took a flyer and her mother stapled it to the pole.

"Can you see it good?" asked Adie.

"Of course I can see it good."

"Have you ever seen a flyer like this before?"

"I see them all the time."

"Have you ever called the number on the flyer before?"

"Well, no."

Adie had tears form in her eyes as she looked down at the ground and struggled to get the words out. "We're not going to find him, are we?"

"We just started looking," said Rhonda as she hugged her daughter. "You have to stay positive. You shouldn't have any negative thoughts until you're married with kids. Now come on. We'll hang some more flyers up."

The two of them walked downtown when they came upon a convenience store. Adie looked at the large front window and told her mother, "We should hang a flyer on the window."

"I think it would be a good place, but we have to ask the store clerk first."

"Why?"

"Because it's the right thing to do."

"Well, you ask."

"Why would I ask?"

"Because I'm too shy."

"Shy? You went to the bathroom in the woods."

"Are you going to bring that up all the time now?"

"If it gives me an argumentative advantage then yes."

Adie rolled her eyes and headed into the store as her mother followed where they stood in line at the counter.

"Maybe you can get you a job here," whispered Rhonda to her daughter.

"I'm too young for a job."

"They used to make kids work in the coalmines back in the early twentieth century."

"They probably didn't get along with their parents either."

The customer in front of them left and they stood in front of the clerk.

"Hi, my daughter lost her dog and we wanted to know if we could hang this flyer in the window."

"Sure. But you have to buy something first," said the clerk in a deadpan voice.

"Buy something?" asked Rhonda as if she wasn't hearing him clearly.

"Yeah. You scratch my back and I'll scratch yours."

"They'll be no back scratching. I don't know where your back has been."

"It seems fair," said Adie.

"How's that fair?"

"You know, that back scratching thing. I'll take a candy bar." Adie took a *Mr. Goodbar* off the rack and placed it on the counter then added, "Can I have a *Mountain Dew* too?"

Rhonda looked at her daughter then the clerk. The clerk said, "Get this beautiful little girl a *Mountain Dew.*"

"Okay."

Adie got her drink; Rhonda paid the ransom and they walked over to the window and taped the flyer up.

Adie told her mother, "I'll go outside and see how it looks."

"Okay."

Adie went out and stood in front of the window. "It's not straight."

"We're hanging a flyer here not a Norman Rockwell painting. It'll be fine."

"I'll change it," said Adie as she started inside while holding her photocopies, tape and stapler in which her soda slipped out of her hands and bounced on the sidewalk. Rhonda quickly went to her daughter.

"I'll open it for you," said Rhonda as she picked the soda up, twisted the cap opened to which it spewed all over the place. Rhonda paid it no mind and took a drink.

"Why are you drinking my pop?"

"I paid for it so I get first drink," said Rhonda as she took the tape and stapler from her daughter's hands.

"Actually, the sidewalk got the first drink. Come on."

The two of them canvassed the city for several hours, but to no avail. Tiger was gone. The two stopped and sat on a park bench for a quick rest when snowflakes began falling from the sky and accumulated quickly on the ground.

"Looks like we might get us a white Christmas," observed Rhonda in hopes that it would cheer her daughter up, but it didn't. She then reluctantly added, "We need to get back home before it gets bad out."

"We can't go yet! We have to find Tiger!"

"Baby, we need to get back. We can't find him in the snow."

Adie looked down at the snow accumulating on the ground and began to cry. "I let him down. He's lost and alone waiting for me to find him and I didn't."

Rhonda put her arm around her daughter to help reassure her. "Everything will be okay."

"I can't believe I'm crying."

"Tiger is your little buddy. I understand."

"Dad would be ashamed of me for crying."

"What? No, he wouldn't."

"I saw him hit his finger with a hammer and he didn't cry. He didn't even use any

pirate language."

"Pirate language?"

"Bad words."

"Oh. Well, he probably didn't want to use pirate language because you were there with him."

"Do men cry?"

"Of course they do."

"I've never seen a man cry. Where do they go when they cry?"

"Wrigley Field."

The two of them got up off the bench and headed back home. As they approached their driveway Tiger came running up to them barking and Adie's eyes lit up like a Christmas tree.

"He came back!" shouted Adie as Tiger began licking her in the face and she took off into the backyard with Tiger chasing after her.

Ron came outside and met Rhonda.

"You're early," said Rhonda as she wrapped her arm around his waist.

"The office let us go early today. Tiger was here when I got back. I guess that means you wasted your Christmas Eve looking for a lost dog that wasn't lost."

"It wasn't a waste of time nor did it feel like Christmas Eve. It was more like Mother's Day."

The two of them then went inside as the snow began to blanket the ground and church bells could be heard in the distance.

End.

From 1895
# "Purple Cow"

A Poem by Gelett Burgess

*I never saw a Purple Cow,*
*I never hope to see one;*
*But I can tell you, anyhow,*
*I'd rather see than be one.*

# A STORY OF THE DAYS TO COME

## BY H.G. WELLS

# I

## THE CURE FOR LOVE

The excellent Mr. Morris was an Englishman, and he lived in the days of Queen Victoria the Good. He was a prosperous and very sensible man; he read the Times and went to church, and as he grew towards middle age an expression of quiet contented contempt for all who were not as himself settled on his face. He was one of those people who do everything that is right and proper and sensible with inevitable regularity. He always wore just the right and proper clothes, steering the narrow way between the smart and the shabby, always subscribed to the right charities, just the judicious compromise between ostentation and meanness, and never failed to have his hair cut to exactly the proper length.

Everything that it was right and proper for a man in his position to possess, he possessed; and everything that it was not right and proper for a man in his position to possess, he did not possess.

And among other right and proper possessions, this Mr. Morris had a wife and children. They were the right sort of wife, and the right sort and number of children, of course; nothing imaginative or highty-flighty about any of them, so far as Mr. Morris could see; they wore perfectly correct clothing, neither smart nor hygienic nor faddy in any way, but just sensible; and they lived in a nice sensible house in the later Victorian sham Queen Anne style of architecture, with sham half-timbering of chocolate-painted plaster in the gables, Lincrusta Walton sham carved oak panels, a terrace of terra cotta to imitate stone, and cathedral glass in the front door. His boys went to good solid schools, and were put to respectable professions; his girls, in spite of a fantastic protest or so, were all married to suitable, steady, oldish young men with good prospects. And when it was a fit and proper thing for him to do so, Mr. Morris died. His tomb was of marble, and, without any art nonsense or laudatory inscription, quietly imposing— such being the fashion of his time.

He underwent various changes according to the accepted custom in these cases, and long before this story begins his bones even had become dust, and were scattered to the four quarters of heaven. And his sons and his grandsons and his great-grandsons and his great-great-grandsons, they too were dust and ashes, and were scattered likewise. It was a thing he could not have imagined, that a day would come when even his great-great-grandsons would be scattered to the four winds of heaven. If any one had suggested it to him he would have resented it. He was one of those worthy people who take no interest in the future of mankind at all. He had grave doubts, indeed, if there was any future for mankind after he was dead.

It seemed quite impossible and quite uninteresting to imagine anything happening after he was dead. Yet the thing was so, and when even his great-great-grandson was dead and decayed and forgotten, when the sham half-timbered house had gone the way of all shams, and the Times was extinct, and the silk hat a ridiculous antiquity, and the modestly imposing stone that had been sacred to Mr. Morris had been burnt to make lime for mortar, and all that Mr. Morris had found real and important was sere and dead, the world was still going on, and people were still going about it, just as heedless and impatient of the Future, or, indeed, of anything but their own selves and property, as Mr. Morris had been.

And, strange to tell, and much as Mr. Morris would have been angered if any one had foreshadowed it to him, all over the world there were scattered a multitude of people, filled with the breath of life, in whose veins the blood of Mr. Morris flowed. Just as some day the life which is gathered now in the reader of this very story may also be scattered far and wide about this world, and mingled with a thousand alien strains, beyond all thought and tracing.

And among the descendants of this Mr. Morris was one almost as sensible and clear-headed as his ancestor. He had just the same stout, short frame as that ancient man of the nineteenth century, from whom his name of Morris—he spelt it Mwres—came; he had the same half-contemptuous expression of face. He was a prosperous person, too, as times went, and he disliked the "new-fangled," and bothers about the future and the lower classes, just as much as the ancestral Morris had done. He did not read the Times: indeed, he did not know there ever had been a Times—that institution had foundered somewhere in the intervening gulf of years; but the phonograph machine, that talked to him as he made his toilet of a morning, might have been the voice of a reincarnated Blowitz when it dealt with the world's affairs. This phonographic machine was the size and shape of a Dutch clock, and down the front of it were electric barometric indicators, and an electric clock and calendar, and automatic engagement reminders, and where the clock would have been was the mouth of a trumpet. When it had news the trumpet gobbled like a turkey, "Galloop, galloop," and then brayed out its message as, let us say, a trumpet might bray. It would tell Mwres in full, rich, throaty tones about the overnight accidents to the omnibus flying-machines that plied around the world, the latest arrivals at the fashionable resorts in Tibet, and of all the great monopolist company meetings of the day before, while he was dressing. If Mwres did not like hearing what it said, he had only to touch a stud, and it would choke a little and talk about something else.

Of course his toilet differed very much from that of his ancestor. It is doubtful which would have been the more shocked and pained to find himself in the clothing of the other. Mwres would certainly have sooner gone forth to the world stark naked than in the silk hat, frock coat, grey trousers and watch-chain that had filled Mr. Morris with sombre self-respect in the past. For Mwres there was no shaving to do: a skilful operator had long ago removed every hair-root from his face. His legs he encased in pleasant pink and amber garments of an air-tight material, which with the help of an ingenious little pump he distended so as to suggest enormous muscles. Above this he also wore pneumatic garments beneath an amber silk tunic, so that he was clothed in air and admirably protected against sudden extremes of heat or cold. Over this he flung a scarlet cloak with its edge fantastically curved. On his head, which had been skilfully deprived of every scrap of hair, he adjusted a pleasant little cap of bright scarlet, held on by suction and inflated with hydrogen, and curiously like the comb of a cock. So his toilet was complete; and, conscious of being soberly and becomingly attired, he was ready to face his fellow-beings with a tranquil eye.

This Mwres—the civility of "Mr." had vanished ages ago—was one of the officials under the Wind Vane and Waterfall Trust, the great company that owned every wind wheel and waterfall in the world, and which pumped all the water and supplied all the electric energy that people in these latter days required. He lived in a vast hotel near that part of London called Seventh Way, and had very large and comfortable apartments on the seventeenth floor. Households and family life had long since disappeared with the progressive refinement of manners; and indeed the steady rise in rents and land values, the disappearance of domestic servants, the elaboration of cookery, had rendered the separate domicile of Victorian times impossible, even had any one desired such a savage seclusion. When his toilet was completed he went towards one of the two doors of his apartment—there were doors at opposite ends, each marked with a huge arrow pointing one one way and one the other—touched a stud to open it, and emerged on a wide passage, the centre of which bore chairs and was moving at a steady pace to the left. On some of these chairs were seated gaily-dressed men and women. He nodded to an acquaintance—it was not in those days etiquette to talk before breakfast—and seated himself on one of these chairs, and in a few seconds he had been carried to the doors of a lift, by which he descended to the great and splendid hall in which his breakfast would be automatically served.

It was a very different meal from a Victorian breakfast. The rude masses of bread needing to be carved and smeared over with animal fat before they could be made palatable, the still recognisable fragments of recently killed animals, hideously charred and hacked, the eggs torn ruthlessly from beneath some protesting hen,—such things as these, though they constituted the ordinary fare of Victorian times, would have awakened only horror and disgust in the refined minds of the people of these latter days. Instead were pastes and cakes of agreeable and variegated design, without any suggestion in colour or form of the unfortunate animals from which their substance and juices were derived. They appeared on little dishes sliding out upon a rail from a little box at one side of the table. The surface of the table, to judge by touch and eye, would have appeared to a nineteenth-century person to be covered with fine white damask, but this was really an oxidised metallic surface, and could be cleaned instantly after a meal. There were hundreds of such little tables in the hall, and at most of them were other latter-day citizens singly or in groups. And as Mwres seated himself before his elegant repast, the invisible orchestra, which had been resting during an interval, resumed and filled the air with music.

But Mwres did not display any great interest either in his breakfast or the music; his eye wandered incessantly about the hall, as though he expected a belated guest. At last he rose eagerly and waved his hand, and simultaneously across the hall appeared a tall dark figure in a costume of yellow and olive green. As this person, walking amidst the tables with measured steps, drew near, the pallid earnestness of his face and the unusual intensity of his eyes became apparent. Mwres reseated himself and pointed to a chair beside him.

"I feared you would never come," he said. In spite of the intervening space of time, the English language was still almost exactly the same as it had been in England under Victoria the Good. The invention of the phonograph and suchlike means of recording sound, and the gradual replacement of books by such contrivances, had not only saved the human eyesight from decay, but had also by the establishment of a sure standard arrested the process of change in accent that had hitherto been so inevitable.

"I was delayed by an interesting case," said the man in green and yellow. "A prominent politician—ahem!—suffering from overwork." He glanced at the breakfast and seated himself. "I have been awake for forty hours."

"Eh dear!" said Mwres: "fancy that! You hypnotists have your work to do."

The hypnotist helped himself to some attractive amber-coloured jelly. "I happen to be a good deal in request," he said modestly.

"Heaven knows what we should do without you."

"Oh! we're not so indispensable as all that," said the hypnotist, ruminating the flavour of the jelly. "The world did very well without us for some thousands of years. Two hundred years ago even—not one! In practice, that is. Physicians by the thousand, of course—frightfully clumsy brutes for the most part, and following one another like sheep—but doctors of the mind, except a few empirical flounderers there were none."

He concentrated his mind on the jelly.

"But were people so sane—?" began Mwres.

The hypnotist shook his head. "It didn't matter then if they were a bit silly or faddy. Life was so easy-going then. No competition worth speaking of—no pressure. A human being had to be very lopsided before anything happened. Then, you know, they clapped 'em away in what they called a lunatic asylum."

"I know," said Mwres. "In these confounded historical romances that every one is listening to, they always rescue a beautiful girl from an asylum or something of the sort. I don't know if you attend to that rubbish."

"I must confess I do," said the hypnotist. "It carries one out of oneself to hear of those quaint, adventurous, half-civilised days of the nineteenth century, when men were stout and women simple. I like a good swaggering story before all things. Curious times they were, with their smutty railways and puffing old iron trains, their rum little houses and their horse vehicles. I suppose you don't read books?"

"Dear, no!" said Mwres, "I went to a modern school and we had none of that old-fashioned nonsense. Phonographs are good enough for me."

"Of course," said the hypnotist, "of course"; and surveyed the table for his next choice. "You know," he said, helping himself to a dark blue confection that promised well, "in those days our business was scarcely thought of. I daresay if any one had told them that in two hundred years' time a class of men would be entirely occupied in impressing things upon the memory, effacing unpleasant ideas, controlling and overcoming instinctive but undesirable impulses, and so forth, by means of hypnotism, they would have refused to believe the thing possible. Few people knew that an order made during a mesmeric trance, even an order to forget or an order to desire, could be given so as to be obeyed after the trance was over. Yet there were men alive then who could have told them the thing was as absolutely certain to come about as—well, the transit of Venus."

"They knew of hypnotism, then?"

"Oh, dear, yes! They used it—for painless dentistry and things like that! This blue stuff is confoundedly good: what is it?"

"Haven't the faintest idea," said Mwres, "but I admit it's very good. Take some more."

The hypnotist repeated his praises, and there was an appreciative pause.

"Speaking of these historical romances," said Mwres, with an attempt at an easy, off-hand manner, "brings me—ah—to the matter I—ah—had in mind when I asked you—when I expressed a wish to see you." He paused and took a deep breath.

The hypnotist turned an attentive eye upon him, and continued eating.

"The fact is," said Mwres, "I have a—in fact a—daughter. Well, you know I have given her—ah—every educational advantage. Lectures—not a solitary lecturer of ability in the world but she has had a telephone direct, dancing, deportment, conversation, philosophy, art criticism ..." He indicated catholic culture by a gesture of his hand. "I had intended her to marry a very good friend of mine—Bindon of the Lighting Commission—plain little man, you know, and a bit unpleasant in some of his ways, but an excellent fellow really—an excellent fellow."

"Yes," said the hypnotist, "go on. How old is she?"

"Eighteen."

"A dangerous age. Well?"

"Well: it seems that she has been indulging in these historical romances—excessively. Excessively. Even to the neglect of her philosophy. Filled her mind with unutterable nonsense about soldiers who fight—what is it?—Etruscans?"

"Egyptians."

"Egyptians—very probably. Hack about with swords and revolvers and things—bloodshed galore—horrible!—and about young men on torpedo catchers who blow up—Spaniards, I fancy—and all sorts of irregular adventurers. And she has got it into her head that she must marry for Love, and that poor little Bindon—"

"I've met similar cases," said the hypnotist. "Who is the other young man?"

Mwres maintained an appearance of resigned calm. "You may well ask," he said. "He is"—and his voice sank with shame—"a mere attendant upon the stage on which the flying-machines from Paris alight. He has—as they say in the romances—good looks. He is quite young and very eccentric. Affects the antique—he can read and write! So can she. And instead of communicating by telephone, like sensible people, they write and deliver—what is it?"

"Notes?"

"No—not notes.... Ah—poems."

The hypnotist raised his eyebrows. "How did she meet him?"

"Tripped coming down from the flying-machine from Paris—and fell into his arms. The mischief was done in a moment!"

"Yes?"

"Well—that's all. Things must be stopped. That is what I want to consult you about. What must be done? What _can_ be done? Of course I'm not a hypnotist; my knowledge is limited. But you—?"

"Hypnotism is not magic," said the man in green, putting both arms on the table.

"Oh, precisely! But still—!"

"People cannot be hypnotised without their consent. If she is able to stand out against marrying Bindon, she will probably stand out against being hypnotised. But if once she can be hypnotised—even by somebody else—the thing is done."

"You can—?"

"Oh, certainly! Once we get her amenable, then we can suggest that she _must_ marry Bindon—that that is her fate; or that the young man is repulsive, and that when she sees him she will be giddy and faint, or any little thing of that sort. Or if we can get her into a sufficiently profound trance we can suggest that she should forget him altogether—"

"Precisely."

"But the problem is to get her hypnotised. Of course no sort of proposal or suggestion must come from you—because no doubt she already distrusts you in the matter."

The hypnotist leant his head upon his arm and thought.

"It's hard a man cannot dispose of his own daughter," said Mwres irrelevantly.

"You must give me the name and address of the young lady," said the hypnotist, "and any information bearing upon the matter. And, by the bye, is there any money in the affair?"

Mwres hesitated.

"There's a sum—in fact, a considerable sum—invested in the Patent Road Company. From her mother. That's what makes the thing so exasperating."

"Exactly," said the hypnotist. And he proceeded to cross-examine Mwres on the entire affair.

It was a lengthy interview.

And meanwhile "Elizebeth Mwres," as she spelt her name, or "Elizabeth Morris" as a nineteenth-century person would have put it, was sitting in a quiet waiting-place beneath the great stage upon which the flying-machine from Paris descended. And beside her sat her slender, handsome lover reading her the poem he had written that morning while on duty upon the stage. When he had finished they sat for a time in silence; and then, as if for their special entertainment, the great machine that had come flying through the air from America that morning rushed down out of the sky.

At first it was a little oblong, faint and blue amidst the distant fleecy clouds; and then it grew swiftly large and white, and larger and whiter, until they could see the separate tiers of sails, each hundreds of feet wide, and the lank body they supported, and at last even the swinging seats of the passengers in a dotted row. Although it was falling it seemed to them to be rushing up the sky, and over the roof-spaces of the city below its shadow leapt towards them. They heard the whistling rush of the air about it and its yelling siren, shrill and swelling, to warn those who were on its landing-stage of its arrival. And abruptly the note fell down a couple of octaves, and it had passed, and the sky was clear and void, and she could turn her sweet eyes again to Denton at her side.

Their silence ended; and Denton, speaking in a little language of broken English that was, they fancied, their private possession—though lovers have used such little languages since the world began—told her how they too would leap into the air one morning out of all the obstacles and difficulties about them, and fly to a sunlit city of delight he knew of in Japan, half-way about the world.

She loved the dream, but she feared the leap; and she put him off with "Some day, dearest one, some day," to all his pleading that it might be soon; and at last came a shrilling of whistles, and it was time for him to go back to his duties on the stage. They parted—as lovers have been wont to part for thousands of years. She walked down a passage to a lift, and so came to one of the streets of that latter-day London, all glazed in with glass from the weather, and with incessant moving platforms that went to all parts of the city. And by one of these she returned to her apartments in the Hotel for Women where she lived, the apartments that were in telephonic communication with all the best lecturers in the world. But the sunlight of the flying stage was in her heart, and the wisdom of all the best lecturers in the world seemed folly in that light.

She spent the middle part of the day in the gymnasium, and took her midday meal with two other girls and their common chaperone—for it was still the custom to have a chaperone in the case of motherless girls of the more prosperous classes. The chaperone had a visitor that day, a man in green and yellow, with a white face and vivid eyes, who talked amazingly. Among other things, he fell to praising a new historical romance that one of the great popular story-tellers of the day had just put forth. It was, of course, about the spacious times of Queen Victoria; and the author, among other pleasing novelties, made a little argument before each section of the story, in imitation of the chapter headings of the old-fashioned books: as for example, "How the Cabmen of Pimlico stopped the Victoria Omnibuses, and of the Great Fight in Palace Yard," and "How the Piccadilly Policeman was slain in the midst of his Duty." The man in green and yellow praised this innovation. "These pithy sentences," he said, "are admirable. They show at a glance those headlong, tumultuous times, when men and animals jostled in the filthy streets, and death might wait for one at every corner. Life was life then! How great the world must have seemed then! How marvellous! They were still parts of the world absolutely unexplored. Nowadays we have almost abolished wonder, we lead lives so trim and orderly that courage, endurance, faith, all the noble virtues seem fading from mankind."

And so on, taking the girls' thoughts with him, until the life they led, life in the vast and intricate London of the twenty-second century, a life interspersed with soaring excursions to every part of the globe, seemed to them a monotonous misery compared with the dædal past.

At first Elizabeth did not join in the conversation, but after a time the subject became so interesting that she made a few shy interpolations. But he scarcely seemed to notice her as he talked. He went on to describe a new method of entertaining people. They were hypnotised, and then suggestions were made to them so skilfully that they seemed to be living in ancient times again. They played out a little romance in the past as vivid as reality, and when at last they awakened they remembered all they had been through as though it were a real thing.

"It is a thing we have sought to do for years and years," said the hypnotist. "It is practically an artificial dream. And we know the way at last. Think of all it opens out to us—the enrichment of our experience, the recovery of adventure, the refuge it offers from this sordid, competitive life in which we live! Think!"

"And you can do that!" said the chaperone eagerly.

"The thing is possible at last," the hypnotist said. "You may order a dream as you wish."

The chaperone was the first to be hypnotised, and the dream, she said, was wonderful, when she came to again.

The other two girls, encouraged by her enthusiasm, also placed themselves in the hands of the hypnotist and had plunges into the romantic past. No one suggested that Elizabeth should try this novel entertainment; it was at her own request at last that she was taken into that land of dreams where there is neither any freedom of choice nor will....

And so the mischief was done.

One day, when Denton went down to that quiet seat beneath the flying stage, Elizabeth was not in her wonted place. He was disappointed, and a little angry. The next day she did not come, and the next also. He was afraid. To hide his fear from himself, he set to work to write sonnets for her when she should come again....

For three days he fought against his dread by such distraction, and then the truth was before him clear and cold, and would not be denied. She might be ill, she might be dead; but he would not believe that he had been betrayed. There followed a week of misery. And then he knew she was the only thing on earth worth having, and that he must seek her, however hopeless the search, until she was found once more.

He had some small private means of his own, and so he threw over his appointment on the flying stage, and set himself to find this girl who had become at last all the world to him. He did not know where she lived, and little of her circumstances; for it had been part of the delight of her girlish romance that he should know nothing of her, nothing of the difference of their station. The ways of the city opened before him east and west, north and south. Even in Victorian days London was a maze, that little London with its poor four millions of people; but the London he explored, the London of the twenty-second century, was a London of thirty million souls. At first he was energetic and headlong, taking time neither to eat nor sleep. He sought for weeks and months, he went through every imaginable phase of fatigue and despair, over-excitement and anger. Long after hope was dead, by the sheer inertia of his desire he still went to and fro, peering into faces and looking this way and that, in the incessant ways and lifts and passages of that interminable hive of men.

At last chance was kind to him, and he saw her.

It was in a time of festivity. He was hungry; he had paid the inclusive fee and had gone into one of the gigantic dining-places of the city; he was pushing his way among the tables and scrutinising by mere force of habit every group he passed.

He stood still, robbed of all power of motion, his eyes wide, his lips apart. Elizabeth sat scarcely twenty yards away from him, looking straight at him. Her eyes were as hard to him, as hard and expressionless and void of recognition, as the eyes of a statue.

She looked at him for a moment, and then her gaze passed beyond him.

Had he had only her eyes to judge by he might have doubted if it was indeed Elizabeth, but he knew her by the gesture of her hand, by the grace of a wanton little curl that floated over her ear as she moved her head. Something was said to her, and she turned smiling tolerantly to the man beside her, a little man in foolish raiment knobbed and spiked like some odd reptile with pneumatic horns—the Bindon of her father's choice.

For a moment Denton stood white and wild-eyed; then came a terrible faintness, and he sat before one of the little tables. He sat down with his back to her, and for a time he did not dare to look at her again. When at last he did, she and Bindon and two other people were standing up to go. The others were her father and her chaperone.

He sat as if incapable of action until the four figures were remote and small, and then he rose up possessed with the one idea of pursuit. For a space he feared he had lost them, and then he came upon Elizabeth and her chaperone again in one of the streets of moving platforms that intersected the city. Bindon and Mwres had disappeared.

He could not control himself to patience. He felt he must speak to her forthwith, or die. He pushed forward to where they were seated, and sat down beside them. His white face was convulsed with half-hysterical excitement.

He laid his hand on her wrist. "Elizabeth?" he said.

She turned in unfeigned astonishment. Nothing but the fear of a strange man showed in her face.

"Elizabeth," he cried, and his voice was strange to him: "dearest—you know me?"

Elizabeth's face showed nothing but alarm and perplexity. She drew herself away from him. The chaperone, a little grey-headed woman with mobile features, leant forward to intervene. Her resolute bright eyes examined Denton. "What do you say?" she asked.

"This young lady," said Denton,—"she knows me."

"Do you know him, dear?"

"No," said Elizabeth in a strange voice, and with a hand to her forehead, speaking almost as one who repeats a lesson. "No, I do not know him. I know—I do not know him."

"But—but ... Not know me! It is I—Denton. Denton! To whom you used to talk. Don't you remember the flying stages? The little seat in the open air? The verses—"

"No," cried Elizabeth,—"no. I do not know him. I do not know him. There is something.... But I don't know. All I know is that I do not know him." Her face was a face of infinite distress.

The sharp eyes of the chaperone flitted to and fro from the girl to the man. "You see?" she said, with the faint shadow of a smile. "She does not know you."

"I do not know you," said Elizabeth. "Of that I am sure."

"But, dear—the songs—the little verses—"

"She does not know you," said the chaperone. "You must not.... You have made a mistake. You must not go on talking to us after that. You must not annoy us on the public ways."

"But—" said Denton, and for a moment his miserably haggard face appealed against fate.

"You must not persist, young man," protested the chaperone.

"Elizabeth!" he cried.

Her face was the face of one who is tormented. "I do not know you," she cried, hand to brow. "Oh, I do not know you!"

For an instant Denton sat stunned. Then he stood up and groaned aloud.

He made a strange gesture of appeal towards the remote glass roof of the public way, then turned and went plunging recklessly from one moving platform to another, and vanished amidst the swarms of people going to and fro thereon. The chaperone's eyes followed him, and then she looked at the curious faces about her.

"Dear," asked Elizabeth, clasping her hand, and too deeply moved to heed observation, "who was that man? Who was that man?"

The chaperone raised her eyebrows. She spoke in a clear, audible voice. "Some half-witted creature. I have never set eyes on him before."

"Never?"

"Never, dear. Do not trouble your mind about a thing like this."

AND SOON AFTER THIS THE CELEBRATED HYPNOTIST WHO DRESSED IN GREEN and yellow had another client. The young man paced his consulting-room, pale and disordered. "I want to forget," he cried. "I must forget."

The hypnotist watched him with quiet eyes, studied his face and clothes and bearing. "To forget anything—pleasure or pain—is to be, by so much-less. However, you know your own concern. My fee is high."

"If only I can forget—"

"That's easy enough with you. You wish it. I've done much harder things. Quite recently. I hardly expected to do it: the thing was done against the will of the hypnotised person. A love affair too—like yours. A girl. So rest assured."

The young man came and sat beside the hypnotist. His manner was a forced calm. He looked into the hypnotist's eyes. "I will tell you. Of course you will want to know what it is. There was a girl. Her name was Elizabeth Mwres. Well ..."

He stopped. He had seen the instant surprise on the hypnotist's face. In that instant he knew. He stood up. He seemed to dominate the seated figure by his side. He gripped the shoulder of green and gold. For a time he could not find words.

"Give her me back!" he said at last. "Give her me back!"

"What do you mean?" gasped the hypnotist.

"Give her me back."

"Give whom?"

"Elizabeth Mwres—the girl—"

The hypnotist tried to free himself; he rose to his feet. Denton's grip tightened.

"Let go!" cried the hypnotist, thrusting an arm against Denton's chest.

In a moment the two men were locked in a clumsy wrestle. Neither had the slightest training—for athleticism, except for exhibition and to afford opportunity for betting, had faded out of the earth—but Denton was not only the younger but the stronger of the two. They swayed across the room, and then the hypnotist had gone down under his antagonist. They fell together....

Denton leaped to his feet, dismayed at his own fury; but the hypnotist lay still, and suddenly from a little white mark where his forehead had struck a stool shot a hurrying band of red. For a space Denton stood over him irresolute, trembling.

A fear of the consequences entered his gently nurtured mind. He turned towards the door. "No," he said aloud, and came back to the middle of the room. Overcoming the instinctive repugnance of one who had seen no act of violence in all his life before, he knelt down beside his antagonist and felt his heart. Then he peered at the wound. He rose quietly and looked about him. He began to see more of the situation.

When presently the hypnotist recovered his senses, his head ached severely, his back was against Denton's knees and Denton was sponging his face.

The hypnotist did not speak. But presently he indicated by a gesture that in his opinion he had been sponged enough. "Let me get up," he said.

"Not yet," said Denton.

"You have assaulted me, you scoundrel!"

"We are alone," said Denton, "and the door is secure."

There was an interval of thought.

"Unless I sponge," said Denton, "your forehead will develop a tremendous bruise."

"You can go on sponging," said the hypnotist sulkily.

There was another pause.

"We might be in the Stone Age," said the hypnotist. "Violence! Struggle!"

"In the Stone Age no man dared to come between man and woman," said Denton.

The hypnotist thought again.

"What are you going to do?" he asked.

"While you were insensible I found the girl's address on your tablets. I did not know it before. I telephoned. She will be here soon. Then—"

"She will bring her chaperone."

"That is all right."

"But what—? I don't see. What do you mean to do?"

"I looked about for a weapon also. It is an astonishing thing how few weapons there are nowadays. If you consider that in the Stone Age men owned scarcely anything but weapons. I hit at last upon this lamp. I have wrenched off the wires and things, and I hold it so." He extended it over the hypnotist's shoulders. "With that I can quite easily smash your skull. I will—unless you do as I tell you."

"Violence is no remedy," said the hypnotist, quoting from the "Modern Man's Book of Moral Maxims."

"It's an undesirable disease," said Denton.

"Well?"

"You will tell that chaperone you are going to order the girl to marry that knobby little brute with the red hair and ferrety eyes. I believe that's how things stand?"

"Yes—that's how things stand."

"And, pretending to do that, you will restore her memory of me."

"It's unprofessional."

"Look here! If I cannot have that girl I would rather die than not. I don't propose to respect your little fancies. If anything goes wrong you shall not live five minutes. This is a rude makeshift of a weapon, and it may quite conceivably be painful to kill you. But I will. It is unusual, I know, nowadays to do things like this—mainly because there is so little in life that is worth being violent about."

"The chaperone will see you directly she comes—"

"I shall stand in that recess. Behind you."

The hypnotist thought. "You are a determined young man," he said, "and only half civilised. I have tried to do my duty to my client, but in this affair you seem likely to get your own way...."

"You mean to deal straightly."

"I'm not going to risk having my brains scattered in a petty affair like this."

"And afterwards?"

"There is nothing a hypnotist or doctor hates so much as a scandal. I at least am no savage. I am annoyed.... But in a day or so I shall bear no malice...."

"Thank you. And now that we understand each other, there is no necessity to keep you sitting any longer on the floor."

# II

## THE VACANT COUNTRY

THE WORLD, THEY SAY, CHANGED MORE BETWEEN THE YEAR 1800 AND THE year 1900 than it had done in the previous five hundred years. That century, the nineteenth century, was the dawn of a new epoch in the history of mankind—the epoch of the great cities, the end of the old order of country life.

In the beginning of the nineteenth century the majority of mankind still lived upon the countryside, as their way of life had been for countless generations. All over the world they dwelt in little towns and villages then, and engaged either directly in agriculture, or in occupations that were of service to the agriculturist. They travelled rarely, and dwelt close to their work, because swift means of transit had not yet come. The few who travelled went either on foot, or in slow sailing-ships, or by means of jogging horses incapable of more than sixty miles a day. Think of it!—sixty miles a day. Here and there, in those sluggish times, a town grew a little larger than its neighbours, as a port or as a centre of government; but all the towns in the world with more than a hundred thousand inhabitants could be counted on a man's fingers. So it was in the beginning of the nineteenth century. By the end, the invention of railways, telegraphs, steamships, and complex agricultural machinery, had changed all these things: changed them beyond all hope of return. The vast shops, the varied pleasures, the countless conveniences of the larger towns were suddenly possible, and no sooner existed than they were brought into competition with the homely resources of the rural centres. Mankind were drawn to the cities by an overwhelming attraction. The demand for labour fell with the increase of machinery, the local markets were entirely superseded, and there was a rapid growth of the larger centres at the expense of the open country.

The flow of population townward was the constant preoccupation of Victorian writers. In Great Britain and New England, in India and China, the same thing was remarked: everywhere a few swollen towns were visibly replacing the ancient order. That this was an inevitable result of improved means of travel and transport—that, given swift means of transit, these things must be—was realised by few; and the most puerile schemes were devised to overcome the mysterious magnetism of the urban centres, and keep the people on the land.

Yet the developments of the nineteenth century were only the dawning of the new order. The first great cities of the new time were horribly inconvenient, darkened by smoky fogs, insanitary and noisy; but the discovery of new methods of building, new methods of heating, changed all this. Between 1900 and 2000 the march of change was still more rapid; and between 2000 and 2100 the continually accelerated progress of human invention made the reign of Victoria the Good seem at last an almost incredible vision of idyllic tranquil days.

The introduction of railways was only the first step in that development of those means of locomotion which finally revolutionised human life. By the year 2000 railways and roads had vanished together. The railways, robbed of their rails, had become weedy ridges and ditches upon the face of the world; the old roads, strange barbaric tracks of flint and soil, hammered by hand or rolled by rough iron rollers, strewn with miscellaneous filth, and cut by iron hoofs and wheels into ruts and puddles often many inches deep, had been replaced by patent tracks made of a substance called Eadhamite. This Eadhamite—it was named after its patentee—ranks with the invention of printing and steam as one of the epoch-making discoveries of the world's history.

When Eadham discovered the substance, he probably thought of it as a mere cheap substitute for india rubber; it cost a few shillings a ton. But you can never tell all an invention will do. It was the genius of a man named Warming that pointed to the possibility of using it, not only for the tires of wheels, but as a road substance, and who organised the enormous network of public ways that speedily covered the world.

These public ways were made with longitudinal divisions. On the outer on either side went foot cyclists and conveyances travelling at a less speed than twenty-five miles an hour; in the middle, motors capable of speed up to a hundred; and the inner, Warming (in the face of enormous ridicule) reserved for vehicles travelling at speeds of a hundred miles an hour and upward.

For ten years his inner ways were vacant. Before he died they were the most crowded of all, and vast light frameworks with wheels of twenty and thirty feet in diameter, hurled along them at paces that year after year rose steadily towards two hundred miles an hour. And by the time this revolution was accomplished, a parallel revolution had transformed the ever-growing cities. Before the development of practical science the fogs and filth of Victorian times vanished. Electric heating replaced fires (in 2013 the lighting of a fire that did not absolutely consume its own smoke was made an indictable nuisance), and all the city ways, all public squares and places, were covered in with a recently invented glass-like substance.

The roofing of London became practically continuous. Certain short-sighted and foolish legislation against tall buildings was abolished, and London, from a squat expanse of petty houses—feebly archaic in design—rose steadily towards the sky. To the municipal responsibility for water, light, and drainage, was added another, and that was ventilation.

But to tell of all the changes in human convenience that these two hundred years brought about, to tell of the long foreseen invention of flying, to describe how life in households was steadily supplanted by life in interminable hotels, how at last even those who were still concerned in agricultural work came to live in the towns and to go to and fro to their work every day, to describe how at last in all England only four towns remained, each with many millions of people, and how there were left no inhabited houses in all the countryside: to tell all this would take us far from our story of Denton and his Elizabeth. They had been separated and reunited, and still they could not marry. For Denton—it was his only fault—had no money. Neither had Elizabeth until she was twenty-one, and as yet she was only eighteen. At twenty-one all the property of her mother would come to her, for that was the custom of the time. She did not know that it was possible to anticipate her fortune, and Denton was far too delicate a lover to suggest such a thing. So things stuck hopelessly between them. Elizabeth said that she was very unhappy, and that nobody understood her but Denton, and that when she was away from him she was wretched; and Denton said that his heart longed for her day and night. And they met as often as they could to enjoy the discussion of their sorrows.

They met one day at their little seat upon the flying stage. The precise site of this meeting was where in Victorian times the road from Wimbledon came out upon the common. They were, however, five hundred feet above that point. Their seat looked far over London. To convey the appearance of it all to a nineteenth-century reader would have been difficult. One would have had to tell him to think of the Crystal Palace, of the newly built "mammoth" hotels—as those little affairs were called—of the larger railway stations of his time, and to imagine such buildings enlarged to vast proportions and run together and continuous over the whole metropolitan area. If then he was told that this continuous roof-space bore a huge forest of rotating wind-wheels, he would have begun very dimly to appreciate what to these young people was the commonest sight in their lives.

To their eyes it had something of the quality of a prison, and they were talking, as they had talked a hundred times before, of how they might escape from it and be at last happy together: escape from it, that is, before the appointed three years were at an end. It was, they both agreed, not only impossible but almost wicked, to wait three years. "Before that," said Denton—and the notes of his voice told of a splendid chest—"we might both be dead!"

Their vigorous young hands had to grip at this, and then Elizabeth had a still more poignant thought that brought the tears from her wholesome eyes and down her healthy cheeks. "One of us," she said, "one of us might be—"

She choked; she could not say the word that is so terrible to the young and happy.

Yet to marry and be very poor in the cities of that time was—for any one who had lived pleasantly—a very dreadful thing. In the old agricultural days that had drawn to an end in the eighteenth century there had been a pretty proverb of love in a cottage; and indeed in those days the poor of the countryside had dwelt in flower-covered, diamond-windowed cottages of thatch and plaster, with the sweet air and earth about them, amidst tangled hedges and the song of birds, and with the ever-changing sky overhead. But all this had changed (the change was already beginning in the nineteenth century), and a new sort of life was opening for the poor— in the lower quarters of the city.

In the nineteenth century the lower quarters were still beneath the sky; they were areas of land on clay or other unsuitable soil, liable to floods or exposed to the smoke of more fortunate districts, insufficiently supplied with water, and as insanitary as the great fear of infectious diseases felt by the wealthier classes permitted. In the twenty-second century, however, the growth of the city storey above storey, and the coalescence of buildings, had led to a different arrangement. The prosperous people lived in a vast series of sumptuous hotels in the upper storeys and halls of the city fabric; the industrial population dwelt beneath in the tremendous ground-floor and basement, so to speak, of the place.

In the refinement of life and manners these lower classes differed little from their ancestors, the East-enders of Queen Victoria's time; but they had developed a distinct dialect of their own. In these under ways they lived and died, rarely ascending to the surface except when work took them there. Since for most of them this was the sort of life to which they had been born, they found no great misery in such circumstances; but for people like Denton and Elizabeth, such a plunge would have seemed more terrible than death.

"And yet what else is there?" asked Elizabeth.

Denton professed not to know. Apart from his own feeling of delicacy, he was not sure how Elizabeth would like the idea of borrowing on the strength of her expectations.

The passage from London to Paris even, said Elizabeth, was beyond their means; and in Paris, as in any other city in the world, life would be just as costly and impossible as in London.

Well might Denton cry aloud: "If only we had lived in those days, dearest! If only we had lived in the past!" For to their eyes even nineteenth-century Whitechapel was seen through a mist of romance.

"Is there nothing?" cried Elizabeth, suddenly weeping. "Must we really wait for those three long years? Fancy three years—six-and-thirty months!" The human capacity for patience had not grown with the ages.

Then suddenly Denton was moved to speak of something that had already flickered across his mind. He had hit upon it at last. It seemed to him so wild a suggestion that he made it only half seriously. But to put a thing into words has ever a way of making it seem more real and possible than it seemed before. And so it was with him.

"Suppose," he said, "we went into the country?"

She looked at him to see if he was serious in proposing such an adventure.

"The country?"

"Yes—beyond there. Beyond the hills."

"How could we live?" she said. "Where could we live?"

"It is not impossible," he said. "People used to live in the country."

"But then there were houses."

"There are the ruins of villages and towns now. On the clay lands they are gone, of course. But they are still left on the grazing land, because it does not pay the Food Company to remove them. I know that—for certain. Besides, one sees them from the flying machines, you know. Well, we might shelter in some one of these, and repair it with our hands. Do you know, the thing is not so wild as it seems. Some of the men who go out every day to look after the crops and herds might be paid to bring us food...."

She stood in front of him. "How strange it would be if one really could...."

"Why not?"

"But no one dares."

"That is no reason."

"It would be—oh! it would be so romantic and strange. If only it were possible."

"Why not possible?"

"There are so many things. Think of all the things we have, things that we should miss."

"Should we miss them? After all, the life we lead is very unreal—very artificial." He began to expand his idea, and as he warmed to his exposition the fantastic quality of his first proposal faded away.

She thought. "But I have heard of prowlers—escaped criminals."

He nodded. He hesitated over his answer because he thought it sounded boyish. He blushed. "I could get some one I know to make me a sword."

She looked at him with enthusiasm growing in her eyes. She had heard of swords, had seen one in a museum; she thought of those ancient days when men wore them as a common thing. His suggestion seemed an impossible dream to her, and perhaps for that reason she was eager for more detail. And inventing for the most part as he went along, he told her, how they might live in the country as the old-world people had done. With every detail her interest grew, for she was one of those girls for whom romance and adventure have a fascination.

His suggestion seemed, I say, an impossible dream to her on that day, but the next day they talked about it again, and it was strangely less impossible.

"At first we should take food," said Denton. "We could carry food for ten or twelve days." It was an age of compact artificial nourishment, and such a provision had none of the unwieldy suggestion it would have had in the nineteenth century.

"But—until our house," she asked—"until it was ready, where should we sleep?"

"It is summer."

"But ... What do you mean?"

"There was a time when there were no houses in the world; when all mankind slept always in the open air."

"But for us! The emptiness! No walls—no ceiling!"

"Dear," he said, "in London you have many beautiful ceilings. Artists paint them and stud them with lights. But I have seen a ceiling more beautiful than any in London...."

"But where?"

"It is the ceiling under which we two would be alone...."

"You mean...?"

"Dear," he said, "it is something the world has forgotten. It is Heaven and all the host of stars."

Each time they talked the thing seemed more possible and more desirable to them. In a week or so it was quite possible. Another week, and it was the inevitable thing they had to do. A great enthusiasm for the country seized hold of them and possessed them. The sordid tumult of the town, they said, overwhelmed them. They marvelled that this simple way out of their troubles had never come upon them before.

One morning near Midsummer-day, there was a new minor official upon the flying stage, and Denton's place was to know him no more.

Our two young people had secretly married, and were going forth manfully out of the city in which they and their ancestors before them had lived all their days. She wore a new dress of white cut in an old-fashioned pattern, and he had a bundle of provisions strapped athwart his back, and in his hand he carried—rather shame-facedly it is true, and under his purple cloak—an implement of archaic form, a cross-hilted thing of tempered steel.

Imagine that going forth! In their days the sprawling suburbs of Victorian times with their vile roads, petty houses, foolish little gardens of shrub and geranium, and all their futile, pretentious privacies, had disappeared: the towering buildings of the new age, the mechanical ways, the electric and water mains, all came to an end together, like a wall, like a cliff, near four hundred feet in height, abrupt and sheer. All about the city spread the carrot, swede, and turnip fields of the Food Company, vegetables that were the basis of a thousand varied foods, and weeds and hedgerow tangles had been utterly extirpated. The incessant expense of weeding that went on year after year in the petty, wasteful and barbaric farming of the ancient days, the Food Company had economised for ever more by a campaign of extermination. Here and there, however, neat rows of bramble standards and apple trees with whitewashed stems, intersected the fields, and at places groups of gigantic teazles reared their favoured spikes. Here and there huge agricultural machines hunched under waterproof covers. The mingled waters of the Wey and Mole and Wandle ran in rectangular channels; and wherever a gentle elevation of the ground permitted a fountain of deodorised sewage distributed its benefits athwart the land and made a rainbow of the sunlight.

By a great archway in that enormous city wall emerged the Eadhamite road to Portsmouth, swarming in the morning sunshine with an enormous traffic bearing the blue-clad servants of the Food Company to their toil. A rushing traffic, beside which they seemed two scarce-moving dots. Along the outer tracks hummed and rattled the tardy little old-fashioned motors of such as had duties within twenty miles or so of the city; the inner ways were filled with vaster mechanisms—swift monocycles bearing a score of men, lank multicycles, quadricycles sagging with heavy loads, empty gigantic produce carts that would come back again filled before the sun was setting, all with throbbing engines and noiseless wheels and a perpetual wild melody of horns and gongs.

Along the very verge of the outermost way our young people went in silence, newly wed and oddly shy of one another's company. Many were the things shouted to them as they tramped along, for in 2100 a foot-passenger on an English road was almost as strange a sight as a motor car would have been in 1800. But they went on with steadfast eyes into the country, paying no heed to such cries.

Before them in the south rose the Downs, blue at first, and as they came nearer changing to green, surmounted by the row of gigantic wind-wheels that supplemented the wind-wheels upon the roof-spaces of the city, and broken and restless with the long morning shadows of those whirling vanes. By midday they had come so near that they could see here and there little patches of pallid dots—the sheep the Meat Department of the Food Company owned. In another hour they had passed the clay and the root crops and the single fence that hedged them in, and the prohibition against trespass no longer held: the levelled roadway plunged into a cutting with all its traffic, and they could leave it and walk over the greensward and up the open hillside.

Never had these children of the latter days been together in such a lonely place.

They were both very hungry and footsore—for walking was a rare exercise—and presently they sat down on the weedless, close-cropped grass, and looked back for the first time at the city from which they had come, shining wide and splendid in the blue haze of the valley of the Thames. Elizabeth was a little afraid of the unenclosed sheep away up the slope—she had never been near big unrestrained animals before—but Denton reassured her. And overhead a white-winged bird circled in the blue.

They talked but little until they had eaten, and then their tongues were loosened. He spoke of the happiness that was now certainly theirs, of the folly of not breaking sooner out of that magnificent prison of latter-day life, of the old romantic days that had passed from the world for ever. And then he became boastful. He took up the sword that lay on the ground beside him, and she took it from his hand and ran a tremulous finger along the blade.

"And you could," she said, "you—could raise this and strike a man?"

"Why not? If there were need."

"But," she said, "it seems so horrible. It would slash.... There would be"—her voice sank,—"blood."

"In the old romances you have read often enough ..."

"Oh, I know: in those—yes. But that is different. One knows it is not blood, but just a sort of red ink.... And you—killing!"

She looked at him doubtfully, and then handed him back the sword.

After they had rested and eaten, they rose up and went on their way towards the hills. They passed quite close to a huge flock of sheep, who stared and bleated at their unaccustomed figures. She had never seen sheep before, and she shivered to think such gentle things must needs be slain for food. A sheep-dog barked from a distance, and then a shepherd appeared amidst the supports of the wind-wheels, and came down towards them.

When he drew near he called out asking whither they were going.

Denton hesitated, and told him briefly that they sought some ruined house among the Downs, in which they might live together. He tried to speak in an off-hand manner, as though it was a usual thing to do. The man stared incredulously.

"Have you done anything?" he asked.

"Nothing," said Denton. "Only we don't want to live in a city any longer. Why should we live in cities?"

The shepherd stared more incredulously than ever. "You can't live here," he said.

"We mean to try."

The shepherd stared from one to the other. "You'll go back to-morrow," he said. "It looks pleasant enough in the sunlight.... Are you sure you've done nothing? We shepherds are not such great friends of the police."

Denton looked at him steadfastly. "No," he said. "But we are too poor to live in the city, and we can't bear the thought of wearing clothes of blue canvas and doing drudgery. We are going to live a simple life here, like the people of old."

The shepherd was a bearded man with a thoughtful face. He glanced at Elizabeth's fragile beauty.

"They had simple minds," he said.

"So have we," said Denton.

The shepherd smiled.

"If you go along here," he said, "along the crest beneath the wind-wheels, you will see a heap of mounds and ruins on your right-hand side. That was once a town called Epsom. There are no houses there, and the bricks have been used for a sheep pen. Go on, and another heap on the edge of the root-land is Leatherhead; and then the hill turns away along the border of a valley, and there are woods of beech. Keep along the crest. You will come to quite wild places. In some parts, in spite of all the weeding that is done, ferns and bluebells and other such useless plants are growing still. And through it all underneath the wind-wheels runs a straight lane paved with stones, a roadway of the Romans two thousand years old. Go to the right of that, down into the valley and follow it along by the banks of the river. You come presently to a street of houses, many with the roofs still sound upon them. There you may find shelter."

They thanked him.

"But it's a quiet place. There is no light after dark there, and I have heard tell of robbers. It is lonely. Nothing happens there. The phonographs of the story-tellers, the kinematograph entertainments, the news machines— none of them are to be found there. If you are hungry there is no food, if you are ill no doctor ..." He stopped.

"We shall try it," said Denton, moving to go on. Then a thought struck him, and he made an agreement with the shepherd, and learnt where they might find him, to buy and bring them anything of which they stood in need, out of the city.

And in the evening they came to the deserted village, with its houses that seemed so small and odd to them: they found it golden in the glory of the sunset, and desolate and still. They went from one deserted house to another, marvelling at their quaint simplicity, and debating which they should choose. And at last, in a sunlit corner of a room that had lost its outer wall, they came upon a wild flower, a little flower of blue that the weeders of the Food Company had overlooked.

That house they decided upon; but they did not remain in it long that night, because they were resolved to feast upon nature. And moreover the houses became very gaunt and shadowy after the sunlight had faded out of the sky. So after they had rested a little time they went to the crest of the hill again to see with their own eyes the silence of heaven set with stars, about which the old poets had had so many things to tell. It was a wonderful sight, and Denton talked like the stars, and when they went down the hill at last the sky was pale with dawn. They slept but little, and in the morning when they woke a thrush was singing in a tree.

So these young people of the twenty-second century began their exile. That morning they were very busy exploring the resources of this new home in which they were going to live the simple life. They did not explore very fast or very far, because they went everywhere hand-in-hand; but they found the beginnings of some furniture. Beyond the village was a store of winter fodder for the sheep of the Food Company, and Denton dragged great armfuls to the house to make a bed; and in several of the houses were old fungus-eaten chairs and tables—rough, barbaric, clumsy furniture, it seemed to them, and made of wood. They repeated many of the things they had said on the previous day, and towards evening they found another flower, a harebell. In the late afternoon some Company shepherds went down the river valley riding on a big multicycle; but they hid from them, because their presence, Elizabeth said, seemed to spoil the romance of this old-world place altogether.

In this fashion they lived a week. For all that week the days were cloudless, and the nights nights of starry glory, that were invaded each a little more by a crescent moon.

Yet something of the first splendour of their coming faded—faded imperceptibly day after day; Denton's eloquence became fitful, and lacked fresh topics of inspiration; the fatigue of their long march from London told in a certain stiffness of the limbs, and each suffered from a slight unaccountable cold. Moreover, Denton became aware of unoccupied time. In one place among the carelessly heaped lumber of the old times he found a rust-eaten spade, and with this he made a fitful attack on the razed and grass-grown garden—though he had nothing to plant or sow. He returned to Elizabeth with a sweat-streaming face, after half an hour of such work.

"There were giants in those days," he said, not understanding what wont and training will do. And their walk that day led them along the hills until they could see the city shimmering far away in the valley. "I wonder how things are going on there," he said.

And then came a change in the weather. "Come out and see the clouds," she cried; and behold! they were a sombre purple in the north and east, streaming up to ragged edges at the zenith. And as they went up the hill these hurrying streamers blotted out the sunset. Suddenly the wind set the beech-trees swaying and whispering, and Elizabeth shivered. And then far away the lightning flashed, flashed like a sword that is drawn suddenly, and the distant thunder marched about the sky, and even as they stood astonished, pattering upon them came the first headlong raindrops of the storm. In an instant the last streak of sunset was hidden by a falling curtain of hail, and the lightning flashed again, and the voice of the thunder roared louder, and all about them the world scowled dark and strange.

Seizing hands, these children of the city ran down the hill to their home, in infinite astonishment. And ere they reached it, Elizabeth was weeping with dismay, and the darkling ground about them was white and brittle and active with the pelting hail.

Then began a strange and terrible night for them. For the first time in their civilised lives they were in absolute darkness; they were wet and cold and shivering, all about them hissed the hail, and through the long neglected ceilings of the derelict home came noisy spouts of water and formed pools and rivulets on the creaking floors. As the gusts of the storm struck the worn-out building, it groaned and shuddered, and now a mass of plaster from the wall would slide and smash, and now some loosened tile would rattle down the roof and crash into the empty greenhouse below. Elizabeth shuddered, and was still; Denton wrapped his gay and flimsy city cloak about her, and so they crouched in the darkness. And ever the thunder broke louder and nearer, and ever more lurid flashed the lightning, jerking into a momentary gaunt clearness the steaming, dripping room in which they sheltered.

Never before had they been in the open air save when the sun was shining. All their time had been spent in the warm and airy ways and halls and rooms of the latter-day city. It was to them that night as if they were in some other world, some disordered chaos of stress and tumult, and almost beyond hoping that they should ever see the city ways again.

The storm seemed to last interminably, until at last they dozed between the thunderclaps, and then very swiftly it fell and ceased. And as the last patter of the rain died away they heard an unfamiliar sound.

"What is that?" cried Elizabeth.

It came again. It was the barking of dogs. It drove down the desert lane and passed; and through the window, whitening the wall before them and throwing upon it the shadow of the window-frame and of a tree in black silhouette, shone the light of the waxing moon....

Just as the pale dawn was drawing the things about them into sight, the fitful barking of dogs came near again, and stopped. They listened. After a pause they heard the quick pattering of feet seeking round the house, and short, half-smothered barks. Then again everything was still.

"Ssh!" whispered Elizabeth, and pointed to the door of their room.

Denton went half-way towards the door, and stood listening. He came back with a face of affected unconcern. "They must be the sheep-dogs of the Food Company," he said. "They will do us no harm."

He sat down again beside her. "What a night it has been!" he said, to hide how keenly he was listening.

"I don't like dogs," answered Elizabeth, after a long silence.

"Dogs never hurt any one," said Denton. "In the old days—in the nineteenth century—everybody had a dog."

"There was a romance I heard once. A dog killed a man."

"Not this sort of dog," said Denton confidently. "Some of those romances—are exaggerated."

Suddenly a half bark and a pattering up the staircase; the sound of panting. Denton sprang to his feet and drew the sword out of the damp straw upon which they had been lying. Then in the doorway appeared a gaunt sheep-dog, and halted there. Behind it stared another. For an instant man and brute faced each other, hesitating.

Then Denton, being ignorant of dogs, made a sharp step forward. "Go away," he said, with a clumsy motion of his sword.

The dog started and growled. Denton stopped sharply. "Good dog!" he said.

The growling jerked into a bark.

"Good dog!" said Denton. The second dog growled and barked. A third out of sight down the staircase took up the barking also. Outside others gave tongue—a large number it seemed to Denton.

"This is annoying," said Denton, without taking his eye off the brutes before him. "Of course the shepherds won't come out of the city for hours yet. Naturally these dogs don't quite make us out."

"I can't hear," shouted Elizabeth. She stood up and came to him.

Denton tried again, but the barking still drowned his voice. The sound had a curious effect upon his blood. Odd disused emotions began to stir; his face changed as he shouted. He tried again; the barking seemed to mock him, and one dog danced a pace forward, bristling. Suddenly he turned, and uttering certain words in the dialect of the underways, words incomprehensible to Elizabeth, he made for the dogs. There was a sudden cessation of the barking, a growl and a snapping. Elizabeth saw the snarling head of the foremost dog, its white teeth and retracted ears, and the flash of the thrust blade. The brute leapt into the air and was flung back.

Then Denton, with a shout, was driving the dogs before him. The sword flashed above his head with a sudden new freedom of gesture, and then he vanished down the staircase. She made six steps to follow him, and on the landing there was blood. She stopped, and hearing the tumult of dogs and Denton's shouts pass out of the house, ran to the window.

Nine wolfish sheep-dogs were scattering, one writhed before the porch; and Denton, tasting that strange delight of combat that slumbers still in the blood of even the most civilised man, was shouting and running across the garden space. And then she saw something that for a moment he did not see. The dogs circled round this way and that, and came again. They had him in the open.

In an instant she divined the situation. She would have called to him. For a moment she felt sick and helpless, and then, obeying a strange impulse, she gathered up her white skirt and ran downstairs. In the hall was the rusting spade. That was it! She seized it and ran out.

She came none too soon. One dog rolled before him, well-nigh slashed in half; but a second had him by the thigh, a third gripped his collar behind, and a fourth had the blade of the sword between its teeth, tasting its own blood. He parried the leap of a fifth with his left arm.

It might have been the first century instead of the twenty-second, so far as she was concerned. All the gentleness of her eighteen years of city life vanished before this primordial need. The spade smote hard and sure, and cleft a dog's skull. Another, crouching for a spring, yelped with dismay at this unexpected antagonist, and rushed aside. Two wasted precious moments on the binding of a feminine skirt.

The collar of Denton's cloak tore and parted as he staggered back; and that dog too felt the spade, and ceased to trouble him. He sheathed his sword in the brute at his thigh.

"To the wall!" cried Elizabeth; and in three seconds the fight was at an end, and our young people stood side by side, while a remnant of five dogs, with ears and tails of disaster, fled shamefully from the stricken field.

For a moment they stood panting and victorious, and then Elizabeth, dropping her spade, covered her face, and sank to the ground in a paroxysm of weeping. Denton looked about him, thrust the point of his sword into the ground so that it was at hand, and stooped to comfort her.

AT LAST THEIR MORE TUMULTUOUS EMOTIONS SUBSIDED, AND THEY COULD talk again. She leant upon the wall, and he sat upon it so that he could keep an eye open for any returning dogs. Two, at any rate, were up on the hillside and keeping up a vexatious barking.

She was tear-stained, but not very wretched now, because for half an hour he had been repeating that she was brave and had saved his life. But a new fear was growing in her mind.

"They are the dogs of the Food Company," she said. "There will be trouble."

"I am afraid so. Very likely they will prosecute us for trespass."

A pause.

"In the old times," he said, "this sort of thing happened day after day."

"Last night!" she said. "I could not live through another such night."

He looked at her. Her face was pale for want of sleep, and drawn and haggard. He came to a sudden resolution. "We must go back," he said.

She looked at the dead dogs, and shivered. "We cannot stay here," she said.

"We must go back," he repeated, glancing over his shoulder to see if the enemy kept their distance. "We have been happy for a time.... But the world is too civilised. Ours is the age of cities. More of this will kill us."

"But what are we to do? How can we live there?"

Denton hesitated. His heel kicked against the wall on which he sat. "It's a thing I haven't mentioned before," he said, and coughed; "but ..."

"Yes?"

"You could raise money on your expectations," he said.

"Could I?" she said eagerly.

"Of course you could. What a child you are!"

She stood up, and her face was bright. "Why did you not tell me before?" she asked. "And all this time we have been here!"

He looked at her for a moment, and smiled. Then the smile vanished. "I thought it ought to come from you," he said. "I didn't like to ask for your money. And besides—at first I thought this would be rather fine."

There was a pause.

"It has been fine," he said; and glanced once more over his shoulder. "Until all this began."

"Yes," she said, "those first days. The first three days."

They looked for a space into one another's faces, and then Denton slid down from the wall and took her hand.

"To each generation," he said, "the life of its time. I see it all plainly now. In the city—that is the life to which we were born. To live in any other fashion ... Coming here was a dream, and this—is the awakening."

"It was a pleasant dream," she said,—"in the beginning."

For a long space neither spoke.

"If we would reach the city before the shepherds come here, we must start," said Denton. "We must get our food out of the house and eat as we go."

Denton glanced about him again, and, giving the dead dogs a wide berth, they walked across the garden space and into the house together. They found the wallet with their food, and descended the blood-stained stairs again. In the hall Elizabeth stopped. "One minute," she said. "There is something here."

She led the way into the room in which that one little blue flower was blooming. She stooped to it, she touched it with her hand.

"I want it," she said; and then, "I cannot take it...."

Impulsively she stooped and kissed its petals.

Then silently, side by side, they went across the empty garden-space into the old high road, and set their faces resolutely towards the distant city—towards the complex mechanical city of those latter days, the city that had swallowed up mankind.

# THE WAYS OF THE CITY

Prominent if not paramount among world-changing inventions in the history of man is that series of contrivances in locomotion that began with the railway and ended for a century or more with the motor and the patent road. That these contrivances, together with the device of limited liability joint stock companies and the supersession of agricultural labourers by skilled men with ingenious machinery, would necessarily concentrate mankind in cities of unparallelled magnitude and work an entire revolution in human life, became, after the event, a thing so obvious that it is a matter of astonishment it was not more clearly anticipated. Yet that any steps should be taken to anticipate the miseries such a revolution might entail does not appear even to have been suggested; and the idea that the moral prohibitions and sanctions, the privileges and concessions, the conception of property and responsibility, of comfort and beauty, that had rendered the mainly agricultural states of the past prosperous and happy, would fail in the rising torrent of novel opportunities and novel stimulations, never seems to have entered the nineteenth-century mind. That a citizen, kindly and fair in his ordinary life, could as a shareholder become almost murderously greedy; that commercial methods that were reasonable and honourable on the old-fashioned countryside, should on an enlarged scale be deadly and overwhelming; that ancient charity was modern pauperisation, and ancient employment modern sweating; that, in fact, a revision and enlargement of the duties and rights of man had become urgently necessary, were things it could not entertain, nourished as it was on an archaic system of education and profoundly retrospective and legal in all its habits of thought. It was known that the accumulation of men in cities involved unprecedented dangers of pestilence; there was an energetic development of sanitation; but that the diseases of gambling and usury, of luxury and tyranny should become endemic, and produce horrible consequences was beyond the scope of nineteenth-century thought. And so, as if it were some inorganic process, practically unhindered by the creative will of man, the growth of the swarming unhappy cities that mark the twenty-first century accomplished itself.

The new society was divided into three main classes. At the summit slumbered the property owner, enormously rich by accident rather than design, potent save for the will and aim, the last avatar of Hamlet in the world. Below was the enormous multitude of workers employed by the gigantic companies that monopolised control; and between these two the dwindling middle class, officials of innumerable sorts, foremen, managers, the medical, legal, artistic, and scholastic classes, and the minor rich, a middle class whose members led a life of insecure luxury and precarious speculation amidst the movements of the great managers.

Already the love story and the marrying of two persons of this middle class have been told: how they overcame the obstacles between them, and how they tried the simple old-fashioned way of living on the countryside and came back speedily enough into the city of London. Denton had no means, so Elizabeth borrowed money on the securities that her father Mwres held in trust for her until she was one-and-twenty.

The rate of interest she paid was of course high, because of the uncertainty of her security, and the arithmetic of lovers is often sketchy and optimistic. Yet they had very glorious times after that return. They determined they would not go to a Pleasure city nor waste their days rushing through the air from one part of the world to the other, for in spite of one disillusionment, their tastes were still old-fashioned. They furnished their little room with quaint old Victorian furniture, and found a shop on the forty-second floor in Seventh Way where printed books of the old sort were still to be bought. It was their pet affectation to read print instead of hearing phonographs. And when presently there came a sweet little girl, to unite them further if it were possible, Elizabeth would not send it to a creche, as the custom was, but insisted on nursing it at home. The rent of their apartments was raised on account of this singular proceeding, but that they did not mind. It only meant borrowing a little more.

Presently Elizabeth was of age, and Denton had a business interview with her father that was not agreeable. An exceedingly disagreeable interview with their money-lender followed, from which he brought home a white face. On his return Elizabeth had to tell him of a new and marvellous intonation of "Goo" that their daughter had devised, but Denton was inattentive. In the midst, just as she was at the cream of her description, he interrupted. "How much money do you think we have left, now that everything is settled?"

She stared and stopped her appreciative swaying of the Goo genius that had accompanied her description.

"You don't mean...?"

"Yes," he answered. "Ever so much. We have been wild. It's the interest. Or something. And the shares you had, slumped. Your father did not mind. Said it was not his business, after what had happened. He's going to marry again.... Well—we have scarcely a thousand left!"

"Only a thousand?"

"Only a thousand."

And Elizabeth sat down. For a moment she regarded him with a white face, then her eyes went about the quaint, old-fashioned room, with its middle Victorian furniture and genuine oleographs, and rested at last on the little lump of humanity within her arms.

Denton glanced at her and stood downcast. Then he swung round on his heel and walked up and down very rapidly.

"I must get something to do," he broke out presently. "I am an idle scoundrel. I ought to have thought of this before. I have been a selfish fool. I wanted to be with you all day...."

He stopped, looking at her white face. Suddenly he came and kissed her and the little face that nestled against her breast.

"It's all right, dear," he said, standing over her; "you won't be lonely now—now Dings is beginning to talk to you. And I can soon get something to do, you know. Soon.... Easily.... It's only a shock at first. But it will come all right. It's sure to come right. I will go out again as soon as I have rested, and find what can be done. For the present it's hard to think of anything...."

"It would be hard to leave these rooms," said Elizabeth; "but——"

"There won't be any need of that—trust me."

"They are expensive."

Denton waved that aside. He began talking of the work he could do. He was not very explicit what it would be; but he was quite sure that there was something to keep them comfortably in the happy middle class, whose way of life was the only one they knew.

"There are three-and-thirty million people in London," he said: "some of them _must_ have need of me."

"Some must."

"The trouble is ... Well—Bindon, that brown little old man your father wanted you to marry. He's an important person.... I can't go back to my flying-stage work, because he is now a Commissioner of the Flying Stage Clerks."

"I didn't know that," said Elizabeth.

"He was made that in the last few weeks ... or things would be easy enough, for they liked me on the flying stage. But there's dozens of other things to be done—dozens. Don't you worry, dear. I'll rest a little while, and then we'll dine, and then I'll start on my rounds. I know lots of people—lots."

So they rested, and then they went to the public dining-room and dined, and then he started on his search for employment. But they soon realised that in the matter of one convenience the world was just as badly off as it had ever been, and that was a nice, secure, honourable, remunerative employment, leaving ample leisure for the private life, and demanding no special ability, no violent exertion nor risk, and no sacrifice of any sort for its attainment. He evolved a number of brilliant projects, and spent many days hurrying from one part of the enormous city to another in search of influential friends; and all his influential friends were glad to see him, and very sanguine until it came to definite proposals, and then they became guarded and vague. He would part with them coldly, and think over their behaviour, and get irritated on his way back, and stop at some telephone office and spend money on an animated but unprofitable quarrel. And as the days passed, he got so worried and irritated that even to seem kind and careless before Elizabeth cost him an effort—as she, being a loving woman, perceived very clearly.

After an extremely complex preface one day, she helped him out with a painful suggestion. He had expected her to weep and give way to despair when it came to selling all their joyfully bought early Victorian treasures, their quaint objects of art, their antimacassars, bead mats, repp curtains, veneered furniture, gold-framed steel engravings and pencil drawings, wax flowers under shades, stuffed birds, and all sorts of choice old things; but it was she who made the proposal. The sacrifice seemed to fill her with pleasure, and so did the idea of shifting to apartments ten or twelve floors lower in another hotel. "So long as Dings is with us, nothing matters," she said. "It's all experience." So he kissed her, said she was braver than when she fought the sheep-dogs, called her Boadicea, and abstained very carefully from reminding her that they would have to pay a considerably higher rent on account of the little voice with which Dings greeted the perpetual uproar of the city.

His idea had been to get Elizabeth out of the way when it came to selling the absurd furniture about which their affections were twined and tangled; but when it came to the sale it was Elizabeth who haggled with the dealer while Denton went about the running ways of the city, white and sick with sorrow and the fear of what was still to come. When they moved into their sparsely furnished pink-and-white apartments in a cheap hotel, there came an outbreak of furious energy on his part, and then nearly a week of lethargy during which he sulked at home. Through those days

Elizabeth shone like a star, and at the end Denton's misery found a vent in tears. And then he went out into the city ways again, and—to his utter amazement—found some work to do.

His standard of employment had fallen steadily until at last it had reached the lowest level of independent workers. At first he had aspired to some high official position in the great Flying or Wind Vane or Water Companies, or to an appointment on one of the General Intelligence Organisations that had replaced newspapers, or to some professional partnership, but those were the dreams of the beginning. From that he had passed to speculation, and three hundred gold "lions" out of Elizabeth's thousand had vanished one evening in the share market. Now he was glad his good looks secured him a trial in the position of salesman to the Suzannah Hat Syndicate, a Syndicate, dealing in ladies' caps, hair decorations, and hats—for though the city was completely covered in, ladies still wore extremely elaborate and beautiful hats at the theatres and places of public worship.

It would have been amusing if one could have confronted a Regent Street shopkeeper of the nineteenth century with the development of his establishment in which Denton's duties lay. Nineteenth Way was still sometimes called Regent Street, but it was now a street of moving platforms and nearly eight hundred feet wide. The middle space was immovable and gave access by staircases descending into subterranean ways to the houses on either side. Right and left were an ascending series of continuous platforms each of which travelled about five miles an hour faster than the one internal to it, so that one could step from platform to platform until one reached the swiftest outer way and so go about the city. The establishment of the Suzannah Hat Syndicate projected a vast façade upon the outer way, sending out overhead at either end an overlapping series of huge white glass screens, on which gigantic animated pictures of the faces of well-known beautiful living women wearing novelties in hats were thrown. A dense crowd was always collected in the stationary central way watching a vast kinematograph which displayed the changing fashion. The whole front of the building was in perpetual chromatic change, and all down the façade—four hundred feet it measured—and all across the street of moving ways, laced and winked and glittered in a thousand varieties of colour and lettering the inscription—

## SUZANNA! 'ETS! SUZANNA! 'ETS!

A broadside of gigantic phonographs drowned all conversation in the moving way and roared "hats" at the passer-by, while far down the street and up, other batteries counselled the public to "walk down for Suzannah," and queried, "Why don't you buy the girl a hat?"

For the benefit of those who chanced to be deaf—and deafness was not uncommon in the London of that age, inscriptions of all sizes were thrown from the roof above upon the moving platforms themselves, and on one's hand or on the bald head of the man before one, or on a lady's shoulders, or in a sudden jet of flame before one's feet, the moving finger wrote in unanticipated letters of fire "'ets r chip t'de," or simply "'ets." And spite of all these efforts so high was the pitch at which the city lived, so trained became one's eyes and ears to ignore all sorts of advertisement, that many a citizen had passed that place thousands of times and was still unaware of the existence of the Suzannah Hat Syndicate.

To enter the building one descended the staircase in the middle way and walked through a public passage in which pretty girls promenaded, girls who were willing to wear a ticketed hat for a small fee. The entrance chamber was a large hall in which wax heads fashionably adorned rotated gracefully upon pedestals, and from this one passed through a cash office to an interminable series of little rooms, each room with its salesman, its three or four hats and pins, its mirrors, its kinematographs, telephones and hat slides in communication with the central depôt, its comfortable lounge and tempting refreshments. A salesman in such an apartment did Denton now become. It was his business to attend to any of the incessant stream of ladies who chose to stop with him, to behave as winningly as possible, to offer refreshment, to converse on any topic the possible customer chose, and to guide the conversation dexterously but not insistently towards hats. He was to suggest trying on various types of hat and to show by his manner and bearing, but without any coarse flattery, the enhanced impression made by the hats he wished to sell. He had several mirrors, adapted by various subtleties of curvature and tint to different types of face and complexion, and much depended on the proper use of these.

Denton flung himself at these curious and not very congenial duties with a good will and energy that would have amazed him a year before; but all to no purpose. The Senior Manageress, who had selected him for appointment and conferred various small marks of favour upon him, suddenly changed in her manner, declared for no assignable cause that he was stupid, and dismissed him at the end of six weeks of salesmanship. So Denton had to resume his ineffectual search for employment.

This second search did not last very long. Their money was at the ebb. To eke it out a little longer they resolved to part with their darling Dings, and took that small person to one of the public creches that abounded in the city. That was the common use of the time. The industrial emancipation of women, the correlated disorganisation of the secluded "home," had rendered creches a necessity for all but very rich and exceptionally-minded people. Therein children encountered hygienic and educational advantages impossible without such organisation. Creches were of all classes and types of luxury, down to those of the Labour Company, where children were taken on credit, to be redeemed in labour as they grew up.

But both Denton and Elizabeth being, as I have explained, strange old-fashioned young people, full of nineteenth-century ideas, hated these convenient creches exceedingly and at last took their little daughter to one with extreme reluctance. They were received by a motherly person in a uniform who was very brisk and prompt in her manner until Elizabeth wept at the mention of parting from her child. The motherly person, after a brief astonishment at this unusual emotion, changed suddenly into a creature of hope and comfort, and so won Elizabeth's gratitude for life. They were conducted into a vast room presided over by several nurses and with hundreds of two-year-old girls grouped about the toy-covered floor. This was the Two-year-old Room. Two nurses came forward, and Elizabeth watched their bearing towards Dings with jealous eyes. They were kind—it was clear they felt kind, and yet ...

Presently it was time to go. By that time Dings was happily established in a corner, sitting on the floor with her arms filled, and herself, indeed, for the most part hidden by an unaccustomed wealth of toys. She seemed careless of all human relationships as her parents receded.

They were forbidden to upset her by saying good-bye.

At the door Elizabeth glanced back for the last time, and behold! Dings had dropped her new wealth and was standing with a dubious face. Suddenly Elizabeth gasped, and the motherly nurse pushed her forward and closed the door.

"You can come again soon, dear," she said, with unexpected tenderness in her eyes. For a moment Elizabeth stared at her with a blank face. "You can come again soon," repeated the nurse. Then with a swift transition Elizabeth was weeping in the nurse's arms. So it was that Denton's heart was won also.

And three weeks after our young people were absolutely penniless, and only one way lay open. They must go to the Labour Company. So soon as the rent was a week overdue their few remaining possessions were seized, and with scant courtesy they were shown the way out of the hotel. Elizabeth walked along the passage towards the staircase that ascended to the motionless middle way, too dulled by misery to think. Denton stopped behind to finish a stinging and unsatisfactory argument with the hotel porter, and then came hurrying after her, flushed and hot. He slackened his pace as he overtook her, and together they ascended to the middle way in silence. There they found two seats vacant and sat down.

"We need not go there—yet?" said Elizabeth.

"No—not till we are hungry," said Denton.

They said no more.

Elizabeth's eyes sought a resting-place and found none. To the right roared the eastward ways, to the left the ways in the opposite direction, swarming with people. Backwards and forwards along a cable overhead rushed a string of gesticulating men, dressed like clowns, each marked on back and chest with one gigantic letter, so that altogether they spelt out:

"PURKINJE'S DIGESTIVE PILLS."

An anæmic little woman in horrible coarse blue canvas pointed a little girl to one of this string of hurrying advertisements.

"Look!" said the anæmic woman: "there's yer father."

"Which?" said the little girl.

"'Im wiv his nose coloured red," said the anæmic woman.

The little girl began to cry, and Elizabeth could have cried too.

"Ain't 'e kickin' 'is legs!—just!" said the anæmic woman in blue, trying to make things bright again. "Looky—now!"

On the façade to the right a huge intensely bright disc of weird colour span incessantly, and letters of fire that came and went spelt out—

"DOES THIS MAKE YOU GIDDY?"

Then a pause, followed by

"TAKE A PURKINJE'S DIGESTIVE PILL."

A vast and desolating braying began. "If you love Swagger Literature, put your telephone on to Bruggles, the Greatest Author of all Time. The Greatest Thinker of all Time. Teaches you Morals up to your Scalp! The very image of Socrates, except the back of his head, which is like Shakspeare. He has six toes, dresses in red, and never cleans his teeth. Hear HIM!"

Denton's voice became audible in a gap in the uproar. "I never ought to have married you," he was saying. "I have wasted your money, ruined you, brought you to misery. I am a scoundrel.... Oh, this accursed world!"

She tried to speak, and for some moments could not. She grasped his hand. "No," she said at last.

A half-formed desire suddenly became determination. She stood up. "Will you come?"

He rose also. "We need not go there yet."

"Not that. But I want you to come to the flying stages—where we met. You know? The little seat."

He hesitated. "Can you?" he said, doubtfully.

"Must," she answered.

He hesitated still for a moment, then moved to obey her will.

And so it was they spent their last half-day of freedom out under the open air in the little seat under the flying stages where they had been wont to meet five short years ago. There she told him, what she could not tell him in the tumultuous public ways, that she did not repent even now of their marriage—that whatever discomfort and misery life still had for them, she was content with the things that had been. The weather was kind to them, the seat was sunlit and warm, and overhead the shining aëroplanes went and came.

At last towards sunsetting their time was at an end, and they made their vows to one another and clasped hands, and then rose up and went back into the ways of the city, a shabby-looking, heavy-hearted pair, tired and hungry. Soon they came to one of the pale blue signs that marked a Labour Company Bureau. For a space they stood in the middle way regarding this and at last descended, and entered the waiting-room.

The Labour Company had originally been a charitable organisation; its aim was to supply food, shelter, and work to all comers. This it was bound to do by the conditions of its incorporation, and it was also bound to supply food and shelter and medical attendance to all incapable of work who chose to demand its aid. In exchange these incapables paid labour notes, which they had to redeem upon recovery. They signed these labour notes with thumb-marks, which were photographed and indexed in such a way that this world-wide Labour Company could identify any one of its two or three hundred million clients at the cost of an hour's inquiry. The day's labour was defined as two spells in a treadmill used in generating electrical force, or its equivalent, and its due performance could be enforced by law. In practice the Labour Company found it advisable to add to its statutory obligations of food and shelter a few pence a day as an inducement to effort; and its enterprise had not only abolished pauperisation altogether, but supplied practically all but the very highest and most responsible labour throughout the world. Nearly a third of the population of the world were its serfs and debtors from the cradle to the grave.

In this practical, unsentimental way the problem of the unemployed had been most satisfactorily met and overcome. No one starved in the public ways, and no rags, no costume less sanitary and sufficient than the Labour Company's hygienic but inelegant blue canvas, pained the eye throughout the whole world. It was the constant theme of the phonographic newspapers how much the world had progressed since nineteenth-century days, when the bodies of those killed by the vehicular traffic or dead of starvation, were, they alleged, a common feature in all the busier streets.

Denton and Elizabeth sat apart in the waiting-room until their turn came. Most of the others collected there seemed limp and taciturn, but three or four young people gaudily dressed made up for the quietude of their companions. They were life clients of the Company, born in the Company's creche and destined to die in its hospital, and they had been out for a spree with some shillings or so of extra pay. They talked vociferously in a later development of the Cockney dialect, manifestly very proud of themselves.

Elizabeth's eyes went from these to the less assertive figures. One seemed exceptionally pitiful to her. It was a woman of perhaps forty-five, with gold-stained hair and a painted face, down which abundant tears had trickled; she had a pinched nose, hungry eyes, lean hands and shoulders, and her dusty worn-out finery told the story of her life. Another was a grey-bearded old man in the costume of a bishop of one of the high episcopal sects—for religion was now also a business, and had its ups and downs. And beside him a sickly, dissipated-looking boy of perhaps two-and-twenty glared at Fate.

Presently Elizabeth and then Denton interviewed the manageress—for the Company preferred women in this capacity—and found she possessed an energetic face, a contemptuous manner, and a particularly unpleasant voice. They were given various checks, including one to certify that they need not have their heads cropped; and when they had given their thumb-marks, learnt the number corresponding thereunto, and exchanged their shabby middle-class clothes for duly numbered blue canvas suits, they repaired to the huge plain dining-room for their first meal under these new conditions. Afterwards they were to return to her for instructions about their work.

When they had made the exchange of their clothing Elizabeth did not seem able to look at Denton at first; but he looked at her, and saw with astonishment that even in blue canvas she was still beautiful. And then their soup and bread came sliding on its little rail down the long table towards them and stopped with a jerk, and he forgot the matter. For they had had no proper meal for three days.

After they had dined they rested for a time. Neither talked—there was nothing to say; and presently they got up and went back to the manageress to learn what they had to do.

The manageress referred to a tablet. "Y'r rooms won't be here; it'll be in the Highbury Ward, Ninety-seventh Way, number two thousand and seventeen. Better make a note of it on y'r card. You, nought nought nought, type seven, sixty-four, b.c.d., gamma forty-one, female; you 'ave to go to the Metal-beating Company and try that for a day—fourpence bonus if ye're satisfactory; and you, nought seven one, type four, seven hundred and nine, g.f.b., pi five and ninety, male; you 'ave to go to the Photographic Company on Eighty-first Way, and learn something or other—I don't know—thrippence. 'Ere's y'r cards. That's all. Next! What? Didn't catch it all? Lor! So suppose I must go over it all again. Why don't you listen? Keerless, unprovident people! One'd think these things didn't matter."

Their ways to their work lay together for a time. And now they found they could talk. Curiously enough, the worst of their depression seemed over now that they had actually donned the blue. Denton could talk with interest even of the work that lay before them. "Whatever it is," he said, "it can't be so hateful as that hat shop. And after we have paid for Dings, we shall still have a whole penny a day between us even now. Afterwards—we may improve,—get more money."

Elizabeth was less inclined to speech. "I wonder why work should seem so hateful," she said.

"It's odd," said Denton. "I suppose it wouldn't be if it were not the thought of being ordered about.... I hope we shall have decent managers."

Elizabeth did not answer. She was not thinking of that. She was tracing out some thoughts of her own.

"Of course," she said presently, "we have been using up work all our lives. It's only fair—"

She stopped. It was too intricate.

"We paid for it," said Denton, for at that time he had not troubled himself about these complicated things.

"We did nothing—and yet we paid for it. That's what I cannot understand."

"Perhaps we are paying," said Elizabeth presently—for her theology was old-fashioned and simple.

Presently it was time for them to part, and each went to the appointed work. Denton's was to mind a complicated hydraulic press that seemed almost an intelligent thing. This press worked by the sea-water that was destined finally to flush the city drains—for the world had long since abandoned the folly of pouring drinkable water into its sewers. This water was brought close to the eastward edge of the city by a huge canal, and then raised by an enormous battery of pumps into reservoirs at a level of four hundred feet above the sea, from which it spread by a billion arterial branches over the city. Thence it poured down, cleansing, sluicing, working machinery of all sorts, through an infinite variety of capillary channels into the great drains, the cloacae maximae, and so carried the sewage out to the agricultural areas that surrounded London on every side.

The press was employed in one of the processes of the photographic manufacture, but the nature of the process it did not concern Denton to understand. The most salient fact to his mind was that it had to be conducted in ruby light, and as a consequence the room in which he worked was lit by one coloured globe that poured a lurid and painful illumination about the room. In the darkest corner stood the press whose servant Denton had now become: it was a huge, dim, glittering thing with a projecting hood that had a remote resemblance to a bowed head, and, squatting like some metal Buddha in this weird light that ministered to its needs, it seemed to Denton in certain moods almost as if this must needs be the obscure idol to which humanity in some strange aberration had offered up his life. His duties had a varied monotony. Such items as the following will convey an idea of the service of the press. The thing worked with a busy clicking so long as things went well; but if the paste that came pouring through a feeder from another room and which it was perpetually compressing into thin plates, changed in quality the rhythm of its click altered and Denton hastened to make certain adjustments. The slightest delay involved a waste of paste and the docking of one or more of his daily pence. If the supply of paste waned—there were hand processes of a peculiar sort involved in its preparation, and sometimes the workers had convulsions which deranged their output—Denton had to throw the press out of gear. In the painful vigilance a multitude of such trivial attentions entailed, painful because of the incessant effort its absence of natural interest required, Denton had now to pass one-third of his days. Save for an occasional visit from the manager, a kindly but singularly foul-mouthed man, Denton passed his working hours in solitude.

Elizabeth's work was of a more social sort. There was a fashion for covering the private apartments of the very wealthy with metal plates beautifully embossed with repeated patterns. The taste of the time demanded, however, that the repetition of the patterns should not be exact—not mechanical, but "natural"—and it was found that the most pleasing arrangement of pattern irregularity was obtained by employing women of refinement and natural taste to punch out the patterns with small dies. So many square feet of plates was exacted from Elizabeth as a minimum, and for whatever square feet she did in excess she received a small payment. The room, like most rooms of women workers, was under a manageress: men had been found by the Labour Company not only less exacting but extremely liable to excuse favoured ladies from a proper share of their duties. The manageress was a not unkindly, taciturn person, with the hardened remains of beauty of the brunette type; and the other women workers, who of course hated her, associated her name scandalously with one of the metal-work directors in order to explain her position.

Only two or three of Elizabeth's fellow-workers were born labour serfs; plain, morose girls, but most of them corresponded to what the nineteenth century would have called a "reduced" gentlewoman. But the ideal of what constituted a gentlewoman had altered: the faint, faded, negative virtue, the modulated voice and restrained gesture of the old-fashioned gentlewoman had vanished from the earth. Most of her companions showed in discoloured hair, ruined complexions, and the texture of their reminiscent conversations, the vanished glories of a conquering youth. All of these artistic workers were much older than Elizabeth, and two openly expressed their surprise that any one so young and pleasant should come to share their toil. But Elizabeth did not trouble them with her old-world moral conceptions.

They were permitted, and even encouraged to converse with each other, for the directors very properly judged that anything that conduced to variations of mood made for pleasing fluctuations in their patterning; and Elizabeth was almost forced to hear the stories of these lives with which her own interwove: garbled and distorted they were by vanity indeed and yet comprehensible enough. And soon she began to appreciate the small spites and cliques, the little misunderstandings and alliances that enmeshed about her. One woman was excessively garrulous and descriptive about a wonderful son of hers; another had cultivated a foolish coarseness of speech, that she seemed to regard as the wittiest expression of originality conceivable; a third mused for ever on dress, and whispered to Elizabeth how she saved her pence day after day, and would presently have a glorious day of freedom, wearing ... and then followed hours of description; two others sat always together, and called one another pet names, until one day some little thing happened, and they sat apart, blind and deaf as it seemed to one another's being. And always from them all came an incessant tap, tap, tap, tap, and the manageress listened always to the rhythm to mark if one fell away. Tap, tap, tap, tap: so their days passed, so their lives must pass. Elizabeth sat among them, kindly and quiet, grey-hearted, marvelling at Fate: tap, tap, tap; tap, tap, tap; tap, tap, tap.

So there came to Denton and Elizabeth a long succession of laborious days, that hardened their hands, wove strange threads of some new and sterner substance into the soft prettiness of their lives, and drew grave lines and shadows on their faces. The bright, convenient ways of the former life had receded to an inaccessible distance; slowly they learnt the lesson of the underworld—sombre and laborious, vast and pregnant. There were many little things happened: things that would be tedious and miserable to tell, things that were bitter and grievous to bear—indignities, tyrannies, such as must ever season the bread of the poor in cities; and one thing that was not little, but seemed like the utter blackening of life to them, which was that the child they had given life to sickened and died. But that story, that ancient, perpetually recurring story, has been told so often, has been told so beautifully, that there is no need to tell it over again here. There was the same sharp fear, the same long anxiety, the deferred inevitable blow, and the black silence. It has always been the same; it will always be the same. It is one of the things that must be.

And it was Elizabeth who was the first to speak, after an aching, dull interspace of days: not, indeed, of the foolish little name that was a name no longer, but of the darkness that brooded over her soul. They had come through the shrieking, tumultuous ways of the city together; the clamour of trade, of yelling competitive religions, of political appeal, had beat upon deaf ears; the glare of focussed lights, of dancing letters, and fiery advertisements, had fallen upon the set, miserable faces unheeded. They took their dinner in the dining-hall at a place apart. "I want," said Elizabeth clumsily, "to go out to the flying stages—to that seat. Here, one can say nothing...."

Denton looked at her. "It will be night," he said.

"I have asked,—it is a fine night." She stopped.

He perceived she could find no words to explain herself. Suddenly he understood that she wished to see the stars once more, the stars they had watched together from the open downland in that wild honeymoon of theirs five years ago. Something caught at his throat. He looked away from her.

"There will be plenty of time to go," he said, in a matter-of-fact tone.

And at last they came out to their little seat on the flying stage, and sat there for a long time in silence. The little seat was in shadow, but the zenith was pale blue with the effulgence of the stage overhead, and all the city spread below them, squares and circles and patches of brilliance caught in a mesh-work of light. The little stars seemed very faint and small: near as they had been to the old-world watcher, they had become now infinitely remote. Yet one could see them in the darkened patches amidst the glare, and especially in the northward sky, the ancient constellations gliding steadfast and patient about the pole.

Long our two people sat in silence, and at last Elizabeth sighed.

"If I understood," she said, "if I could understand. When one is down there the city seems everything—the noise, the hurry, the voices—you must live, you must scramble. Here—it is nothing; a thing that passes. One can think in peace."

"Yes," said Denton. "How flimsy it all is! From here more than half of it is swallowed by the night.... It will pass."

"We shall pass first," said Elizabeth.

"I know," said Denton. "If life were not a moment, the whole of history would seem like the happening of a day.... Yes—we shall pass. And the city will pass, and all the things that are to come. Man and the Overman and wonders unspeakable. And yet ..."

He paused, and then began afresh. "I know what you feel. At least I fancy.... Down there one thinks of one's work, one's little vexations and pleasures, one's eating and drinking and ease and pain. One lives, and one must die. Down there and everyday—our sorrow seemed the end of life....

"Up here it is different. For instance, down there it would seem impossible almost to go on living if one were horribly disfigured, horribly crippled, disgraced. Up here—under these stars—none of those things would matter. They don't matter.... They are a part of something. One seems just to touch that something—under the stars...."

He stopped. The vague, impalpable things in his mind, cloudy emotions half shaped towards ideas, vanished before the rough grasp of words. "It is hard to express," he said lamely.

They sat through a long stillness.

"It is well to come here," he said at last. "We stop—our minds are very finite. After all we are just poor animals rising out of the brute, each with a mind, the poor beginning of a mind. We are so stupid. So much hurts. And yet ...

"I know, I know—and some day we shall _see_.

"All this frightful stress, all this discord will resolve to harmony, and we shall know it. Nothing is but it makes for that. Nothing. All the failures—every little thing makes for that harmony. Everything is necessary to it, we shall find. We shall find. Nothing, not even the most dreadful thing, could be left out. Not even the most trivial. Every tap of your hammer on the brass, every moment of work, my idleness even ... Dear one! every movement of our poor little one ... All these things go on for ever. And the faint impalpable things. We, sitting here together.—Everything ...

"The passion that joined us, and what has come since. It is not passion now. More than anything else it is sorrow. Dear ..."

He could say no more, could follow his thoughts no further.

Elizabeth made no answer—she was very still; but presently her hand sought his and found it.

# IV

## UNDERNEATH

UNDER THE STARS ONE MAY REACH UPWARD AND TOUCH RESIGNATION, WHAT-ever the evil thing may be, but in the heat and stress of the day's work we lapse again, come disgust and anger and intolerable moods. How little is all our magnanimity—an accident! a phase! The very Saints of old had first to flee the world. And Denton and his Elizabeth could not flee their world, no longer were there open roads to unclaimed lands where men might live freely—however hardly—and keep their souls in peace. The city had swallowed up mankind.

For a time these two Labour Serfs were kept at their original occupations, she at her brass stamping and Denton at his press; and then came a move for him that brought with it fresh and still bitterer experiences of life in the underways of the great city. He was transferred to the care of a rather more elaborate press in the central factory of the London Tile Trust.

In this new situation he had to work in a long vaulted room with a number of other men, for the most part born Labour Serfs. He came to this intercourse reluctantly. His upbringing had been refined, and, until his ill fortune had brought him to that costume, he had never spoken in his life, except by way of command or some immediate necessity, to the white-faced wearers of the blue canvas. Now at last came contact; he had to work beside them, share their tools, eat with them. To both Elizabeth and himself this seemed a further degradation.

His taste would have seemed extreme to a man of the nineteenth century. But slowly and inevitably in the intervening years a gulf had opened between the wearers of the blue canvas and the classes above, a difference not simply of circumstances and habits of life, but of habits of thought—even of language. The underways had developed a dialect of their own: above, too, had arisen a dialect, a code of thought, a language of "culture," which aimed by a sedulous search after fresh distinction to widen perpetually the space between itself and "vulgarity." The bond of a common faith, moreover, no longer held the race together. The last years of the nineteenth century were distinguished by the rapid development among the prosperous idle of esoteric perversions of the popular religion: glosses and interpretations that reduced the broad teachings of the carpenter of Nazareth to the exquisite narrowness of their lives. And, spite of their inclination towards the ancient fashion of living, neither Elizabeth nor Denton had been sufficiently original to escape the suggestion of their surroundings. In matters of common behaviour they had followed the ways of their class, and so when they fell at last to be Labour Serfs it seemed to them almost as though they were falling among offensive inferior animals; they felt as a nineteenth-century duke and duchess might have felt who were forced to take rooms in the Jago.

Their natural impulse was to maintain a "distance." But Denton's first idea of a dignified isolation from his new surroundings was soon rudely dispelled. He had imagined that his fall to the position of a Labour Serf was the end of his lesson, that when their little daughter had died he had plumbed the deeps of life; but indeed these things were only the beginning. Life demands something more from us than acquiescence. And now in a roomful of machine minders he was to learn a wider lesson, to make the acquaintance of another factor in life, a factor as elemental as the loss of things dear to us, more elemental even than toil.

His quiet discouragement of conversation was an immediate cause of offence—was interpreted, rightly enough I fear, as disdain. His ignorance of the vulgar dialect, a thing upon which he had hitherto prided himself, suddenly took upon itself a new aspect. He failed to perceive at once that his reception of the coarse and stupid but genially intended remarks that greeted his appearance must have stung the makers of these advances like blows in their faces. "Don't understand," he said rather coldly, and at hazard, "No, thank you."

The man who had addressed him stared, scowled, and turned away.

A second, who also failed at Denton's unaccustomed ear, took the trouble to repeat his remark, and Denton discovered he was being offered the use of an oil can. He expressed polite thanks, and this second man embarked upon a penetrating conversation. Denton, he remarked, had been a swell, and he wanted to know how he had come to wear the blue. He clearly expected an interesting record of vice and extravagance. Had Denton ever been at a Pleasure City? Denton was speedily to discover how the existence of these wonderful places of delight permeated and defiled the thought and honour of these unwilling, hopeless workers of the underworld.

His aristocratic temperament resented these questions. He answered "No" curtly. The man persisted with a still more personal question, and this time it was Denton who turned away.

"Gorblimey!" said his interlocutor, much astonished.

It presently forced itself upon Denton's mind that this remarkable conversation was being repeated in indignant tones to more sympathetic hearers, and that it gave rise to astonishment and ironical laughter. They looked at Denton with manifestly enhanced interest. A curious perception of isolation dawned upon him. He tried to think of his press and its unfamiliar peculiarities....

The machines kept everybody pretty busy during the first spell, and then came a recess. It was only an interval for refreshment, too brief for any one to go out to a Labour Company dining-room. Denton followed his fellow-workers into a short gallery, in which were a number of bins of refuse from the presses.

Each man produced a packet of food. Denton had no packet. The manager, a careless young man who held his position by influence, had omitted to warn Denton that it was necessary to apply for this provision. He stood apart, feeling hungry. The others drew together in a group and talked in undertones, glancing at him ever and again. He became uneasy. His appearance of disregard cost him an increasing effort. He tried to think of the levers of his new press.

Presently one, a man shorter but much broader and stouter than Denton, came forward to him. Denton turned to him as unconcernedly as possible. "Here!" said the delegate—as Denton judged him to be—extending a cube of bread in a not too clean hand. He had a swart, broad-nosed face, and his mouth hung down towards one corner.

Denton felt doubtful for the instant whether this was meant for civility or insult. His impulse was to decline. "No, thanks," he said; and, at the man's change of expression, "I'm not hungry."

There came a laugh from the group behind. "Told you so," said the man who had offered Denton the loan of an oil can. "He's top side, he is. You ain't good enough for 'im.'"

The swart face grew a shade darker.

"Here," said its owner, still extending the bread, and speaking in a lower tone; "you got to eat this. See?"

Denton looked into the threatening face before him, and odd little currents of energy seemed to be running through his limbs and body.

"I don't want it," he said, trying a pleasant smile that twitched and failed.

The thickset man advanced his face, and the bread became a physical threat in his hand. Denton's mind rushed together to the one problem of his antagonist's eyes.

"Eat it," said the swart man.

There came a pause, and then they both moved quickly. The cube of bread described a complicated path, a curve that would have ended in Denton's face; and then his fist hit the wrist of the hand that gripped it, and it flew upward, and out of the conflict—its part played.

He stepped back quickly, fists clenched and arms tense. The hot, dark countenance receded, became an alert hostility, watching its chance. Denton for one instant felt confident, and strangely buoyant and serene. His heart beat quickly. He felt his body alive, and glowing to the tips.

"Scrap, boys!" shouted some one, and then the dark figure had leapt forward, ducked back and sideways, and come in again. Denton struck out, and was hit. One of his eyes seemed to him to be demolished, and he felt a soft lip under his fist just before he was hit again—this time under the chin. A huge fan of fiery needles shot open. He had a momentary persuasion that his head was knocked to pieces, and then something hit his head and back from behind, and the fight became an uninteresting, an impersonal thing.

He was aware that time—seconds or minutes—had passed, abstract, uneventful time. He was lying with his head in a heap of ashes, and something wet and warm ran swiftly into his neck. The first shock broke up into discrete sensations. All his head throbbed; his eye and his chin throbbed exceedingly, and the taste of blood was in his mouth.

"He's all right," said a voice. "He's opening his eyes."

"Serve him——well right," said a second.

His mates were standing about him. He made an effort and sat up. He put his hand to the back of his head, and his hair was wet and full of cinders. A laugh greeted the gesture. His eye was partially closed. He perceived what had happened. His momentary anticipation of a final victory had vanished.

"Looks surprised," said some one.

"'Ave any more?" said a wit; and then, imitating Denton's refined accent.

"No, thank you."

Denton perceived the swart man with a blood-stained handkerchief before his face, and somewhat in the background.

"Where's that bit of bread he's got to eat?" said a little ferret-faced creature; and sought with his foot in the ashes of the adjacent bin.

Denton had a moment of internal debate. He knew the code of honour requires a man to pursue a fight he has begun to the bitter end; but this was his first taste of the bitterness. He was resolved to rise again, but he felt no passionate impulse. It occurred to him—and the thought was no very violent spur—that he was perhaps after all a coward. For a moment his will was heavy, a lump of lead.

"'Ere it is," said the little ferret-faced man, and stooped to pick up a cindery cube. He looked at Denton, then at the others.

Slowly, unwillingly, Denton stood up.

A dirty-faced albino extended a hand to the ferret-faced man. "Gimme that toke," he said. He advanced threateningly, bread in hand, to Denton. "So you ain't 'ad your bellyful yet," he said. "Eh?"

Now it was coming. "No, I haven't," said Denton, with a catching of the breath, and resolved to try this brute behind the ear before he himself got stunned again. He knew he would be stunned again. He was astonished how ill he had judged himself beforehand. A few ridiculous lunges, and down he would go again. He watched the albino's eyes. The albino was grinning confidently, like a man who plans an agreeable trick. A sudden perception of impending indignities stung Denton.

"You leave 'im alone, Jim," said the swart man suddenly over the blood-stained rag. "He ain't done nothing to you."

The albino's grin vanished. He stopped. He looked from one to the other. It seemed to Denton that the swart man demanded the privilege of his destruction. The albino would have been better.

"You leave 'im alone," said the swart man. "See? 'E's 'ad 'is licks."

A clattering bell lifted up its voice and solved the situation. The albino hesitated. "Lucky for you," he said, adding a foul metaphor, and turned with the others towards the press-room again. "Wait for the end of the spell, mate," said the albino over his shoulder—an afterthought. The swart man waited for the albino to precede him. Denton realised that he had a reprieve.

The men passed towards an open door. Denton became aware of his duties, and hurried to join the tail of the queue. At the doorway of the vaulted gallery of presses a yellow-uniformed labour policeman stood ticking a card. He had ignored the swart man's hæmorrhage.

"Hurry up there!" he said to Denton.

"Hello!" he said, at the sight of his facial disarray. "Who's been hitting _you_?"

"That's my affair," said Denton.

"Not if it spiles your work, it ain't," said the man in yellow. "You mind that."

Denton made no answer. He was a rough—a labourer. He wore the blue canvas. The laws of assault and battery, he knew, were not for the likes of him. He went to his press.

He could feel the skin of his brow and chin and head lifting themselves to noble bruises, felt the throb and pain of each aspiring contusion. His nervous system slid down to lethargy; at each movement in his press adjustment he felt he lifted a weight. And as for his honour—that too throbbed and puffed. How did he stand? What precisely had happened in the last ten minutes? What would happen next? He knew that here was enormous matter for thought, and he could not think save in disordered snatches.

His mood was a sort of stagnant astonishment. All his conceptions were overthrown. He had regarded his security from physical violence as inherent, as one of the conditions of life. So, indeed, it had been while he wore his middle-class costume, had his middle-class property to serve for his defence. But who would interfere among Labour roughs fighting together? And indeed in those days no man would. In the Underworld there was no law between man and man; the law and machinery of the state had become for them something that held men down, fended them off from much desirable property and pleasure, and that was all. Violence, that ocean in which the brutes live for ever, and from which a thousand dykes and contrivances have won our hazardous civilised life, had flowed in again upon the sinking underways and submerged them. The fist ruled. Denton had come right down at last to the elemental—fist and trick and the stubborn heart and fellowship—even as it was in the beginning.

The rhythm of his machine changed, and his thoughts were interrupted.

Presently he could think again. Strange how quickly things had happened! He bore these men who had thrashed him no very vivid ill-will. He was bruised and enlightened. He saw with absolute fairness now the reasonableness of his unpopularity. He had behaved like a fool. Disdain, seclusion, are the privilege of the strong. The fallen aristocrat still clinging to his pointless distinction is surely the most pitiful creature of pretence in all this clamant universe. Good heavens! what was there for him to despise in these men?

What a pity he had not appreciated all this better five hours ago!

What would happen at the end of the spell? He could not tell. He could not imagine. He could not imagine the thoughts of these men. He was sensible only of their hostility and utter want of sympathy. Vague possibilities of shame and violence chased one another across his mind.

Could he devise some weapon? He recalled his assault upon the hypnotist, but there were no detachable lamps here. He could see nothing that he could catch up in his defence.

For a space he thought of a headlong bolt for the security of the public ways directly the spell was over. Apart from the trivial consideration of his self-respect, he perceived that this would be only a foolish postponement and aggravation of his trouble. He perceived the ferret-faced man and the albino talking together with their eyes towards him. Presently they were talking to the swart man, who stood with his broad back studiously towards Denton.

At last came the end of the second spell. The lender of oil cans stopped his press sharply and turned round, wiping his mouth with the back of his hand. His eyes had the quiet expectation of one who seats himself in a theatre.

Now was the crisis, and all the little nerves of Denton's being seemed leaping and dancing. He had decided to show fight if any fresh indignity was offered him. He stopped his press and turned. With an enormous affectation of ease he walked down the vault and entered the passage of the ash pits, only to discover he had left his jacket—which he had taken off because of the heat of the vault—beside his press. He walked back. He met the albino eye to eye.

He heard the ferret-faced man in expostulation. "'E reely ought, eat it," said the ferret-faced man. "'E did reely."

"No—you leave 'im alone," said the swart man.

Apparently nothing further was to happen to him that day. He passed out to the passage and staircase that led up to the moving platforms of the city.

He emerged on the livid brilliance and streaming movement of the public street. He became acutely aware of his disfigured face, and felt his swelling bruises with a limp, investigatory hand. He went up to the swiftest platform, and seated himself on a Labour Company bench.

He lapsed into a pensive torpor. The immediate dangers and stresses of his position he saw with a sort of static clearness. What would they do to-morrow? He could not tell. What would Elizabeth think of his brutalisation? He could not tell. He was exhausted. He was aroused presently by a hand upon his arm.

He looked up, and saw the swart man seated beside him. He started. Surely he was safe from violence in the public way!

The swart man's face retained no traces of his share in the fight; his expression was free from hostility—seemed almost deferential. "'Scuse me," he said, with a total absence of truculence. Denton realised that no assault was intended. He stared, awaiting the next development.

It was evident the next sentence was premeditated. "Whad—I—was—going—to say—was this," said the swart man, and sought through a silence for further words.

"Whad—I—was—going—to say—was this," he repeated.

Finally he abandoned that gambit. "You're aw right," he cried, laying a grimy hand on Denton's grimy sleeve. "You're aw right. You're a ge'man. Sorry—very sorry. Wanted to tell you that."

Denton realised that there must exist motives beyond a mere impulse to abominable proceedings in the man. He meditated, and swallowed an unworthy pride.

"I did not mean to be offensive to you," he said, "in refusing that bit of bread."

"Meant it friendly," said the swart man, recalling the scene; "but—in front of that blarsted Whitey and his snigger—Well—I 'ad to scrap."

"Yes," said Denton with sudden fervour: "I was a fool."

"Ah!" said the swart man, with great satisfaction. "That's aw right. Shake!"

And Denton shook.

The moving platform was rushing by the establishment of a face moulder, and its lower front was a huge display of mirror, designed to stimulate the thirst for more symmetrical features. Denton caught the reflection of himself and his new friend, enormously twisted and broadened. His own face was puffed, one-sided, and blood-stained; a grin of idiotic and insincere amiability distorted its latitude. A wisp of hair occluded one eye. The trick of the mirror presented the swart man as a gross expansion of lip and nostril. They were linked by shaking hands. Then abruptly this vision passed—to return to memory in the anæmic meditations of a waking dawn.

As he shook, the swart man made some muddled remark, to the effect that he had always known he could get on with a gentleman if one came his way. He prolonged the shaking until Denton, under the influence of the mirror, withdrew his hand. The swart man became pensive, spat impressively on the platform, and resumed his theme.

"Whad I was going to say was this," he said; was gravelled, and shook his head at his foot.

Denton became curious. "Go on," he said, attentive.

The swart man took the plunge. He grasped Denton's arm, became intimate in his attitude. "'Scuse me," he said. "Fact is, you done know 'ow to scrap. Done know 'ow to. Why—you done know 'ow to begin. You'll get killed if you don't mind. 'Ouldin' your 'ands—There!"

He reinforced his statement by objurgation, watching the effect of each oath with a wary eye.

"F'r instance. You're tall. Long arms. You get a longer reach than any one in the brasted vault. Gobblimey, but I thought I'd got a Tough on. 'Stead of which ... 'Scuse me. I wouldn't have 'it you if I'd known. It's like fighting sacks. 'Tisn' right. Y'r arms seemed 'ung on 'ooks. Reg'lar—'ung on 'ooks. There!"

Denton stared, and then surprised and hurt his battered chin by a sudden laugh. Bitter tears came into his eyes.

"Go on," he said.

The swart man reverted to his formula. He was good enough to say he liked the look of Denton, thought he had stood up "amazing plucky. On'y pluck ain't no good—ain't no brasted good—if you don't 'old your 'ands.

"Whad I was going to say was this," he said. "Lemme show you 'ow to scrap. Jest lemme. You're ig'nant, you ain't no class; but you might be a very decent scrapper—very decent. Shown. That's what I meant to say."

Denton hesitated. "But—" he said, "I can't give you anything—"

"That's the ge'man all over," said the swart man. "Who arst you to?"

"But your time?"

"If you don't get learnt scrapping you'll get killed,—don't you make no bones of that."

Denton thought. "I don't know," he said.

He looked at the face beside him, and all its native coarseness shouted at him. He felt a quick revulsion from his transient friendliness. It seemed to him incredible that it should be necessary for him to be indebted to such a creature.

"The chaps are always scrapping," said the swart man. "Always. And, of course—if one gets waxy and 'its you vital ..."

"By God!" cried Denton; "I wish one would."

"Of course, if you feel like that—"

"You don't understand."

"P'raps I don't," said the swart man; and lapsed into a fuming silence.

When he spoke again his voice was less friendly, and he prodded Denton by way of address. "Look see!" he said: "are you going to let me show you 'ow to scrap?"

"It's tremendously kind of you," said Denton; "but—"

There was a pause. The swart man rose and bent over Denton.

"Too much ge'man," he said—"eh? I got a red face.... By gosh! you are—you are a brasted fool!"

He turned away, and instantly Denton realised the truth of this remark.

The swart man descended with dignity to a cross way, and Denton, after a momentary impulse to pursuit, remained on the platform. For a time the things that had happened filled his mind. In one day his graceful system of resignation had been shattered beyond hope. Brute force, the final, the fundamental, had thrust its face through all his explanations and glosses and consolations and grinned enigmatically. Though he was hungry and tired, he did not go on directly to the Labour Hotel, where he would meet Elizabeth. He found he was beginning to think, he wanted very greatly to think; and so, wrapped in a monstrous cloud of meditation, he went the circuit of the city on his moving platform twice. You figure him, tearing through the glaring, thunder-voiced city at a pace of fifty miles an hour, the city upon the planet that spins along its chartless path through space many thousands of miles an hour, funking most terribly, and trying to understand why the heart and will in him should suffer and keep alive.

When at last he came to Elizabeth, she was white and anxious. He might have noted she was in trouble, had it not been for his own preoccupation. He feared most that she would desire to know every detail of his indignities, that she would be sympathetic or indignant. He saw her eyebrows rise at the sight of him.

"I've had rough handling," he said, and gasped. "It's too fresh—too hot. I don't want to talk about it." He sat down with an unavoidable air of sullenness.

She stared at him in astonishment, and as she read something of the significant hieroglyphic of his battered face, her lips whitened. Her hand—it was thinner now than in the days of their prosperity, and her first finger was a little altered by the metal punching she did—clenched convulsively. "This horrible world!" she said, and said no more.

In these latter days they had become a very silent couple; they said scarcely a word to each other that night, but each followed a private train of thought. In the small hours, as Elizabeth lay awake, Denton started up beside her suddenly—he had been lying as still as a dead man.

"I cannot stand it!" cried Denton. "I will not stand it!"

She saw him dimly, sitting up; saw his arm lunge as if in a furious blow at the enshrouding night. Then for a space he was still.

"It is too much—it is more than one can bear!"

She could say nothing. To her, also, it seemed that this was as far as one could go. She waited through a long stillness. She could see that Denton sat with his arms about his knees, his chin almost touching them.

Then he laughed.

"No," he said at last, "I'm going to stand it. That's the peculiar thing. There isn't a grain of suicide in us—not a grain. I suppose all the people with a turn that way have gone. We're going through with it—to the end."

Elizabeth thought grayly, and realised that this also was true.

"We're going through with it. To think of all who have gone through with it: all the generations—endless—endless. Little beasts that snapped and snarled, snapping and snarling, snapping and snarling, generation after generation."

His monotone, ended abruptly, resumed after a vast interval.

"There were ninety thousand years of stone age. A Denton somewhere in all those years. Apostolic succession. The grace of going through. Let me see! Ninety—nine hundred—three nines, twenty-seven—three thousand generations of men!—men more or less. And each fought, and was bruised, and shamed, and somehow held his own—going through with it—passing it on.... And thousands more to come perhaps—thousands!

"Passing it on. I wonder if they will thank us."

His voice assumed an argumentative note. "If one could find something definite ... If one could say, 'This is why—this is why it goes on....'"

He became still, and Elizabeth's eyes slowly separated him from the darkness until at last she could see how he sat with his head resting on his hand. A sense of the enormous remoteness of their minds came to her; that dim suggestion of another being seemed to her a figure of their mutual understanding. What could he be thinking now? What might he not say next? Another age seemed to elapse before he sighed and whispered: "No. I don't understand it. No!" Then a long interval, and he repeated this. But the second time it had the tone almost of a solution.

She became aware that he was preparing to lie down. She marked his movements, perceived with astonishment how he adjusted his pillow with a careful regard to comfort. He lay down with a sigh of contentment almost. His passion had passed. He lay still, and presently his breathing became regular and deep.

But Elizabeth remained with eyes wide open in the darkness, until the clamour of a bell and the sudden brilliance of the electric light warned them that the Labour Company had need of them for yet another day.

That day came a scuffle with the albino Whitey and the little ferret-faced man. Blunt, the swart artist in scrapping, having first let Denton grasp the bearing of his lesson, intervened, not without a certain quality of patronage. "Drop 'is 'air, Whitey, and let the man be," said his gross voice through a shower of indignities. "Can't you see 'e don't know 'ow to scrap?" And Denton, lying shamefully in the dust, realised that he must accept that course of instruction after all.

He made his apology straight and clean. He scrambled up and walked to Blunt. "I was a fool, and you are right," he said. "If it isn't too late ..."

That night, after the second spell, Denton went with Blunt to certain waste and slime-soaked vaults under the Port of London, to learn the first beginnings of the high art of scrapping as it had been perfected in the great world of the underways: how to hit or kick a man so as to hurt him excruciatingly or make him violently sick, how to hit or kick "vital," how to use glass in one's garments as a club and to spread red ruin with various domestic implements, how to anticipate and demolish your adversary's intentions in other directions; all the pleasant devices, in fact, that had grown up among the disinherited of the great cities of the twentieth and twenty-first centuries, were spread out by a gifted exponent for Denton's learning. Blunt's bashfulness fell from him as the instruction proceeded, and he developed a certain expert dignity, a quality of fatherly consideration. He treated Denton with the utmost consideration, only "flicking him up a bit" now and then, to keep the interest hot, and roaring with laughter at a happy fluke of Denton's that covered his mouth with blood.

"I'm always keerless of my mouth," said Blunt, admitting a weakness. "Always. It don't seem to matter, like, just getting bashed in the mouth— not if your chin's all right. Tastin' blood does me good. Always. But I better not 'it you again."

Denton went home, to fall asleep exhausted and wake in the small hours with aching limbs and all his bruises tingling. Was it worth while that he should go on living? He listened to Elizabeth's breathing, and remembering that he must have awaked her the previous night, he lay very still. He was sick with infinite disgust at the new conditions of his life. He hated it all, hated even the genial savage who had protected him so generously. The monstrous fraud of civilisation glared stark before his eyes; he saw it as a vast lunatic growth, producing a deepening torrent of savagery below, and above ever more flimsy gentility and silly wastefulness. He could see no redeeming reason, no touch of honour, either in the life he had led or in this life to which he had fallen. Civilisation presented itself as some catastrophic product as little concerned with men—save as victims— as a cyclone or a planetary collision. He, and therefore all mankind, seemed living utterly in vain. His mind sought some strange expedients of escape, if not for himself then at least for Elizabeth. But he meant them for himself. What if he hunted up Mwres and told him of their disaster? It came to him as an astonishing thing how utterly Mwres and Bindon had passed out of his range. Where were they? What were they doing? From that he passed to thoughts of utter dishonour. And finally, not arising in any way out of this mental tumult, but ending it as dawn ends the night, came the clear and obvious conclusion of the night before: the conviction that he had to go through with things; that, apart from any remoter view and quite sufficient for all his thought and energy, he had to stand up and fight among his fellows and quit himself like a man.

The second night's instruction was perhaps less dreadful than the first; and the third was even endurable, for Blunt dealt out some praise.

The fourth day Denton chanced upon the fact that the ferret-faced man was a coward. There passed a fortnight of smouldering days and feverish instruction at night; Blunt, with many blasphemies, testified that never had he met so apt a pupil; and all night long Denton dreamt of kicks and counters and gouges and cunning tricks. For all that time no further outrages were attempted, for fear of Blunt; and then came the second crisis. Blunt did not come one day—afterwards he admitted his deliberate intention—and through the tedious morning Whitey awaited the interval between the spells with an ostentatious impatience. He knew nothing of the scrapping lessons, and he spent the time in telling Denton and the vault generally of certain disagreeable proceedings he had in mind.

Whitey was not popular, and the vault disgorged to see him haze the new man with only a languid interest. But matters changed when Whitey's attempt to open the proceedings by kicking Denton in the face was met by an excellently executed duck, catch and throw, that completed the flight of Whitey's foot in its orbit and brought Whitey's head into the ash-heap that had once received Denton's. Whitey arose a shade whiter, and now blasphemously bent upon vital injuries. There were indecisive passages, foiled enterprises that deepened Whitey's evidently growing perplexity; and then things developed into a grouping of Denton uppermost with Whitey's throat in his hand, his knee on Whitey's chest, and a tearful Whitey with a black face, protruding tongue and broken finger endeavouring to explain the misunderstanding by means of hoarse sounds. Moreover, it was evident that among the bystanders there had never been a more popular person than Denton.

Denton, with proper precaution, released his antagonist and stood up. His blood seemed changed to some sort of fluid fire, his limbs felt light and supernaturally strong. The idea that he was a martyr in the civilisation machine had vanished from his mind. He was a man in a world of men.

The little ferret-faced man was the first in the competition to pat him on the back. The lender of oil cans was a radiant sun of genial congratulation.... It seemed incredible to Denton that he had ever thought of despair.

Denton was convinced that not only had he to go through with things, but that he could. He sat on the canvas pallet expounding this new aspect to Elizabeth. One side of his face was bruised. She had not recently fought, she had not been patted on the back, there were no hot bruises upon her face, only a pallor and a new line or so about the mouth. She was taking the woman's share. She looked steadfastly at Denton in his new mood of prophecy. "I feel that there is something," he was saying, "something that goes on, a Being of Life in which we live and move and have our being, something that began fifty—a hundred million years ago, perhaps, that goes on—on: growing, spreading, to things beyond us—things that will justify us all.... That will explain and justify my fighting—these bruises, and all the pain of it. It's the chisel—yes, the chisel of the Maker. If only I could make you feel as I feel, if I could make you! You will, dear, I know you will."

"No," she said in a low voice. "No, I shall not."

"So I might have thought—"

She shook her head. "No," she said, "I have thought as well. What you say—doesn't convince me."

She looked at his face resolutely. "I hate it," she said, and caught at her breath. "You do not understand, you do not think. There was a time when you said things and I believed them. I am growing wiser. You are a man, you can fight, force your way. You do not mind bruises. You can be coarse and ugly, and still a man. Yes—it makes you. It makes you. You are right. Only a woman is not like that. We are different. We have let ourselves get civilised too soon. This underworld is not for us."

She paused and began again.

"I hate it! I hate this horrible canvas! I hate it more than—more than the worst that can happen. It hurts my fingers to touch it. It is horrible to the skin. And the women I work with day after day! I lie awake at nights and think how I may be growing like them...."

She stopped. "I am growing like them," she cried passionately.

Denton stared at her distress. "But—" he said and stopped.

"You don't understand. What have I? What have I to save me? You can fight. Fighting is man's work. But women—women are different.... I have thought it all out, I have done nothing but think night and day. Look at the colour of my face! I cannot go on. I cannot endure this life.... I cannot endure it."

She stopped. She hesitated.

"You do not know all," she said abruptly, and for an instant her lips had a bitter smile. "I have been asked to leave you."

"Leave me!"

She made no answer save an affirmative movement of the head.

Denton stood up sharply. They stared at one another through a long silence.

Suddenly she turned herself about, and flung face downward upon their canvas bed. She did not sob, she made no sound. She lay still upon her face. After a vast, distressful void her shoulders heaved and she began to weep silently.

"Elizabeth!" he whispered—"Elizabeth!"

Very softly he sat down beside her, bent down, put his arm across her in a doubtful caress, seeking vainly for some clue to this intolerable situation.

"Elizabeth," he whispered in her ear.

She thrust him from her with her hand. "I cannot bear a child to be a slave!" and broke out into loud and bitter weeping.

Denton's face changed—became blank dismay. Presently he slipped from the bed and stood on his feet. All the complacency had vanished from his face, had given place to impotent rage. He began to rave and curse at the intolerable forces which pressed upon him, at all the accidents and hot desires and heedlessness that mock the life of man. His little voice rose in that little room, and he shook his fist, this animalcule of the earth, at all that environed him about, at the millions about him, at his past and future and all the insensate vastness of the overwhelming city.

# V

## BINDON INTERVENES

In Bindon's younger days he had dabbled in speculation and made three brilliant flukes. For the rest of his life he had the wisdom to let gambling alone, and the conceit to believe himself a very clever man. A certain desire for influence and reputation interested him in the business intrigues of the giant city in which his flukes were made. He became at last one of the most influential shareholders in the company that owned the London flying stages to which the aëroplanes came from all parts of the world. This much for his public activities. In his private life he was a man of pleasure. And this is the story of his heart.

But before proceeding to such depths, one must devote a little time to the exterior of this person. Its physical basis was slender, and short, and dark; and the face, which was fine-featured and assisted by pigments, varied from an insecure self-complacency to an intelligent uneasiness. His face and head had been depilated, according to the cleanly and hygienic fashion of the time, so that the colour and contour of his hair varied with his costume. This he was constantly changing.

At times he would distend himself with pneumatic vestments in the rococo vein. From among the billowy developments of this style, and beneath a translucent and illuminated headdress, his eye watched jealously for the respect of the less fashionable world. At other times he emphasised his elegant slenderness in close-fitting garments of black satin. For effects of dignity he would assume broad pneumatic shoulders, from which hung a robe of carefully arranged folds of China silk, and a classical Bindon in pink tights was also a transient phenomenon in the eternal pageant of Destiny. In the days when he hoped to marry Elizabeth, he sought to impress and charm her, and at the same time to take off something of his burthen of forty years, by wearing the last fancy of the contemporary buck, a costume of elastic material with distensible warts and horns, changing in colour as he walked, by an ingenious arrangement of versatile chromatophores. And no doubt, if Elizabeth's affection had not been already engaged by the worthless Denton, and if her tastes had not had that odd bias for old-fashioned ways, this extremely _chic_ conception would have ravished her. Bindon had consulted Elizabeth's father before presenting himself in this garb—he was one of those men who always invite criticism of their costume—and Mwres had pronounced him all that the heart of woman could desire. But the affair of the hypnotist proved that his knowledge of the heart of woman was incomplete.

Bindon's idea of marrying had been formed some little time before Mwres threw Elizabeth's budding womanhood in his way. It was one of Bindon's most cherished secrets that he had a considerable capacity for a pure and simple life of a grossly sentimental type. The thought imparted a sort of pathetic seriousness to the offensive and quite inconsequent and unmeaning excesses, which he was pleased to regard as dashing wickedness, and which a number of good people also were so unwise as to treat in that desirable manner. As a consequence of these excesses, and perhaps by reason also of an inherited tendency to early decay, his liver became seriously affected, and he suffered increasing inconvenience when travelling by aëroplane. It was during his convalescence from a protracted bilious attack that it occurred to him that in spite of all the terrible fascinations of Vice, if he found a beautiful, gentle, good young woman of a not too violently intellectual type to devote her life to him, he might yet be saved to Goodness, and even rear a spirited family in his likeness to solace his declining years. But like so many experienced men of the world, he doubted if there were any good women. Of such as he had heard tell he was outwardly sceptical and privately much afraid.

When the aspiring Mwres effected his introduction to Elizabeth, it seemed to him that his good fortune was complete. He fell in love with her at once. Of course, he had always been falling in love since he was sixteen, in accordance with the extremely varied recipes to be found in the accumulated literature of many centuries. But this was different. This was real love. It seemed to him to call forth all the lurking goodness in his nature. He felt that for her sake he could give up a way of life that had already produced the gravest lesions on his liver and nervous system. His imagination presented him with idyllic pictures of the life of the reformed rake. He would never be sentimental with her, or silly; but always a little cynical and bitter, as became the past. Yet he was sure she would have an intuition of his real greatness and goodness. And in due course he would confess things to her, pour his version of what he regarded as his wickedness—showing what a complex of Goethe, and Benvenuto Cellini, and Shelley, and all those other chaps he really was—into her shocked, very beautiful, and no doubt sympathetic ear. And preparatory to these things he wooed her with infinite subtlety and respect. And the reserve with which Elizabeth treated him seemed nothing more nor less than an exquisite modesty touched and enhanced by an equally exquisite lack of ideas.

Bindon knew nothing of her wandering affections, nor of the attempt made by Mwres to utilise hypnotism as a corrective to this digression of her heart; he conceived he was on the best of terms with Elizabeth, and had made her quite successfully various significant presents of jewellery and the more virtuous cosmetics, when her elopement with Denton threw the world out of gear for him. His first aspect of the matter was rage begotten of wounded vanity, and as Mwres was the most convenient person, he vented the first brunt of it upon him.

He went immediately and insulted the desolate father grossly, and then spent an active and determined day going to and fro about the city and interviewing people in a consistent and partly-successful attempt to ruin that matrimonial speculator. The effectual nature of these activities gave him a temporary exhilaration, and he went to the dining-place he had frequented in his wicked days in a devil-may-care frame of mind, and dined altogether too amply and cheerfully with two other golden youths in their early forties. He threw up the game; no woman was worth being good for, and he astonished even himself by the strain of witty cynicism he developed. One of the other desperate blades, warmed with wine, made a facetious allusion to his disappointment, but at the time this did not seem unpleasant.

The next morning found his liver and temper inflamed. He kicked his phonographic-news machine to pieces, dismissed his valet, and resolved that he would perpetrate a terrible revenge upon Elizabeth. Or Denton. Or somebody. But anyhow, it was to be a terrible revenge; and the friend who had made fun at him should no longer see him in the light of a foolish girl's victim. He knew something of the little property that was due to her, and that this would be the only support of the young couple until Mwres should relent. If Mwres did not relent, and if unpropitious things should happen to the affair in which Elizabeth's expectations lay, they would come upon evil times and be sufficiently amenable to temptation of a sinister sort. Bindon's imagination, abandoning its beautiful idealism altogether, expanded the idea of temptation of a sinister sort. He figured himself as the implacable, the intricate and powerful man of wealth pursuing this maiden who had scorned him. And suddenly her image came upon his mind vivid and dominant, and for the first time in his life Bindon realised something of the real power of passion.

His imagination stood aside like a respectful footman who has done his work in ushering in the emotion.

"My God!" cried Bindon: "I will have her! If I have to kill myself to get her! And that other fellow——!"

After an interview with his medical man and a penance for his overnight excesses in the form of bitter drugs, a mitigated but absolutely resolute Bindon sought out Mwres. Mwres he found properly smashed, and impoverished and humble, in a mood of frantic self-preservation, ready to sell himself body and soul, much more any interest in a disobedient daughter, to recover his lost position in the world. In the reasonable discussion that followed, it was agreed that these misguided young people should be left to sink into distress, or possibly even assisted towards that improving discipline by Bindon's financial influence.

"And then?" said Mwres.

"They will come to the Labour Company," said Bindon. "They will wear the blue canvas."

"And then?"

"She will divorce him," he said, and sat for a moment intent upon that prospect. For in those days the austere limitations of divorce of Victorian times were extraordinarily relaxed, and a couple might separate on a hundred different scores.

Then suddenly Bindon astonished himself and Mwres by jumping to his feet. "She shall divorce him!" he cried. "I will have it so—I will work it so. By God! it shall be so. He shall be disgraced, so that she must. He shall be smashed and pulverised."

The idea of smashing and pulverising inflamed him further. He began a Jovian pacing up and down the little office. "I will have her," he cried. "I will have her! Heaven and Hell shall not save her from me!" His passion evaporated in its expression, and left him at the end simply histrionic. He struck an attitude and ignored with heroic determination a sharp twinge of pain about the diaphragm. And Mwres sat with his pneumatic cap deflated and himself very visibly impressed.

And so, with a fair persistency, Bindon sat himself to the work of being Elizabeth's malignant providence, using with ingenious dexterity every particle of advantage wealth in those days gave a man over his fellow-creatures. A resort to the consolations of religion hindered these operations not at all. He would go and talk with an interesting, experienced and sympathetic Father of the Huysmanite sect of the Isis cult, about all the irrational little proceedings he was pleased to regard as his heaven-dismaying wickedness, and the interesting, experienced and sympathetic Father representing Heaven dismayed, would with a pleasing affectation of horror, suggest simple and easy penances, and recommend a monastic foundation that was airy, cool, hygienic, and not vulgarised, for viscerally disordered penitent sinners of the refined and wealthy type. And after these excursions, Bindon would come back to London quite active and passionate again. He would machinate with really considerable energy, and repair to a certain gallery high above the street of moving ways, from which he could view the entrance to the barrack of the Labour Company in the ward which sheltered Denton and Elizabeth. And at last one day he saw Elizabeth go in, and thereby his passion was renewed.

So in the fullness of time the complicated devices of Bindon ripened, and he could go to Mwres and tell him that the young people were near despair.

"It's time for you," he said, "to let your parental affections have play. She's been in blue canvas some months, and they've been cooped together in one of those Labour dens, and the little girl is dead. She knows now what his manhood is worth to her, by way of protection, poor girl. She'll see things now in a clearer light. You go to her—I don't want to appear in this affair yet—and point out to her how necessary it is that she should get a divorce from him...."

"She's obstinate," said Mwres doubtfully.

"Spirit!" said Bindon. "She's a wonderful girl—a wonderful girl!"

"She'll refuse."

"Of course she will. But leave it open to her. Leave it open to her. And some day—in that stuffy den, in that irksome, toilsome life they can't help it—they'll have a quarrel. And then—"

Mwres meditated over the matter, and did as he was told.

Then Bindon, as he had arranged with his spiritual adviser, went into retreat. The retreat of the Huysmanite sect was a beautiful place, with the sweetest air in London, lit by natural sunlight, and with restful quadrangles of real grass open to the sky, where at the same time the penitent man of pleasure might enjoy all the pleasures of loafing and all the satisfaction of distinguished austerity. And, save for participation in the simple and wholesome dietary of the place and in certain magnificent chants, Bindon spent all his time in meditation upon the theme of Elizabeth, and the extreme purification his soul had undergone since he first saw her, and whether he would be able to get a dispensation to marry her from the experienced and sympathetic Father in spite of the approaching "sin" of her divorce; and then ... Bindon would lean against a pillar of the quadrangle and lapse into reveries on the superiority of virtuous love to any other form of indulgence. A curious feeling in his back and chest that was trying to attract his attention, a disposition to be hot or shiver, a general sense of ill-health and cutaneous discomfort he did his best to ignore. All that of course belonged to the old life that he was shaking off.

When he came out of retreat he went at once to Mwres to ask for news of Elizabeth. Mwres was clearly under the impression that he was an exemplary father, profoundly touched about the heart by his child's unhappiness. "She was pale," he said, greatly moved; "She was pale. When I asked her to come away and leave him—and be happy—she put her head down upon the table"—Mwres sniffed—"and cried."

His agitation was so great that he could say no more.

"Ah!" said Bindon, respecting this manly grief. "Oh!" said Bindon quite suddenly, with his hand to his side.

Mwres looked up sharply out of the pit of his sorrows, startled. "What's the matter?" he asked, visibly concerned.

"A most violent pain. Excuse me! You were telling me about Elizabeth."

And Mwres, after a decent solicitude for Bindon's pain, proceeded with his report. It was even unexpectedly hopeful. Elizabeth, in her first emotion at discovering that her father had not absolutely deserted her, had been frank with him about her sorrows and disgusts.

"Yes," said Bindon, magnificently, "I shall have her yet." And then that novel pain twitched him for the second time.

For these lower pains the priest was comparatively ineffectual, inclining rather to regard the body and them as mental illusions amenable to contemplation; so Bindon took it to a man of a class he loathed, a medical man of extraordinary repute and incivility. "We must go all over you," said the medical man, and did so with the most disgusting frankness. "Did you ever bring any children into the world?" asked this gross materialist among other impertinent questions.

"Not that I know of," said Bindon, too amazed to stand upon his dignity.

"Ah!" said the medical man, and proceeded with his punching and sounding. Medical science in those days was just reaching the beginnings of precision. "You'd better go right away," said the medical man, "and make the Euthanasia. The sooner the better."

Bindon gasped. He had been trying not to understand the technical explanations and anticipations in which the medical man had indulged.

"I say!" he said. "But do you mean to say ... Your science ..."

"Nothing," said the medical man. "A few opiates. The thing is your own doing, you know, to a certain extent."

"I was sorely tempted in my youth."

"It's not that so much. But you come of a bad stock. Even if you'd have taken precautions you'd have had bad times to wind up with. The mistake was getting born. The indiscretions of the parents. And you've shirked exercise, and so forth."

"I had no one to advise me."

"Medical men are always willing."

"I was a spirited young fellow."

"We won't argue; the mischief's done now. You've lived. We can't start you again. You ought never to have started at all. Frankly—the Euthanasia!"

Bindon hated him in silence for a space. Every word of this brutal expert jarred upon his refinements. He was so gross, so impermeable to all the subtler issues of being. But it is no good picking a quarrel with a doctor. "My religious beliefs," he said, "I don't approve of suicide."

"You've been doing it all your life."

"Well, anyhow, I've come to take a serious view of life now."

"You're bound to, if you go on living. You'll hurt. But for practical purposes it's late. However, if you mean to do that—perhaps I'd better mix you a little something. You'll hurt a great deal. These little twinges ..."

"Twinges!"

"Mere preliminary notices."

"How long can I go on? I mean, before I hurt—really."

"You'll get it hot soon. Perhaps three days."

Bindon tried to argue for an extension of time, and in the midst of his pleading gasped, put his hand to his side. Suddenly the extraordinary pathos of his life came to him clear and vivid. "It's hard," he said. "It's infernally hard! I've been no man's enemy but my own. I've always treated everybody quite fairly."

The medical man stared at him without any sympathy for some seconds. He was reflecting how excellent it was that there were no more Bindons to carry on that line of pathos. He felt quite optimistic. Then he turned to his telephone and ordered up a prescription from the Central Pharmacy.

He was interrupted by a voice behind him. "By God!" cried Bindon; "I'll have her yet."

The physician stared over his shoulder at Bindon's expression, and then altered the prescription.

So soon as this painful interview was over, Bindon gave way to rage. He settled that the medical man was not only an unsympathetic brute and wanting in the first beginnings of a gentleman, but also highly incompetent; and he went off to four other practitioners in succession, with a view to the establishment of this intuition. But to guard against surprises he kept that little prescription in his pocket. With each he began by expressing his grave doubts of the first doctor's intelligence, honesty and professional knowledge, and then stated his symptoms, suppressing only a few more material facts in each case. These were always subsequently elicited by the doctor. In spite of the welcome depreciation of another practitioner, none of these eminent specialists would give Bindon any hope of eluding the anguish and helplessness that loomed now close upon him. To the last of them he unburthened his mind of an accumulated disgust with medical science. "After centuries and centuries," he exclaimed hotly; "and you can do nothing—except admit your helplessness. I say, 'save me'—and what do you do?"

"No doubt it's hard on you," said the doctor. "But you should have taken precautions."

"How was I to know?"

"It wasn't our place to run after you," said the medical man, picking a thread of cotton from his purple sleeve. "Why should we save you in particular? You see—from one point of view—people with imaginations and passions like yours have to go—they have to go."

"Go?"

"Die out. It's an eddy."

He was a young man with a serene face. He smiled at Bindon. "We get on with research, you know; we give advice when people have the sense to ask for it. And we bide our time."

"Bide your time?"

"We hardly know enough yet to take over the management, you know."

"The management?"

"You needn't be anxious. Science is young yet. It's got to keep on growing for a few generations. We know enough now to know we don't know enough yet.... But the time is coming, all the same. _You_ won't see the time. But, between ourselves, you rich men and party bosses, with your natural play of the passions and patriotism and religion and so forth, have made rather a mess of things; haven't you? These Underways! And all that sort of thing. Some of us have a sort of fancy that in time we may know enough to take over a little more than the ventilation and drains. Knowledge keeps on piling up, you know. It keeps on growing. And there's not the slightest hurry for a generation or so. Some day—some day, men will live in a different way." He looked at Bindon and meditated. "There'll be a lot of dying out before that day can come."

Bindon attempted to point out to this young man how silly and irrelevant such talk was to a sick man like himself, how impertinent and uncivil it was to him, an older man occupying a position in the official world of extraordinary power and influence. He insisted that a doctor was paid to cure people—he laid great stress on "paid"—and had no business to glance even for a moment at "those other questions." "But we do," said the young man, insisting upon facts, and Bindon lost his temper.

His indignation carried him home. That these incompetent impostors, who were unable to save the life of a really influential man like himself, should dream of some day robbing the legitimate property owners of social control, of inflicting one knew not what tyranny upon the world. Curse science! He fumed over the intolerable prospect for some time, and then the pain returned, and he recalled the made-up prescription of the first doctor, still happily in his pocket. He took a dose forthwith.

It calmed and soothed him greatly, and he could sit down in his most comfortable chair beside his library (of phonographic records), and think over the altered aspect of affairs. His indignation passed, his anger and his passion crumbled under the subtle attack of that prescription, pathos became his sole ruler. He stared about him, at his magnificent and voluptuously appointed apartment, at his statuary and discreetly veiled pictures, and all the evidences of a cultivated and elegant wickedness; he touched a stud and the sad pipings of Tristan's shepherd filled the air. His eye wandered from one object to another. They were costly and gross and florid—but they were his. They presented in concrete form his ideals, his conceptions of beauty and desire, his idea of all that is precious in life. And now—he must leave it all like a common man. He was, he felt, a slender and delicate flame, burning out. So must all life flame up and pass, he thought. His eyes filled with tears.

Then it came into his head that he was alone. Nobody cared for him, nobody needed him! at any moment he might begin to hurt vividly. He might even howl. Nobody would mind. According to all the doctors he would have excellent reason for howling in a day or so. It recalled what his spiritual adviser had said of the decline of faith and fidelity, the degeneration of the age. He beheld himself as a pathetic proof of this; he, the subtle, able, important, voluptuous, cynical, complex Bindon, possibly howling, and not one faithful simple creature in all the world to howl in sympathy. Not one faithful simple soul was there—no shepherd to pipe to him! Had all such faithful simple creatures vanished from this harsh and urgent earth? He wondered whether the horrid vulgar crowd that perpetually went about the city could possibly know what he thought of them. If they did he felt sure _some_ would try to earn a better opinion. Surely the world went from bad to worse. It was becoming impossible for Bindons. Perhaps some day ... He was quite sure that the one thing he had needed in life was sympathy. For a time he regretted that he left no sonnets—no enigmatical pictures or something of that sort behind him to carry on his being until at last the sympathetic mind should come....

It seemed incredible to him that this that came was extinction. Yet his sympathetic spiritual guide was in this matter annoyingly figurative and vague. Curse science! It had undermined all faith—all hope. To go out, to vanish from theatre and street, from office and dining-place, from the dear eyes of womankind. And not to be missed! On the whole to leave the world happier!

He reflected that he had never worn his heart upon his sleeve. Had he after all been too unsympathetic? Few people could suspect how subtly profound he really was beneath the mask of that cynical gaiety of his. They would not understand the loss they had suffered. Elizabeth, for example, had not suspected....

He had reserved that. His thoughts having come to Elizabeth gravitated about her for some time. How little Elizabeth understood him!

That thought became intolerable. Before all other things he must set that right. He realised that there was still something for him to do in life, his struggle against Elizabeth was even yet not over. He could never overcome her now, as he had hoped and prayed. But he might still impress her!

From that idea he expanded. He might impress her profoundly—he might impress her so that she should for evermore regret her treatment of him. The thing that she must realise before everything else was his magnanimity. His magnanimity! Yes! he had loved her with amazing greatness of heart. He had not seen it so clearly before—but of course he was going to leave her all his property. He saw it instantly, as a thing determined and inevitable. She would think how good he was, how spaciously generous; surrounded by all that makes life tolerable from his hand, she would recall with infinite regret her scorn and coldness. And when she sought expression for that regret, she would find that occasion gone forever, she should be met by a locked door, by a disdainful stillness, by a white dead face. He closed his eyes and remained for a space imagining himself that white dead face.

From that he passed to other aspects of the matter, but his determination was assured. He meditated elaborately before he took action, for the drug he had taken inclined him to a lethargic and dignified melancholy. In certain respects he modified details. If he left all his property to Elizabeth it would include the voluptuously appointed room he occupied, and for many reasons he did not care to leave that to her. On the other hand, it had to be left to some one. In his clogged condition this worried him extremely.

In the end he decided to leave it to the sympathetic exponent of the fashionable religious cult, whose conversation had been so pleasing in the past. "He will understand," said Bindon with a sentimental sigh. "He knows what Evil means—he understands something of the Stupendous Fascination of the Sphinx of Sin. Yes—he will understand." By that phrase it was that Bindon was pleased to dignify certain unhealthy and undignified departures from sane conduct to which a misguided vanity and an ill-controlled curiosity had led him. He sat for a space thinking how very Hellenic and Italian and Neronic, and all those things, he had been. Even now—might one not try a sonnet? A penetrating voice to echo down the ages, sensuous, sinister, and sad. For a space he forgot Elizabeth. In the course of half an hour he spoilt three phonographic coils, got a headache, took a second dose to calm himself, and reverted to magnanimity and his former design.

At last he faced the unpalatable problem of Denton. It needed all his newborn magnanimity before he could swallow the thought of Denton; but at last this greatly misunderstood man, assisted by his sedative and the near approach of death, effected even that. If he was at all exclusive about Denton, if he should display the slightest distrust, if he attempted any specific exclusion of that young man, she might—misunderstand. Yes—she should have her Denton still. His magnanimity must go even to that. He tried to think only of Elizabeth in the matter.

He rose with a sigh, and limped across to the telephonic apparatus that communicated with his solicitor. In ten minutes a will duly attested and with its proper thumb-mark signature lay in the solicitor's office three miles away. And then for a space Bindon sat very still.

Suddenly he started out of a vague reverie and pressed an investigatory hand to his side.

Then he jumped eagerly to his feet and rushed to the telephone. The Euthanasia Company had rarely been called by a client in a greater hurry.

So it came at last that Denton and his Elizabeth, against all hope, returned unseparated from the labour servitude to which they had fallen. Elizabeth came out from her cramped subterranean den of metal-beaters and all the sordid circumstances of blue canvas, as one comes out of a nightmare. Back towards the sunlight their fortune took them; once the bequest was known to them, the bare thought of another day's hammering became intolerable. They went up long lifts and stairs to levels that they had not seen since the days of their disaster. At first she was full of this sensation of escape; even to think of the underways was intolerable; only after many months could she begin to recall with sympathy the faded women who were still below there, murmuring scandals and reminiscences and folly, and tapping away their lives.

Her choice of the apartments they presently took expressed the vehemence of her release. They were rooms upon the very verge of the city; they had a roof space and a balcony upon the city wall, wide open to the sun and wind, the country and the sky.

And in that balcony comes the last scene in this story. It was a summer sunsetting, and the hills of Surrey were very blue and clear. Denton leant upon the balcony regarding them, and Elizabeth sat by his side. Very wide and spacious was the view, for their balcony hung five hundred feet above the ancient level of the ground. The oblongs of the Food Company, broken here and there by the ruins—grotesque little holes and sheds—of the ancient suburbs, and intersected by shining streams of sewage, passed at last into a remote diapering at the foot of the distant hills. There once had been the squatting-place of the children of Uya. On those further slopes gaunt machines of unknown import worked slackly at the end of their spell, and the hill crest was set with stagnant wind vanes. Along the great south road the Labour Company's field workers in huge wheeled mechanical vehicles, were hurrying back to their meals, their last spell finished. And through the air a dozen little private aëroplanes sailed down towards the city. Familiar scene as it was to the eyes of Denton and Elizabeth, it would have filled the minds of their ancestors with incredulous amazement. Denton's thoughts fluttered towards the future in a vain attempt at what that scene might be in another two hundred years, and, recoiling, turned towards the past.

He shared something of the growing knowledge of the time; he could picture the quaint smoke-grimed Victorian city with its narrow little roads of beaten earth, its wide common-land, ill-organised, ill-built suburbs, and irregular enclosures; the old countryside of the Stuart times, with its little villages and its petty London; the England of the monasteries, the far older England of the Roman dominion, and then before that a wild country with here and there the huts of some warring tribe. These huts must have come and gone and come again through a space of years that made the Roman camp and villa seem but yesterday; and before those years, before even the huts, there had been men in the valley. Even then—so recent had it all been when one judged it by the standards of geological time—this valley had been here; and those hills yonder, higher, perhaps, and snow-tipped, had still been yonder hills, and the Thames had flowed down from the Cotswolds to the sea. But the men had been but the shapes of men, creatures of darkness and ignorance, victims of beasts and floods, storms and pestilence and incessant hunger. They had held a precarious foothold amidst bears and lions and all the monstrous violence of the past. Already some at least of these enemies were overcome....

For a time Denton pursued the thoughts of this spacious vision, trying in obedience to his instinct to find his place and proportion in the scheme.

"It has been chance," he said, "it has been luck. We have come through. It happens we have come through. Not by any strength of our own....

"And yet... No. I don't know."

He was silent for a long time before he spoke again.

"After all—there is a long time yet. There have scarcely been men for twenty thousand years—and there has been life for twenty millions. And what are generations? What are generations? It is enormous, and we are so little. Yet we know—we feel. We are not dumb atoms, we are part of it—part of it—to the limits of our strength and will. Even to die is part of it. Whether we die or live, we are in the making....

"As time goes on—perhaps—men will be wiser.... Wiser....

"Will they ever understand?"

He became silent again. Elizabeth said nothing to these things, but she regarded his dreaming face with infinite affection. Her mind was not very active that evening. A great contentment possessed her. After a time she laid a gentle hand on his beside her. He fondled it softly, still looking out upon the spacious gold-woven view. So they sat as the sun went down. Until presently Elizabeth shivered.

Denton recalled himself abruptly from these spacious issues of his leisure, and went in to fetch her a shawl.

The End

# MOMENT IN HISTORY

*A happy gent delivering milk and other dairy goods to the people.*
*Photo from 1950s.*

# Southwest Scenarios

**COMMENTARIES FROM RURAL ARIZONA**
**BY DARRYLE PURCELL**

## Free Speech is a Right

*From April 2017*

WRITING ABOUT WHITE-HATTED COWBOY GOOD GUYS IS OUT OF THE QUESTION this week. Today's topic is on the other side of the spectrum – contemporary villains. These are people who know nothing about the values of the Code of the West. They don't respect anyone else's rights to live and speak freely. And they have channeled their lack of values into a destructive, Machiavellian hatred. Obviously, I'm referring to the current crop of violent, anti-free-speech protesters.

The people who scream the loudest while destroying property just to make sure other opinions aren't voiced do not deserve our attention. They deserve the attention of law enforcement. Break the law; go to jail.

You know the protest gatherings I'm referring to. On the other hand, there are many valuable rallies and parades in this country that profess a point of view. And, in Arizona, most of them are peaceful and end up being a lot of fun. I wouldn't be surprised to see a Pit-Bull-Pride Parade on Bullhead City's Miracle Mile this year as a replacement for the River Regatta. But I digress.

This country has bent over backward to accommodate political expression of all kinds. Americans have the right to say some very wacky things, as long as they do so peacefully. Since the 1960s, protesters have taken to the streets to rally for every issue from anti-war to anti-death penalty, anti-vaccination, anti-meat, anti-guns and anti-restroom "discrimination." And no one steps in the way to stop these naysayers while the law is being followed. Peaceful protest is our First Amendment right; violence is not.

Today, whenever protesters seem to be being ignored, they tend to get out of hand. And just like our parents used to say in the 1950s and '60s when a bunch of us kids would get carried away with our toy swords and BB-guns, "It's all fun and games until someone loses an eye." Many current protests seem to be premeditated crimes of violence and should be dealt with as such.

I've noticed issues are now less important to protesters than personalities. For instance, in California (the land of openness, diversity and acceptance), professional agitators always gather to disrupt any speaker to the right of Ho Chi Minh or Jerry Brown. Civilized discourse has become a thing of the past for the Golden State. Of course that state looks upon current federal immigration laws a lot like southern states once viewed the Emancipation Proclamation. (Just thinking about that brought an odd image of Nancy Pelosi in a Confederate general's uniform to mind.)

Anyway, lots of things have been said in this paper and others about the behavior of today's protesters. I believe lawbreakers need to be dealt with by the law. But I also think that many liberals who share the anti-Trump, anti-wall, anti-Republican values of the protesters also do not believe that violence is the answer. And those folks should unite with the rest of us and denounce the violence. Then, maybe, we could get back to civil discourse.

And I, for one, would look forward to a peaceful Bullhead City Pit-Bull-Pride Parade, as long as there is no discrimination against Jack Russell terriers, Weimaraners, Shih Tzus, miniature Pinschers or Pekingese pups. I'm sure we could all get along. But cats can be prohibited.

# Southwest Scenarios

The commentaries here and in future issues were originally published by *The Mohave Valley Daily News between 1993 & 2013--and* in many ways they apply to today.
We are grateful to republish these commentaries written by Darryle Purcell in full and unedited. His own brand of humor and style can deliver insight, provoke thought, and even boil blood.

FROM 1912: VAUDEVILLE ENTERTAINER MARY DORR

# THE CHRISTMAS MASQUERADE

## BY MARY E. WILKINS FREEMAN

*From 1912: Vaudeville entertainer Mary Dorr*

On Christmas Eve the Mayor's stately mansion presented a beautiful appearance. There were rows of different coloured wax candles burning in every window, and beyond them one could see the chandeliers of gold and crystal blazing with light. The fiddles were squeaking merrily, and lovely little forms flew past the windows in time to the music.

There were gorgeous carpets laid from the door to the street, and carriages were constantly arriving and fresh guests tripping over them. They were all children. The Mayor was giving a Christmas Masquerade tonight to all the children in the city, the poor as well as the rich. The preparation for this ball had been making an immense sensation for the last three months. Placards had been up in the most conspicuous points in the city, and all the daily newspapers had at least a column devoted to it, headed with

**"THE MAYOR'S CHRISTMAS MASQUERADE,"** in very large letters.

The Mayor had promised to defray the expenses of all the poor children whose parents were unable to do so, and the bills for their costumes were directed to be sent in to him.

Of course there was great excitement among the regular costumers of the city, and they all resolved to vie with one another in being the most popular, and the best patronized on this gala occasion. But the placards and the notices had not been out a week before a new Costumer appeared who cast all the others into the shade directly. He set up his shop on the corner of one of the principal streets, and hung up his beautiful costumes in the windows. He was a little fellow, not much bigger than a boy of ten. His cheeks were as red as roses, and he had on a long curling wig as white as snow. He wore a suit of crimson velvet knee-breeches, and a little swallow-tailed coat with beautiful golden buttons. Deep lace ruffles fell over his slender white hands, and he wore elegant knee buckles of glittering stones. He sat on a high stool behind his counter and served his customers himself; he kept no clerk.

It did not take the children long to discover what beautiful things he had, and how superior he was to the other costumers, and they begun to flock to his shop immediately, from the Mayor's daughter to the poor ragpicker's. The children were to select their own costumes; the Mayor had stipulated that. It was to be a children's ball in every sense of the word.

So they decided to be fairies and shepherdesses, and princesses according to their own fancies; and this new Costumer had charming costumes to suit them.

It was noticeable that, for the most part, the children of the rich, who had always had everything they desired, would choose the parts of goose-girls and peasants and such like; and the poor children jumped eagerly at the chance of being princesses or fairies for a few hours in their miserable lives.

When Christmas Eve came and the children flocked into the Mayor's mansion, whether it was owing to the Costumer's art, or their own adaptation to the characters they had chosen, it was wonderful how lifelike their representations were. Those little fairies in their short skirts of silken gauze, in which golden sparkles appeared as they moved with their little funny gossamer wings, like butterflies, looked like real fairies. It did not seem possible, when they floated around to the music, half supported on the tips of their dainty toes, half by their filmy purple wings, their delicate bodies swaying in time, that they could be anything but fairies. It seemed absurd to imagine that they were Johnny Mullens, the washerwoman's son, and Polly Flinders, the charwoman's little girl, and so on.

The Mayor's daughter, who had chosen the character of a goose-girl, looked so like a true one that one could hardly dream she ever was anything else. She was, ordinarily, a slender, dainty little lady rather tall for her age. She now looked very short and stubbed and brown, just as if she had been accustomed to tend geese in all sorts of weather. It was so with all the others—the Red Riding-hoods, the princesses, the Bo-Peeps and with every one of the characters who came to the Mayor's ball; Red Riding-hood looked round, with big, frightened eyes, all ready to spy the wolf, and carried her little pat of butter and pot of honey gingerly in her basket; Bo-Peep's eyes looked red with weeping for the loss of her sheep; and the princesses swept about so grandly in their splendid brocaded trains, and held their crowned heads so high that people half-believed them to be true princesses.

But there never was anything like the fun at the Mayor's Christmas ball. The fiddlers fiddled and fiddled, and the children danced and danced on the beautiful waxed floors. The Mayor, with his family and a few grand guests, sat on a dais covered with blue velvet at one end of the dancing hall, and watched the sport. They were all delighted. The Mayor's eldest daughter sat in front and clapped her little soft white hands. She was a tall, beautiful young maiden, and wore a white dress, and a little cap woven of blue violets on her yellow hair. Her name was Violetta.

The supper was served at midnight—and such a supper! The mountains of pink and white ices, and the cakes with sugar castles and flower gardens on the tops of them, and the charming shapes of gold and ruby-coloured jellies. There were wonderful bonbons which even the Mayor's daughter did not have every day; and all sorts of fruits, fresh and candied. They had cowslip wine in green glasses, and elderberry wine in red, and they drank each other's health. The glasses held a thimbleful each; the Mayor's wife thought that was all the wine they ought to have. Under each child's plate there was a pretty present and every one had a basket of bonbons and cake to carry home.

At four o'clock the fiddlers put up their fiddles and the children went home; fairies and shepherdesses and pages and princesses all jabbering gleefully about the splendid time they had had.

But in a short time what consternation there was throughout the city. When the proud and fond parents attempted to unbutton their children's dresses, in order to prepare them for bed, not a single costume would come off. The buttons buttoned again as fast as they were unbuttoned; even if they pulled out a pin, in it would slip again in a twinkling; and when a string was untied it tied itself up again into a bowknot. The parents were dreadfully frightened. But the children were so tired out they finally let them go to bed in their fancy costumes and thought perhaps they would come off better in the morning. So Red Riding-hood went to bed in her little red cloak holding fast to her basket full of dainties for her grandmother, and Bo-Peep slept with her crook in her hand.

The children all went to bed readily enough, they were so very tired, even though they had to go in this strange array. All but the fairies—they danced and pirouetted and would not be still.

"We want to swing on the blades of grass," they kept saying, "and play hide and seek in the lily cups, and take a nap between the leaves of the roses."

The poor charwomen and coal-heavers, whose children the fairies were for the most part, stared at them in great distress. They did not know what to do with these radiant, frisky little creatures into which their Johnnys and their Pollys and Betseys were so suddenly transformed. But the fairies went to bed quietly enough when daylight came, and were soon fast asleep.

There was no further trouble till twelve o'clock, when all the children woke up. Then a great wave of alarm spread over the city. Not one of the costumes would come off then. The buttons buttoned as fast as they were unbuttoned; the pins quilted themselves in as fast as they were pulled out; and the strings flew round like lightning and twisted themselves into bow-knots as fast as they were untied.

And that was not the worst of it; every one of the children seemed to have become, in reality, the character which he or she had assumed.

The Mayor's daughter declared she was going to tend her geese out in the pasture, and the shepherdesses sprang out of their little beds of down, throwing aside their silken quilts, and cried that they must go out and watch their sheep. The princesses jumped up from their straw pallets, and wanted to go to court; and all the rest of them likewise. Poor little Red Riding-hood sobbed and sobbed because she couldn't go and carry her basket to her grandmother, and as she didn't have any grandmother she couldn't go, of course, and her parents were very much doubled. It was all so mysterious and dreadful. The news spread very rapidly over the city, and soon a great crowd gathered around the new Costumer's shop for every one thought he must be responsible for all this mischief.

The shop door was locked; but they soon battered it down with stones. When they rushed in the Costumer was not there; he had disappeared with all his wares. Then they did not know what to do. But it was evident that they must do something before long for the state of affairs was growing worse and worse.

The Mayor's little daughter braced her back up against the tapestried wall, and planted her two feet in their thick shoes firmly. "I will go and tend my geese," she kept crying. "I won't eat my breakfast. I won't go out in the park. I won't go to school. I'm going to tend my geese—I will, I will, I will!"

And the princesses trailed their rich trains over the rough unpainted floors in their parents' poor little huts, and held their crowned heads very high and demanded to be taken to court. The princesses were mostly geese-girls when they were their proper selves, and their geese were suffering, and their poor parents did not know what they were going to do and they wrung their hands and wept as they gazed on their gorgeously apparelled children.

Finally the Mayor called a meeting of the Aldermen, and they all assembled in the City Hall. Nearly every one of them had a son or a daughter who was a chimney-sweep, or a little watch-girl, or a shepherdess. They appointed a chairman and they took a great many votes and contrary votes but they did not agree on anything, until every one proposed that they consult the Wise Woman. Then they all held up their hands, and voted to, unanimously.

So the whole board of Aldermen set out, walking by twos, with the Mayor at their head, to consult the Wise Woman. The Aldermen were all very fleshy, and carried gold-headed canes which they swung very high at every step. They held their heads well back, and their chins stiff, and whenever they met common people they sniffed gently. They were very imposing.

The Wise Woman lived in a little hut on the outskirts of the city. She kept a Black Cat, except for her, she was all alone. She was very old, and had brought up a great many children, and she was considered remarkably wise.

But when the Aldermen reached her hut and found her seated by the fire, holding her Black Cat, a new difficulty presented itself. She had always been quite deaf and people had been obliged to scream as loud as they could in order to make her hear; but lately she had grown much deafer, and when the Aldermen attempted to lay the case before her she could not hear a word. In fact, she was so very deaf that she could not distinguish a tone below G-sharp. The Aldermen screamed till they were quite red in the faces, but all to no purpose: none of them could get up to G-sharp of course.

So the Aldermen all went back, swinging their gold-headed canes, and they had another meeting in the City Hall. Then they decided to send the highest Soprano Singer in the church choir to the Wise Woman; she could sing up to G-sharp just as easy as not. So the high Soprano Singer set out for the Wise Woman's in the Mayor's coach, and the Aldermen marched behind, swinging their gold-headed canes.

The High Soprano Singer put her head down close to the Wise Woman's ear, and sung all about the Christmas Masquerade and the dreadful dilemma everybody was in, in G-sharp—she even went higher, sometimes, and the Wise Woman heard every word.

She nodded three times, and every time she nodded she looked wiser.

"Go home, and give 'em a spoonful of castor-oil, all 'round," she piped up; then she took a pinch of snuff, and wouldn't say any more.

So the Aldermen went home, and every one took a district and marched through it, with a servant carrying an immense bowl and spoon, and every child had to take a dose of castor-oil.

But it didn't do a bit of good. The children cried and struggled when they were forced to take the castor-oil; but, two minutes afterward, the chimney-sweeps were crying for their brooms, and the princesses screaming because they couldn't go to court, and the Mayor's daughter, who had been given a double dose, cried louder and more sturdily: "I want to go and tend my geese. I will go and tend my geese."

So the Aldermen took the high Soprano Singer, and they consulted the Wise Woman again. She was taking a nap this time, and the Singer had to sing up to B-flat before she could wake her. Then she was very cross and the Black Cat put up his back and spit at the Aldermen.

"Give 'em a spanking all 'round," she snapped out, "and if that don't work put 'em to bed without their supper."

Then the Aldermen marched back to try that; and all the children in the city were spanked, and when that didn't do any good they were put to bed without any supper. But the next morning when they woke up they were worse than ever.

The Mayor and Aldermen were very indignant, and considered that they had been imposed upon and insulted. So they set out for the Wise Woman again, with the high Soprano Singer.

She sang in G-sharp how the Aldermen and the Mayor considered her an impostor, and did not think she was wise at all, and they wished her to take her Black Cat and move beyond the limits of the city.

She sang it beautifully; it sounded like the very finest Italian opera music.

"Deary me," piped the Wise Woman, when she had finished, "how very grand these gentlemen are." Her Black Cat put up his back and spit.

"Five times one Black Cat are five Black Cats," said the Wise Woman. And directly there were five Black Cats spitting and miauling.

"Five times five Black Cats are twenty-five Black Cats." And then there were twenty-five of the angry little beasts.

"Five times twenty-five Black Cats are one hundred and twenty-five Black Cats," added the Wise Woman with a chuckle.

Then the Mayor and the Aldermen and the high Soprano Singer fled precipitately out the door and back to the city. One hundred and twenty-five Black Cats had seemed to fill the Wise Woman's hut full, and when they all spit and miauled together it was dreadful. The visitors could not wait for her to multiply Black Cats any longer.

As winter wore on and spring came, the condition of things grew more intolerable. Physicians had been consulted, who advised that the children should be allowed to follow their own bents, for fear of injury to their constitutions. So the rich Aldermen's daughters were actually out in the fields herding sheep, and their sons sweeping chimneys or carrying newspapers; and while the poor charwomen's and coal-heavers, children spent their time like princesses and fairies. Such a topsy-turvy state of society was shocking. While the Mayor's little daughter was tending geese out in the meadow like any common goose-girl, her pretty elder sister, Violetta, felt very sad about it and used often to cast about in her mind for some way of relief.

When cherries were ripe in spring, Violetta thought she would ask the Cherry-man about it. She thought the Cherry-man quite wise. He was a very pretty young fellow, and he brought cherries to sell in graceful little straw baskets lined with moss. So she stood in the kitchen door one morning and told him all about the great trouble that had come upon the city. He listened in great astonishment; he had never heard of it before. He lived several miles out in the country.

"How did the Costumer look?" he asked respectfully; he thought Violetta the most beautiful lady on earth.

Then Violetta described the Costumer, and told him of the unavailing attempts that had been made to find him. There were a great many detectives out, constantly at work.

"I know where he is!" said the Cherry-man. "He's up in one of my cherry-trees. He's been living there ever since cherries were ripe, and he won't come down."

Then Violetta ran and told her father in great excitement, and he at once called a meeting of the Aldermen, and in a few hours half the city was on the road to the Cherry-man's.

He had a beautiful orchard of cherry-trees all laden with fruit. And, sure enough in one of the largest, way up amongst the topmost branches, sat the Costumer in his red velvet and short clothes and his diamond knee-buckles. He looked down between the green boughs. "Good-morning, friends!" he shouted.

The Aldermen shook their gold-headed canes at him, and the people danced round the tree in a rage. Then they began to climb. But they soon found that to be impossible. As fast as they touched a hand or foot to a tree, back it flew with a jerk exactly as if the tree pushed it. They tried a ladder, but the ladder fell back the moment it touched the tree, and lay sprawling upon the ground. Finally, they brought axes and thought they could chop the tree down, Costumer and all; but the wood resisted the axes as if it were iron, and only dented them, receiving no impression itself.

Meanwhile, the Costumer sat up in the tree, eating cherries and throwing the stones down. Finally he stood up on a stout branch, and, looking down, addressed the people.

"It's of no use, your trying to accomplish anything in this way," said he; "you'd better parley. I'm willing to come to terms with you, and make everything right on two conditions."

The people grew quiet then, and the Mayor stepped forward as spokesman, "Name your two conditions," said he rather testily. "You own, tacitly, that you are the cause of all this trouble."

"Well" said the Costumer, reaching out for a handful of cherries, "this Christmas Masquerade of yours was a beautiful idea; but you wouldn't do it every year, and your successors might not do it at all. I want those poor children to have a Christmas every year. My first condition is that every poor child in the city hangs its stocking for gifts in the City Hall on every Christmas Eve, and gets it filled, too. I want the resolution filed and put away in the city archives."

"We agree to the first condition!" cried the people with one voice, without waiting for the Mayor and Aldermen.

"The second condition," said the Costumer, "is that this good young Cherry-man here has the Mayor's daughter, Violetta, for his wife. He has been kind to me, letting me live in his cherry-tree and eat his cherries and I want to reward him."

"We consent," cried all the people; but the Mayor, though he was so generous, was a proud man. "I will not consent to the second condition," he cried angrily.

"Very well," replied the Costumer, picking some more cherries, "then your youngest daughter tends geese the rest of her life, that's all."

The Mayor was in great distress; but the thought of his youngest daughter being a goose-girl all her life was too much for him. He gave in at last.

"Now go home and take the costumes off your children," said the Costumer, "and leave me in peace to eat cherries."

Then the people hastened back to the city, and found, to their great delight, that the costumes would come off. The pins stayed out, the buttons stayed unbuttoned, and the strings stayed untied. The children were dressed in their own proper clothes and were their own proper selves once more. The shepherdesses and the chimney-sweeps came home, and were washed and dressed in silks and velvets, and went to embroidering and playing lawn-tennis. And the princesses and the fairies put on their own suitable dresses, and went about their useful employments. There was great rejoicing in every home. Violetta thought she had never been so happy, now that her dear little sister was no longer a goose-girl, but her own dainty little lady-self.

The resolution to provide every poor child in the city with a stocking full of gifts on Christmas was solemnly filed, and deposited in the city archives, and was never broken.

Violetta was married to the Cherry-man, and all the children came to the wedding, and strewed flowers in her path till her feet were quite hidden in them. The Costumer had mysteriously disappeared from the cherry-tree the night before, but he left at the foot some beautiful wedding presents for the bride—a silver service with a pattern of cherries engraved on it, and a set of china with cherries on it, in hand painting, and a white satin robe, embroidered with cherries down the front.

## The End

*Photo possibly from 1930; Actress Anna May Wong*

# WHEN EAST MET WEST

## BY W.C. TUTTLE

This Story was published in 1925,
in *The Blue Book Magazine*

Some poetical person once wrote:

For East is East and West is West.

And never the twain shall meet.

He was all wrong, that feller—all wrong. And I'll tell you how I know he was wrong.

I ain't no pessimist. Not by a danged sight, I ain't. If a little kid burns his fingers on a red-hot stove and keeps away from the fire from that time on, you don't call him a pessimist. That's me—burnt to a caution.

All the Harper tribe, as far back as I can figure out, was cautious. We bred more runners than we did fighters. Of course there ain't as many of us as there is Smiths. Smiths predominate, as it were. Anyway, the Smith tribe ain't got nothin' to do with this.

I ain't been in Piperock for several weeks. Me and "Dirty Shirt" Jones has been prospectin' back in the Whisperin' Creek hills, with our usual good luck—of gettin' back before all our food was gone. And we finds my pardner, "Magpie" Simpkins, settin' at the table in our shack, wearin' his Sunday clothes.

Magpie is so danged tall that it takes him all day to find out whether a certain pain is indigestion or inflammation of the kneecaps. He's solemn, Magpie is. And when that elongated, pious-faced cross between a scientific lecture and a — fool statement gets pouches under his eyes and droops his eyelids like a blood-hound—caution cometh to me.

Magpie is writin'. He's got ink plumb to his elbow and the floor is plumb littered with paper. Does he welcome us effusively? Like — he does. He just looks at us, kinda reprovin'-like, as if we should 'a' knocked.

"Well, you old cattywampus, howdy!" greets Dirty Shirt.

Dirty has one eye that kinda oscillates, as it were. Not bein' what an astronomer would call 'a fixed orbit,' it does a lot of jigglin' before it picks up what Dirty's lookin' at.

But it don't noways affect Dirty's aim, bein' as he shoots with both eyes open, and most of the time with both legs workin'. Magpie looks him over solemnly and says—

"Mr. Jones, I give you good afternoon."

Dirty spits in the general direction of the stove.

"I'll take it," says he.

"Mr. Harper," says Magpie dignified-like.

I kicks the door shut, slides my gun around where I can get it real quick and looks my old pardner over. He's shaved. Yeah, you can always tell when Magpie has shaved, because he's got so danged many wounds. He's got on a celluloid collar—one of them kind that it ain't safe to smoke in. I can smell stove polish, which Magpie has used on his boots.

Take it all the way around, Magpie Simpkins is a dude.

"You ain't got yore days mixed, have yuh?" I asked.

"Days mixed?"

He speaks like an actor—kinda runnin' the scale in G flat, as yuh might say.

"This ain't Sunday," says I.

"I am well aware of it."

"Then what's the idea of dressin' up thisaway?"

"The idea? Hah!" He kinda swells up with importance. "I'm the president."

I looks quick at Dirty, who is starin' at Magpie with his mouth wide open. Then he looks at me and shakes his head.

"Ike," says he hoarse-like, "I knowed it. By ——, the human brain can jist stand so much. He's been feeblin' up in the head for a long time. I've seen it comin' on by degrees, and I ain't a mite surprized. There ain't nothin' yuh can do, except to hopple 'em so they can't hurt nobody."

Magpie looks at Dirty kinda funny and Dirty edges toward the door.

"Better git a rope, Ike," advises Dirty, backin' agin' the door. "Them high-minded first symptoms is apt to degenerate into vi'lence, and we don't want him to hurt nobody."

"Set down, you —— fool," says Magpie. "I ain't crazy."

"Proves it on himself," declares Dirty nervous-like. "They all swear they ain't. Look out for his first rush, Ike."

But I holds firm. To me he's always been crazy so I ain't scared of an extra degree.

"Democrat or Republican president?" I asks. "We didn't git back in time for the convention, you remember."

"Don't try to be smart, Ike," says he. "I plumb forgot that you fellers has been away. Since you was here, Piperock has advanced by leaps and bounds. Right now I am writin' a biography of our fair city for all to read and appreciate how we have advanced. It is marvelous."

"What is? The biography?" asks Dirty.

"No—our advancement. Gentlemen, we are on the threshold of a wonderful era for Piperock. No more shall the rest of the world point a finger of scorn at our community. No more shall they say that Piperock is uncivilized, unbalanced. From this day henceforth we shall blossom like the rose. Our ideals shall and will be realized to the fullest extremity. How is that, Ike?"

"Fits in with what we've just heard," says I.

"And with the dawnin' of a new day—" Magpie squints at his paper— "all these—that's as far as I've got."

"And that's a —— of a long ways, if you ask me," said Dirty Shirt solemn-like.

"Now about bein' president," says I. "Yuh hadn't ought to go that far, Magpie."

"Hadn't I? Huh! That's who I am, Ike. Look upon me. I am the first president of the Piperock Chamber of Commerce."

"What the — kind of a thing is that?" asked Dirty.

"Chamber of Commerce? Dirty Shirt, I'm surprized at you. It is an organization."

"It's the same thing as the Chamber of Horrors," says I, "only they deals in commerce mostly. This one will prob'ly have horrors as a side-line."

"Nothin' of the kind, Ike," protests Magpie. "Piperock is past the age of swaddlin' clothes. We has emerged into the sunlight and it will be well for all other cities to look to their laurels. I wouldn't be surprized to see Piperock one of the big cities of the world. We have everythin' to make it big."

"Yeah, we've got a lot of country," admits Dirty Shirt. "Me and Ike came across twenty miles of it today, and there was more beyond where we started from. If you want to go east, west, north or south from here yuh can find a lot of open country. We've got room to build, that's a cinch."

"But what would bring anybody here?" I asks. "Folks won't even come from Paradise, except to a dance; and then they come to pick a fight. We ain't got a — of a lot to offer—except to somebody that wants trouble, Magpie."

"We will have, Ike. The idea was started in Paradise originally. Me and Wick Smith was down there last week and we went to see a tent show. It wasn't much good and it wasn't doin' no business. Me and Wick got to talkin' to the feller that owned the show and he told us all about his hard luck.

"He says that a circus is a drug on the market now, and that animiles ain't worth nothin', except in a zoo. He says that he's really surprised that some of our towns don't have no zoo. He says they're all puttin' 'em in in the East, and that no town can ever be an attraction unless it's got a zoo.

"Well, me and Wick has a few drinks with him and got to talkin' it over with him. He says he's got the ingredients of a first-class zoological menagerie, and that he's got a idea of puttin' the proposition up to Paradise. He's got a elephant. Of course it ain't no first class elephant, bein' as it's kinda run down from travelin' so much.

"The camel is—well, it ain't noways in full plumage, but it's a camel. The tiger seems to be as good as tigers go. He says he'll take a thousand dollars for the whole bunch. 'Course he tells us how much we'd have to pay if we bought them animiles at retail price; but he kinda lumps 'em together and gives 'em to us at cost.

"Wick Smith is public-spirited, and after I tells him what we'll do about organizin' a Chamber of Commerce, he ups and buys them animiles on the spot. The feller throws in the cage free gratis for nothin'; so that saves us quite a lot. I figures that we can pick up a grizzly and a wolf and mebbe a mountain lion to kinda add to our zoo. Folks will come a long ways to look at wild animiles, Ike—a long ways."

Me and Dirty looks at each other and goes out to unpack, while Magpie goes ahead on Piperock's epitaph.

It's been quite a while since we put our foot on the rail; so we hurries up to Buck Masterson's saloon, where we runs into Wick Smith and "Mighty" Jones. Mighty and Dirty Shirt ain't no relation. Mighty is a little jigger, who thinks he's big enough to hold his own. That's one reason why Mighty is mostly always on crutches. He swears in a tenor voice and chaws his tobacco.

Buck greets us gladly, but Wick don't seem so happy.

"You fellers been prospectin' again?" asks Buck.

"Yeah, and we're goin' ag'in," says Dirty Shirt. "This here town is gettin' too danged effete to suit me and Ike."

"It is effete," agrees Mighty. "Ain't been nobody killed for two weeks."

"Cheer up, brother," says Wick solemn-like. "There's allus a lull before a storm."

"You preparin' to massacre?" I asks.

"Well, I ain't been treated right," says Wick. "I done paid a thousand cold dollars for some jungle insects, and I'm wonderin' jist how I'm goin' to cash in on said contraptions. Magpie Simpkins got me drunk and talked me into bein' a public benefactor, dang his hide.

"Got me to procure the ingredients of a zoological garden, that's what he done. Got the whole — town heated up over a thing he calls the Piperock Chamber of Commerce, and then goes out and gits himself elected president. That's a — of a way to do, ain't it?"

"You wanted to be president, eh?" I asks.

"Well, —, why not. I bought the — thing, didn't I? Magpie said that Piperock would pay me back for it. How'll they do it, I'd like to know. Mebbe I'm supposed to raffle 'em off, eh?"

"I won't buy no chances," says Buck. "I've been down to the livery-stable and got a look at them there animals, and I'm free to state that I don't want none. Magpie orates that we'll have 'em to attract more folks to Piperock. My —, that bunch will drive away what we've got."

"If I had that elephant," said Mighty, "I'd shore take a reef in him. His hide don't fit him no place. He ain't no attraction—he's a disgrace. From the rear he looks like 'Polecat' Perkins in his Sunday pants. Wick, you ort to give him a belt to take up the slack."

"That's why he's an attraction," declared Wick. "The feller I bought him from said that Gunga Din was a rare species of elephant. His name's Gunga Din. My —, he ort to be good. I paid three hundred and thirty-three dollars and thirty-three and one-third cents for him. That camel and the tiger cost the same."

"I think that Magpie's crazy," say I.

"How about me?" wails Wick. "I paid for 'em myself."

"Yore wife's callin' yuh, Wick," observed Buck.

Wick squints toward the door and nods sadly.

"Yeah, I left her to run the store while I talks over my sorrow. Now I've got to go back and git — agin'. She don't believe in Chambers of Commerce, she don't; and I'm commencin' to wonder if she ain't right."

Wick pilgrims across the street, while me and Dirty goes down to the livery stable to see what Wick bought. "Hassayampa" Harris is runnin' the stable.

"Howdy, Hassayampa," says I. "How are you?"

"Liver trouble," says he, diagnosin' himself. "Spots before m' eyes, dizziness and kinda sluggish-like."

He does look kinda pale and walks antegodlin'.

"How comes you to git them there symptoms?" asks Dirty.

"Ignorance," says Hassayampa. "I tried to take a bale of hay away from Exhibit A of the Chamber of Commerce."

"Meanin' Gunga Din?"

"That accordion-skinned thing," says Hassayampa painful-like, kinda pluckin' at his Adam's apple. "I ain't jist right in m' mind yet. It grabbed me by the slack of the pants and took m' pants plumb off while I'm still in the air. Them kinda shocks ain't noways good for the human form. Then the —— thing slapped me across the face with my own pants and knocked me plumb across the stable and into the oat-bin. I ain't been right since."

"You ort to read up on things like that," says Dirty.

"Read? What in —— can a man read at a time like that?"

"Wasn't there no directions with 'em?" I asks.

"No. Direction don't mean nothin' to a thing like that, Ike. Do you want to gaze upon 'em?"

"Yeah, we'll look," nods Dirty.

"Cost two-bits per each," informs Hassayampa. "Magpie says they're worth it—and they are. My ——, there ain't no questions about it."

"That's a —— of a idea!" snorts Dirty. "Two-bits to see a elephant. I'll tell you what we will do, Hassayampa; we'll pay the two-bits to see you try to take another bale away from Gunga Din."

"You never will," sighs Hassayampa. "I'm cured. Anyway, I'm about half out of hay. I've got a bill of seven dollars agin' them critters right now. By golly, that tagger c'n go plumb to ——. Meat costs money."

We left Hassayampa talkin' to himself and went back up town, where we leans on Buck's bar.

We ain't been there long when Mike Pelly, Ricky Henderson and "Old Testament" Tilton rides in from Paradise. Mike is the saloon-keeper and Ricky runs the barber shop. The third member of this here trio represents the other element of Paradise.

Testament looks a heap like some old buzzard that had been disappointed in love. He wears one of them beetle-backed coats, a pair of pants that sure follers the contour of his skinny legs and a pair of boots that sag a heap at the top and shows that Testament don't noways pinch his feet.

Mike parts his hair on one side, slicks one side down until she almost reaches the bridge of his nose, where it retreats some sudden-like. He smells a heap of heel-yuh-tripe perfume.

Ricky is a barber. He looks, smells and acts like one. When he gets excited he applauds, like he was stroppin' a razor. Testament used to think that he had snatched Ricky and Mike from the burnin'. When Testament first comes to that country he has an idea that there was a lot of brands to snatch from the burnin'; but he got scorched a few times and let things go as they lay.

Them three angles up to the bar, shakes hands with us, just like they cared to meet us, and asks us to drink. Testament has his usual lemonade and a wink, and then we discusses conditions.

"How is everythin' in this village of iniquity?" asks Testament kinda offhanded.

"Iniquity, ——!" snorts Buck. "There ain't no iniquity in Piperock. We're clean-minded and antiseptic of condition. If there's any infection in this city it's brought here from Paradise. By golly, some day you'll be glad to be knowed as bein' a suburb of Piperock City."

"Haw-haw-haw-haw!" says Ricky. "Suburb of Piperock. Paradise will be a mee-trop-polis when Piperock goes back to the prairie-dogs."

It's difference of opinion that makes horse races, wars and so many kinds of whisky—all out of one barrel. Me and Dirty Shirt are plumb full of civic pride, and we're willin' to fight for our fair city—if we had one— but Piperock and Paradise ain't worth no supreme effort; so we slides out kinda graceful-like and pilgrims back to our shack.

Magpie is just goin' away, carryin' complete dignity and a lot of stationery. I tells him about the three men from Paradise.

"The word has reached," says Magpie, swellin' his chest. "We shall not hide our light under a bushel."

"Then you better hide yore carcass behind a wood-pile," says Dirty Shirt. "Them three antagonizers didn't jist ride up here to git a drink of liquor."

"We are a peaceable aggregation," says Magpie. "No more shall the war-cry sever, nor the runnin' rivers be red. We are about to shed the things that have held us back. Uncivilization must bow to the tread of wisdom. The wheel of progress is turnin', and woe unto him who gits under the tire. The people of Piperock have risen in their might, unleashed the bonds which have held them in darkness and are comin' out into the light of a new day."

"And," says Dirty kinda awed-like, "if that ain't a —— of a lot to say all in one bunch, I'll eat the garment that made me famous."

Magpie snorts and pilgrims on up the street. In spite of the mighty proclamation he emits to us, I notices that he's got a six-gun shoved into the waistband of his pants. Me and Dirty stretches out on the two bunks and rolls up a little sleep.

In the course of human events some queer things happen. And the queerest thing I can think of is the fact that Jasmine Greenbaum came to teach school at Piperock. Jasmine ain't the kind you'd imagine would take a job like that.

She's plumb decorative, if yuh know what I mean. I ain't goin' to describe her, 'cause I ain't got words enough. Her eyes would make a man lift his head when somebody is shootin' at him. She lives with Wick Smith's family while she's teachin' the young of Piperock to not shoot at each other.

Me and Dirty runs into her that evenin' after we've been stationary at Buck's bar for an hour or more. Dirty's active eye jiggles convulsive-like for a while, and he seems to be wearin' about six too many hands.

"I'm sure you remember me," says she, smilin' at us.

"If I lives to be a million, I won't forget," pants Dirty.

"I am Mister Harper," says I. "And the Harper fambly has the longest memories of any fambly on earth."

"Outside of the Jones's," says Dirty. "My old pa could remember before they started puttin' aces in the decks of cards."

"Memories don't figure," says I. "We're glad to meetcha, Miss Greenbaum. What can I do for yuh, ma'am?"

"Same here," says Dirty, kinda elbowin' me aside.

"I told them that you were always willing to do anything for the public good," says she, smilin' sweet-like.

"To whom did yoo tell this, ma'am?" I asks.

Somehow I kinda gets a hunch that everythin' ain't just right.

"Mr. Simpkins, the president of the Chamber of Commerce," says she. "He and Mr. Smith seemed to think——"

"Since when did they start thinkin'?" asks Dirty. "That shore is a novelty to my ears, ma'am."

"Mr. Simpkins is a very brilliant man," says she. "He has some wonderful ideas."

"With parts missin'," says I.

"Perhaps you do not appreciate what he is doing for Piperock, Mr. Harper," says she. "I have just come from a meeting of the new Chamber of Commerce, where Mr. Simpkins presided and read us some wonderful plans for the betterment of this town.

"As you know we already have the nucleus of a zoological garden. Mr. Smith, who is heart and soul in the advancement of Piperock, purchased these three jungle animals. Our meeting this afternoon was to decide upon a plan to reimburse Mr. Smith and to acquire the animals for the city.

"Next Monday is Labor Day. I have been lead to understand that Piperock has never celebrated Labor Day."

"They've sure celebrated everythin' else," says Dirty Shirt. "My —, ma'am, don't let 'em celebrate. You don't know Piperock."

"It will be a harmless celebration. I spoke about having you two gentlemen assist, and Mr. Simpkins and Mr. Smith assured me that neither of you had any civic pride. They said that both of you were uncivilized, unprogressive and not at all in accord with any movement that would curb your savage tendencies. I'm sure it is prejudice on their part."

"Yo're danged right!" says Dirty. "Them pelicans sure did lie to you in fine shape, ma'am. Piperock don't mean a whole lot to either one of us, but I'm willin' to do anythin' yuh say."

I'm cautious, as I said before. This here idea of havin' a pretty school teacher come to us and hoodle us into doin' somethin' that our hearts tell us is dangerous don't set so good. I've heard this same kind of stuff before, and so has Dirty; but any old time a pretty girl smiles at Dirty, it's just another old Garden of Eden and a lot of apples.

She don't tell us what we're supposed to do, but she does ask us to promise to help 'em out. Well, what can yuh do in a case like that? Me and Dirty goes back to Buck's place, where we massages our insides with Buck's Best.

And lemme tell you somethin'—Buck's liquor sure tempers the wind to the sheared sheep. Ten years ago he bought a barrel of it. He sells on an average of two or three gallons a day, and that barrel is still over half-full. It has never weakened, as far as we can taste.

After while Magpie and Wick comes into the place. Dignified? My —, they act like a pair of royal flushes.

"Greetin's, Mr. Masterson," says Magpie lofty-like. "How goes things this day and date?"

"Well, all right," says Buck, bein' kinda dazed. "How did the meetin' go?"

"Perfect," says Magpie. "The die is cast. The ladies' auxiliary is in complete accord with us and we all feel that it will be a day to date time from. Piperock will emerge from her shell and take her place among the cities of the world."

"The ladies' what?" asks Dirty.

"Auxiliary," explains Wick. "My wife is president. It is an a-ad—uh—"

"Adjunct," prompts Magpie.

"I know it," says Wick. "There's my wife, who is president, and the followin', to wit: Mrs. Wick Smith, Mrs. Pete Gonyer, Mrs. Yuma Yates, Mrs. Mighty Jones, and Miss Hilda Hansen. Of course the list is not complete, as it were, and we expect more. However, we have a quorum, et cettery, *ad libitum*."

"I s'd hope sho," says Dirty, gettin' dignified. "What 'bout Mish Jasm'n Greenbaum? Ain't she invited t' j'in?"

"Miss Jasmine Greenbaum is actin' in an advisory capacity," explains Magpie. "It kinda makes her feel free to do as she wishes. We're leavin' a lot of it to her imagination."

"What was Testament and Ricky and Mike doin' up here?" asks Buck.

"Kinda gropin' around," says Magpie. "They heard that we was due to progress, and of course they had to come and see what it was about. I told 'em about Piperock acquirin' a Chamber of Commerce and three jungle curiosities. They don't *sabe* the idea of the Chamber, but they offers to take the animals at a slight advance over what Piperock paid."

"What did you say?" asks Wick anxious-like.

"I told 'em to go to ——. Them animals ain't for sale."

"Ain't they?" asks Wick. "At more'n I paid? Magpie, I'd like to have the say-so over them critters myself. I own 'em, don't I? They ain't Piperock's animals until Piperock has a bill-of-sale for 'em. I sure as —— don't thank yuh for what you've done to me."

"Where's yore public spirit?" asks Magpie.

"Thassall right," complains Wick. "I've got more public spirit than most folks, I reckon; but a thousand dollars is a thousand dollars. If Paradise wants to pay me more'n I paid—they git 'em, by gosh!"

"You'd make a fine president for the Chamber of Commerce," says Magpie.

"All right," says Wick. "If you can think of anythin' else that's funny, I'll listen."

"Yore livestock are eatin' up dollars," says I.

"Yeah, and that's another thing," wails Wick, pawin' at Magpie's sleeve. "Who's goin' to pay their board?"

"Gunga Din eats a bale of hay every fifteen minutes," offers Dirty Shirt solemn-like.

"He—he does?"

"He—he do," nods Dirty. "The last bale was two pounds short; so Gunga Din ate Hassayampa's pants for dessert. Them there tigers will eat a whole cow for a meal and you know what cows are worth right now."

"Magpie—" Wick is almost cryin' by this time—"Magpie, I asks you as a friend—what'll I do?"

"Have patience, Wickie."

"Have —! I'll go down there and massacree all three of them monstrosities, that's what I'll do, by gosh!"

"And lose yore thousand dollars, eh?" Magpie shakes his head. "Wick Smith, you ain't hardly fit to help us build up Piperock."

"It's for the glory of our fair city," says Buck.

Wick turns around and walks out. He's kinda all choked up, but I know danged well it ain't emotion. Me and Dirty feels that the fair city of Piperock ain't so badly in need of our assistance; so we saddles up our rollin' stock and goes to Paradise town.

PARADISE RUNS A DEAD HEAT WITH PIPEROCK, AS FAR AS CITY IS CONCERNED. When P. T. Barnum said that a fool is born every minute, he might have added that they were all pointed toward Yellowrock County.

We finds several of the above in Mike Pelly's saloon, and among them is "Chuck" Warner, "Muley" Bowles, "Telescope" Tolliver and Henry Clay Peck. These four disgraces are from the Cross J ranch, but claims Paradise as their native haunt. Also we finds "Liniment" Lucas and "Tombstone" Todd and "Hard-Pan" Hawkins.

Tombstone is so tough that he can wear tight boots on his bunions, and "Hard-Pan" Hawkins keeps books on his crimes. Tombstone draws me aside and gnaws on one end of his mustache, while he cuffs his sombrero plentiful.

"Ike," says he hoarse-like, "what's this I'm hearin' about the hamlet of Piperock? Somebody was a-tellin' me that they've convened up there to respectablize the town somewhat."

"It's kinda hard to per-fume the rose," says I.

Tombstone gnaws a little more and fights his hat.

"Yeah, I s'pose that's right, Ike. Are you and Dirty Shirt part and parcel of this here movement?"

"Not knowin'ly, Tombstone," says I. "You can speak to me with perfect confidence and go away feelin' that I won't exaggerate what you've told me."

"There has been braggin' goin' on," stated Tombstone. "If there's anythin' Paradise hates it's braggin'. Piperock orates that she's leapin' ahead like a bee-stung bear. She ain't, Ike. It jist ain't no ways possible for her to leap thataway. She ain't active like Paradise. We're able to do things.

"Whereabouts in — does Piperock compare with Paradise, I asks yuh to answer honestly? She don't. We've got spirit, climate and brain power. We've got courageous men, wimmin and children. Why, our offspring are equal to two grown men of Piperock. We've got everythin', Ike."

"Except a elephant, a camel and a tiger," says I.

"What's them amount to?"

"And a Chamber of Commerce, Tombstone."

"Mm-m-m, yeah. Well?"

"Well—right back at yuh. I never started this argument."

"It ain't no argument, Ike," he explains. "Paradise is the legitimate place for them things. We could do it up right."

Tombstone invites me back to the bar, which I accepts. Dirty is arguin' with the Cross J outfit and Liniment Lucas, and from Dirty's talk I'd gather that he's body and soul with Piperock.

"From this day henceforth, Piperock shall rossom like a blose," orates Dirty Shirt. "The people of Piperock have rosin in their might, and we are comin' out into the dight of a lew day. And if that ain't a — of a lot to say at once, I'll eat the garment that made me what I am today."

From that time on things get kinda hazy. Mike Pelly peddles a brand that would make a cotton-tail rabbit grow fangs in his mouth and rattles on his tail. I'm led to understand that Paradise is jealous of Piperock, and that Paradise hankers for them three animals, like a calf hankerin' for its ma.

Me and Dirty balances on the edge of the sidewalk in front of Mike's place and begins to cheer for Piperock, when some careless son of a gun moved a heavy chair plumb out of Mike's doorway and it hits me and Dirty Shirt at the same time.

And when we woke up we finds ourselves in jail. Hank Padden, our estimable sheriff, tells us that we're in jail for disturbin' the peace.

"You be —!" wails Dirty Shirt. "Paradise never had no peace to disturb. I can prove it to any judge, jury or collection of folks which has two ideas above a monkey."

"I done my duty," says Hank firm-like. "I was hired for this kind of work. You'll prob'ly git six months apiece."

This was sure cheerin' news. The Paradise jail don't feed none too good. We had a idea that Piperock would arise in its wrath and come down to drag us forth—but they didn't. I sent word to Magpie, and he answered it.

I sent him this word—

Me and Dirty Shirt are in jail for upholdin' Piperock.

And this is what he sent to me—

Good for you. We appreciate yore civic pride.

He didn't sign his name, but he didn't need to. I *sabe* that *hombre* like a book. Dirty gets kinda gloomy over it all and swears that he's all through with Piperock. Right there and then I adds my voice to his.

"If that's patriotism," says Dirty, "gimme death. Our own town has turned us down, Ike Harper. I didn't think they'd do it. And they wouldn't, if they wasn't gettin' civilized."

A little later on cometh Chuck Warner, Liniment Lucas and Testament Tilton.

"You can take the preacher back," says Dirty. "We ain't in for murder, you know."

"I'm not in my clerical capacity," says Testament. "Be ye both of good cheer."

"— of a fine chance, the way Hank runs his place here," snorts Dirty.

"I've been up to Piperock," says Chuck, wigglin' his ears. Chuck's got flexible ears and he can wiggle 'em like a mule.

"And nobody shot yuh?" gasps Dirty. "My gosh, they're sure gittin' forgivin', Chuck."

"They ain't no friends to you two," says Chuck seriouslike. "They're glad yo're in jail down here."

Chuck Warner is the biggest liar west of the Atlantic Ocean—but this time I believed him.

"Magpie and Wick Smith hope yuh stay in jail," says he.

"It kinda looks like they'd git their hopes," Dirty acts kinda mournful.

"It kinda does," agrees Liniment.

He's got one of them long, wet-lookin' noses and sad eyes. I reckon his folks intended him to be a undertaker, but Old Lady Fate had "horse-thief" marked after his name in the Big Book.

"Is this here a party of condolence, or did yuh come to gloat?" I asks. I hate like — to have folks lookin' at me through the bars.

"Condolence and good cheer," says Testament, hitchin' up his pants. "You might call it a parley. I will go now, as it would not be meet for me to be party to it. Not that I ain't in accord with it entirely, you understand."

"It sure must be a tough proposition to drive you away," observed Dirty.

Old Testament pulled out, Hank unlocks the cell door, and they all comes in.

And what follered kinda touched upon my heart-strings. It was Chuck's idea. I listened to Chuck, Hank and Liniment Lucas, as they unfolds what's on their minds. It has been said that every man has his price. Ours was one elephant, one camel and a tiger.

They wants us to steal them three animals for Paradise. All we've got to do is to hand 'em over to Paradise and all is forgiven. But they're square about it, at that; they will pay Wick Smith what he paid for 'em; and give us a hundred apiece.

"And Piperock ain't treated you two square," says Chuck.

"Thassall right," says I, "but yuh can't get away with anything like that, Chuck. It wouldn't be hard for Piperock to prove that they owned 'em, 'cause they're all there is of the species in Yaller Rock County."

"We've fixed that all up," says Chuck. "Don'tcha worry about that end of it. You fellers go back home, feelin' sore at Paradise, and nobody will expect yuh to raid the zoo; *sabe?*"

WHEN WE WENT HOME, AFTER SWEARIN' TO DO OUR LITTLE BEST, AND WE finds Magpie in the shack, composin' some more stuff. We don't say nothin' about his kind note to us, and he don't mention it to us.

"Still tryin' to uplift Piperock on paper?" I asks.

"Combatin' a evil influence, Ike. We are the pioneers—others foller. Some one is tryin' to steal our thunder."

"You got plenty of it," declares Dirty. "They could swipe a lot of it from you and still leave enough for a dozen men."

"Sarcasm is the weapon of the ignorant," says Magpie. "What heard ye in Paradise?"

"Nothin' much."

"No? Huh. Did yuh know that Paradise is emulatin' us—or is goin' to?"

"All fools ain't dead yet," opines Dirty Shirt.

"They've ordered a elephant, camel and a tiger," says Magpie. "They're payin' a big price for 'em, just to keep Piperock from leadin' the procession. Telescope Tolliver and Muley Bowles told us about it today. Telescope said he thought we ought to know about it."

"Yeah, we heard about it," says Dirty Shirt, kinda off-handed like. "It didn't mean nothin' to us."

"Well, we're holdin' a indignation meetin' tomorrow night," says Magpie. "We aims to protest openly against such practise. It ain't ethical. You and Ike be there, will yuh? Up in the Mint Hall. The ladies auxiliary will be there, et cettery. We don't wish for blood to be spilled. It's ag'in our principles and regulations; but, by grab, they'll go too far pretty soon—and have to get helped back."

The next day is kinda quiet in Piperock; but when Piperock is quiet she's dangerous. Wick Smith ain't at the store, and Mrs. Smith ain't got much use for me and Dirty; so we keep away. After samplin' some wobble water we pilgrims down to the livery-stable to see how Hassayampa is comin'.

But we don't find Hassayampa in charge. Wick Smith meets us at the door, and he looks as wise as a owl.

"Whatcha want?" he asks.

"Whatcha got?" asks Dirty.

Wick clears his throat kinda hoarse-like.

"I've got civic pride, by ——!"

"You've showed it, Wick," says I.

"Uh-huh. If I had more sense and less pride I'd be better off. Hassayampa Harris hands me a bill for thirty-six dollars' worth of feed—and I got so —— full of pride that I kicked him out and took charge.

"My ——, that elephant is jist like a hay-baler. Yuh can't fill it up, I tell yuh. And he was feedin' Cleo-patree meat! Can yuh beat that? Cleo-patree is the tiger. That son of a gun has cost me one hundred dollars per stripe."

"Wick," says I, "wouldst be rid of 'em?"

Wick looks at me for quite a while, spits painful-like and nods slowly.

"Wouldst."

"I can get yuh a thousand dollars for the layout."

"Ike, I hope yuh ain't lyin' to me."

"C. O. D.," says I.

"That's the joker," says he kinda wailin'. "C. O. D., eh? How in —— can yuh deliver a thing like these, I'd ask you? Half of Piperock is guardin' this here stable. Over across the street is Pete Gonyer. Farther down the street is Mighty Jones, and up the other way is Olaf Hansen. One of them three has his eye on this place. They're watchin' to see that Paradise don't come and take them things away.

"And at night they're guardin' this place with sawed-off shotguns. They heard that Paradise was goin' to take away the menagerie; that's what they heard."

"It's kinda easy to see why Paradise wants to shift the job to me and Dirty Shirt Jones," says I. "Can't yuh do as yuh want to with yore own animals?"

"I can't," wails Wick. "Magpie got me drunk, Judge Steele wrote out a option—and I signed it. I can't sell until thirty days after Labor Day. By that time I'll be in the poor house."

"What do these here animals look like?" asks Dirty.

Wick leads up back in the stable and makes us used to the dangdest lookin' trio of animals I ever seen. Cleopatra is in a cage on wheels, and if there ever was a meaner-lookin' tiger I've never seen it. She's jist skin and bones and a big mouth full of teeth.

The camel opens his mouth and grins at us, kinda asthmatic-like. His name is Sahara, and he looks like ——. If it wasn't for his humps he'd look like a moth-eaten burro.

"Here's the *e pluribus peritonitis*," says Wick, pointin' at the next stall. "There stands Gunga Din. I tied the son of a gun up a while ago."

We steps over and takes a close look. It's kinda dark in that stall.

Whap!

Somethin' hit me in the face and I done a foot-race backward plumb to the rear door, where I hits my shoulders first, followed by the rest of my anatomy, makin' a sound like the couplin'-up of an engine on a train of cars. Kinda clunkety, clinkety, clank!

Through the haze I sees Dirty Shirt fade out through the front doorway, and I seen Wick Smith climb up a post, where he hangs harness. He got hold of the harness peg and tries to lift himself up; but the peg busted and he landed back on the floor under two sets of heavy harness.

I got up and went weavin' down the stable, feelin' kinda light and airy. I seen Wick come up from under that harness and go gallopin' out of the place with a horse collar around his neck and a set of tugs sailin' out behind, holdin' a hame in each hand, like a man carryin' two flags.

I fell down twice before I got outside, where I found Dirty and Wick. Wick got a tug caught in the sidewalk and ain't got sense enough to let loose of the hame. There he is, yankin' and haulin', while Dirty is standin' in front of him, legs wide apart, wavin' his hat in Wick's face and yellin'.

"Whoa! Whoa! Whoa, you —— fool!"

I fell over the tug and sat down on the edge of the sidewalk. Dirty manages to get Wick calmed down, and we looks each other over. Dirty has got a pair of sleeves on, but no shirt. His jiggly eye does a lot of cavortin', as he looks at me.

"I never expected to see any of us alive," says he.

"You don't need to start cheerin'," says I. "What in —— was the matter, Wick?"

"Ignorance!" snorts Dirty. "If I didn't know any more natural history than that I'd hang my head in shame, Wick. You tied him up, did yuh? Well, by golly you ort to find out which is the head end of a elephant. You tied him by the tail."

"Well, I-I-I-I tut-tied him," wails Wick. "Ends don't mean nothin' to me. They both hang down. The only danged way I can tell which is which is to give it some hay and see which end turns toward it. He didn't kill either one of yuh, did he?"

"Don't give Gunga Din any credit," says I. "If that back door hadn't been shut I'd be in Canada right now. Go back and make pets of them things, if you must, but spare me from havin' anythin' more to do with 'em."

We helped Wick back into the stable, stole a bottle of horse liniment and went home to recuperate. Dirty walks like his rudder was cramped just a little, and I'm kinda reared back to take the strain off my shoulders, hips and ankles.

IT WAS KINDA LATE THAT EVENIN' WHEN ME AND DIRTY LIMPED UP TO THE Mint Hall and found Piperock assembled. Magpie is on the platform, and the argument seems to be gettin' warm. On the platform with him is Mrs. Wick Smith and Miss Jasmine Greenbaum. When she sees us, she hops off the platform, comes and leads me and Dirty up to the front of the room and asks us to sit down.

"These two gentlemen have offered to help me in this," says she. "They have the interests of Piperock at heart. I know they are brave and full of courage, and for that reason I have selected them."

"Brave and full of courage!" snorts Yuma Yates. "Full of rheumatism, from the way they walk."

"I'm goin' to remember most everythin' I hear said here," says Dirty. "That's remark number one, Yuma."

"My list shows number one for Yuma Yates," says I.

Magpie hitches up his belt and moves to the edge of the platform, where he glares at me and Dirty Shirt.

"Threats are out of order," he tells us. "Piperock is passin' from such things. From now onward we are promoters of brotherly love—not battle. Heed this and save yourself trouble. We welcome both to the fold, and thank yuh for offerin' yore assistance to Miss Greenbaum. Sincerely yours, Piperock Chamber of Commerce."

"In reply to yore letter of today," says I, "I can say that yore fold don't appeal to us; so am sendin' it back by return mail. Sincerely yours, Ike Harper and Dirty Shirt Jones. P. S. And if you don't know what I mean—ask us."

Magpie glares at us for several moments and then turns to Miss Jasmine.

"Miss Greenbaum," says he, "I told you that I was sure them two jiggers was drunk when they offered to help yuh. Probably they'll deny ever sayin' it now."

Dirty Shirt hops to his feet.

"Magpie Simpkins, yo're a—a—exaggeratin' things. By golly, we said we'd help Miss Greenbaum, and we'll do it. Anythin' she asks us to do is jist the same as done. Ain't that right, Ike?"

"Well," says I, "I hate to have anybody doubt that I don't know what I'm sayin'—drunk or sober. I'm with you, Dirty."

"I knew it," says Miss Greenbaum. "I knew they would do it for me. It isn't often that I make a mistake in human nature. When I first saw these two gentlemen, something told me that they were to be depended upon. Mr. Harper and Mr. Jones, I thank you."

"Yo're welcome," says Dirty. "You sure are awful welcome."

"Well, now that we've settled that part of it, I move that we adjourn. Tomorrow will be spent in preparin' things. We've got a lot of work to do. 'Scenery,' you'll bring yore autymobile in tomorrow?"

Scenery Sims admits that he will. Scenery is a little, thin son of a gun, with a E-string voice, and owns the only horseless vehicle in Yaller Rock County.

"The ladies will be busy on their costumes," says Magpie, "and there will be much decoratin' to be did. The time is kinda short to complete all the details; but it is goin' to be the biggest thing ever pulled off in the West. Our grandchildren will be proud of us."

"Yours won't be," says Dirty Shirt.

It's kind of a mean remark, bein' as Magpie never was married. Nobody laughed, but those directly behind us kinda eased themselves aside out of the line of fire.

Magpie shook his head and polished the nail of his trigger finger on his right ear.

"We've got to be meek," says he. "'The meek shall inherit the earth.'"

"That won't be a — of a lot of fun, if there ain't nothin' but meek ones left," says I.

"There'll be a — of a lot of earth to divide, too," says Dirty Shirt.

And that's all we knew about the meetin'. I've got a hunch that Dirty spoke up too quick. I told him that they've been arguin' about me and him before we got there, but he don't care. There ain't a chance to steal them animals for Paradise, even if we was so inclined—which we ain't—so we decided to let nature take its course.

Early the next mornin' we finds Magpie paintin' a big sign. He ain't noways artistic, but readable. At the top is one word, in letters two feet high—

PAGEANT

And just below that is two more big words—

OF PROGRESS

"What's that, Magpie?" asks Dirty Shirt.

"Depictin'," says Magpie, wipin' some black paint out of his mustache, "the progress of Piperock. Pageant means a high-toned parade. There has been parades before, but this is the first pageant. If you two fellers will go up to Wick Smith's house you'll prob'ly find Mrs. Smith and Miss Greenbaum workin' on yore costumes. They was goin' to make 'em first thing today."

"Our costumes?" I asks. "Whyfor costumes for us, Magpie?"

"Have to have 'em, Ike."

"Oh, well, if we have to have 'em."

Me and Dirty spells out the next thing on the list:

WHEN EAST MEETS WEST

THE EAST IS AMAZED AT THE PROGRESS OF THE WEST

THEY MINGLE LIKE BROTHERS

THE COMING OF THE WHITE MAN VICTORY

THE SPIRIT OF PIPEROCK—PROGRESS

DON'T FORGET THE BIG DANCE AT THE MINT HALL

THATCHER'S COMBINED ORCHESTRA WILL FURNISH THE
STRAINS AND SCENERY

SIMS WILL DO THE CALLIN'

COME ONE AND ALL

TWO DOLLARS PER EACH WILL COVER THE PAGEANT
AND DANCE

PIPEROCK CHAMBER OF COMMERCE

MAGPIE SIMPKINS, President

We found Wick Smith at the store. He hoodled Hassayampa into takin' charge of the animals again and is runnin' his own store; but he ain't cheerful.

"Tomorrow is Labor Day," says he with tears in his voice. "I ort to be happy, I s'pose, 'cause the proceeds of the pag-unt is to help pay me for them animals; but somehow I can't seem to rend the veil, as Old Testament says, and see the silver linin'."

"Aw, it'll be all right," says Dirty. "Parades ain't much to worry about."

"Thasso?" Wick squints at Dirty. "You've survived some of our parades, ain't yuh, Dirty?"

"Yeah, but you've got to figure that Piperock is civilized. It ain't noways what she used to be, Wick. Right now Piperock is meek and mild."

"I'll betcha," nods Wick. "Well, I still has hopes, but—I dunno. I can't quite figure out my wife lookin' like a statoo of Victory, nor I can't figure out Mrs. Pete Gonyer and Mrs. Mighty Jones depictin' Progress. My —, my wife don't look like Victory."

"You ain't never won a battle from her yet, have yuh?" I asks.

"No, that's a cinch. Well, mebbe it'll be all right. You fellers ain't got no easy chore yoreselves."

"We ain't?" I asks. "What have we got to do with it, Wick?"

"You two depicts the East, Ike. Anyway, that's what they've proclaimed for yuh."

"—, I don't look like no East!" snorts Dirty.

321

"I don't think I do either," says I. "Anyway, I ain't seen nobody from the East that looks a — of a lot like me. How does she come that we're inflicted with this idea, Wick?"

"Don't ask me. My —, it ain't none of my doin's. I've got all the grief I can stand. You better ask Magpie or Jasmine. They fixed it all up between 'em."

"Do we wear costumes?" asks Dirty.

"Search me. My wife does. Mosquito-bar! My —, can yuh see my wife in a mosquito-bar dress?"

"I'd like to," says Dirty.

And then we left. Wick hadn't ought to be so finicky. His wife is about five feet four inches tall and weighs two hundred and fifty. She also wheezes considerable in her talk. Mrs. Gonyer is six feet two inches tall, and so danged thin that she rattles when she walks. Mrs. Mighty Jones ain't no taller than Mrs. Smith, and she don't weigh a hundred.

ME AND DIRTY DON'T GET MUCH SATISFACTION AROUND THAT TOWN. MAGPIE goes to Paradise to advertise the affair, and to probably do a lot of braggin' about himself. We runs into Scenery Sims, who has his eyes focused on the wine when it is red, and he ain't exactly what you'd call coherent.

"I—I ain't much," he tells us tearful-like.

We agrees with him, which don't help him none.

"I can't do nothin'," he tells us.

"—, that ain't news," agrees Dirty. "Everybody knows that."

"In the pay-jint," says he. "I want to be somethin'."

"All right," says I. "You be a hump in the road for the wagons to run over."

"That's all right f'r you two pelicans," says he. "You've got things to do. I've been shoved aside, that's what I've been done to, by gosh. Mebbe Piperock is progressin', but I'm right where I was a week ago. Have a drink?"

We would. In fact we had several. We got to a point where Dirty gets to braggin' about bein' East. He orates that he's also effete. Magpie comes back from Paradise, all swelled up over himself, and invades Buck's place.

"They'll come," he tells the world. "Paradise will be here in copious gobs. From Curlew we'll poll a big majority, and there'll be a sprinklin' from Yaller Horse. I prognosticate that Piperock will hold about all there is in Yaller Rock County. We has spread the gospel of progress, and the world responds."

"Has Paradise got her animals yet?" asks Buck.

"Not yet. Mike Pelly tells me that they're on the way. It's goin' to be nip and tuck between us towns. Well, I've got to go and see how things is goin'. Is Pete and Yuma workin' on that float?"

"All day," says Buck. "It'll be a dinger."

"Float?" says Dirty. "My ——, they're ignorant, Ike. There ain't water enough in this town to float a cork. We've done give our word to see that this here pe-rade is a howlin' success; but after it's over, me and you starts a pilgrimage. I sicken of the flesh-pots, jack-pots, et cettery. Long may she wave. Let's have another libation to old man Backus."

And that's the way she went. Bill Thatcher and his orchestra showed up a little later on—a bull-fiddle, a squeeze-organ and a jews-harp. Bill's boy, Ham, is the squeeze-organist, and old "Frenchy" Deschamps is doin' the moanin' on the harp.

"Kinda wanted t' know what kind of music Magpie wanted us to play," explains Bill. "We've got all kinds."

"You fellers graduated from 'Sweet Marie'?" asked Dirty.

"That's good music," says Bill kinda indignant-like. "If yuh don't like that, we can play it any old way you want it."

Some of Paradise comes that night, and among 'em is the gang from the Cross J. Chuck gets me aside and asks how we're comin' on the animal stealin'. I points out the difficulties, showin' him how close Piperock is guardin' their zoo.

"Get 'em durin' the parade," says Chuck. "Everybody will be interested in that, don'tcha see?"

"Can't be did," says I. "I'm part of the parade."

"What part are you, Ike?"

"I'm half of the east end," says I. "Now you know as much as I do."

"Who's guardin' 'em now, Ike?"

"I ain't sure, but I reckon Hassayampa is on duty."

Chuck goes away, leavin' me to nod at the bartender and lean against Dirty Shirt. Then cometh Polecat Perkins and his pack of high-class mongrels. He's got eight of 'em, all on ropes, and they proceeds to tangle themselves around our legs.

"Greetin's, everybody," says Polecat. "Lay down, dogs!"

Polecat joins our convention and gets enthusiastic over the fact that tomorrow is Labor Day and that we're goin' to have a jollification.

"Take them dogs outside," orders Buck. "My —, this ain't no doggery, Polecat. Take 'em away so folks will have a chance to git to the bar."

Just about that time Hassayampa Harris comes into that saloon. I dunno how far he jumped from the outside, but I know he scraped his head on the top of the doorway and landed plumb in the middle of the room

"Yeeow-w-w-w! Look out!" he yelps.

Right behind Hassayampa comes Cleopatra. She comes among us, like a striped streak, hits in the middle of the room, lands on the pool table and goes plumb out through the back door, which has just been opened by Mighty Jones. Mighty's feet flip up where his hat had been, and over him goes Polecat's flock of dogs, each one tryin' to yell louder than the rest.

"That's our tiger!" explodes Buck.

"You—you can huh-have it!" pants Hassayampa.

"How did it get loose?"

"Go and ask it. I—I was talkin to Chuck Warner at the front door of the stable when all to once I hears somebody yell, and here comes Cleopatra."

"Somebody yell?" snorts Buck. "By golly, I'll bet some of that Paradise gang turned her loose while you was at the front door. Git down there, everybody, before they turn 'em all loose."

They all went down there, except me and Dirty and Buck. They could turn 'em loose as far as me and Dirty are concerned. A few minutes after they're gone Old Testament and Muley Bowles comes in. Testament ain't got no hat and his coat is split up the back. Muley don't track very well and he's got a swellin' over one eye.

"'In the midst of life we are in death,'" says Testament, indicatin' that he don't want his lemonade straight.

Buck looks 'em over.

"You two been fightin' each other?" he asks.

"It—it was a mistake," says Muley, drinkin' the water and pourin' his liquor in the cuspidor. "I thought Testament was a—a—"

"He thought I was a door," finished Testament, "and tried to go through me. Perhaps we had better go home, Muley."

"Yeah—and stay home," says Muley painful-like.

They went out just before the crowd came back. It seems that Gunga Din and Sahara are all right, but they left five guards in the stable.

"We found a hat," said Mighty. "Hassayampa said that they ain't fed that tiger for two days, and I'm kinda scared that we won't never find the man to put under that hat."

I'm goin' to draw a veil over the rest of that night. It will be sufficient to say that mornin' came apace, the sun came up in its usual way, and among us was brotherly love and the sweet spirit of progress. Civilization is sweet to the civilized.

Magpie found us the next day. He looks us over, tells us what he thinks of our ancestors, takes our guns away and leads us down to Wick Smith's home. I'm kinda hazy on just what happened to us, but it seems that me and Dirty went to sleep on a bed.

I DUNNO WHAT TIME I WOKE UP, BUT I SUPPOSE IT WAS AFTERNOON. I SETS UP on that bed and looks at the dangest person I ever seen. He was settin' there, lookin' at me. He's kind of a dirty, brown-complected *hombre*, with somethin' white wrapped around his head, and his body is covered with a striped gown of some kind.

I bats my eyes a couple of times, but he don't disappear.

"I'm dead and in —," says the apparation.

It has the voice and eye of Dirty Shirt Jones, but the rest of it don't look like him. Right then and there I marks an X after my name for a temperance vote.

"Yessir, I'm dead," says the person. "I've had delirium tremens enough times to know that this ain't it."

I looks across the room and sees another jigger of the same brand. Then I starts to get out of bed, intendin' to head for the door and this second dirty-faced thing moves right along with me. I've been lookin' in a mirror. Then I lifts one hand to my face, and it comes away the color of chocolate. There's a strong odor of turpentine in the place.

"What in — has been happenin'?" I asks.

"Are you Ike Harper?" he asks, kinda awed-like.

"If that's a mirror, I ain't," says I. "Who are you?"

"I used to be Dirty Shirt Jones."

I starts to scratch my head and finds it all wrapped up in cloth.

"Did we get hurt, or somethin'?" I asks.

Before he can answer me, Wick Smith, Yuma Yates and Mighty Jones come in. They looks us over, and Wick Smith says—

"Thank gosh, they're sober enough to ride."

"Who done this to us?" asks Dirty. "I'll kill the man that painted me thisaway!"

"There was six of us done it," says Yuma. "It sure is one good job. By golly, nobody will know yuh, that's a cinch. Haw-haw-haw-haw!"

I got off that bed, intendin' to maul somebody; but Yuma pulled his gun and backed me onto the bed again.

"The worst is over, Ike," says he. "Be docile and gain great fame for yourself—you and Dirty."

"We better be goin'," opines Wick. "The crowd is anxious for us to get started. C'om, you East Injuns."

"East Injuns?" says I. "Is that what we look like?"

"Accordin' to the book," nods Yuma. "C'mon."

What could we do, I ask yuh? We went out with them, wearin' bandaged heads, house-paint and mother-hubbards. That paint is beginnin' to dry on my face, and the turpentine stings like a lot of bees. I opened my mouth and I can't get it shut.

"H'rah for —!" wails Dirty. "Who's 'fraid of fire?"

We follers 'em up to the corner of Holt's hotel, and there we finds Gunga Din and Sahara, which are bein' held by Pete Gonyer, Olaf Hansen, Hassayampa Harris, Scenery Sims and "Half-Mile" Smith.

"Gunga Din is broke to ride," stated Hassayampa, "but I dunno about Sahara. Ike can ride the elephant, 'cause he's the biggest, and Dirty Shirt can mount the camel."

"Just a short moment," says I. "Nobody asked us. When I ride, I choose a horse; *sabe*? I ain't no elephant scratcher."

"Ain't yuh?" asks Yuma. "You swore to do what Miss Greenbaum asked yuh to, Ike. She asks yuh to ride the elephant."

"But what for?" I asks.

By golly, I ain't got no idea what it's all about. I can hear folks yellin' out in the street, and when they start to yellin' in Piperock, I don't wish to be there.

"Here's what yuh got to do," says Yuma. "You two ride down the street. About in front of Wick's store yuh will meet old Chief Cod Liver Oil and old Runnin' Dog. They'll have on their war-bonnets, et cettery, and they know what to do. They represent the old West; *sabe*?

"They give yuh the peace-sign, and it seems like yo're all talkin'. That's the part of it which is knowed as the West meetin' the East. Then comes Pete in an old covered wagon. That is the comin' of the white man. The Injuns act surprized. Behind his wagon comes Scenery Sims' autymobeel, which has been made into a float, and on it is the three figures, which represent Victory and the Progress of Piperock; *sabe*?

"Then that's about all, I reckon. I dunno what else there's to be done, Ike. Magpie explains that much to me. Thatcher's orchestra will be playin' all the time, I reckon. Anyway, it'll be good. Hassayampa, you and Half Mile help Ike up on Gunga Din."

"It'll be good all right," grunts Mighty. "Cod Liver Oil and Runnin' Dog done split a quart of lemon extract and a bottle of perfume between 'em."

I let 'em put me up on the back of that India-rubber ox, which ain't wearin' saddle nor bridle. Behind my animal is Dirty Shirt, settin' on the hump of Sahara, his face twisted kinda funny. He's got a pair of reins to hang on to.

Just then Gunga Din starts ahead. There ain't nothin' I can do but set there and let things go. We went surgin' around the corner and into the main street. Yaller Rock County sure was there. Every hitchrack is packed with horses, and between the racks and the middle of the street stands the population of a county, waitin' for us to show up.

They lets out a cheer when we showed up, and we ain't more than halfway to 'em, when up the street comes old Cod Liver Oil and Runnin' Dog, both of 'em decked out in war-paint, nose-paint, war-bonnets, and ridin' painted ponies.

I reckon it was a sight worth seein'. Honest to gosh, I sure did feel aboriginal. I was stoical, too. The only emotion I can show is with my right leg—the left one has gone to sleep. Then the East met the West.

We got within twenty feet of each other before them pinto horses got a good look at Gunga Din and Sahara. Cod Liver Oil's pinto just spread its legs, bawled like a calf—and fell down, sendin' the old buck into a somersault almost under Gunga Din. Runnin' Dog's pinto turns around on one hind leg, shuckin' old Runnin' Dog, and went past us like a streak.

Gunga Din reached down, wrapped his trunk around Cod Liver Oil, and stood the old boy on his head twenty feet away.

"Yee-ow-w-w!" yelps Liniment Lucas. "Some show!"

And into it all comes Pete Gonyer, drivin' a team of broncs hitched to a covered wagon. He is the Comin' of the White Man. He came—I'll say that much for him. The yellin' is too much for that team of broncs, and here comes Pete, feet braced against the front-gate of that wagon, haulin' short on the lines, while behind him billows that wagon-cover, like a anchored balloon.

Runnin' Dog has got to his feet, with the war-bonnet over one eye and blood in the other one.

"Whoo!" he screams. "Hyas masahchie mokst la tet!"

It was the first elephant he ever seen, and he called it a big evil with two heads.

There ain't no chance for me to move Gunga Din out of the path of them two broncs; so I sets supine and lets death rush down upon us. But it don't rush all the way.

About twenty feet away, them two broncs get their first look at the East, and they don't like it. They dig their heels into that hard street, set down in their harness, and out of that cloud of dust comes Pete Gonyer, all spread out like a flyin' squirrel, and he lands all spraddled out on the head of Gunga Din, still hangin' onto his lines.

As old Judge Steele might say—"Pandyammonium reigns."

The two broncs regains their equilibrium, ducks sideways and tries to go around us. They were goin' pretty good when they took up the slack on them lines, and Pete Gonyer lifted right off the dome of Gunga Din, sailed off through the air and butted Dirty Shirt plumb off his camel. He not only butted him off, but took him along.

Then Gunga Din lifted his trunk high in the air and bugles loud and free—

"Ra-a-a-a te ta-a-a-a ta ta-a-a-a!"

Right then I want to get down. I don't reckon that any Harper ever lived that wanted to get down as badly as I do; but there ain't no safety on the ground. Every horse at them hitch-racks are heavin' and surgin, folks yelpin'. I want to yell, but that darned paint has set, with my mouth half open, and all I can do is say—

"Hoo, hoo, hoo!" like a darned owl.

Then cometh Victory—and Progress. Pete Gonyer has made a riggin' to fit over the top of Scenery Sims' automobile, kinda like a platform, and there's a railin' all around it, decorated with flags and colored cloth. The driver ain't in sight, and the danged thing looks like a runaway raft.

On the front of the arrangement stand Mrs. Wick Smith, all gauded up in cheese-cloth and a silver crown, which is settin' down over one ear, kinda rakish-like. One hand is grippin' the rail, while the other hangs to a big banner.

Behind her stands Mrs. Gonyer, dressed in white, tryin' to hold up one hand, like an Injun givin' a peace-sign, and hangin' onto her is Mrs. Mighty Jones, wearin' a nightgown and a pair of paper wings, one of which has climbed up on her shoulder, makin' her look like a broken-winged duck.

I seen all this in a lot less time than it takes to tell it. The thing is comin' too danged fast, I *sabe* that much, and I know that an automobile don't scare at elephants. A runaway horse goes past me, hits its rump against the platform of Victory and Progress and skids the thing aside.

Mrs. Smith goes down in a lump, and Mrs. Gonyer lands on her knees, with that one hand still up in the air. Then Victory and Progress hits the East.

They knocked Gunga Din loose from the street, but they didn't remove him. I got Mrs. Smith in my arms, but Mrs. Mighty Jones went past me so fast that I didn't have no chance to make a collection. Then Gunga Din got his four feet on to the terry-firma agin' and started out.

He bowed his head, put it against that float and started for Buck's saloon front. I seen Magpie's head come up from among the wreckage and he starts hammerin' Gunga Din over the head with a piece of two-by-four, but he might as well 'a' kissed him, for all the good it done.

Wick Smith comes gallopin' alongside of us, yellin'—

"Leggo my wife! Leggo my wife! Dang you, Ike—leggo her!"

"Tell it to her!" I yelps back at him. "You — fool, I ain't doin' the holdin'."

The rear wheels of that equipage hits the sidewalk, lifts up real sudden, and we begins to shove that whole works plumb through Buck's saloon front. It was then that I managed to get loose from another man's wife, and proceeds to fall backward off that elephant.

I dunno what in — Sahara was doin' right behind Gunga Din, unless he was supposed to be there; but I do know that I lit kinda folded up across his long neck, and he starts to run with me. We went around in a circle three times before I fell off, and that — camel walked all over me.

Then I sets up in that dusty street and tries to see what is goin' on. Horses are runnin' around like they was in a circus ring, and some of 'em are draggin' wagons and buggies behind 'em, which makes the street a dangerous place for to be. One wagon circled the street twice before I notices that Dirty Shirt is standin' up in the wagon, kinda balancin' himself, with his arms spread out wide.

Then the wagon hit the sidewalk and Dirty turned over twice before landed sittin' down on the sidewalk. I managed to limp and crawl over to him. His good eye is plumb closed, and the bad one won't keep still.

He's singin' soft and low, and kinda beatin' time with that jiggly eye. I has to listen real close, but above the roar of destruction I hears his singin'—

"Littul birdie in the tree, in the tree, in the tree;

Littul birdie in the tree-e-e-e-e, sing a song for me-e-e-e-e."

"There ain't no tree, Dirty," says I.

"Ain't there?" he asks soft-like. "There ort to be—there's so — many birds."

Over around Buck's place there's folks yellin' to beat four of a kind, and some misguided jigger starts shootin'. I can see that there ain't no regular doorway left in Buck's saloon—just an openin' about ten feet wide.

Just about that time Gunga Din comes around the corner. He ain't got nobody on his back now, but he's got a chair hooked around one hind leg.

He runs into the hitch-rack, tried to go under it, and lifts it plumb out of the ground. This kinda makes him sore; so he wraps his trunk around one of the posts and starts for us, packin' and draggin' it along with him, while on the far end of it is tied a piebald bronc from Paradise.

The most of the crowd stampeded for the Mint Hall, Wick's store and other places of safety, and it sure don't take long to clear the street of spectators. I *sabe* that Gunga Din is on a regular bust; so I picks Dirty Shirt up in my arms and staggers toward Buck's place.

I ain't in no shape to pack anybody, 'cause my right leg acts too short, which makes me circle a little to the right and I'm close to Gunga Din before I realize it.

There's just a whap and a rip, and outside of Dirty's headgear he's as naked as the day he was born. Gunga Din shucked him like an ear of corn. But Dirty don't know it, and I don't care; so we staggers on through the haze.

We fell into Buck's place, and it don't take a normal man to see that everythin' ain't right in there.

Old Testament Tilton is settin' up on what used to be the back-bar, squattin' there like a wise old owl, lookin' over the world; settin' there like a statue, sayin' nothin'. Piled up against the bar is what is left of the float. Buck is flat on his back, with his feet up over the pool-table, which has been moved over against the wall.

All to once that mass which used to be the float begins to heave upward, and from among the busted two-by-fours, twisted wires and colored cloth, cometh Sahara. How in — that camel got mixed up in that float, I don't know, but there he is.

He comes out of there, plumb decorated, and hanging to his tail like grim death comes Magpie Simpkins, the president of Piperock's Chamber of Commerce.

Magpie has still got on one boot, a suit of red underwear and the crown of his hat, and in his eyes is a stern resolve. And behind him, pawin' out of the wreck, comes Wick Smith. They all gets clear of the wreck and Sahara stops. Wick has a two-foot piece of two-by-four in his hands, and he braces his feet far apart.

"Mum-Magpie," says he kinda thin-like. "You has made me a widder man, gol ding yuh."

But Magpie don't hear it. His mind is far behind that pageant of progress. He bows and kinda smiles, as he says:

"The wheel of progress is turnin', and wo unto him who gits under the tire. The people of Piperock has risen in their might, unleashed their bonds which has held them in darkness——"

Tunk! Wick Smith's two-by-four ended the speech.

"You didn't have to blame him entirely, Wick," says I.

He turns and looks at me, kinda weavin' on his feet.

"You?" he whispers. "You come bub-back? Where's my wife?"

"I dunno, Wick."

"You had her, dang you! I seen you huggin' her!"

I seen that piece of scantlin' comin', but didn't have flexibility enough to dodge. I distinctly heard it clank against my head, and then I finds myself out in the street again. I can hear a lot of dogs wailin', and I wonders if I can hear this because I've gone to the dogs. Ain't it funny what a feller will think about in a case like that?

A lot of folks are yellin' at somebody or somethin'; so I sets up and concentrates on the present. A bullet digs into the dirt beside me, but I don't mind. I kinda wonders why they're shootin' at me, of course. Then somethin' hooks me off the ground and begins to give me a ride.

I managed to get one eye open and finds that I'm on one end of that hitch-rack, and the motive power is furnished by Gunga Din. They've picked me up in the angle between one post and the top-pole, and the friction on that part of me which wasn't on the pole was somethin' awful.

Then Gunga Din let out another of them awful bugles, shucked the hitch-rack and headed for Buck's place again——and hangin' to the slack skin of Gunga Din's rear end was Cleopatra. Behind them came Polecat Perkins' pack of hounds, run to a frazzle, but still able to stagger on and wail plenty loud and long.

Them dogs has run that tiger all night, and it ain't no wonder that the tiger is huntin' for somethin' to climb on to. Right into the wreck of Buck's place they went, while the crowd, which is located in places of safety, yelled, shot and generally decided that — was havin' a recess.

It's only about five minutes since East met West, but there has been several things come to pass. Gunga Din has gone back into Buck's place, tryin' to get rid of Cleopatra, when here comes Chief Cod Liver Oil, packin' an old Sharps rifle. The old war-whoop sure must 'a' been fortified against fear by much flavorin' extract, 'cause he heads straight for Buck's shattered entrance, soundin' his tribal war-whoop regular.

I got to my feet. I reckon they were my feet. There ain't no feelin' in 'em, but they hold me up; so they must be mine. An armless man could count all the Harper heroes on the fingers of his hands, but just the same I goes pawin' toward Buck's place to see what I can salvage from Gunga Din, Cleopatra and Cod Liver Oil.

I don't quite get there, when Cod Liver Oil comes out. He came out of there, end over end, missed me about a foot, and stood on his head and shoulders in the street. His Sharps lit just outside the doorway; so I picked it up and went in.

Cleopatra is settin' on what used to be the end of Buck's mahogany bar, her mouth wide open and her eyes shut. Gunga Din is standin' in the middle of the room, with one hind foot on Magpie's pant-leg, and Sahara is half-in and half-out of a rear window. And every time Gunga Din weaves the whole building shakes.

Dirty Shirt has got to his feet, and there he stands, plumb out of clothes, kinda rockin' on his feet and grinnin' foolish.

"Dud-do somethin'!" whispers Magpie. "Ain't nobody goin' to do somethin'?"

"Call on the Chamber of Commerce," says I.

From under a smashed card-table, Wick Smith shoves up his head. He's got the brim of his hat in his teeth, but manages to work it loose with his tongue.

"I give up," he wheezes. "I know when I've got enough."

Old Testament is still settin' on the back-bar, but now he shakes loose and falls into Cleopatra. He kinda takes that big striped cat into a lovin' embrace, but Cleopatra yowled once, kicked Testament backward and jumped straight at me.

I throwed up that old Sharps, took a wing-shot at Cleopatra and then a great weight settled upon me. I ain't no fighter. None of my family ever won any diamond belts; but there never was a Harper that wouldn't fight to save his own life. And I sure went into a clinch with that tiger.

My eyes are too full of dust and pain for me to see just how the battle is comin'. We just kept on fightin', thassall. Once we got separated and it takes us quite a while to get together again, but we did. I can't see a danged thing and I don't reckon Cleopatra can either; so we locates each other by sense of smell.

I dunno how long we fought. Scientists would probably differ as to how long a man and a tiger can fight without one or both of 'em dyin'. I ain't got no feelin' left within' me. I reckon I'm kinda primitive just now, and I fights with tooth and claw. I hears voices around me, kinda cheerin'; so I puts up a supreme effort, as it were, and feels the tiger go limp.

"My —!" I hears Dirty gasp hoarse-like. "They're still at it."

"I licked him—her," says I.

I ain't got more than enough breath to say that. And then I kinda passed out.

It seems like I heard somebody say:

"Let him alone, dang yuh! He done jist what I've wanted to see done for a long time."

It was probably quite a some time before I woke up again. For quite a while I can't figure out just where I am and what's goin' on. I seem to be layin' across somethin' that heaves and surges a heap. I manages to get one eye open and discovers that I'm on my stummick across a saddle.

Out in front of me and the horse is a queer-lookin' figure. It's got on a pair of overalls, which won't stay up, barefooted, bareheaded. It looks back at me, and I recognize Dirty Shirt by his jiggly eye.

Then I slides off and sets down beside the trail.

"Where we goin'?" I asks.

Dirty comes back and sits down beside me.

"It don't make no difference, does it?" he asks. "They said that we was mostly to blame; so I took you away from 'em and went away. It wasn't our fault, Ike; but they have to blame somebody."

"Magpie was mostly to blame," says I. "We done the best we could. I dunno what you done, Dirty, but I know I saved Piperock from a lot of heartaches."

"You sure did, Ike," says Dirty.

"That critter would 'a' been the ruination of Piperock."

"That's a cinch, Ike. But the worst of it is, you only stops the plague temp'rarily."

"Thasso?" says I. "I done my best, Dirty Shirt. I wish I had the hide for a souvenir."

Dirty looks queer-like at me.

"I dunno," says he kinda sad-like. "A shock sometimes causes a feller to jerk back to his cannibal ancestors."

I dunno what he's talkin' about, but I'm too bunged up to care much, and my face is beginnin' to crack.

"How in — did it finish?" I asks.

"All right, Ike. The animals all hived up in the livery-stable, and Wick Smith sold 'em to Paradise."

"The — he did!" I exclaimed, or as much of an exclamation as I can use in my condition. "And didn't the Piperock Chamber of Commerce stop him?"

"There was only one to vote agin' it—and he was too danged near death to even squawk. They never even give him credit for tryin' to save the tiger. I seen it all, Ike. When you lifted that old Sharps to shoot Cleopatry, Magpie got loose from Gunga Din and fell into yuh."

"Uh-uh-huh," says I, feelin' weak. "And then what did I do to the tiger, Dirty."

"Nothin' a-tall. The wheels of progress got to turnin', and Magpie got under the tire, thasall. In the language of Magpie Simpkins, I wouldn't be surprized to see Piperock one of the big cities of the world."

"Well," says I, "in the language of Ike Harper, whose spirit, liver, lights and gizzard has been busted to make a Piperock holiday, let's get to — out of here, before the place grows too big. I don't want to even be seen in the suburbs."

But she hasn't grown any since.

The End

# Thank you for reading!

| 2 | 9 | 5 | 6 | 1 | 7 | 3 | 4 | 8 |
|---|---|---|---|---|---|---|---|---|
| 6 | 7 | 1 | 3 | 8 | 4 | 9 | 5 | 2 |
| 3 | 4 | 8 | 5 | 9 | 2 | 6 | 7 | 1 |
| 9 | 2 | 3 | 7 | 4 | 8 | 1 | 6 | 5 |
| 5 | 8 | 7 | 9 | 6 | 1 | 4 | 2 | 3 |
| 1 | 6 | 4 | 2 | 3 | 5 | 7 | 8 | 9 |
| 4 | 1 | 6 | 8 | 2 | 3 | 5 | 9 | 7 |
| 7 | 3 | 2 | 4 | 5 | 9 | 8 | 1 | 6 |
| 8 | 5 | 9 | 1 | 7 | 6 | 2 | 3 | 4 |

**Next issue is coming out this Spring...**